Praise for Debra Parmley's
A Desperate Journey

"A stunning debut! A Desperate Journey is an enchanting tale of love, forgiveness, redemption, and passion. Don't miss this one."
~ *Gerri Russell, author of Warrior's Bride*

"Debra Parmley is a promising new writer!"
~ *Bobbi Smith, NYT bestselling author, Queen of the western romance*

Rating: 4 Cups "I absolutely enjoyed A Desperate Journey. It is filled with trust issues, evil people, betrayal, and even love and romance sprinkled along the way. The plot is wonderfully woven with some twists and turns I never expected. Debra Parmley produces an outstanding read that pricks the heart."
~ *Cherokee, Coffee Time Romance*

"The characters in American Title II contestant Parmley's debut are very well developed, and the descriptive language transports readers to the past."
~ *Keitha Hart, Romantic Times*

Rating: 5 Hearts "A Desperate Journey is a well-written, historical romance set in the middle of the nineteenth century when cowboys ruled this land."
~ *Margo Arthur, The Romance Studio*

A Desperate Journey

Debra Parmley

A Samhain Publishing, Ltd. publication.

Samhain Publishing, Ltd.
577 Mulberry Street, Suite 1520
Macon, GA 31201
www.samhainpublishing.com

A Desperate Journey
Print ISBN: 978-1-60504-276-3
Digital ISBN: 1-60504-074-6

Editing by Bethany Morgan
Cover by Angela Waters

First Samhain Publishing, Ltd. electronic publication: July 2008
First Samhain Publishing, Ltd. print publication: March 2009

Dedication

To Trixie
In memoriam.
Who waited patiently by my side throughout
the creation of this book.

Writing is a solitary journey, but there are many people who helped along the way and I would like to take this opportunity to thank them. My utmost appreciation goes to:

Dusty Richards of the Ozark Creative Writers Conference for issuing the challenge.

The Antioch Writers Workshop, where Clint McCown critiqued that first chapter.

Bobbi Smith, for her Creative Challenge Contest, for taking the time after the manuscript finalled to tell me the story really needed to start in chapter three, for her continued encouragement, advice and friendship.

Everyone who voted for *A Desperate Journey* in the American Title II contest and to Dorchester Publishing and Romantic Times magazine for sponsoring the contest that has launched so many authors. To my American Title II sisters for our sisterhood.

My agent. My first wonderful editor, Carrie Jackson. Bethany Morgan, the excellent editor who inherited me, and who made editing this manuscript a joy. Angela Waters, for creating the beautiful cover. And the entire Samhain Publishing family for their hard work and dedication to the quality of the book.

Lucy Monroe, mentor and friend. My former critique groups. Ernie Lancaster, of the Memphis SWAT team for critiquing the gunfight. Michael W. for his advice and encouragement. My family for their unfailing support. But especially to Mike, for supporting me, making it possible to follow this dream.

Prologue

Kansas, 1859

Luke slid his hands around Sally's waist, pulling her close.

She gasped as her hips met his and she felt his hard body against her, throbbing.

Luke's eyes darkened with desire. "From the moment I first saw you, I wanted you."

Her eyes widened in surprise.

"I wanted to take you like this and kiss you."

He'd kissed her before, soft and gentle, but he'd never held her like this. There had always been people around. The entire wagon train had followed their brief courtship.

"Tonight I'm going to kiss every inch of you."

A shiver of nervous anticipation ran down her spine along with a tiny touch of fear of the unknown, and she giggled.

He bent down and slowly his lips teased hers. She relaxed into his arms, giving him all her love.

She had nothing to fear. Tonight was their wedding night and she would trust him. She loved him with her whole heart.

He broke off and turned her to face away from him, lifting her long unbraided hair over her left shoulder.

"I've waited all day to do this."

He unbuttoned the top of her wedding dress and bent to kiss her neck. With each button he added another kiss, his breath tickling her heated skin until his lips caressed her.

When he reached the small of her back, the dress slid to the floor in a rush, leaving her standing in front of the fireplace in her underclothes.

His lips brushed the small of her back, then he turned her back around to face him and brushed his thumbs across her hardened nipples, the thin chemise the only fabric between them.

Breathless, she waited for his next move, wondering what he would do, longing for him to touch her there again.

"I want to see all of you."

He removed the rest of her clothing until she stood naked before him. She reached with her hands to cover herself.

"Stand still." He pulled her hands away. "I want to see what kind of wife I've got."

He circled around her, turning to look her up and down as he passed, unbuttoning his shirt. He circled her until the heat within his eyes, the heat within her body made her want to reach out and touch him.

She waited for him to speak, watching his face, to see if he was pleased with her.

"I knew you'd make a good wife." A grin lit his face.

She exhaled.

He stripped off his shirt and tossed it in the corner. Then he reached out and pulled her against him and she felt his hardness again, pushing against her insistently as he gave her a bold kiss and his grip tightened.

Sudden panic rose within her and she tried to pull away. He was too rough. Too fast.

He broke away and his eyes narrowed. Then his eyes lit.

"Did you listen to the vows? You promised to obey me."

"Yes."

She'd vowed to obey a man she barely knew. A man she'd met just two weeks ago. This was a side of him she'd never seen.

"Then stop fighting me. Get into bed."

She crawled under the covers and waited.

He stalked to the bed, flipped the covers back and knelt over her. "I told you I was going to kiss you all over. Relax and lay still."

His tongue teasing her nipple sent a moist heat down to her loins. He rained kisses across her breasts and down her belly until she could no longer think.

In a hazy fog, she felt his finger enter her folds.

"So sweet. So wet. So ready."

His finger flicked at a sensitive spot and she jumped.

He stopped, loosened his trousers and let them drop to the floor.

She'd never seen a naked man before and his hard length shocked her with the thought that he would soon enter her body.

She backed up against the headboard.

He was too big.

"Come back here. Open your legs for me, wife."

Wife. It was her duty to obey her new husband, trusting him to be easy with her. She loved him, and surely he loved her. And she wanted babies. As many as the good Lord gave her. She slid back down, opened her legs and waited.

He entered her quickly and the pain was sharp.

She closed her eyes to hide her tears but he saw them.

"The first time always hurts a woman."

He paused then reached down to that sensitive spot again and rubbed it until she moved beneath him.

"Now that's more like it, wife."

She soon forgot the initial pain as he taught her things about her body she'd never known. He wanted her again and again through that long night, and she wanted only for him to say those three little words. Luke taught her body to crave his touch but he never once said he loved her.

Kansas, 1867

"Sally." Mr. Harper shook her shoulder to wake her where she sat in the rocker holding Mrs. Harper's newborn child. "Reverend Miller is ready to take you home."

Sally hadn't thought about that night for a long time. That night she had conceived Matthew, and nothing had been the same since. She tried to be a loving wife, but she waited for words she would never hear.

She nodded, rose and gave the baby to Mrs. Harper. "He's beautiful."

As beautiful as her son Matthew who waited at home. The only good that had come from their marriage was her children.

Chapter One

"'Gone to Texas.'" Reverend James Miller read the letter Luke had left pinned to the front door. "'I told you I ain't no farmer. I'm taking Matthew. It's time he learned to be a man.'"

"He's lying," Sally gasped.

Luke had never taken an interest in the children.

"No, Sally, I'm afraid not. That's what the letter says."

Sally Wheeler's world spun as she sagged against the door.

Texas. So far away.

His words hit her.

No. It couldn't be. He'd taken Matthew.

Speechless, she looked at Reverend Miller.

"You've had a shock." Reverend Miller touched her arm, his gaze warm and kind. "And I know you're exhausted."

He couldn't begin to know how battered and worn she felt. The note had swept away her last bit of strength, leaving her completely drained. Her mind couldn't quite grasp the news. Her husband and son gone? This couldn't be real.

She'd gone without sleep for two nights helping Mrs. Harper birth her first baby. Reverend Miller had shown up the second night prepared to baptize and bury, but thankfully both mother and child had lived. Then the reverend had been kind enough to give Sally a ride home.

She'd known Luke would be angry with her for staying away so long, but this—this was nothing like what she'd expected.

"How could he? He knew the auction was today."

She stepped inside and glanced about the bare cabin where

her mother's furniture had once stood. His guns were gone from over the fireplace, her things were scattered about and a kitchen chair lay broken on the floor.

"Sally, what happened here?"

The reverend's voice reminded her she wasn't alone. It pained her to have him see the way they'd lived, the evidence of her poverty so clear. She hadn't been raised to live like this. She frowned. "I don't know."

All she knew was that she had only a few hours to pack.

"I'd planned to come back for the auction. But I'll stay and help you pack your things."

"Thank you."

"Do you have any idea what you'll do?"

"No."

I've left everything up to Luke and look where that has gotten me. I'll never make that mistake again.

"I thought Luke had a plan."

Well, apparently he did, just not one that included his wife and daughter.

"You and Carolyn can ride back with me to the parsonage when the auction is over and stay with us until you sort things out."

Yes, she had much to sort out. But she had to hurry.

"There isn't much time." She glanced down at her dress, stained from the birthing. "I need to change my dress."

"I'll check on Carolyn then."

Sally nodded and glanced out the doorway to where her three-year-old daughter lay curled in peaceful slumber on the seat of the wagon.

She hurried to change while darting anxious glances at the floor.

Are my treasures safe?

Reaching under the mattress, she removed the long iron rod she'd hidden. Most nights Luke had returned home late with liquored breath and empty hands. She wished she'd had the courage to use it on him.

She slid the rod under a floorboard and wrenched, lifting the wood until it cracked. From the exposed cavity she retrieved the carved box her grandfather had made and opened it.

Thank God the jewelry is still here.

She pulled out Mama's locket, Grandfather's pocket watch and Grandmother's black oval brooch. Luke had gone into a rage when he'd thought she lost them. Her fingers traced the brooch. The only permanent things she owned were from her family.

Reverend Miller knocked on the doorframe and she jumped.

"Sally, Carolyn just woke up." He stepped inside holding her daughter, who rubbed one small fist across her eye.

Sally hugged the jewelry to her chest. There was no time to hide it. "Promise you won't tell."

He put Carolyn down. "Sally, if you have enough to save the farm..." His voice trailed off as he rubbed his chin. "I don't suppose it matters now that Luke is gone."

"You can't tell anyone. Not even Martha."

He paused before answering. "You have my word." He turned away and headed for the door. "Hide them. If anyone asks, I can honestly say I don't know where they are."

She held out her hand to Carolyn. "Come help me pack your things, sweetheart. We're staying with the Millers tonight."

"Where my new dolly lives?"

Sally had promised her a new rag doll after they moved. But she hadn't had time to make one.

"No, she lives in our new home. We're going for a visit."

Reverend Miller pushed a large trunk he'd found in the barn into the cabin. "I'll load it when you're ready."

Sally opened the trunk, lifted the quilt and felt for the coins sewn inside.

They were still there.

Luke hadn't known about them. She'd almost told him, but one glance around the bare room where her mother's furniture had stood proved she had been smart not to.

Luke wasted money hand over fist and sold anything of value. He wouldn't have used her treasures to save the farm.

Surrounded by family heirlooms, Sally felt more like her old self. The quilt she'd made with Mama for her hope chest lay on the bed. She ran her hand over the knots and stitches, touching part of Mama's apron and Grandfather's plaid shirt. Here were

13

the pieces of her family history stitched together.

"I understand how hard this must be," Reverend Miller said.

How could he begin to understand?

"And I'm sorry that you've lost your home."

Not as sorry as Luke is going to be.

She bit back the retort.

This is all Luke's fault. He gambled away every dime. He took and took and took. But this time he isn't going to get away with it. Somehow I will get my son back.

Sally nodded to the reverend then glanced about the cabin. Her children had been born here. Despite the misery, she'd had moments of joy. She knew each crack in the wall like her own hand.

She found herself straining to hear Matthew's voice as she packed her things, though she knew he wasn't there. Only the wind whistled through cracks in the walls.

The front door hadn't closed properly. It swung and banged in the wind. Swing, bump, bang. Each time it slapped, she jumped. Like a ghost town, the cabin showed only a shadow of its former self.

She walked to the flower garden Luke had made fun of, telling her she couldn't grow anything but scrawny brats for him to feed. Words that stung like the back of his hand. But he continued to share her bed, uncaring that she might conceive.

The garden had been the one thing she did for herself. Wild mint had taken over, but the sunflowers grew tall.

She gazed across the flat Kansas land that went on forever. Once she'd thought it spread clear to the blue skies of heaven.

Sally gathered sunflowers into her apron. Carolyn called them "sun babies" and rocked them in her arms. She would save the seeds so Carolyn wouldn't lose her sun babies.

The auctioneer arrived, and in the distance she saw the wagons. Most of the town would turn out. Not because they wanted to buy the place, but for the entertainment the auction provided. And the gossip.

Sally felt like she'd fallen through the dry cracks in the Kansas soil.

Sally's ears rang with the final pounding of the gavel as the auctioneer called out, "Sold!"

The small gray cabin that Luke had never whitewashed was someone else's problem now, and as the townsfolk said goodbye, Sally's face stiffened from holding a forced smile.

She'd endured the curious looks and whispers of the crowd, the speculation of why Luke wasn't there and what the pastor was doing holding her elbow as Carolyn stood holding on to her skirt. The feeling she might faint had passed, though her knees still trembled with fatigue.

"Sally?"

Hearing the familiar voice took her by surprise and she turned. "Ozzie Moss!" He'd led the wagon train that took her family to Kansas eight years ago. "It's been years."

He'd come by after Matthew was born, but Luke had made it clear he wasn't welcome. Luke didn't like anyone coming around, especially Ozzie. The feeling was mutual. Ozzie had warned her not to marry Luke.

"I'm so glad you've come." In spite of his rough trail-worn appearance, he looked wonderful. Though he smelled ripe and looked as if he hadn't bathed in months, she hugged him like a long lost friend.

Unaccustomed to showing emotion, he patted her awkwardly on the back. "I was bringin' a load through an' heard about yer troubles. I come to see how ye was."

Relief flooded through her. Now she knew what to do.

She would convince him to take her to Texas.

"Luke took Matthew and I need you to help me find him."

Ozzie frowned as she told him of Luke's note. He shook his head. "I knew he weren't no good. Now why would ye want to go chasin' after him?"

"I'm not going after him. I'm going to get Matthew back."

"Well, I ain't goin' clear to Texas this time. My route ends 'bout halfway."

"Please, Moss."

"Trail rides is rough. More so fer a woman. An' Sally, ye got a young 'un to care for. It's a powerful lot to take on."

"Sally and Carolyn are welcome to stay at the parsonage as long as they need," Reverend Miller said.

"Well, then, yer safe here with good folks to look after ye." Moss nodded. "Good to see ye, Sally." He glanced overhead. "I'd best get to town an' find me a room afore the storm comes." He gestured to his mules. "An' they've waited long enough fer supper."

Reverend Miller hurried to lash down the oiled canvas over the buckboard wagon. "Ready, Sally? Martha will have dinner on."

"More than ready." Her stomach growled.

Wind lifted her skirt as she climbed into the wagon and large drops of rain pelted her face. The rain stung, but nothing like the sting of losing Matthew.

She didn't look back at her home as they rode away. The farm was lost. She couldn't work the land alone, and it had become obvious Luke would never put the effort into it. It had been their home but she would never see it again. She didn't care to see it again. Not after all she'd lived through.

She only wanted to see Matthew. To hold him, muddy knees, rumpled hair and all. She closed her eyes and pictured the light dusting of freckles across his nose and his gap-toothed grin where he'd lost a tooth.

As she pictured his freckled face and his serious expression, she thought of how he never laughed when Luke was near. She thought of the dark side of her husband, the side she'd seen glimpses of. She couldn't help but feel Matthew wouldn't be safe with him. Even when Luke meant well, he was reckless and self-involved.

But Luke had stolen her son. She could no longer make excuses for him. She could no longer believe he meant well. She could no longer listen to his lies.

Amid the shock she'd felt since hearing the note, her anger stirred. The anger she'd never dared to show Luke.

She would never forgive him for this. But she *would* get her son back. Before something worse happened.

Riding to the parsonage on the wagon's hard bench, Sally felt jolted to pieces. Water collected in rows in the muddy fields where the corn never grew.

Carolyn tugged at her skirt. "Mama, I'm hungry."

"I know, sweetheart. We'll eat soon."

Reverend Miller stopped in front of the parsonage and helped them down. "Tell Martha I'll be in once I settle the horses."

Sally grasped Carolyn's hand and led her to the one-story house with the lace curtains. "Now, be on your best behavior."

"Yes, Mama."

Sally knocked on the door and then cracked it. "Martha?"

"Why, Sally, what a surprise," Martha said. "Come in."

Observing Martha's tidy chignon, Sally tucked the loose strands of hair from her long braid behind her ear and smoothed her faded dress.

"Come sit down."

Sally eased into a chair, and Carolyn climbed onto her lap.

Martha sat beside her and leaned forward. "Sally, dear, what's wrong?" The intensity in her eyes heightened the sharpness of her nose. "It's late for visiting. Why, it will be dark soon."

Reverend Miller entered. "Sally and Carolyn are staying with us for a while." He held out his hand. "Come along, Carolyn, we'll go milk Bessie." She slipped off of Sally's lap and ran to join him, placing her hand in his.

Sally rolled one shoulder then the other to ease the tension, and her spine creaked with each movement.

"Where's Matthew?"

"Gone." Sally glanced at her work-worn hands, so rough compared with Martha's. "To Texas."

"Texas?" Shock filled Martha's face.

"I came home from the Harpers and Luke was gone. He took Matthew."

A sharp pain tore through her chest. She couldn't catch her breath. Saying the words aloud stabbed like a knife.

He'd taken her son.

"Mercy. And you had no idea?"

Sally took a deep breath. "He left a note."

"Oh, you poor dear. And you not being able to read."

The silence of the farmyard had been her first inkling something was wrong. Matthew should have run to meet her once he heard the wagon. And Luke met any man who rode

17

onto their place with his rifle in hand.

"So he left you here to deal with the auction."

"Yes." Sally pursed her lips, unwilling to say more.

"My biscuits." Martha rushed into the kitchen.

Carolyn giggled as Reverend Miller carried her in. He settled her in a chair and Sally sat beside her.

Thank God I still have my daughter.

"Carolyn," he said. "Our heavenly father looks down upon us every night and hears our prayers. Let's pray, shall we?"

Carolyn dropped her head as she'd been taught. While they prayed, Sally added a silent prayer.

Please, Lord, keep my son safe.

"Mm, dinner smells heavenly," Reverend Miller said as Martha flitted around him like a moth to an oil lamp.

"It's a good thing I know how to prepare a chicken properly, seeing as how your parishioners pay you with poultry."

Martha scurried about, winding Sally's already tight nerves until she felt they'd snap.

As Carolyn devoured her food, Martha exchanged knowing glances with her husband. Sally's face heated. Carolyn ate as if she hadn't been fed in days.

"You can stay as long as you need," Reverend Miller said.

"Thank you." Martha was lucky to have such a kind husband.

If only she'd been half as lucky.

"Perhaps Luke will find work and send for you," he said.

"No." She shook her head. "He won't."

"Men say things in anger they don't mean. You mustn't give up hope."

Men do things in anger too. She touched her jaw, remembering, and shuddered. *I don't want him back. But I want my son. Luke had no right to take him.*

Sally forced herself to swallow past the lump in her throat and held back her tears. She couldn't let herself fall apart.

After dinner, Martha showed her to the guestroom then left her alone with her daughter.

As she wiped Carolyn's face and combed her daughter's

tangled hair, the nightly ritual calmed her unsteady hands.

Rain pinged on the tin roof. A streak of lightning outside the window illuminated the yard, then thunder rumbled off in the distance. For months they'd been without a drop. Now it poured. Matthew could be out in this storm. She had no way of knowing when they'd left or how far they'd ridden. But Luke wouldn't stop for Matthew's sake.

Carolyn sniffled, and Sally stroked her cheek the way she had when she was a baby until the comforting motion lulled her to sleep. Sally kissed her forehead, and then lay back in bed to stare at the ceiling.

No one will tuck Matthew in tonight.

She squeezed her eyes closed as the thought tore at her. Luke was wrong. He had to know seven was too young to learn to be a man. Only last week Matthew had lost a tooth and said another was "wiggly". She had to be there when it came out. She couldn't bear to miss a moment of her children's lives.

Her life had gone from bad to worse from the day she'd said, "I do". Marrying Luke had been the biggest mistake of her life, but at least she had the children.

Just when she'd taught herself to bear one more burden, another was piled on. She only had so much strength.

How much more can I take?

The wind howled outside as if echoing the loss within her soul. She wanted to stand on the front porch and scream, but she forced the feeling down. Luke had taught her that. Stay quiet. Don't show your emotions. Attract as little attention as possible. Now she was full of all the bubbling emotions she'd held back for so long.

Rain pelted the roof. Sally wrapped her arms around her stomach and curled on her side as the tears she'd held back finally burst free. She cried until, in exhaustion, she drifted off to sleep.

Matthew stood on a hill, calling for her.

Luke rode up and lifted him onto his saddle.

"Come home," she called. Just when he turned toward her, she woke with a start to a crack of thunder. Her dream left her with a deep sense of loss.

The rains still fell, and her dream washed away like the

topsoil on the Kansas prairie. Yet the strong feeling lingered that Matthew was in danger.

Reverend Miller drove them to town for supplies. He lifted Carolyn down, and she ran onto the porch.

"Mr. Walls!"

The short pear-shaped man with ruddy cheeks settled his hands on his rounded hips. "My, look how you've grown. What can I get you today?"

"Lemon drops!"

"Oho." He chuckled. "This sweet child needs some lemon."

Sally turned to Martha. "Could you watch her while I run an errand?"

"Why certainly, Sally."

She hurried to the livery stable. As she'd suspected, Ozzie was there with his mules.

"Mornin', Sally."

"Good morning. How soon are you planning to leave, Moss?"

"Once Tar gits shoed."

"Take us along. I'll be glad to pay you."

He snorted. "I don't need yer money, missy. Keep it to feed that young 'un."

"Moss, I'm going after Luke, and if you won't take me, I'm buying the stage tickets today."

He squinted at her. "I done tracked many a critter, but fellers is harder. Some fellers ain't never found."

"We'll find them, Moss. I'm going to get my boy back if it's the last thing I do." She placed her hands on her hips. "With you or without you, I'm going to Texas."

Moss muttered under his breath, "Changin' a woman's mind is harder then tyin' down a bobcat with a piece of string."

"I'm already packed."

"Cain't let ye head off alone." He shook his head. "I'll come by the parsonage fer ye. But be ready. I ain't waitin'."

"Thank you, Moss." She gave him a quick hug, which made him turn red, and then hurried back to the store.

Sally placed coins on the counter. "Carolyn needs shoes."

"I don't have her size, but I can order them."

"No, there isn't time."

Carolyn pouted.

"Mercy, child. That lip will fall right off." Martha turned to Sally. "What do you mean there's no time?"

"Ozzie is taking us to Texas."

"Mercy, do you think that's wise? And who is Ozzie?"

Sally didn't have time to explain. "We have to hurry or he'll leave us behind. We'll need new dresses." She pointed to one in the window. "How about that one?"

Carolyn's eyes followed Sally's finger, and she lost her pout in a giggle. "Yellow, like my sun babies."

"I have another just like it in your size, Sally."

She had to be careful with the coins, but they needed warm clothes to travel. Carolyn could hardly travel in her worn flour-sack dress, and Sally hadn't owned a store-bought dress since marrying Luke. She nodded.

Mr. Walls tallied the purchases and tied them with string. "A man was here earlier, asking about Luke."

Sally froze.

"Who was he?" Martha asked. "What did he want?"

"He didn't say, but he's not from around these parts."

Sally bit her lip. Who was this stranger and why was he looking for Luke? He'd disappeared suddenly. What had he done?

The bell over the door jingled as a customer entered.

Sally turned to look, as if drawn by an invisible thread.

A tall shadowy figure of a man scanned the room, his gaze lighting on her. Gray-blue eyes pinned her to the floor and she held her breath.

"I'll be with you once I help these folks," Mr. Walls said.

The stranger broke his gaze, nodded once and walked to the corner where he turned his back to examine the rifles.

A shiver crawled up her spine, sending her nerves on edge.

Who was that man? Could he be the same stranger Mr. Walls said was looking for Luke?

Robert Truman focused his attention on the rifles to take

his mind off of the striking woman who stood holding the hand of a small girl at the counter. Her curly red-gold hair and large blue eyes in a pale face had drawn his attention the minute he walked in. He'd briefly forgotten why he'd entered the store.

"There you are." The shopkeeper handed her a package.

"Sally, are you ready?" the other woman asked.

Sally clutched her purchases and nodded, sending Rob a nervous glance from beneath her lashes.

For a moment, Rob wondered if she was the same Sally the saloonkeeper had spoken of. But he'd said nothing about Luke having children and the child showed no resemblance.

Sally smiled at the shopkeeper and her smile lit up her whole face. Rob pushed his thoughts aside.

No, she was much too pretty and wholesome to be mixed up with the likes of Luke Wheeler.

The shopkeeper hurried them out while ignoring Rob.

Why hadn't the shopkeeper told him about Luke's wife?

Rob watched through the window as a man lifted the child into the wagon, and then helped the women up. The shopkeeper stood outside waving good-bye.

What a friendly little town. He frowned as the wagon drove down the street and the shopkeeper stayed outside, avoiding him.

He stepped out onto the porch and cleared his throat. "You neglected to tell me about Luke's wife."

The shopkeeper blanched. "She doesn't need any trouble."

Anyone who took up with Luke had more than enough trouble, and that was a fact.

"You'll have to get your answers elsewhere."

"I already know where to find her." Rob fingered his holster as he watched the man's eyes. "There's something you aren't telling me. Something you're foolishly gloating over."

The man swallowed hard.

"Out with it."

"The woman in the wagon," he took a nervous step back, "was Sally Wheeler."

Rob whipped his head around to spot the wagon in the distance. He should have suspected something when the shopkeeper rushed them out the door.

With two steps he was off the porch and mounting his horse.

So she *was* Luke's wife. He spurred his horse to a gallop.

Luke had an eye for pretty women, and he preferred redheads. But Sally was more than just another pretty face. Something in her vulnerable blue eyes had called to him.

He shook the thought away.

A woman could blind a man. Make him forget what he came here for.

Luke's trail had led him here. He'd waited a long time for revenge and no woman was going to get in his way.

Sally tucked her hair under her bonnet. She had felt the stranger's gaze on her back. A chill swept over her and she shivered. Her fingers rubbed the brooch at her throat. Winter would arrive soon.

She rode to the parsonage in silent worry as Martha alternated between speculating about what the stranger might want and trying to convince Sally that she was making a mistake going after her son.

When the wagon approached the parsonage, Sally saw a tall, darkly clad man seated in the shadows of the porch steps.

Luke? She caught her breath.

Her heart leapt and she immediately looked for Matthew.

But as the man rose in one fluid motion, her heart sank. He was taller than her husband and Matthew was still missing.

She and the Millers climbed down from the wagon and headed for the porch.

"Good evening!" Reverend Miller extended his hand. "Reverend James Miller."

An air of isolation shrouded the man wearing the long duster. He removed his hat but ignored Reverend Miller's outstretched hand.

She gasped.

The man with gray-blue eyes from the store. He must have arrived when Martha had insisted we stop to talk with a neighbor.

He barely nodded at Reverend Miller. "Robert Truman." His voice was low and smooth as he stepped closer, and it sent a shiver through her body. "Sally Wheeler," he spoke with an edge to his voice, "I'd like a word with you, alone."

His gray-blue gaze pierced the distance between them, as if to pin her there.

"No." She backed away one step at a time, sensing danger in the quiet man who followed her every step.

His eyes bore into her as if reaching for her secrets.

"I insist."

His hand closed around her wrist in a firm, warm grip.

She froze at the shock of his touch.

Her senses came alive as if lit by a spark, which ran through her entire body.

His eyes flared in surprise even as his fingers tightened.

He stood so close her breath hitched. She could count the freckles under his tanned skin, trace the slight lines across his forehead and touch the rough bristles on his chin and jaw above his upper lip. His lip gave a slight twitch, drawing her gaze even more.

She swallowed hard and forced her eyes back up to meet his.

Every inch of her wanted to pull away and run, but his grip was too strong.

Unshaven and rough, he smelled of horses, sweat and leather. She crinkled her nose. He needed a bath and a shave. She took a slow breath to calm herself, but his scent filled her senses, making her aware of his masculinity.

"Anything you have to say to me, say it here."

"Mr. Truman." Reverend Miller moved beside her as if to protect her. "What do you want?"

He released her wrist and answered without taking his eyes off her. "I'm looking for Luke Wheeler."

His steady gaze made her knees tremble.

"I went out to his place, but it was deserted. The saloonkeeper said to talk to Sally."

His cold gray-blue eyes looked her up and down with a cool appraisal that stunned her. Men just didn't look at women that way. His eyes shone like silver lightning, and the tiny hairs on the back of her neck tingled.

Under his beard, the planes of his face looked hard, as if he never smiled. She flushed under his gaze.

Robert Truman appeared to be Luke's age. Yet age was hard to judge in the West, where the land wore everything and everyone down before their time. How did he know Luke?

"What do you want with him?" Reverend Miller asked.

Robert dusted off his hat. His gray-blue eyes became flat and unreadable as stone. "He owes me." He placed the hat back on and finished with absolute authority. "I've come to collect."

Her spine tingled with each word. Her nagging misgivings for Luke flared. What had he done?

Once Robert's hat was back on, Sally could no longer see his eyes under the hat brim. She could only see his straight nose, and firm jaw beneath the stubble. His jaw moved.

She couldn't tell if he still watched her, but she had a feeling he did, and she didn't like it. She fingered her brooch as strange, disquieting thoughts raced through her mind.

Who was he? What debt did Luke owe him?

She wanted to ask, but the words froze in her throat.

"I'm afraid you're too late," Reverend Miller said. "Luke took off, and his place was auctioned." He nodded to Sally. "This lady is his wife, and that's their daughter. So you see you're not the only one who'd like to know where he is."

If possible, Robert's features hardened even more, and the look in his eyes as he stared into hers only made her more nervous. He glanced at Carolyn. "I'll be in town, if you hear from him."

"We know where to find you," Reverend Miller said.

"Ladies." Robert tipped his hat.

The scent of campfires and horses followed him as he walked past. He swung up on his horse in one swift movement, and didn't look back.

As she watched him ride away, Sally's anger toward Luke flamed into a raging fire.

What kind of danger had he placed Matthew in?

Whatever he was involved in, he'd drag Matthew right into the middle of it. There was no doubt in her mind.

Robert Truman was a dangerous man.

Chapter Two

Reverend Miller gave Sally a look of concern. "Do you have any idea what Mr. Truman wants with Luke?"

"No. Strange men came by, but Luke never introduced them."

"That man must be an outlaw," Martha said.

"Now, Martha, you don't know that," Reverend Miller said. "We'll pray about it. All will be well, Sally."

But all would not be well. It hadn't been for a long time.

It was easy for the Millers to say wait and pray. Nothing bad ever happened to them. She'd prayed until her knees ached. She'd prayed Luke would change, she'd prayed they wouldn't lose the farm. She was tired of waiting and she wasn't listening to Reverend Miller any more.

Sally turned away as her thoughts churned. She'd thought if she only tried hard enough, she could make her marriage work.

That was a foolish dream.

Luke had walked out on their marriage, and now her only concern was getting her son back. Luke's problems were his own.

She would deal with her own problems now. She'd listened to her father, then Luke, then Reverend Miller. She was tired of following the advice of men. Where had that ever gotten her? She was tired of meekly accepting her lot in life. She no longer believed that by doing all the right things and trying harder, her life would turn out all right.

Rob tossed his saddlebags onto the dresser in his room

above the saloon, and then headed downstairs for a drink. He was filled with a sense of satisfaction. Soon he would find Luke. *Luke owed him.*

Five years spent in that miserable jail for a crime he didn't commit had taught him to wait for vengeance.

It surprised him to learn Luke had married. It didn't seem possible a man like him would settle with one woman for any length of time.

As Rob gathered information on Luke, he hoped Luke felt the noose tightening. No man on earth knew more about Luke Wheeler than he did. Like a hound catching a scent on the breeze, Rob sensed how close he was to obtaining his goal. But Luke had vanished, almost as if he'd known Rob was coming. The man had a way of slipping off just before the noose cut off his air.

No man's luck held forever.

He'd find Luke, and then he'd be made to pay for five years of Rob's life, his good name and May Belle. After all these years Rob would finally have justice. He found the thought extremely satisfying.

Rob sipped his drink as a vision of Sally filled his head. She had a slim waist that flared into rounded hips, and her red-gold hair hung down to her waist in a braid. He wondered how it would look loose and falling over her bare shoulders.

Luke had good taste in women.

A pity Sally had married him. His gut told him she would lead him to Luke. He would keep watching her until she did.

He tossed back the last of his drink and thought back to when he'd first seen her in the store, looking like an angel with those big blue eyes against her pale skin. The attraction had hit him with surprising force. No other woman had turned his head since his fiancée died.

Revenge left no time for women.

He wasn't about to let one twist her way around his heart again, turning his head.

Until he'd seen Sally, none had even come close. He'd briefly entertained the thought he would gladly share her blankets.

From the first moment he'd seen her, he'd wanted her, like

a stallion filled with blood lust for his mare.

Rob snorted.

Like that could ever happen. Douse those thoughts now. I've been without a woman far too long. She's married to Luke. The last woman on earth to get tangled up with.

He pulled out a deck of cards and tapped them on the table. Cards would take his mind off thoughts of Sally. Thoughts of long red-gold hair spread across his blankets.

He shook his head and willed the image away as he shuffled the cards.

Sally listened to the clock in the parlor tick and watched Carolyn playing with her dolly in the corner. Moss would arrive soon. She wished he would hurry. She hugged her arms around herself and stepped out onto the porch to wait.

Sally agreed with Martha.

Robert Truman is an outlaw. One who will eventually find my missing husband.

She'd looked into his eyes and seen the determination there. Why, she could even see his face in front of her if she closed her eyes. She wished she could clear that vision from her mind.

She couldn't believe Luke had done this to her.

What kind of a man is he, really? He allowed no questions, no talk of his past. What secrets does he have?

Luke wasn't a responsible father. She hadn't been comfortable leaving Matthew with him when she'd gone to help Mrs. Harper.

If I had taken Matthew with me, he would be with me now.

The thought tore at her.

With outlaws hunting for Luke, he would drag Matthew right into the worst sort of trouble. Her stomach clenched. She had to find him. Each day Luke took him further away.

The tragic circumstances of her life had tied her hands for far too long.

From this day forward, things are going to change.

There were many things she'd do once she had her son

back, and one of the first was to find someone to teach her how to read.

Ozzie halted his mule team in front of the house.

Sally turned to Martha who'd joined her on the porch. "Martha, this is Ozzie Moss. He led our wagon train to Kansas."

Ozzie climbed down and held out his hand. He removed his hat and dust fell. "Pleased to meet ye, ma'am."

Martha's nose twitched and she hesitated, eyeing his grubby hand as he grabbed hers and shook it. She brushed her hand on her apron. "Likewise."

"Time to git a move on," Ozzie said.

Sally said goodbye to the Millers, handed Carolyn up to Moss and climbed aboard the wagon. Carolyn caught Sally's excitement as if it were a fever. She peeked into and under things.

"Git on now," Moss urged the mules forward and soon the parsonage was only a speck in the distance.

Winter was coming fast, but Sally refused to worry about the weather. Moss had rubbed the canvas-covered wagon with oil to waterproof it so the supplies would be safe.

A sense of strength came to her. Soon she'd see her son.

Carolyn fell asleep to the creaking and rocking of the wagon. Sally covered her then sat back and wrapped the horse blanket around herself. The rough material scratched and she didn't care for the smell, but it was warm. She'd get used to the smell. She'd have to get used to many things. She grinned, thinking of how Martha's nose had twitched when Moss came near. He smelled like his mules.

The movement of the wagon lulled Sally to sleep, and as she dozed she dreamed of Robert Truman. Each detail of his face was etched in her memory as his eyes looked into hers. His words repeated in her head over and over again. She woke with a start when they stopped.

They camped for the night near a stream. Moss took care of the mules while Sally and Carolyn gathered kindling. Then Sally took out the skillet and plates from the wooden crate hanging off the back of the wagon.

"Mama always said, 'cook the easily spoiled foods first'. Better use the eggs since they might crack."

She reached into the flour barrel for eggs. By the time Moss finished caring for his mules, she'd scrambled the eggs.

Carolyn giggled with glee. "Mama, this is breakfast food. So I don't have to go to bed."

"Them biscuits sure do smell good." Moss chuckled. "But little fillies don't git to hear stories unless they go to bed."

"Will you tell me a story?"

"I reckon."

As he ate, Moss told stories of trail rides, mining and cow poking. It seemed he'd done almost everything legal, and he hinted of things that weren't.

Carolyn listened with wide eyes.

Sally wondered how old he was to have done all those things. His crinkled face was hidden behind a full beard and mustache.

Moss caught Carolyn staring. "Well, little miss, what're ye looking at?" He winked then stuck out his tongue to lick the food off his mustache. "I was savin' it fer later."

Carolyn giggled.

Moss winked at Sally then continued his tale. He had wiry, taut arms from driving mules, and his laugh was infectious.

When was the last time I've had a good laugh?

It felt good after all the tension she'd been under.

After dinner he patted his girth. "I need to walk these here vittles off."

Sally washed the dishes and then tucked Carolyn in.

"Mama, one more story?"

Sally told her the story of Noah's ark.

"Can we take animals too?" Carolyn asked.

"It would be fun, wouldn't it? But no, there'll be plenty of animals where we're going."

"Where are we going?" asked Carolyn.

"Texas."

"Will Matthew and Papa be there?" Carolyn yawned, barely able to keep her eyes open as Sally stroked her forehead.

"Yes. Now go to sleep." She smiled as Carolyn closed her eyes.

"Let's have us a talk," Moss said.

"What's on your mind?"

He gestured to the land around them. "We're in God's country. Ain't no other men nor women about, no townsfolk to tell ye what ain't fittin'."

"I'm glad to be away from all the wagging tongues."

Moss gave her a stern look and continued. "No protection against nature, no law, no safety fer women nor children. Just us here, Sally. No one to know if'n ye change yer mind. Ye kin settle in the next town an' start fresh."

She placed her hands on her hips. "No. I'm going to Texas. My son needs me." Pacing, she looked away south and clenched her fists. "Luke had no right to take him." She turned back to Moss with frown. "And when I find him he's going to wish he hadn't."

Moss raised his hands. "I ain't gonna argue with ye. But don't never say ole Moss didn't give ye a chance to change yer mind."

"I know you're only thinking of me, Moss, but there'll be no changing my mind. I have to find my son."

He slapped his hat on his trouser leg and stomped away from the campsite. "Tarnation," he muttered, "what've ye got yerself into this time, ye ole fool."

His mule brayed in response.

"Talkin' to a woman's like barkin' at a knot."

One thing she'd have to get used to was the way Moss muttered to his mules constantly, as if she couldn't hear him.

The supplies in the wagon left little room for sleeping. Carolyn slept inside while Sally slept under the wagon. Along with her excitement over being on the trail, a hoot owl kept Sally awake well into the night.

That and a sense that someone was there in the dark, watching her.

But it was only nerves from sleeping out under the stars.

Once she slept, she dreamed of wagons, dust, heat, thirst and Matthew calling to her on the wind as a firm hand closed around her wrist.

In the darkness, Rob studied Sally. Silhouetted as she

paced in front of the fire, she couldn't see him as he sat on his horse, watching.

Pensively, he peered through the darkness and wondered if she could sense he'd followed her. Her hand rose to play with the brooch at her neck, a nervous mannerism. She paced back and forth like a caged animal. Each time she turned, her hair flipped in the air. She crossed her arms and placed her hands on her hips.

The motion emphasized the curve of her hips.

Rob blew out a whistle as he watched her in the dark.

The way the campfire silhouetted her figure and lit her unbound hair sent his thoughts in an unwanted direction.

He willed them away.

She shook her head at the old man.

Who was the old codger? Was he taking her to Luke?

Rob had kept back far enough so no one would notice, but Sally had a way of looking around as if she knew he was there. He sat on his horse watching until she slipped into her bedroll. Then he rode back to his own campsite.

He sat cleaning his gun and wondered what her true feelings were toward Luke. Luke's abandonment could be his way of getting out of debt without facing consequences. The question was whether Sally was in on the scheme.

Luke has been good at avoiding his responsibilities so far. But all that will change soon.

Rob finished cleaning his empty gun then pointed it at an imaginary target and dry fired. The day of reckoning couldn't be postponed forever.

I'll find you, Luke. Then you'll pay.

The question of Sally remained. Was she in cahoots with Luke? The storekeeper claimed Sally only wanted to find her son, but the man was obviously protecting Sally.

Luke is a smooth one who can sweet-talk a woman into anything. And she is his wife.

She'd taken off before he had a chance to talk to her again. It irked him. But he would have another chance.

There are hundreds of miles between here and Texas. A few days on the trail will wear her down. The old man is no protection. One old man, one woman and a small child traveling so far at the start of winter and through Indian Territory don't stand a chance.

Rob shook his head. Sally was lucky he'd followed her. He wouldn't let anything happen to her. She was his quickest route to Luke. But she was skittish as a colt. He had no intention of approaching her until the time was right.

He put the gun away and lay down on his bedroll. For now he'd sleep and try to put thoughts of Sally out of his mind.

He closed his eyes and the image of Sally standing in front of the fire filled his mind.

Damn it. If I can just stop thinking about the woman.

The next morning Sally woke stiff and tired.

"Don't look like ye slept none," Moss said.

As she nodded, her head throbbed. "No. I didn't."

"Go rest in back. Carolyn ken ride with me. Won't do ye no good to wear yerself out. Ye'll walk when them mules tire."

Sally climbed in the back then curled up between two barrels. She fell asleep immediately and dreamed.

Robert Truman's gray-blue eyes were watching her. Steady, without blinking they seared her to her very soul. His hand closed over her wrist and a light feeling came over her body as he rose into the air, pulling her along beside him until they rested on a milky white cloud, floating without touching a solid thing in the blue sky.

Sally looked down and saw she was naked. Then she looked at him. The cloud covered him like a mist, but she knew beneath it he was naked too.

She waited, without fear or embarrassment for what would happen next. Still his gaze never wavered from hers.

He pulled her close and suddenly they were falling into the clouds, as he planted a kiss in the hollow of her neck. The sky turned dark as his kiss sang through her body, and she closed her eyes as she felt her body rising. Rising as a heat built within her and they rose higher into the clouds.

His lips moved from her neck to her ear, raining kisses all the way down to her breasts. She gave herself freely to him, and with each kiss they rose a little further until she felt she would burst with the feeling. And as his lips moved down her belly to her pleasure point, they soared higher until his tongue touched her there and she exploded into a million glowing stars in the night sky.

It was then that she woke, heart pounding, with a sense of unreality at seeing where she was, and trying to make sense of it all.

Moss was telling Carolyn of their wagon train to Kansas.

Hearing Moss speak of the hardships they'd endured brought her back to earth with a crash.

Those were long hot days on the trail. Papa had made Kansas sound magical with its free land for farming. He'd never had a chance to plow the first row.

On the trail, Mama had caught the fever and died.

Sally could still picture the open field they'd buried Mama in. The sun had beat down as they'd piled rocks on the grave to keep wolves out. Moss had said to hurry before Indians came.

Out of the twenty buried in the long row of graves, Mama's stood out forever in her mind.

Carolyn was asleep. Sally moved her into the back of the wagon then sat beside Moss.

"Did ye sleep good, Sally Mae?"

She hadn't been called that since Papa died. "Yes, I did."

"I was tellin' Carolyn of our ride to Kansas."

"I heard. It brought back sad memories."

"Ye did yer best takin' care of yer sisters."

She'd cared for them after Mama died until the fever took them too.

"Papa was never the same."

"He jus' give up on life."

Sally nodded but couldn't speak and Moss patted her knee. "We'll get to Texas."

"I should have listened to you when you told me not to marry Luke."

He grunted. "Ye ain't never took my advice."

She'd met Luke right after her father died. He was devilishly handsome and charmed her before she could think.

She'd been occupied with illness and death, and his words were like a breath of fresh air. Soon he had her smiling like a candle that hadn't been lit for a long time. With Luke's coaxing and teasing, her appetite returned. She turned to him like a daisy turns toward the sun, soaking up the attention. Soaking up what she'd thought was love. But he'd never used the word. Not once.

After the wedding he changed. He became secretive and moody. He would ride off for weeks. His temper was short. Having a son hadn't changed him one lick. She'd learned quickly to keep the children away as she bore the brunt of his temper.

Why would Luke take Matthew when he doesn't even like children?

All those nights he'd come home with whiskey breath and hard fists. She shook her head to force back the bad memories. Every memory she had of Luke was soured in some way.

Kansas was Papa's dream and my nightmare.

"Moss, how many weeks before we reach Texas?"

"Now, Sally Mae, ye know there ain't any way of tellin'. On a good day a wagon might travel twenty miles an' in winter it won't go near as fast if'n the weather don't hold."

After a time, Sally walked beside the wagon. Moss claimed the more weight the mules pulled, the quicker they'd tire.

Here on the trail, she had hours full of nothing to do but walk along beside the wagon, retracing Luke's actions over the last two weeks. His behavior had been stranger than usual.

The day Mr. Harper came to get Sally because his wife was in early labor, Luke had pushed her into the barn, locked the door and demanded she lift her skirts.

He'd known he'd be gone before I would return.

She thought again of her embarrassment when she emerged from the barn. She could tell by the way Mr. Harper reddened and turned away that he'd known what Luke had done.

Luke had laughed and said, "A wife has to see to her own man's needs before she runs off to another man's house. Especially a man with a pregnant wife who ain't had any."

Sally had lifted Carolyn into Mr. Harper's wagon before she

quickly climbed in herself. In her hurry to get away from Luke, she'd forgotten to hug Matthew.

"Mind your father," she'd called out, as Mr. Harper cracked the whip. That had been the way she'd said goodbye to Matthew.

Tears filled her eyes and ran down her cheeks.

It had all happened so fast.

Anger overtook the place of pain in her heart, numbing it. He'd known he was leaving days before the auction, and the last thing he'd said to her was "get in here and lift your skirt". Bruises were all he'd left her with.

Setting her jaw, she determined to do whatever it took to get her son back from the monster that was her husband.

And heaven help anyone who stands in my way.

Chapter Three

Carolyn bounced on the seat. "Look, Mama, look!"

"Yes, sunshine, that's Fort Riley."

"We'll stop here for a day or two, an' I'll ask if anyone has seen Luke," Moss said.

"We can't stay long." Sally frowned. "Each day Luke gets farther away. I had no idea we'd travel so slow."

"Cain't go no faster lessen' ye got fresh mules. And them we ain't got. Hep." He urged his team on toward the fort.

"It looks like the soldiers are preparing for trouble."

The fort was a buzz of activity as they rode in.

Carolyn stared at the soldiers in fascination.

Moss stopped the wagon as a soldier held up one hand. "All civilians report to Sergeant Keener. Follow me."

Sally and Carolyn trailed along behind the men until they reached a small, white tent. Inside, a sergeant with a pencil-thin mustache shuffled through papers on his desk. He rose when they entered, lifted his hat and nodded to Sally. "Ma'am."

He gestured to two chairs and they sat. Sally held Carolyn on her lap.

"Name?"

"Sally Wheeler. This is my daughter Carolyn and my friend Ozzie Moss."

The sergeant made a notation then leaned back and tapped his fingers together. "Where are you headed?"

"To Texas to find my husband and son."

Husband. The word tasted bitter in her mouth.

The sergeant raised his eyebrows and watched her for a

long moment without speaking. "That's quite a distance for a woman and child to travel without protection."

"Now look here." Moss stood, sputtering.

The sergeant held up his hand. "No offense. You'll stay in the Fort. Later you can travel with a group headed south."

"Do you know of any such group?" Sally asked.

"No." He eyed Sally up and down as an odd look crossed his face. Then he glanced over at Moss. "We'll speak of your missing husband later."

He knows something about Luke.

Sally nodded, barely able to contain her questions. He obviously wasn't going to tell her now. The dismissal in his tone was evident.

"My birthday is tomorrow," Carolyn piped up.

The sergeant smiled down at her. "How old will you be?"

She held up four fingers.

Sergeant Keener turned to Sally. "I don't have time to talk now, but I'd be pleased if you'd join me for dinner tomorrow night."

"Thank you." She would ask him about Luke then.

"I must return to my duties. You'll camp with the others."

Holding Carolyn's hand, Sally left the tent. The settlers' area was full of wagons, tents, cook fires and children running. Moss chose a spot for the wagon then tended his mules.

Sally washed the dust from her face then accepted a glass of cider from the woman camped beside them as Carolyn played with the woman's two daughters.

"What are the soldiers preparing for?" Sally asked.

The woman stared. "Haven't you heard? Them Indians raided five homesteads. The army ordered us into the fort for safety."

Matthew.

She could only hope and pray Luke would keep him safe. Luke's vicious streak could be the one thing protecting Matthew.

"The sergeant said to find a group headed south."

"You won't find one. Not now. We're all staying here."

"I can't stay. I have to find my husband and son."

"You should be thankful to be safe in this fort." The woman shivered. "Lord knows what them savages might do." Sally had heard terrible tales of Indian raids. But Luke and Matthew had to travel through Indian Territory to reach Texas, and so would she. She wrapped her arms around Carolyn and held her close, unable to bear the thought of anyone hurting either of her children.

I have to find my son, and no threat of Indians is going to stop me. I'll do whatever it takes to get him away from Luke. To get him away from danger and safe, back in my arms where he belongs.

She gave Carolyn a squeeze and breathed in her sweet little girl scent, closing her eyes.

No one gets between my children and me. Not even Luke.

After settling Carolyn in bed, Sally lay awake watching the stars and listening to the noises in the fort.

A soldier on watch called, "All's well".

It didn't reassure her.

All the dangers Matthew could encounter played themselves through her head. Despite her determination to force the thoughts away, her mind kept returning to them. She wanted to saddle a horse and ride after him as fast as she could. But she couldn't with Carolyn to consider. If only Luke's bad temper was enough to keep her son alive. Luke wasn't a man to cross.

Sally rolled onto her side. She longed to sleep next to Carolyn in the wagon, holding her. But there was no room.

Dozens of supplies filled the back of the wagon. Twenty pounds of coffee, twenty pounds of sugar, ten pounds of rice and one hundred pounds of flour. Then there was the load Moss had to deliver.

She fingered the locket she wore even when she slept. She'd lost so many family heirlooms already. Each time Luke had sold one she'd cried. Tears made Luke angry.

Tonight tears spilled down her cheeks. No one could see her in the darkness and the night noises muffled the sound. A dog barked, a baby cried and somewhere a man snored.

Here in the dark it was safe to cry.

Questions raced through her head. Was Matthew sleeping

under the stars or with a roof over his head? Was he warm enough? And the most nagging question of all—why had Luke taken him? Did he hate her that much? He had to have known what this would do to her.

Imagining where Matthew was tonight would make her wild with worry. Wherever Luke was, he was playing cards. Matthew would eat according to Luke's luck.

Luke held his secrets like cards, close to himself. Why hadn't he warned her that a man might come looking for him? Where had he gone? And what had he done to make Robert come after him? Luke was capable of anything. Except honest work.

The last time he'd stayed out all night, she'd found a bit of courage. Or was it fear of losing the farm? She'd told him not to come home again stinking of whiskey. She'd said the next time he went riding off, it had better be to find a job.

She'd thought he would hit her, but instead he smirked. Now she pictured his smirk and wondered if he'd taken Matthew for spite.

All she'd ever wanted was to be a good wife and mother. She'd tried so hard to do whatever he'd asked. Yet it had never been enough. She'd thought she married one kind of man only to find herself married to another. From the first week of their marriage, she'd learned to give him what he wanted.

He enjoys hurting me.

"I'm glad he's gone," she whispered into the night.

Her thoughts turned to Robert Truman.

Strange how she could close her eyes and see each detail of his face yet she could not say the same of Luke. Perhaps it was that she didn't want to remember Luke and all the bad memories.

Robert Truman's eyes haunted her, the way his gaze searched her, as if looking for her every secret, the way his gaze penetrated her deeper than any man's ever had.

She tried to put him out of her mind, but it was impossible. Each time she saw a shadow, she had the feeling he was there watching her. But when she turned to look, no one was there. Though she felt sure he was miles away, the feeling lingered.

If he discovered where Luke had gone, would he find Luke before she did?

She pictured the way the muscle clenched in his jaw when he spoke Luke's name. What had Luke done to put that look in his eyes and what would he do about it?

There was bound to be shooting. She had to make sure her son didn't stand in the way between the two most dangerous men she'd ever met.

Rob entered the fort and told the sentry on duty he was traveling to Oklahoma to find an old friend. Half-truths had served him well since he'd begun the search for Luke.

He'd once counted Luke a passing acquaintance. May Belle had enjoyed the man's company and Rob had wanted to please her.

Love had blinded him. He should have trusted his instincts. If not for Luke, his fiancée would still be alive.

His fists clenched.

Beautiful unfaithful May Belle.

He was no longer the trusting fool he'd once been. There was only one person he could trust. Himself.

He wanted to talk to Sally again, but she'd left before he'd had a chance. Once he got her alone, he'd get answers. Now that she had only the old man to keep her company, he'd have a better chance of talking to her on the trail.

It would be easy to watch her undetected with people milling about the fort.

He'd just finished grooming his horse when Lee Clark, his former prison mate, rode up.

"I've been chasing you for the last three days. You said you'd meet me in Marysville."

"Sally took off and I had to catch up. I knew you'd be able to find me. What news do you have?"

"Luke isn't married to that woman you've been following."

"That's not what I heard."

As a former Pinkerton man, Lee was capable of tracking the craftiest outlaw and he was very thorough.

"You want to hear the rest?"

"You know I do."

"Luke was busy while you were locked up. Managed to

marry three different women."

Rob snorted. "Figures."

"It gets even better."

"Go on."

"He's played them all for fools. He finds lonely women who have no family, convinces them to marry him then brings in a traveling minister to do the honors. But he's no minister. He's one of Luke's gang."

"Three women." Rob shook his head. "Damn, he *has* been busy. And let me guess. He takes all their money, and then disappears."

"That's what he did to Sally. He borrowed so heavily on their farm there was no chance they'd ever get it back. Rose is a dancehall girl, she never had any money to begin with. She was his first wife, before you met him. Their son ought to be about thirteen now. She's still carrying a torch for him but he doesn't come around."

"And the other?"

"The other is the most recent. Young girl who lived with her mother and helped her run a boarding house before the girl took up with Luke and got pregnant. She's working in a saloon now."

Another life ruined. Luke was good at that.

"Her mother said I'd be doing her a favor if I put a bullet between his eyes."

"I'll be more than happy to oblige her."

"You'll want to talk to the girl. She's the one most likely to know where he is, if Sally isn't going to meet him."

"She claims she's married to him and he's taken her son. Says she's going to get the boy back."

"She'll need help if it's just her and the old man. What do you plan to do?"

"First I'm going to find out what she knows about where Luke has headed and if she's in league with him."

"You going to tell her she isn't married?"

Rob looked off toward the wagon. "When the time is right."

"That might change her mind if she's thinking kindly toward him. Give her another reason to be mad."

Rob stared off into the distance and frowned.

So Sally isn't married. That doesn't change a thing.

But even as he told himself that, deep down he knew one reason to fight the attraction to her had just been removed.

Lee watched him for a minute without speaking. "Never thought a woman would get under your skin again."

"She hasn't."

"I wouldn't be so sure."

"Lee, you know why I'm here. And nothing and no one is going to get in my way."

"Do you want my help?"

"Don't need it. But I'm much obliged to you for finding out what you did and coming all this way to tell me."

Lee grasped his shoulder. "Some debts can never be repaid. Any time you need me, I've got your back."

Rob clasped his shoulder in return. "I appreciate that. But this one is for me and me alone."

Lee nodded and they stepped apart.

"Come on, I'll buy you a drink. If you've been chasing me for three days you must be a mite thirsty."

"That I am."

Rob contemplated what Sally would do once she heard the news as they headed for the bar.

The next day Carolyn and Sally wore their new yellow dresses. Sally wanted to look respectable. The threadbare dress she'd been wearing wasn't even fit for quilt scraps.

She kept to the wagon keeping an eye on Carolyn while Moss made inquiries about Luke. By dinnertime he'd still learned nothing of value.

"He ain't one to tell folks his business," Moss said.

"Perhaps the sergeant knows something," Sally said.

"You gals are purty as a picture." Moss winked.

"Lovely." Sergeant Keener appeared in front of the wagon, smiled and extended his arm. "Ma'am, may I have the honor?"

"Yes, sir, you may." Sally linked her arm through his and they walked to his tent for dinner.

Moss trailed along behind to chaperone. Earlier he'd

pointed out that a lone woman was an invitation to some men, missing husband or not.

"Can I touch your sword?" Carolyn asked.

"If you are very careful."

She touched it with her index finger and giggled. "It's shiny."

At the sergeant's tent they were served chicken, cornbread, and for dessert, a birthday cake. After dinner, the sergeant gave Carolyn a rag doll. She danced with it, singing.

The sergeant stood. "I'll walk you back to your wagon."

They strolled back and Moss went to check on his mules.

Sally lifted Carolyn into the wagon and then turned back to the sergeant. "I want to thank you for all you've done."

Her surprise at the gift was mingled with suspicion. He'd gone out of his way to give Carolyn a present, yet he'd only met them yesterday.

It was quite inappropriate.

Carolyn hugged the doll tight as she settled in to play. Sally couldn't refuse the gift now. Carolyn was too young to understand. But it made Sally uncomfortable.

"My pleasure, ma'am." He moved toward Sally. "We'll have dinner in my tent tomorrow night. Just the two of us."

"No, I couldn't." She stepped back, suddenly wary. Her back touched the wagon and she jumped. All through dinner she'd hoped he'd tell her what he knew. Yet when pressed, he claimed to know nothing of Luke or her son. Her hand rose to her brooch as he leaned nearer. "I must find my husband and son."

"I can't allow you to leave the fort. It's too dangerous."

"What do you mean you can't allow it?"

He gripped her arm. "Listen. I can't protect you outside this fort. You must stay."

She stiffened as her heart hammered in her chest. The look in his eyes made her nervous.

He pulled her closer. "You mustn't leave."

Why is he behaving this way? He knows I am married. It isn't proper.

She glanced at Carolyn, who was completely engrossed in

her new dolly.

Sergeant Keener followed the direction of her glance. "Think of your child if you won't think of yourself."

"I am thinking of my child."

She thought of nothing but. Nothing but her missing child.

He reached up and released the wagon flap. "Think long and hard, Sally." His thumb rubbed her arm inside her elbow. "I'd hate to see you captured for an Indian's slave. That red hair of yours makes you quite a prize."

"I'll be careful."

He yanked her close against his body, his arousal evident. "I'll take care of you."

She gasped and tried to pull away.

His fingers tightened.

She froze, his manner suddenly reminding her of Luke.

Don't make him angry.

"It's a hard journey. But that's not the only thing that's hard." He pushed her against the wagon, knocking the wind out of her as his fingers bit into her arm and his other hand yanked up her skirt.

She struggled, trying to push him away. "No!"

Carolyn called out, "Mama?"

"Go to sleep, birthday girl, I'll take care of your mama." His hand forced her underclothes away and he growled in her ear, "Stay quiet. You don't want your daughter to see."

"Leave me alone," she whispered, frantically struggling. "I'm married."

"I like a woman with fire." His hand cupped her bare bottom and squeezed, pulling her close to rub against her. "And when I met Luke Wheeler he said nothing of a wife or son."

Sally gasped.

Matthew wasn't with him? Where had he hidden Matthew so that the sergeant hadn't seen him?

"He didn't seem the marrying type."

His lips took hers in a harsh, controlling kiss.

Sally's mind spun as she struggled to get away.

He let her up for air. "If you're good to me, I'll escort you south myself. It's been a long time since I had a woman."

Debra Parmley

The click of a gun cocking behind the sergeant's head made him freeze.

"Let her go." Robert Truman stood behind the sergeant with a look of fury on his face, his voice dead calm.

"This is none of your business." The sergeant let her go and turned to face him. "If you know what's good for you, you'll move along."

"This woman *is* my business. So it's you who'll be moving along." Robert's gaze narrowed. "Now."

The sergeant moved away one slow step at a time, his hands raised. "Sally, I'll see you tomorrow."

Not if I can help it.

"Sally, are you all right?" Robert's voice was gentle, his profile strong and sure.

"Yes." She adjusted her clothes nervously and smoothed her skirt. "Thank you for stopping him."

"No thanks are necessary. If there's anything else I can do for you..."

He could hold her until her limbs stopped shaking. No, she couldn't tell him that. She shouldn't even be thinking of it. But he'd saved her and she couldn't seem to stop herself as he stood before her, strength radiating from him like the rays of the sun.

It would be so easy to fall into his arms.

Yet she couldn't. She twisted the wedding band on her finger. She'd taken vows to be true to her husband, scoundrel that he was. And she wouldn't break them.

She glanced away. "No. Moss will be back soon."

If Moss knew an outlaw was looking for her husband, he might change his mind about taking her to Texas. She couldn't tell him about Robert.

"Who is Moss?"

"Ozzie Moss is an old family friend." She looked about for Ozzie. "You should go."

"It would be best if I waited for your friend to return. In case the sergeant comes back."

"No. I'll be fine." Her fingers touched the brooch and she bit her lip with a frown. Moss would be here any minute. Then she would have to explain Robert's presence. "Really."

He sized her up in silence, his gray-blue eyes lingering over

46

her with a warmth that made her flush. Finally he nodded. "Then I'll be going. You take care, Sally."

"Thank you again. Good night."

Sally looked into the wagon where Carolyn had fallen asleep and sighed with relief. Her daughter had been spared the scene.

Moss came up. "I spoke to the sergeant when ye was fixin' up fer dinner. We'd best lay low here 'til it's safe."

"Why, Moss, I didn't think you were afraid of anything."

"'Fraid, no, course not," he sputtered. "Jus' makes more work fer a man to set his sails 'gainst a pervailin' wind, and them winds is pervailin' right now."

She placed her hands on her hips. "We have to leave tonight. I *can't* stay here. How soon can you be ready?"

He stared at her. "Ozzie Moss is always ready, even when he don't want ter be. Tarnation, Sally, cain't it wait 'til mornin'?"

"No. The sergeant tried to...seduce me." She didn't like lying to Ozzie, but if she told the truth she'd have to explain about Robert. "I wouldn't sleep a wink, knowing he was nearby."

He shook his head and stomped off muttering, "Women folks always has to have their way. Cain't reason with 'em, wors'n mules. Have to leave tonight. Humph."

Sally ignored him. She'd take her chances outside the fort, Indians and all. She couldn't stay here another minute.

Rob had watched and listened from the shadows as the sergeant manhandled Sally. His hand had closed over his gun and flexed before he forced it away.

No. All Sally has to do is cry out.

But she had made no sound other than a whisper he couldn't hear from where he hid.

She must know her marriage isn't valid. Why else is she carrying on with the sergeant? Or is she one of those women who likes a little on the side?

Is the man going to take her right there, with her little girl inside the wagon? Now that just isn't right.

She had begun to struggle, and as he saw the sergeant raise her skirt baring her leg, Rob had moved out of the shadows and pulled his gun.

When it was over, he had stepped back into the shadows to watch over her as he had before.

She seemed to attract the worst sort of men. Keeping the woman safe clear to Texas might prove to be more of a job than he'd thought. It would be much better if he were to travel with her. He wondered how that could be arranged.

Rob smiled to himself as he heard Sally tell the old man she was leaving tonight. That suited him just fine. He'd be right behind her, keeping back far enough that she wouldn't realize he followed her.

He was drawn to her like no woman he'd ever met before. She made his blood surge. It would have been easier if she were truly married. Then she would have been off limits.

If not for Luke, things would be very different. He would have gathered her in his arms, comforting her after her scare. If not for Luke, she wouldn't have been in this position in the first place. Neither would he.

He watched her until he was sure they were ready to head out, pushing away the thought of holding her in his arms.

What were her feelings toward Luke and what secrets did she hide? Did she hide Luke's secrets?

She was a puzzle he would solve.

He considered her recent behavior. She seemed in a great hurry to find Luke. She was probably following his instructions to meet.

Women aren't to be trusted.

He had learned that lesson the hard way.

"Moss, hurry."

Will the sergeant bar me from leaving the fort?

Moss grumbled to his mules, "Dang woman, cain't wait to run into trouble in the middle of the night. Has to leave now." He climbed onto the wagon. "Dang if it ain't aggravatin' followin' a woman's direction."

Sally pretended not to hear him as they rode away south.

Once on the trail, Moss kept silent, brooding.

"I'm sorry, Moss, but I had to get away from that man. I doubt the Indians will bother us."

"If yer in their territory, they'll bother ye all right. Don't matter who ye are or if ye travel by day or night."

"I had no choice. And we'll find Matthew quicker."

"Ain't no point in arguin' with a woman anyhow," Moss muttered. "Get on now," he called to his mules.

They drove all night and Sally dozed with the intention of offering to take a turn driving the mules after they stopped.

"I reckon we gone as far as we kin. I'm mighty hungry an' my mules need restin'."

"I'll fix us a nice big meal. We didn't see one Indian. Now aren't you glad we didn't hide in the fort?"

"I ain't never hid, but I laid low many a time. It ain't the same. Not seein' Indians on the first night don't mean we ain't gonna see Indians later."

"I'm not afraid. I've seen one."

"When? Where?" Moss frowned, glanced around and squinted off into the distance.

"Not here. On our ride to Kansas, I saw a girl in a canoe."

"Humph. If you'd seen a warrior, you'd a been more skeered, I reckon."

"Well, just the same, nothing bad happened."

"Ye gonna fix them vittles or yap all day?" He stomped off.

She called after him, "I promised you a big meal, and that's what you'll have."

Hungry men were grouchy men. This wasn't the time to argue with him about Indians. She thought of all the stories her grandfather had told of their people in Scotland and Ireland fighting over land. Men always fought over land. She couldn't fault the Indians for fighting for theirs, though she knew it wasn't a popular opinion.

Sally sliced sweet potatoes, fried them in hot fat then sprinkled them with molasses. A gust of wind blew, causing her skirt to catch and rise toward the fire.

She backed away quickly, remembering the woman who'd caught fire during the Kansas trip. She'd have to be more careful.

She mixed an ashcake with cornmeal, the last of the buttermilk and fat. Then she kneaded the thick dough and placed it in the skillet to bake.

Food would be harder to come by as the trail went on. Much would depend on what Moss could shoot.

After they ate, she walked to the stream to wash the dishes and pans. On the other side of the stream, a black horse pawed the ground. There must be a rider nearby. But she didn't see anyone. The only sounds were the trickling of the water and the horse's huffing. Still, someone had to have ridden the horse. It wore a blanket.

A man crouched in the bushes, his dark eyes watching her.

Her breath caught. She froze.

The Indian warrior didn't appear to move or breathe. His dark eyes locked onto her, his penetrating gaze dark and fierce, his shoulders powerful as if carved of stone. He didn't blink.

She couldn't move or scream and her breath roared in her ears, while her mind told her to run.

His fierce chiseled face held smudges of dirt as if he'd stepped out of the land, like no civilized man. He wore two feathers in his hair and three necklaces, one made from claws.

Would he kill her?

Carolyn!

She was with Moss. He'd fire a shot if there were trouble.

All was quiet.

What was the warrior waiting for? Was he alone?

His eyes continued to bore into hers. It seemed like days and still he didn't move. His horse shuffled and she noticed it was lame. The man's shoulder bled from a wound.

His chest rose slightly. So he was breathing, but still he barely moved. How bad was his wound? She had medicine back at the wagon. Would he let her clean the wound?

Water dripped through the rinsing cloth, past her fingers, down her arm. Still, she stood frozen, afraid to lay it down. Sudden movement might startle him into doing something.

What should she do? Try to help him? Scream or run? If only Moss would come.

Could he be hungry? Slowly she reached for the pan that held the remaining sweet potatoes and held it out toward him.

His dark eyes, which rooted her to the edge of the stream, darted past her to their campsite. He listened then shot her a sharp glance as he moved back into the bushes, taking cover until she no longer saw him.

She looked back at the campsite. What had startled him?

"Sally, where did ye run off to?" Moss called.

Quickly she set the pan of food down and gathered the other dishes. She'd return for the pan later.

"I was washing dishes," she called as she hurried back to the wagon.

"It ain't safe to go off alone."

"I'm perfectly fine." She walked quickly away from the tree line toward the wagon.

Later, Sally slipped back to the creek. She saw no sign of the warrior, but on her side of the stream on the flat rock where she'd sat to gather water, a necklace of blue-green rocks lay next to the empty pan.

She slipped the necklace over her head and tucked it inside her blouse. If she wore the gift openly she'd have to explain it to Moss. Yet another secret she kept from him.

Moss said they'd start back on the trail the next morning.

Sally watched the tree line for signs of the Indian as she listened to every little sound.

"Morning," Sally said.

Moss stretched like the old hunting dog her grandfather once had. He'd aged since their last journey. Back then he'd always been the first up. A niggling bit of doubt made her wonder if she'd been wise in asking him to help her.

Though he prided himself on his tracking and wilderness skills, his eyes weren't as sharp as she remembered. He hadn't noticed the eagle circling overhead earlier, and he had trouble finding things in the wagon.

"Mornin'. Coffee made yit?"

"Almost." She placed her hands on her hips. "It's high time you let me take a turn driving the wagon."

She'd pull her own weight on the trail.

"Well, now. If yer sure ye kin handle 'em."

"I can."

He seemed pleased and she was glad she'd made the offer.

Once they'd finished breakfast and she'd driven for a bit to show him she really could handle the team, they stopped and he unhitched one of the mules.

"Reckon I'll scout ahead jus' fer a short bit." He rode off with a nod to her, as the team started forward.

The rhythm of the wagon put Carolyn to sleep. Sally gazed ahead as the sense of being alone came over her. She should be used to the feeling by now. Even when Luke was home, she was alone. She'd give anything to have her sisters and her parents back again. To hear the chatter of female voices. Anything but the mournful prairie wind.

The wagon lurched. Sally's hands tightened on the reins as something gave a loud crack.

The wagon tipped to the side.

Carolyn screamed.

"Carolyn!" Sally reached for her as they slid sideways.

The corner of the wagon hit the ground with a thud and they tumbled off the seat onto the hard soil, Sally cushioning Carolyn's fall.

She fought to hold onto the three startled mules.

They moved about frantically and as she stood, they almost threw her off her feet again.

After she had them settled and tied the reins, she turned to Carolyn, who stood sucking her thumb, as her rag doll hung limp in her other hand.

A tear ran down Carolyn's cheek as she began to cry. "Mama, I was scared."

Sally hugged her. "You're all right, sunshine. Moss will be back soon. He'll tell us what to do."

She surveyed the damage, looking to see what they'd hit.

They'd hit a rock. It looked bad.

How could she have hit such a large rock? Why hadn't she paid attention as she drove the wagon? Moss would be angry. It was all her fault. She wished now that she hadn't offered to drive his team.

How long it would be until he returned? And what would he do? Even if he yelled, at least he'd know what to do. He'd have to fix the wagon out here in the middle of nowhere.

Sally and Carolyn sat on the ground and waited under the

gray sky, which grew darker by the minute. Raindrops sprinkled down. They moved near the wagon for protection. Carolyn whimpered and hugged her dolly tight.

She heard a rider rapidly approaching.

Sally jumped up and ran around to the other side of the wagon shouting, "Oh, I'm so glad you've come!"

Her smile faded as her eyes locked on the man's long, lean form. A flicker of apprehension coursed through her. She placed a hand over her brooch, took a step back and froze.

No, not him again.

"Well, Sally, what a surprise."

What was *he* doing here? Was he following her?

"Looks like you could use a hand." Robert Truman got down off his horse and strode toward her.

Sally put her arms around Carolyn, pulling her close.

It seemed the world stopped as he drew closer.

He stood in front of her, tall and straight like a towering spruce, as he looked down into her eyes, his sharp gray-blue eyes assessing her. He'd bathed and shaved. The angles of his chin now stood out on his chiseled face.

This was the second time in two days Robert Truman had come to her rescue.

She stared as if she'd never seen him before. He was incredibly handsome now that he'd cleaned up. His mouth curved into a smile, deepening the lines of his face as he glanced down at Carolyn. A butterfly fluttered in Sally's stomach.

"There's no reason to be afraid," he said.

"I'm not afraid," Carolyn replied.

He looked pointedly at Sally's hands, which were holding her daughter too tight.

She let loose and Carolyn moved away to find her dolly.

As Sally continued to look into his eyes, a sense came over her that he wouldn't hurt them.

She realized she was staring and blushed. He was much taller than Luke. He towered over her, making her feel small. And he was looking at her in a way that made her cheeks even warmer. In fact, her body was growing warmer by the minute and the memory of the feel of his hand over her wrist returned.

Flustered, she looked down at her wrist.

He was disturbing to her in every way.

Robert moved closer in front of her with a commanding air of self-confidence that made her glance up at him again.

"Have you heard from Luke?"

"No," she answered quickly over her rapidly beating heart. She would not be attracted to this man. He was dangerous. She tried not to look at his dark hair and sun-tanned face. She dared not look into his eyes again.

He was doing strange things to her insides and she had to remind herself she was married.

"Would you tell me if you had?"

Her gaze dropped to his gun belt then darted away again.

Martha was right. He looks like a gunfighter. Outlaw or lawman, either way he is dangerous.

His commanding presence frightened her. But not enough to tell him anything, even if she'd known where Luke had gone.

"That's what I thought." His voice was harsh and she shivered as she felt his gaze on her.

She kept her eyes averted and didn't speak.

The very air around them seemed alive. Even though she didn't look at him, she felt it all around her.

It made no difference if he worked for the law or for himself. He still wanted Luke, and it wasn't for anything good. And that would put Matthew right in the middle of danger. But if he was asking her, then he must not know where Luke had gone.

"Let me have a look at the damage."

"All right," she replied in a small voice.

Moss, hurry back soon.

It was unlikely Robert would ride on. But surely there was no harm in him looking at the wagon. He couldn't do more damage to it than she'd already done.

He laid his hat on the ground and crawled under the wagon.

She watched the muscles in his legs as he scooted beneath.

Suddenly her throat was dry and she moved to get a drink of water. She splashed a bit of it on her face to cool down, then sat to wait and bit her lip, wondering how bad the damage was to the wagon.

Carolyn's tears had stopped the minute Robert rode up. Now she squatted playing with her dolly, completely unaware of how the air crackled between her mother and the stranger.

Carolyn, who was usually afraid of strange men.

The rain stopped though dark clouds still threatened overhead.

Rob mused over Sally's reaction to him as he checked the wagon. It wasn't maidenly virtue that made her look away. Her eyes had shown considerable interest in his appearance, now that he'd bathed and shaved, and though he'd noticed a note of fear, she was definitely attracted to him.

The attraction was mutual. She was a beauty, and under other circumstances he'd enjoy seeing how far it would take them. But he wanted her to lead him to Luke, and anything else would just get in the way. Beauty like hers could lead him off-track quicker than a rattlesnake.

Though Sally had an innocent look to her, that didn't mean she *was* innocent. He couldn't imagine how she could have stayed that way while married to Luke. That she was chasing after Luke told him all he needed to know.

Though for a few long minutes his heart had risen into his throat as he'd watched the wagon tip and heard their screams. It was with relief that he'd seen they were unharmed.

Sally watched him beneath the wagon and wondered what he was doing. What was taking so long?

After what seemed like forever, he scooted back out and she watched those hard muscles again. He stood and dusted off his trousers. Then he picked up his hat, knocked it against his leg and studied her with intent.

She was acutely aware of his tall, rangy body. A swath of dark hair fell across his forehead and his clear, observant gray-blue eyes watched her.

She traced the pattern on her brooch until she realized he was watching her every move, then her hand dropped to her side. She couldn't let him know he frightened her.

"It doesn't look good." He shook his head. "Can't be fixed. And it's too far to the nearest town." He settled his hat back on his head.

She could no longer read his unfathomable eyes. A new wave of apprehension swept through her as she listened to his voice. She was alone with a man she barely knew. A man who wanted Luke for some reason. Something big enough that he'd lingered instead of moving on.

He's followed me. It couldn't be a coincidence he'd just happened along so suddenly. He'd been waiting to rescue her each time. This meant he'd never been far.

His face, bronzed by wind and sun, remained neutral, but she felt his gray-blue eyes under the hat watching her intently.

"You're looking for Luke," he said.

"Yes." She bit back the questions racing through her mind.

If only he'd ride on.

But then he'd likely find Luke first and she couldn't allow that to happen. She had no doubt he'd find Luke. He seemed capable of anything. And that scared her. She shivered.

"You're headed to Texas. You've heard from him."

"No. I don't know where he is." Sudden panic at the thought of Matthew getting between the two dangerous men made her blurt out, "Travel with me and we'll find him sooner."

As soon as the words left her mouth, she regretted them.

What did I do?

Chapter Four

"Unload your belongings. We'll pack what we can on the mules, then I'll take you to town." Robert had an air of authority and a tone that demanded instant obedience.

Sally hesitated. Already she regretted her hasty words. What had she been thinking, inviting him to travel with her?

He was the sort of man who would take control, and as Martha had said, he was probably an outlaw.

It was too late to take her words back. Still, she wasn't going anywhere alone with him and Moss would return soon. But traveling with an outlaw wasn't the only danger. He was disturbing to her in every way, and each time she saw him, the pull was stronger. Even now her heart was hammering foolishly.

"I'm waiting for Ozzie Moss."

"Where is he?"

"He went ahead to scout. It's his wagon and he'll decide what to do. He always carries extra wagon wheels."

He surveyed the landscape and shrugged, making her notice the way his muscles rippled beneath his shirt.

"Won't be anything he can do. Wheels are useless. That axle is cracked." Gray-blue eyes under his hat's brim studied her face thoughtfully, gauging her reaction.

Oh, no. Moss will be upset over the loss of his wagon. It is his livelihood and he has a load to deliver. There's no telling how he will react to the news.

"You'd best decide what to take before he returns. He won't want to wait while you pick through your things."

"I suppose you're right." Taking Carolyn by the hand, Sally

led her to the back of the wagon. "Stay right here."

Carolyn nodded, sat and watched Robert with wide eyes.

If only Moss would hurry back before I do something I might regret.

Her nerves were strung tighter than a fiddle's bow. She'd do anything to keep her son safe, even if it meant traveling with a dangerous man. But now she'd be under his watchful eyes until they found her son. And it was a long way to Texas. The thought made her shiver in a combination of anticipation and dread. She couldn't stand not knowing where he was on the trail, and she couldn't stand being so near him.

Sally climbed into the wagon, feeling his gaze on her.

Rob watched her bend to climb into the wagon and fought the urge to follow her. Everything took on a clean brightness when she was around until he could almost forget what he'd come for.

He couldn't help wondering what she'd do if he kissed her. The image of her bared skin when the sergeant had pushed her skirt up was burned into his mind—scorching him with desire.

Rob shook his head. He had to stay on track and not allow unwanted thoughts to distract him.

With the old man gone, this was the perfect opportunity to speak to her alone. As alone as a woman with a small child would ever be.

Knowing Luke had tricked her into a false marriage, he'd begun to feel sympathy for her. Sympathy he couldn't afford. He still didn't know if she was in cahoots with Luke and planning to meet him somewhere. But he needed to find out. And the best way to start was to tell her about her marriage. See what her reaction would be. And he needed to do it before the old man returned.

Sally rolled her quilts, which they would need as the weather turned colder, all the while listening to Carolyn's voice singing outside the wagon. The sound reassured her.

Lifting the christening gown both of her children had worn, she held it to her breast and closed her eyes. There wasn't room. Maybe some other mother would find a use for it.

"I'll feed the mules before we leave."

His voice behind her ear made her jump and her eyes flew

open. He'd crept up on her and now her heart raced.

"Fine." Her voice shook. He made her nervous and now he knew it. "Go ahead."

He edged around in front of her until they were almost nose-to-nose. Though with his height she had to look up at him. They were so close she could see a faint scar on his forehead below a wave of hair and wrinkles in the corners of his eyes as they smiled down into hers with compassion.

Her breath caught in her throat.

"You can't take everything." His voice softened, like velvet. Soothing. Warm. "Only the essentials."

Flushed, she held the christening gown away from her breast where his gaze had caressed her briefly. Briefly, but long enough to make a heat rise in her body.

"Yes, I know."

She had to say something, anything to mask the way she longed for him to touch her breasts, even as his hand closed over her hand and the christening gown.

His touch was warm and firm, and it was as if every fiber in her body screamed out for him to stay here, touching her.

There was no sound other than the beating of her heart, as she watched his chest rise and fall, his muscles firm beneath his shirt.

Say something. Anything.

She forced her gaze away and slid her hand free, clearing her throat. "Do you think my things will still be here if we came back?"

"No." He shook his head. "By the time you make it back, this wagon will be picked clean, either by Indians, settlers or both. It'll be nothing but a shell."

She swallowed. She'd suspected as much. Moss had never let their wagon train stop by broken-down wagons for fear they carried illnesses or had been set upon by Indians. The most he'd do was call out for survivors before hurrying on past. He claimed "broke-down wagons are bad luck". She could only imagine what he'd think seeing his own wagon "broke-down".

"Sally, now that we're alone..." he tipped her chin up to look at him again, "...I have something to tell you."

Alone. We are alone.

She forgot to breathe.

A part of her wanted to scream and run. A part of her wanted him to kiss her. Wanted to feel that warm hand holding her chin on other parts of her body.

His eyes turned a darker shade and he bent, brushing her lips gently as her eyes closed.

Less than a kiss but more. Oh so much more.

He straightened, looking down at her with longing and regret in his eyes as a warmth curled in her belly and her breath came back to her.

It was wrong, oh so wrong. But it felt so right.

"I can't do this. Luke did me wrong but that doesn't make me any less a married woman."

Inhaling sharply, he spoke in a rush. "Sally, listen to me. I need to tell you something before your friend returns."

His gaze searched hers, delving into her deepest places, and he tipped his head to the side as if to gauge her reaction. She caught her breath, suddenly reading him in a way she'd never thought possible.

Whatever he had to say, he wasn't happy to share it.

"Luke Wheeler isn't your husband."

She gave him a sad smile, humoring him. "Then who is he?"

That question had plagued her for years. Luke never talked about his past. He said his life began when he met her, and at first she'd found that charming. But now she knew it to be a lie given to evade the subject.

Robert gave her a frustrated frown. "He *is* Luke Wheeler, but your marriage isn't legal."

What does he mean my marriage isn't legal?

"I don't understand."

He took a deep breath before he spoke. "Luke hired a friend of his to pretend to be a circuit preacher. And he's done this with two other women."

"No," Sally gasped. "That can't be true."

A hint of pity crept into his eyes. "I wouldn't lie to you. But if you doubt my word, just ask the other two women he tricked. One has a thirteen-year-old son and the other has a baby on the way."

She stared at him in shock.

Luke was a known liar. But this...she'd never expected something like this. Beneath her shock one thought ran through her mind.

There'd been signs she hadn't paid attention to.

Things he'd said came back to her. Private things. The times he'd called out another woman's name in his sleep. The morning when she'd asked who Rose was and his anger turned on her. She glanced down at the white scar, a reminder of that time, which stretched across her wrist. He'd made sure she knew never to ask him about Rose again.

"Rose," she murmured with a frown.

"She was his first so-called wife. She's an actress who dances at the Red Slipper Saloon in New Mexico. They have a son, Hank."

"Hank," she repeated after him in a dead tone.

She felt like the wind had been knocked out of her. Her marriage to Luke was a lie. Luke had lied to her from the moment he met her. How foolish she'd been to marry him.

And the last thing he'd said to her before he left was "get in here and lift your skirt". She wasn't his wife, yet he'd claimed a husband's rights as his last words to her.

Sally closed her eyes.

She felt as used as an old rag and as worn out.

Luke had a lot to answer for when she caught up with him.

The liar.

Her eyes flew open.

And Robert Truman was no better.

Her eyes narrowed as she glared at him. "And you figured since I wasn't an honest woman you could just up and kiss me any time you felt like it. Since I wasn't married after all."

He frowned and his gaze flickered away and back again. "I just thought you should know."

The rifle was in his hand before she could think to react.

"I'll just pack the ammunition and this rifle. Leave you some time alone." He turned and leapt down from the wagon.

Her jaw dropped and she stared out the wagon at his back as he walked over to the mules.

"Well, I'll have you know I'm not that kind of woman!" she yelled at him as he walked away.

He didn't slow or turn to look back at her.

Men. Kissing and grabbing and whatnot whenever they felt like it. Like a woman didn't have any feelings. Taking without ever asking.

She wished he'd come back and go through it all again so she could slap him. If only she were faster thinking of these things before instead of after the fact.

Sally sat on a flour barrel and took a deep breath to calm herself. While she'd been reacting to Robert's kiss and his closeness in the confines of the wagon, he'd been checking out the contents. Everything the outlaw did had a purpose.

He was no different than Luke, doing whatever it took to get what he wanted.

She'd be wise to remember that.

Sally hurried to bundle her personal belongings before Moss returned. She left her nightgowns. As long as Rob was going with them, she'd sleep in her clothing. She'd keep him at a distance and be sure he didn't touch her again.

Moss galloped up, holding his rifle. "Sally, you an' Carolyn all right?"

Sally peered out from the back of the wagon, then climbed down and went over to stand by Carolyn. "Yes, we're fine." She gestured at Robert. "He stopped to help."

Moss glared as he got down off his mule, still pointing his rifle at Robert. "That right?"

Sally fingered her brooch nervously.

"Yes, that's right." Robert tipped his hat. "Robert Truman, but you can call me Rob."

Rob. It sounded like the name for an outlaw. Like a name one of Luke's friends would have. Luke, who'd robbed her of her child. Luke, who'd tricked her and lied to her from the beginning. She wouldn't have trouble calling him Rob, but it didn't mean she was going to be so friendly as to trust him.

She would not make the mistake again of letting her feelings trick her into loving a worthless no-'count man.

"Ozzie Moss," the old muleskinner ground out.

"We've been waiting for you to return," Rob said. "Your

axle's broke."

"Let me jes' have a look-see." Moss scooted under the wagon, still holding the rifle. His voice roared underneath. "Dagnabbit! Axle's split to pieces."

He scooted out and walked around to the front of the wagon. As soon as he saw the rock, he lifted his hat off his head and threw it to the ground.

"Tarnation, Sally, what did ye do to my wagon? How the blazes could ye not see that big rock?" His face grew redder, and a vein pulsed in the side of his face as stepped toward her.

Sally flinched and stepped back. "I'm sorry. I, I wasn't watching. I only wanted to help."

"It's broke now, an' sorry ain't gonna fix it." He picked up his hat and banged it roughly against his leg. "'Let me drive the wagon,' she says." He scowled. "'We're leavin' in the mornin',' she says." He shook his head and waved his hat at her. His finger stabbed in the air with each word. "Ye. Ain't. Trail boss, Missy. An' don't. Be thinkin'. Ye are."

She opened her mouth to speak, but he held one finger in the air to show he wasn't done.

"This is what comes of rushin' off. From now on ye do as I say. Or get yerself to Texas."

Hesitating she asked, "What do we do now?"

He squinted at her. "What do ye think? We pack them mules down heavy. Ye'll be lucky to ride one."

Sally forced back tears. She wouldn't let the men see her cry. Every day since Mrs. Harper had given birth, one thing after another had gone wrong. She couldn't take one more bad thing happening. Most of the time she could lay the cause of all her troubles at the foot of one man. But this time it was all her fault. If only she'd been more careful.

"That's not the only trouble. I saw an Indian a few miles back," Rob said. "He may be trailing you."

"That so?" Moss glared at him. "Mebbe he ain't the only one trailin' us."

"I was heading in the same direction and saw you needed help." He glanced over at Sally. "Then Sally asked me to travel with you."

"That so?" Moss turned to her with a frown. "Now why

would ye go an' do that?"

"He said he was traveling the same way." She shrugged then threw his words at him. "You always said there was strength in numbers."

Moss had to agree to let Rob travel with them. At least then she'd know he wouldn't reach Luke first. But she couldn't explain her reasons to Moss.

He scowled at her. "Hurry up an' get yer things."

Sally climbed into the wagon, collected another bundle then climbed out.

"Got to get my load on these here mules." Moss shook his head. "I cain't spare but one fer ridin'. I'll take Carolyn."

"Sally can ride with me," Rob said.

No. She couldn't. She glanced at Moss for his reaction. She couldn't tell him Rob was looking for Luke. Not with Rob's eyes boring into her, daring her. Testing to see what she'd do. Who knew how Moss would react?

"I can't ride with you."

Moss spat. "Yer the one invited him, ye ride with him."

He was still angry with her and there was nothing she could say to get back in his good graces right now. "Fine." But it wasn't fine. "I'll get my things."

Amusement hovered in Rob's eyes, along with something unreadable. "Hurry up, Sally."

She climbed back into the wagon then emerged with pots, pans and her three-legged skillet. She walked to Rob's horse.

"This is a horse not a pack mule."

"But..."

"You can't take everything."

"Bring the skillet an' leave the rest," Moss said.

Once the mules were packed, and Sally had handed Carolyn up to Moss, Rob held out his hand for her.

She stood eying it and wished for the first time in years that she lived in circumstances that allowed her to wear gloves. For his touch sent tingles all through her body.

"We ain't got all day," Moss said.

Rob raised an eyebrow as he waited for her to put her hand in his.

The moment they touched, the warmth of his hand sent tingles up her arm and she gave a small gasp.

But his hand clasped hers and he hauled her up onto the horse before she could even think of what her reaction to him meant. Suddenly she was seated behind him, forced to hold onto his waist, which tightened under her fingers as she felt his ridged muscles beneath her fingertips.

Every sense in her body came alive. She felt the warmth of his body and inhaled his musky scent, closing her eyes against the sight of his muscular shoulders, willing her thoughts under control.

"Ready?"

His voice sent alarm racing through her senses as the sensations intensified.

No. Not ready.

But her body said otherwise.

"Move out." Moss's voice forced her to focus on the trail.

"We're right behind you."

Moss muttered, "Wants to hep. Humph. Everywhere I go with the gal another feller comes along to hep. First the sergeant, now this un."

His mutterings could be amusing, but not this time.

Rob could sense Sally's fear, though she attempted to hide it. The thought bothered him. He was unaccustomed to women being afraid of him. Holding the tiny christening gown in the wagon, she'd seemed vulnerable. He'd felt a moment of pity as he'd caught a glimpse into her heart. Then he'd been unable to keep from kissing her.

Though he'd stopped himself before it went far, he could still taste her on his lips, soft and sweet.

One taste will never be enough.

He gritted his teeth.

Now if that wasn't the stupidest damn thing he'd ever done.

He'd felt like the worst sort of brute when he'd seen the pain in her eyes at hearing of the other women and the way Luke had tricked them.

Then to top it all off, he'd gone and kissed her.

He was a damn fool. She had every right to be angry with him for losing control and kissing her like that.

Even if it had been worth every second.

As she'd turned her anger on him, it had occurred to him that she might emerge with the end of a gun pointed right at him if he weren't careful. He hadn't entirely trusted her earlier invitation to join them. So he'd made sure the rifles were well away from her and packed on the mules.

Tempting as she is, I won't kiss her again.

Though he'd just made the situation more difficult, he'd ride it out as far as it took him.

Up until now, all had gone well. He'd try to set Sally at ease, though that could prove difficult. She wasn't the only one having trouble. The minute her hands touched his waist he'd reacted with a tightening of muscle, and the way her breasts brushed against his back before she leaned away from him was hard to ignore.

It will be best if the little girl rides with me next time. Being so close to Sally is a frustration I don't need.

Luke watched Moss deal with the little girl. The old man would soon need a break from the child's incessant chatter.

He'd meant to ingratiate himself with Moss and the old man accepted him, which meant Sally hadn't told the old muleskinner that he was looking for Luke. But why not?

Is she still in love with Luke even though she's learned they aren't married?

She seemed wholesome and a good mother and she *was* responsive to him.

She flares hotter than a blacksmith's fire at my touch.

If she wasn't Luke's woman, they'd get this physical reaction to each other out of the way with a quick tumble. But that wasn't going to happen. She'd made it clear she wasn't that kind of woman.

Once they made camp, Sally prepared stew and cornbread.

"I can't recall when I've had such a good meal," Rob said with a smile. "That's the best supper I've had in a long time."

"Thank you." Sally blushed and ladled out another helping.

She watched the men enjoying their meal. Luke had never commented on her cooking other than to complain. Yet it must not be as bad as he'd made it out to be. Moss and Rob had both eagerly asked for seconds.

Perhaps Luke had been wrong about a lot of things.

She'd caught him in lie after lie. Why would this be any different? Everything Luke had ever said or done was a lie.

Rob was obviously trying his best to put her at ease, acting the gentleman. But that didn't mean she could let down her guard. If she did, he might kiss her again.

Though she wanted him to treat her with respect, and she knew it was wrong, deep down she wanted him to kiss her again.

Who was Robert Truman? Where did he come from, and what did he want? He watched her behind smiling eyes.

She felt shaky all over, but she hid her fear, not wanting either of the men to notice.

She wouldn't do anything to jeopardize Moss taking her to Texas. More than likely Moss already regretted he'd ever agreed to do it.

"Best cook less." Moss frowned. "Cain't carry as much, nor go as far without restocking them vittles now that I ain't got my wagon."

"Sure, Moss, I'll be real careful."

Surely he wouldn't stay angry forever. How long would it be until he got over the loss of his wagon? She hoped soon because she needed to tell him about Rob. And she couldn't when he bristled and moved off every time she tried to speak to him. But then Rob hadn't left them alone, either.

Moss watched Rob scrape the bottom of his bowl with his spoon and scowled. "Funny how you jus' happened to be in the area when my wagon broke."

Rob shrugged. "I was headed this way."

"Where *are* ye headed?"

"South."

"How far?"

"Texas. Thought I'd hire on at one of the ranches."

"Ain't the time of year for hirin'."

Rob shrugged again. "Maybe not."

Sally listened as she fixed a bedroll near the fire for Carolyn. Rob hadn't told Moss he was looking for Luke and he probably wouldn't. Good.

"Move her back. Them sparks'll catch her blanket afire," Moss growled.

Her palm covered the brooch at her neck. "I didn't think of that."

She'd best quit worrying about what Rob wanted or what he'd do and pay attention to what she was doing. But it was hard when his eyes followed her every move. When she was aware of his presence every minute.

Rob pondered as he chewed on a piece of dry grass, watching Sally. What secrets was she hiding?

She hadn't told Moss that he was looking for Luke. Foolish woman. How did she know she wasn't putting her life and her daughter's life in danger? She was obviously afraid. But she hid her fear well enough. Though the old man was suspicious, he had no idea what was going on or he'd have reacted differently.

"I'll sit up an' tend the fire tonight," Moss said.

"I can take a turn," Rob said.

Moss narrowed his eyes. "You insinuatin' I ain't able?"

"No. Only offering to help."

"I got more hep than I need." Moss eyed Sally. "What I ain't got is a wagon. I ain't sleepy nohow."

"Suit yourself." Rob raised his hat brim an inch.

Sally and Carolyn settled in under their covers and Sally began to tell a fairy tale. Moss sat by the fire shaking his head and muttering under his breath.

Rob moved his bedroll to the other side of the fire, to ease Sally's mind. He laid back and nudged his hat down over his eyes.

Might as well sleep. Let the old man wear himself out since he wants to sit up all night brooding.

He closed his eyes and pictured Sally and Carolyn seated together at supper. They'd made quite a picture with the glow of the fire against their red-gold hair and those blue eyes. The little girl was pretty, like her mother. She didn't look a bit like Luke. Carolyn would be a beauty one day. He wondered if that was how Sally had looked as a child.

Sally's voice carried over to him. "Go to sleep, sweetheart, and I'll tell you one more story."

Rob listened to her soft voice telling a tall Texas tale. Lord, that woman could spin a tale. And her voice soothed like music. He thought of her soft lips and forced the thought away.

It can never be. She is only a way for me to find Luke. I will not lose my heart again to a woman.

When Rob woke, the fire had worn down. A cold wind blew across the land and a light snow had begun to fall.

Moss slept, his head nodding.

Soft flakes drifted down, covering Sally's eyelashes. She breathed through parted lips that called to him, and it was all he could do to keep from covering her mouth with his. Needing a distraction, he rose to build up the fire again.

Sally dreamed Rob was kissing her. The long, lingering kiss made her feel sleepy and languid. Heated her skin to a rosy flush. So languid she moved to his rhythm as his lips moved from her lips down to her breasts and belly.

She licked her lips and sighed.

She wanted to stay and sleep under the falling snow as he kissed her farther down and down. His tongue touched her most sensitive spot where she was warm and ready. He licked her again and again until she moaned her release.

She reached out to touch him.

But something was wrong. She felt the sudden cold against her heated body. And she shouldn't be kissing Robert Truman. Shouldn't be letting him kiss her there or anywhere.

She woke and sat up, her heart pounding, one arm outside the blanket touching her hip now, the other hand cupping her sated mound. Her gaze fled immediately to Rob, to find him watching her as he bent over the fire, paused between cooking bacon in the skillet, his mouth open and a mesmerized look in his eyes.

It mattered not that Moss and Carolyn were there, still sleeping. It was as if there was no one left in the world but Rob and her, and the pull toward him was like nothing she'd ever known.

His eyes swept over her approvingly, increasing the languor in her body, warming her. His eyes told her he'd seen her

69

touching herself and knew of the dream she'd had. He wanted her. He crouched by the fire, like a big cat ready to pounce.

Embarrassed, she pulled her blankets up to her chin, for all the good it did to calm her overly responsive body.

Lord help me. All he has to do is look at me to put me in a state.

Had he seen her reach for him as she dreamed? What motions had she made in her sleep?

The scent of her arousal hovered on her fingers. She'd been touching herself. Heat filled her cheeks at the certainty.

He watched her, sharing her secret, his eyes warm with a desire that made her nipples tighten.

He knows.

He gave her a conspiratorial wink before moving toward Moss. "Time the old man was up."

She suddenly felt foolish clutching the blanket. His teasing wink came as a surprise and made her feel like a silly young girl. Which she wasn't. She was a grown woman with a grown woman's needs and desires.

Desires I've been fully aware of ever since I met him.

He'd been nothing but a gentleman since she'd told him she wasn't that kind of woman.

Yet she'd slept only a few feet away from him, dreaming of his touch, his kisses. Traveling together was a bad idea, with her desire raging so far out of control, but it was too late to tell Moss about Rob now. He'd be angry and he'd never take her to Texas.

Rob stood over Moss, looking down at the snoring man. "Maybe next time, the old man will listen to me and let me spell him. He looks worn out."

Next time. He meant to travel with them the whole way to Texas because she'd invited him. She'd dug her own hole and there was no getting out.

Sally turned away from his gaze and went to wake Carolyn. Her daughter's cheeks glowed rosy red against the light snow and all thoughts of Rob fled. Was she ill?

No. She can't get sick. Not here. Not now.

"Wake up, sunshine."

Carolyn blinked and mumbled, "Mama, are we home?"

Sally touched Carolyn's cheeks. They felt as if she had a little stove inside. "No, baby, but we'll stop in the nearest town."

Rob shook Moss's shoulder. "Wake up. Carolyn is sick."

Moss woke fast. "We'd best get her to a doctor."

Rob held out a cup to Moss. "Coffee?"

"Since ye got it made. But we'd best git movin'."

"We'll travel better with full stomachs and I've already cooked breakfast."

Moss's belly rumbled. "Make it fast."

They ate bacon wrapped around biscuits, but Carolyn refused to eat or drink. Sally tore strips of cloth from an old dress. If only she'd been able to buy Carolyn shoes. Her feet felt icy through her stockings.

Sally wound the cloth around Carolyn's feet, held them in her hands and rubbed hard. Her daughter looked like a painted doll in her yellow dress and bright red cheeks. She needed to see a doctor. Sally could hear a rattling in her chest when she breathed. What if she had pneumonia?

Moss moved them out and Carolyn rode with him again after he wrapped her in the smelly horse blanket Sally had objected to earlier. Now she was glad to have the warm woolen blanket.

As they rode south, heavy snowflakes fell. It snowed all afternoon. They rode in silence, urging the mules and horse on. Occasionally Carolyn gave a sharp cough, worrying Sally.

What if the sickness was in her lungs?

Carolyn slept and Sally listened for a rattle in her breath. Her thoughts whirled as wind whipped across the ground in fierce gusts, drowning out other sounds. The sky darkened.

Would they find a doctor in the next town? If only they could they reach one in time. She couldn't bear the thought of losing her little girl.

Then she thought of Matthew. If he got sick, Luke wouldn't know how to care for him. Luke wouldn't care. He'd leave him in the closest town. He had no patience with illness.

Her anger toward Luke deepened. Here she was in the middle of nowhere with a sick child. All because of Luke. If she lost her baby girl she'd never forgive him.

Carolyn coughed again, the sound a bark. Worry wound its

way through Sally's mind. She tried not to think of all the terrible things that could happen, to focus on her daughter.

They had to find a doctor for Carolyn.

They had to hurry.

Chapter Five

The town of Abilene stood quiet in the dark night. Most people were inside, out of the wind and cold. They passed a barbershop and bathhouse, a blacksmith shop, a post office, a store and a one-story hotel. Many of the settlers lived in nondescript huts. The Kansas Pacific Railroad would come through soon, but the tracks hadn't reached the town yet.

Piano keys tinkled as they rode past the hotel saloon.

Rob gave the saloon a wistful glance. Inside he'd find whiskey and a warm woman. He glanced over at Sally, his gaze moving over her curves.

He couldn't stop thinking of her as she'd dreamed. The sound of her moan and the flush in her cheeks were frozen into his mind and he couldn't shake them.

I have to stop constantly thinking of her that way. There were always easy women to be found in a saloon and finding one would make it easier to focus on his goal.

Moss cleared his throat and nodded toward the saloon. "Might want to wet yer whistle."

"There's plenty of time for that once we find a doctor."

When they reached the sheriff's office, Moss got off his mule, handed Carolyn to Sally and went in to ask about a doctor. The sheriff emerged and took one look at Carolyn.

"You're lucky Doc Collins is in town. Before he moved here, I'd have sent you to the barber." He pointed down the street to the end of town. "His house is the new one on the end." A pig waddled past the house in the moonlight and the sheriff chuckled. "Andy's pig is loose again. Doc's wife won't like that."

"Much obliged," Moss said.

They hurried toward the house and Moss knocked on the door.

Sally thought they must present a bedraggled sight to the neatly dressed lady who opened the door. Moss always looked trail-worn. Carolyn was doll-like with her porcelain skin and bright rosy cheeks brought on by the fever.

The woolen blanket smelled of mules and Sally wondered if it offended the lady. If it did, she gave no sign.

Rob leaned against a porch post with an expression that said he'd rather be elsewhere. He appeared rough and ready to ride, like an outlaw.

Which he probably is.

"Step inside," the woman said. "Wait here in the parlor while I fetch Doctor Collins."

The doctor came out from the kitchen, wiping his mouth with a napkin.

"I'm sorry to disturb your dinner," Sally said.

"I'm finished. I don't usually eat this late, but I've been out making calls." He took one glance at Carolyn who was asleep in Sally's arms and his eyes sharpened. "Well, now, have a sick little one, do you? Bring her in here."

Sally followed him into a front room filled with medical instruments and medicine bottles. She laid Carolyn on the bed without waking her and the doctor bent over her to listen with his stethoscope.

Sally waited in silent worry.

He straightened and turned to her. "We need to break the fever. Has she been near others who were sick?"

"We came from Fort Riley but I didn't hear of anyone with the fever while we were there."

"Fort Riley." He shook his head. "She could've caught anything. In a day or two we'll know if it turns into pneumonia or small pox. It's in the early stages."

Sally clutched her throat in alarm. Either disease was deadly. Pneumonia killed many children every year. And smallpox, even if the victims lived, pitted and scarred them for life.

Her fingers rubbed the brooch. "Is there anything you can give her?"

"Yes, but we have to sweat the poison out. Then the fever will break. I see no pox on her yet." He paused and looked the group over. "Where are you staying?"

Moss twisted his hat in his hands, a look of concern on his face. "We just rode in. Ain't found a place yet."

He'd stopped grouching about his wagon once he learned of Carolyn's illness.

Doc Collins gestured to Sally. "You and the child can stay here. The others will have to stay in the hotel. Long ago my wife and I came to an agreement that no men would stay in our house. We had trouble once."

Moss nodded. "Now don't ye worry none, Sally. Jus' get yer little girl to feelin' better. We'll stop back tomorrow an' see how she fares."

Rob touched the brim of his hat and nodded to Sally before stepping outside.

Once the doctor's wife had settled Carolyn in a room, the doctor directed Sally to cover her with heavy quilts.

Carolyn tried to push the covers away.

"No, sunshine, you have to keep the blankets on."

"Mama, I'm hot."

"I know, baby, but you'll be better soon."

Sally tried to believe those words. She bathed Carolyn's face with cool damp cloths. Her flushed face felt hot.

Neither the doctor nor his wife could convince Sally to leave Carolyn's side. The night lingered long and hard. She wept bitter tears remembering all the family she'd lost to fevers and how helpless she'd been, as helpless as she felt now.

The next days ran together. Night and day seemed the same, with nothing but wet cloths to wring and Carolyn's mumbling and tossing and that wretched cough. There were sheets to change and Sally tried to coax Carolyn to swallow fluids.

Icy fear twisted around her heart at the thought of losing her little girl. She wore herself out with worry until the fever finally broke.

Carolyn was left with a slight cough. It hadn't been the smallpox and they'd kept her lungs clear. She'd recover.

The doctor convinced Sally that Carolyn was out of danger

and ordered her to get some sleep. She slept for an entire day.

When she woke, she heard Carolyn in the next room singing, "Pop Goes the Weasel". She laid in bed listening to the sounds she'd feared she'd never hear again and closed her eyes.

"All around the cobblers bench..."

Thank you, Lord, Sally prayed.

She rose, went into the room and hugged her daughter.

"Oh, Carolyn, my little sunshine, I love you so much."

"See my dolly, Mama, her name is Suzy Sunshine."

The doctor's wife had given her a rag doll. They'd had to burn the one the sergeant had given her. The doctor said it might carry disease. Carolyn's new doll had black yarn eyes, and was made from old white sheets with yellow yarn for hair.

Carolyn hugged her doll. "She's mine, Mama. I'm taking her to Texas."

Doc Collins appeared in the doorway. "You shouldn't travel to Texas in this weather. Wait until its warmer."

"Is Carolyn well enough to travel?"

"She needs to stay warm and dry and she needs shoes."

"Yes, doctor. We'll go to the store tomorrow."

"Be sure to bundle her up and keep her warm."

Sally's thoughts turned again to Matthew and Luke. She'd been focused on Carolyn's illness. She'd had no time to worry about catching up with Luke.

How many days had she lost? Each day Luke took Matthew farther away.

Moss stopped by that evening to visit.

"I have to buy Carolyn some shoes tomorrow," Sally said. "And I only have a little money left after paying the doctor and room and board. The medicine was expensive."

"Tomorrow, I'll come by an' we'll git her shoes. I'll do some tradin'." Moss said.

Sally reached for her grandfather's pocket watch.

"I have this."

"Ye don't want to trade that there family piece."

"I do if it means my little girl won't get sick again. Besides, I mean to take extra medicine with us. What if Carolyn gets sick again? What if Matthew is sick when we find him?"

Her stomach churned at the thought of Matthew sick on the trail with no one to care for him.

"Sally, ye got to think sensible. It'll be a while 'fore she ken travel. I ken get you settled in somewhere."

"No." She shook her head. "I'm going to find Matthew. You made a promise and I'm holding you to it."

They'd already spent too much time here in town. Anything could have happened to Matthew by now.

Her fingers closed over the brooch. She had it and the locket with Mama's picture. Now that her gold was gone, she hoped she wouldn't have to sell them, but she'd do whatever it took to get her son back.

"We'll talk later when you ain't thinkin' so foggy."

The one thing they agreed on was the plan to take Carolyn to the store the next day.

It was late in the evening when Rob paid them a visit.

She sensed he was there though she hadn't heard him enter.

She turned to where he stood in the doorway with his hat in his hands, dark hair dropping in waves over his forehead and those intense eyes focused on nothing but her.

His gaze traveled over her face and searched her eyes. "How is she?"

His voice held a warmth and concern that touched something deep inside of her.

"She's over the worst of it." Her hand smoothed Carolyn's forehead where she lay sleeping, yet her gaze was riveted to his. "She just tires quickly."

"Good." He let out a long breath and took a step forward. "I'm glad to hear it."

The moment he came near, the bedroom seemed to shrink. His presence filled the whole of it and her pulse skittered wildly.

"And how are you, Sally?" He added in a lower, huskier tone, "You look tired."

I was so afraid I'd lose her.

She wanted to say the words but she couldn't share how she felt. It was all wrapped up in the tangle of emotion he created whenever he was near.

He moved toward her, cupping her chin and tilting it

upward. "You have dark circles under your eyes."

His gaze was gentle upon her face, his brow concerned, and she knew if she gave in to her desire she would be in his arms in a heartbeat.

She longed for him to hold her.

But it couldn't be.

She was overly tired, her emotions exhausted, and she hadn't the strength to stop at letting him hold her.

She set her jaw and the wall of her determination rose between them. "Yes. I am tired." She turned away. "And Carolyn needs her rest."

She felt his presence behind her pulling at her like taffy.

"Then I'll be going. I'm glad to hear she'll mend."

His voice rumbled into her body and his words rested in a small place in her heart.

This general store was bigger than the one back home, though chickens still ran down the center of town. The store was fully stocked and smelled of dried fruit, vinegar and smoked ham.

"You seem to have everything," Sally said to the owner.

"Once the railroad reaches us, cowboys will come through with longhorns to load on the train. After the cows are loaded, and the men get paid, they'll have plenty of cash to spend and I'll be stocked and ready."

"Would you have any shoes to fit my little girl?"

He looked at Carolyn's feet. "I surely do."

After searching in the back he emerged with a pair that fit her.

Carolyn tapped her toes together and giggled.

Sally watched with a smile.

How easy it was to please her daughter.

On the way back to Doc's house Moss said, "It's too bad you had to trade your Grandpa's watch fer them shoes."

"What use would it be to me if I lost Carolyn? Grandfather would've wanted me to use it as I did." Sally walked briskly and blinked away tears.

"Settle here in town. I ken find Luke an' Matthew."

"No." Sally shook her head. "We're going to Texas and I'm tired of you trying to talk me out of it."

Moss grunted and they walked in silence.

Then she stopped and turned to him. "Let's leave tomorrow morning. But don't tell Rob."

"Yer the one invited him. What changed yer mind?"

"Nothing. I just had second thoughts about traveling with a man I don't know."

A man she was drawn to like no other.

Each time she saw him the feeling grew stronger. She couldn't think when he was near. Or she thought too much about his nearness. But she could have controlled her desires. It was his tenderness that had nearly done her in. She'd had too little of it in her life and her heart cried out for it.

"'Fore ye go rushin' off, what did Doc say?"

"She'll be fine. We'll leave at first light."

"An' if I say no?"

"I'll go on my own, and you'll have broken your word."

"I figured."

They parted and then Sally entered Doc's house.

Carolyn danced around the parlor in her new shoes as Doc's eyes twinkled.

"New shoes are good medicine," he said, "aren't they?"

"Yes, sir. Suzie Sunshine likes them too." She held the doll down near her feet and made the doll dance.

One of Doc's patients came in, and Sally and Carolyn went into the kitchen where his wife was cooking.

Carolyn sat on a little stool near the fireplace playing with her doll while the women baked bread. Sally kneaded the bread dough as her thoughts wandered.

How long would it be until she had her own kitchen again? She didn't mind helping out but it wasn't the same as having her own place and her children needed a home of their own.

How would she ever be able to afford a home? With no husband she'd have to settle for whatever she could afford. Which at the moment was nothing.

What would she do once she had Matthew back? She'd never longed for anything but a happy family. Now she had no home and her husband wasn't really her husband. All she had were her precious children. But she needed a place to raise them.

First though, she'd have to get Matthew back. This time tomorrow they'd be back on the trail, that much closer to her son.

Rob sat in the saloon holding his cards and waiting for the man across the table to make a play. His thoughts returned to Sally. She wouldn't stay any longer than she had to. She was probably itching to leave already. He was glad Carolyn was out of danger, but he wished Sally didn't have her along. They could've traveled straight through without being slowed down by a child. Matthew wouldn't slow Luke down.

It could've been worse. Carolyn could've been sick for a long time. He steered his mind back to his cards and resigned himself to waiting. His luck was good tonight. He won again and raked in the winnings as he thought about the past.

Luke had cheated him, though not at cards. Five years of his life could never be repaid. Five years rotting away in jail. Then the two years he'd spent searching for Luke. Seven lost years that could never be recovered.

While he'd suffered, Luke had played at being a family man. One thing he'd learned about Luke through the long search was the man never stuck with anything. Rob was surprised Luke had stayed with Sally so long. Though she was a beauty, Rob suspected her innocence had been part of the attraction for Luke. The man left a trail of ruined women everywhere he went.

He'd find Luke soon. Sally must know where he was headed. Women could be secretive.

May Belle had been found dead in Rob's room one week before their wedding. And Luke had disappeared, leaving no trail. Rob had been escorted off to jail before he'd even had a chance to prove his innocence. Before he'd learned what secrets May Belle hid.

When he was released, Luke had long vanished. No one knew where he'd come from or where he'd gone. Little was known about his family or childhood.

But it didn't matter now. What mattered was finding the

man and exacting vengeance.

Wherever Luke was, he brought trouble. It was the one constant with Luke; where he went, trouble followed. And that made his trail easier to follow once Rob knew what to look for.

This time trouble was going to find Luke and there'd be no running.

I'll trail him to the ends of the earth.

Luke would face his past. He'd set up the wrong man. One who would never quit, no matter how far Luke ran.

He raked in his winnings with a grim, determined smile.

In the morning, Moss brought the mules to Doc's house. Sally handed Carolyn to him before climbing into the saddle of one of the new mules he'd traded for.

"How far to the next town?" Sally asked.

Moss scowled. "We'd go quicker if'n I still had my wagon."

Sally regretted having said anything to remind him.

"We need to hurry. We've lost too many days already."

And if we hurry, we can get there before Rob does.

Rob finished his breakfast and wondered where Moss was. It wasn't like him to be late to a meal, let alone miss one.

Something had to be wrong. He paid for his meal then hurried to Doc's house.

Had Carolyn taken a turn for the worse?

Though irritated by the delay in his plan to find Luke, he was worried about her.

She is a sweet little girl. It isn't her fault her father is a skunk.

Doc's wife opened the door.

"How is Carolyn?"

A look of surprise came over her face. "Why, they left early this morning."

Damn, not again.

He jammed his hat on his head and ran to the livery stable.

I helped Sally, hell, she'd invited me along, and she'd still snuck off without a word.

What had made her change her mind about him? Had she told Moss he was looking for Luke and the old man convinced her to go without telling him? Or had she heard from Luke?

Twice now she'd secretly taken off at the crack of dawn. He should've known she might do it again. No one had said a word about Carolyn being well enough to travel. Only that she was on the mend.

Rob collected his horse. He'd catch up with them. It wouldn't be hard. They could only travel so fast with a small child and the load Moss still had to deliver.

He gritted his teeth as he rode out of town.

Sneaky woman. She won't lose me this easily.

He shouldn't be surprised, with her being Luke's woman. He'd let the way she cared for Carolyn sway his thinking.

Being a good mother doesn't make her an honest woman.

To be honest with himself, he'd let his attraction to her sway his thinking. Despite all his efforts, he hadn't been able to get her out of his mind. She'd crawled under his skin and into his thoughts.

But she wouldn't distract him from his plan for revenge.

Sally glanced over her shoulder. If only they could travel faster, away from Rob. She'd had plenty of time to regret asking him to join them. This had been a perfect chance to correct her mistake. It felt good to be on the trail again, finally doing something and moving that much closer to Matthew. But she couldn't help worrying about Rob catching up with them.

Carolyn coughed.

Sally shot her a worried glance. Had she made a bad decision leaving today?

Well, the choice is made now. There is no going back.

Moss kept Carolyn bundled in the smelly horse blanket, and her left cheek was pink from dozing on the rough cloth.

The wind blew, whipping dirt across Sally's face. She covered her nose with a handkerchief and urged her mule on.

Moss had warned her before they left that storms this time of year could rage fiercely. On the ferry across the Kansas River just after they left Abilene, Moss had said he hoped they'd be able to make their way as easily across the other big rivers. But he'd sounded worried. Or maybe he was still thinking about his wagon.

She was tired of speculating about what was on men's minds. Luke. Rob. Moss. The only way to know was to ask and hope for an honest answer. At least Moss would be honest.

"What's worrying you, Moss?"

"We got to cross the Cimarron, the North and South Canadian, the Washita and the Red. All them rivers is treacherous."

It was the biggest word Sally had ever heard him use. "All five of them?"

"Yep."

"Why are they so dangerous?"

She'd much rather know what she was getting into than be surprised.

"Quicksand, fast changin' waters. An' if them mules won't want to cross, ye cain't ride across. Ye have to lead 'em. Cain't say as I blame 'em. I ain't lookin' forward to crossin' them rivers neither."

They plodded along against the wind for a while without speaking, as Sally's thoughts worried over the picture Moss had drawn of the dangerous rivers.

She couldn't swim. Neither could Carolyn.

Moss spoke up, startling her, "Yer friend is back."

Sally turned to see. Rob was behind but quickly gaining on them. "He's not my friend. I fear he'll follow us all the way to Texas."

"Now why would he do that?"

"He's looking for Luke."

"What do ye mean lookin' fer Luke?" Moss glared at her. "What else ain't ye told me?"

He was already angry about the wagon. Now he'd really be mad. "Nothing. He's looking for Luke, that's all."

"That's all. Humph. What fer?"

"I don't know. He didn't say and I didn't ask."

Moss shook his head. "Ye ain't been straight with me."

Sally's cheeks flushed. It was true. She hadn't told him about Rob. But she'd had no chance to tell him before. First

Rob had been watching her every move, and then Carolyn had taken sick. She'd hoped they'd ride away and she wouldn't ever have to tell him. Now he'd never trust her and he was even madder.

"An' him bein' so friendly-like."

"He only helped us because he thinks I know where Luke is. I don't want him to find Luke before I do. Matthew could be hurt. So that's why I asked Rob to join us."

Rob rode up beside her. "I thought we had an agreement."

Sally kept silent and twisted the reins in her hands. She didn't know what to say. She'd asked him to join them and he had a right to be upset. But she'd changed her mind. She didn't want to travel with him. She couldn't take the way he watched her, or the way he made her feel when he was near.

"What kind of agreement?" Moss frowned.

"Sally asked me to help her find Luke."

Moss glared at them both. "Ain't neither of ye been straight with me an' I don't like bein' made out to be no dad-blamed fool."

"I did ask Rob to join us," Sally admitted, heat rising in her cheeks.

"But you didn't feel the need to tell me you planned to leave this morning," Rob said.

"It was a last minute decision."

Rob snorted.

"I don't trust you," she said.

"That makes two of us."

"Now listen here," Moss growled, "I aim to take charge of this here trail ride. An' here's my conditions. If'n ye cain't be straight with each other, ye'll at least be straight with me. I don't want no more surprises."

Sally nodded. "All right, Moss."

Rob tipped his head and looked into Moss's eyes for a moment before nodding.

"Do ye know where Luke went?" he asked Rob.

"Do you think I'd be here if I did?"

"No. But she don't know where he is neither. He run off with her son an' we don't know where he is. Texas somewheres.

And that ain't much hep. So it ain't goin' to do ye no good to hang onto her skirts hopin' to find him."

Sally watched Rob for a sign of anger.

A muscle in his jaw clenched. But his eyes and his face remained neutral.

He obviously held a great amount of anger inside and that scared her more than shouting would have.

"We'd best avoid Newton," Rob said, changing the subject. "There's trouble."

Moss squinted at him. "What kind of trouble?"

"Outlaws. They'll rob anyone who comes through town."

"How do ye know this?"

"The sheriff told me."

Moss nodded and they rode off the path to the east of Newton. The mules slowed as the wind picked up.

Some time later, Moss shouted back. "I'd hoped we'd make it to the river, but it ain't likely. We'd best make camp."

They found a place in a cluster of trees.

Moss stopped and handed Carolyn down to Sally. "Get her in a bed roll an' we'll set out the storm. It's blowin' too hard to move on."

Moss and Rob took care of the animals then started a fire, but the wind kept blowing it out. They finally gave up and huddled together under blankets, eating beef jerky.

Sally didn't think she could eat, the way her stomach clenched tight with nerves.

As Rob handed her a piece of jerky, his fingers brushed hers and she jumped. She had the wildest urge to run. But then Carolyn snuggled closer and Sally pushed the urge away.

Carolyn nibbled on her jerky until she fell asleep.

"So Luke took your son." Rob gazed into her eyes as he spoke. "How old is he?"

"Seven. I left him at home when I went to help a neighbor. Luke and Matthew were gone when I came home."

"Why did he take the boy?"

"I have no idea."

Rob chewed for a moment, mulling it over.

"And you have no idea where he's gone?"

Debra Parmley

"No. I told you that already."

"He ever mention Texas before?"

"No."

"Not even in passing?"

"Never. Don't you think I've already been over this a thousand times in my mind? He never told me a thing."

"How did you meet him?"

"We were on a wagon train to Kansas. He joined up with us on the trail."

"Someone he knew was traveling with you?"

"No." She sighed. "He never said where he was going or where he'd come from. When he asked me to marry him, I thought he wanted to work my father's homestead in Kansas."

"He's not the farming type."

"Yes, well I learned that the hard way, didn't I?" She stared off into the distance, away from him.

Her tone was bitter. It was clear she was angry with Luke for taking the boy. And she obviously regretted marrying him.

But that didn't mean she'd lead Rob to Luke. Some women defended their husbands no matter what their husbands did to them. And there was always the chance Luke could sweet-talk her. He must have laid it on thick to make anyone believe he wanted to be a farmer. Hard labor wasn't Luke's style.

As the temperature fell, the group huddled closer together, Moss on one side of Sally and Rob on the other while she held Carolyn.

Though they weren't touching, Sally was aware of Rob's breath and the muscles beneath his blanket each time he shifted. His closeness disturbed her, but they needed as much warmth as possible. She tried not to think of her discomfort but of keeping Carolyn warm.

Eventually exhaustion swept over Sally and she dozed.

Rob was fully aware of Sally's every move. Her shoulder leaned against him and her breasts rose and fell with her breath. The wind blew loose tendrils of her long hair across his face that tickled irritatingly.

Everything about her irritated him. Inviting him to join her and then breaking her word. Taking off with no notice as if she

86

wanted him to chase her.

Now there was a thought.

He smoothed her red-gold hair back and lightly fingered a loose tendril, thinking how soft it felt. Like her lips now parted in sleep. He could lose himself in softness like that.

But no. He had to control himself. She had him following her around like a duckling and mooning over her.

As he yanked his blanket tighter, her head fell slightly onto his shoulder.

The old man leaned forward and turned to watch him with narrowed eyes.

Rob shrugged. He hadn't asked her to fall asleep there, but he wouldn't move or wake her. She felt warm and soft against him with Carolyn snuggled on her lap.

Warmth spread through his body until he thought he'd never sleep, but finally exhaustion had him nodding off.

The next morning, he woke early, before the others. It was a habit from his prison days to always wake before his jailers or the other prisoners. He'd learned to sleep light. Sometimes he wondered if he would ever sleep soundly again.

The tree he was leaning against felt cold and hard, and all his muscles ached from sleeping in that position. He looked down at Sally as she slept. Her head still rested on his shoulder. His elbow seemed to have lost all feeling.

Carolyn snuggled into her blankets with only her nose peeking out. Sally sighed in her sleep.

The gentler sex, the ones men were raised to protect.

In sleep Sally bore the same innocence as her child.

So this must be how it feels to have a family. Waking to this every morning. Feeling a responsibility to care for them.

The strange feeling in his throat made him swallow.

It was enough to choke a man. And all from watching them sleep. Appearances were deceiving.

He thought back to the night he'd asked May Belle to marry him. He'd wanted to spend the rest of his life caring for her. Not a mistake he would make again.

He needed to get up. He moved his arm and Sally relaxed, sinking deeper into his shoulder. He cleared his throat.

Sally slept on.

"Sally?"

She leaned into him, but still she didn't wake. Uncomfortably warm and aroused, he shifted his leg to ease the pressure.

Moss was awake and must have noticed his discomfort. He shook Sally. "Ye goin' to sleep all day?"

He frowned at Rob.

Rob stared back. A man couldn't help his reaction, could he? It wasn't as if he wanted to be attracted to her. His body wasn't listening. And as for his heart, he would never allow it to be hurt the way May Belle had wounded him.

Sally stretched, and then opened her eyes to look into Rob's. Overwhelmed by his nearness, she sat up with a gasp. Her heart pounded an erratic rhythm, and she was aware of warm arousal throughout her body. A tumble of confused thoughts and feelings assailed her.

She watched Rob in confusion. How wonderful it felt waking up next to him. Long ago she'd missed waking to the warmth of Luke's body, before she learned what a harsh man he was.

Sally clenched her fists.

All those nights together, the things he'd done and they hadn't even been married.

She wasn't that kind of woman and she wasn't going to have those kinds of feelings toward Rob. That way led to ruin for a woman.

But this morning the glow had spread throughout her body and she couldn't seem to turn it off, even if she didn't want to feel that way about Rob. Perhaps she was that kind of woman. Apparently she was drawn to the wrong kind of men, she reflected with bitterness. She'd have to fight her wanton nature.

As Rob went to check on his horse, she woke Carolyn, feeling her cheeks for any return of fever. But she was fine.

The wind had died and Moss built a fire for coffee and bacon.

Carolyn wrinkled her nose. "Mama, I don't want bacon," she pouted. "I want cookies."

"No cookies here, sunshine."

The doctor's wife had spoiled her. Cookies were a luxury. Once on the trail Carolyn forgot about cookies as she played with her dolly and sang nonsense songs.

They reached the Arkansas River at dusk. Moss wanted to cross before morning. Wichita had a trading post at the confluence of the Big and Little Arkansas rivers near the Wichita Indian Village and he wasn't comfortable around Indians.

Sally saw a ferry and a store, but no one seemed to be about. There was a sign by the door. "What does the sign say?"

Rob read it for her. "Rates of ferriage. Horseman ten cents, man on foot five cents, one-horse wagon fifteen cents, two-horse team twenty cents, four-horse team thirty cents, the other rates are for cattle and the rates double at night."

He turned to Moss. "I don't mind paying the extra ferriage to save time."

Moss muttered, "Ought to be half what he gets regular, seein' as how I ain't got a wagon no more."

Rob went inside to look for the ferry driver and came back out. "He's too drunk to take anyone across tonight. He's passed out. There are extra beds. We can settle with him in the morning."

Sally settled Carolyn into the bunk nearest the fire. On the other side of the fireplace, the ferryman sat, tipped back in his chair, his jaw hanging open as he kept up a steady snore. The jug in his hand rested on his thigh, while his hat threatened to fall off his bobbing head.

"It's stinky here, Mama," Carolyn said.

"Yes, sunshine, I know." Sally's nose twitched. "Roll onto your side facing the other way and it won't be so bad." She smoothed Carolyn's hair. "Go on to sleep."

Soon her daughter was sleeping soundly. Moss and Rob had settled the animals for the night and stoked the fire, and Sally slid into bed beside Carolyn. Rob and Moss took the bunk against the wall, Moss still muttering under his breath about his wagon and being charged for a full team he didn't even have.

"Hell, old man. I'd pay you just to shut up," Rob said. "First sunlight I aim to be up and crossing that river."

The room fell silent and Sally curled onto her side away from the men with a smile as she hugged Carolyn close.

The next morning, Sally had just fixed the coffee and was starting the bacon when the ferryman woke.

"Well, damn my eyes if it ain't an angel come to save me," the man roared as he stood with a lurch.

Sally jumped and took a step back.

"Ain't you the purtiest thing," he said with a leer.

She smiled nervously, not wanting to anger him.

Rob chose that moment to enter the store. "Morning. It's about time you were awake. Name's Rob."

"Fletcher, but you can call me Fletch."

"We need to buy passage across the river."

The ferryman's gaze drifted back toward Sally. "Cain't take you across." He shook his head. "Not for another two weeks."

"Why the hell not?"

"Water's running too high." Fletch stepped behind Sally. "That bacon sure does smell good." He peered over her shoulder. "You smell mighty good too."

"That's it." Rob's voice hardened.

Sally heard the cock of a gun and turned.

Rob stood with his gun pressed to Fletcher's head.

"I think you'll be taking us across. You'll be taking us across today." He jerked his head. "Sally, get your things."

"Ye heard the man," Moss argued. "That water is too fast, too high."

"We're going now." His tone brooked no argument.

"Ain't we goin' ter eat first?" Moss persisted.

"Lost my appetite." Rob's jaw clenched and he nudged Fletch with his gun. "Now move."

Sally watched Rob force the ferryman out the door and her hands shook as she gathered their things. "Carolyn, you stay away from those men and do as I tell you."

"Yes, Mama."

Even her bubbly daughter was subdued by the force Rob had brought into the store. And just when she'd begun to relax around him.

But he was no better than Luke. He was just another man

who would use force to get what he wanted. And men like that were dangerous.

Sally reached for Carolyn's hand while they silently watched the men load the ferry. Rob stood atop the bank with his hand on his gun as Moss began to coax the mules up the dock and onto the ferry.

"You better pay me double like you said," Fletcher shouted to Rob.

The coolness and steel in Rob's reply made Sally shiver. "You'll get your money when we're on the other side."

"Stupid cowboys," Fletch muttered with a frown. "Water's too high."

Rob's expression did not change, yet Sally knew he'd heard the man.

"Get them mules on up in front, just them two," Fletcher directed Moss, as he squinted against the sun. "Get 'em up on that hitching post."

Moss hitched the first two with a grumble.

"Now them other two in the middle." Fletcher frowned. "And keep them calm. I don't want no animals giving me trouble."

"Don't ye worry none about my mules." Moss hitched the other two. "I know my business good as you know yourn."

Rob led his horse up the ramp next. As Moss took the reigns from him he said, "I hope like hell you know what you're doing."

Rob merely grunted.

Finally Fletcher called to Sally, "Come on, little lady, you get on over here by me." He held out his hand to her.

Though Rob's eyes narrowed, he said nothing, just continued to stand with his hand on his gun as he watched them.

Sally lifted Carolyn up to Moss and reached for Fletcher's hand. Though he was behaving like a gentleman now, his bloodshot eyes took her in. "That's it," he said as he helped her onto the ferry, his sour-whiskey breath making her wish she could hold her nose. His hand was raspy, rough and strong.

She waited till he turned away to push off from the bank to wipe her hand on her dress.

The ferryman grabbed a pole and gave a shove off the bank.

Moss squinted at him when he turned back around. "I 'spose ye expect me to hep ye."

"One of you has to. I let my men off for two weeks till this river is ready to cross, and they'll be at the nearest saloon till I send for them."

They both glanced at Rob who stood by his horse, his right hand never far from his gun. He'd just displayed how fast he was with it.

"It's gonna be hell to get this ferry back across the river by myself." Fletcher grabbed the rope and began walking hand over hand down the length of the ferry.

Though the ride was smooth at first, Sally eyed the rushing waters in the middle of the river and wondered what would happen when they reached it. From the glances of the men, they were wondering the same thing. This did not reassure her.

Carolyn stood with Sally in the middle where it was most stable. She bounced up and down with excitement.

Sally gripped Carolyn's shoulders. "Stand still."

"Ma'am, you got to control your child," Fletcher said as he continued working the ropes.

Sally looked down at the cold, dark, swiftly flowing water, remembering with a shiver of panic that neither she nor Carolyn could swim.

"Carolyn, sit down."

Her daughter obeyed and Sally looked for something to hold onto. The ferry didn't feel so sturdy as it began to creak and shift with the water becoming steadily rougher. Sally's knees shook as her thoughts ran with the dark and dangerous river. The creaking grew louder as the mules shuffled and shifted their hooves.

The whites of their eyes rolled in fear when the boards of the ferry began to moan and groan. They didn't like this raft any more than she did. She briefly touched the brooch at her neck and reached out to balance herself against a mule.

"I told you this river was too fast," Fletch growled at Rob as the creaking and groaning grew louder and the river shook the ferry.

They were three quarters of the way across and the ropes

were straining as Fletcher and Moss strained to pull them across.

Crack!

The rear guide post holding the guide ropes snapped in two.

"Son of a bitch!" Fletcher dropped to the floor of the ferry, holding on, just as the ferry flipped around, lurching and twisting as if it were playing crack the whip.

Carolyn and Sally screamed.

"Damn it! Sally, hold on!" Rob shouted.

The mules brayed and his horse whinnied. The horse and mules struggled against their ropes and the strain snapped the hitching post in half. One mule jumped off into the water, making the ferry tip even more.

"Dang nab it, Critter!" Moss turned and shouted.

His favorite mule was swimming toward shore with all the gear on its back while a second mule followed. At the same time, a third fell onto its hindquarters braying and Moss caught hold of it, fighting to get it under control. The fourth kicked back and Rob's horse, which had been dancing in fear, fell into the water along with the fourth mule. The commotion tipped the ferry, flinging them all into the water, except for Fletcher who clung to the one remaining pole, cursing all the while.

"Mama!" Carolyn screamed as she was flung from Sally's arms.

"Carolyn!" Sally shouted. Raw panic seized her as the current carried Sally downstream in the opposite direction.

"I've got her!" With two long strokes, Rob reached her, grabbed her by the back of her dress and reached for the saddle of his horse.

Moss was already holding the tail of one of his mules as the animals swam to shore.

Sally thrashed and screamed as the rushing water carried her further and further downstream, bobbing her up and down in the water, her heavy wet skirts twisting around her legs, threatening to pull her down.

She bobbed, the river alternating between dunking her and allowing great gasps of air.

She grabbed part of the broken hitching post and clung to it to keep her head above water.

Rob glanced back, realizing Sally hadn't swum to shore. A look of horror crossed his face when he saw how far the river had taken her.

"Help! I can't swim!" Sally screamed and swallowed water as the river carried her swiftly downstream.

"Sally!" Rob called. "Hold on!"

She'd drifted too far beyond his reach.

Chapter Six

He'd never swim to her in time.

Moss reached the other side just minutes before Rob and Carolyn.

Rob pushed Carolyn to Moss, saying, "Take her, I'm going for Sally."

He climbed into the saddle and spurred his horse to a gallop as they raced down the bank.

About a hundred yards downriver, a huge pine tree blown over by a storm had fallen partially into the water, its roots upended.

Sally was swept into the branches of the tree and was caught by the current. She caught hold of a wet, slimy branch as she fought to keep her grip. The limb creaked as if it would break any moment. The river current tugged at her, trying to pull her downstream.

"Hold tight!" Rob yelled. "I'm coming!"

She couldn't catch her breath. Water splashed up into her mouth. Sheer black fright swept through her as the cold water chilled her to the bone. How long could she hold on?

Rob's horse skidded to a stop and Rob leapt off. He climbed down the trunk of the tree and reached for Sally's hand.

"Sally, grab my hand," he called, his eyes asking her to trust him.

But she couldn't let go—terrified that he wouldn't be able to save her.

The branch snapped and she let go and reached for his hand. Strong fingers closed around her wrist just as the branch dropped into the river and was swept away.

His warm hand brought her up until she was almost on top of the tree trunk. He pulled her out, shaking and dripping with water and mud.

Her knees felt weak. Her entire body quivered as they slowly edged back up the tree trunk. He reached the shore first and stood. Teeth chattering, she tried to stand and collapsed into his arms.

"Thank God you're safe," he whispered into her ear, his warm breath sending tingles down her spine.

Gathering her closer, he held her in a snug embrace. Sheltered in the warmth of his arms, her trembling limbs clung to him seeking his strength.

She could have drowned.

As she shivered, great heaving sobs shook her body.

He whispered again, his breath hot against her ear, "You're safe, Sally, I've got you."

His words wrapped around her like a warm blanket as his hands rubbed her back, trying to warm her. "We need to get you warm and into dry clothes."

She was safe.

She took a deep breath and exhaled, feeling his uneven breath on her cheek as he held her close. As she clung to him her body shook again.

"I've got you," he repeated, his lips kissing her temples in a caress, once, twice as he spoke. "Shh, it's all right."

She leaned back and looked up into his eyes, wanting to crawl into his warmth, wanting to be held, safe like this forever.

It felt so right. Like this was her place in the world.

She closed her eyes.

His lips touched hers, gentle as a whisper. Her heart pounded as she responded to his kiss, glad to be alive.

She could have died. But he'd saved her.

Her heart beat a rapid rhythm. As she drew strength from him, his kiss grew bolder, more intimate. She'd never been kissed this way before, as if he breathed with her, waiting for her to relax and invite him further. And she wanted to, God help her but she wanted to.

No one had held her like this since she was a small girl. Luke had certainly never held her this way.

The thought of Luke vanquished the cocoon of warmth.

She stiffened. Her clothing was soaked and dripping and she was pressed up against Rob in a most intimate way. He had to know the way her body responded to him.

He released her and stood watching, his eyes smoldering with desire.

She raised her fingertips to her lips almost without thinking. Still warm and moist from his kiss, they longed for him to continue. Her body tingled.

This couldn't be.

She looked away, her cheeks burning, her body suddenly chilled again yet wanting him at the same time.

"We'd best join the others," he said.

She nodded, unable to speak or look at him.

Rob grasped her elbow with a firm but gentle grip. She took one step and collapsed. He caught her in his arms and carried her to his horse.

He lifted her onto his horse and climbed into the saddle behind her.

As his arms reached around her to grasp the reigns, she shivered again, but with more than the cold. Every inch of her body was suddenly alive with the need to be touched, to be held. She leaned back against his strong chest, feeling the heat of his body and a warmth beginning within her own. He held her for only a moment before urging his horse on. But it was a moment she knew she would remember forever.

When they reached the others, Carolyn stood crying as Moss awkwardly patted her on the head, saying, "Hush now."

They climbed off the horse and Sally sank to her knees and hugged her daughter.

"Mama, I was scared!" Carolyn's arm slid around her neck.

"I was scared too, sunshine."

Moss held out his hand to Rob. "I thank ye fer savin' them gals. Never had no use fer Luke. But yer welcome at my campsite any day."

Rob shook his hand solemnly. "Anyone would have done it.

97

We'd best get them dry and warm."

Sally shivered from the cold. Thoughts of Rob captured her mind. Thoughts she dared not entertain. Thoughts of being held against his strong body. He'd made her feel safe, warm and cared for. Luke had never made her feel like that.

She studied Rob's face. What it would be like to be held in those strong arms each night? To be protected and cared for? She thought she'd faced the harsh realities of loneliness before, but until this moment she'd never known how unloved and alone she'd been all these years. She would never have known what she had missed.

Now she longed for something she could never have.

"We need to build a fire," Rob said.

Shouting came from upriver, and they turned to look at where the Fletcher fought to bring his ferry back to shore. It was too far to hear what he said, though it was clear he was cursing and shaking his fist at Rob.

Rob raised his arms in the air and shrugged.

"How are you going to pay him the other half?" Sally asked.

"I'm not."

She raised her eyebrows.

"He didn't take us all the way and there's no way to take it to him. Old drunk should have taken better care of his equipment."

The men built a huge fire. Supplies like flour and sugar were ruined and many others had washed away, but Moss had saved the whiskey. He offered it to Sally.

"Warm ye up. Careful ye don't take too much now. That booze will do yer mind."

Sally opened her wooden box and removed the cross-stitched wedding sampler she'd wrapped her family Bible in. Everything in the box had stayed dry as it floated. She tossed the sampler on the fire.

Rob watched the sad look on Sally's face as the sampler caught fire. She sat silently staring into the fire as it devoured the cloth, her fingers tracing over her brooch.

Sally glanced at Rob. Her pale, chilled cheeks colored before she hastily looked away.

Ever since he'd kissed her, she'd avoided meeting his gaze.

He could have controlled the urge, had it only been physical. Other feelings had almost swallowed him. He'd wanted to calm her fears, wanted to run his fingers along her face. He'd needed gentleness. Needed to give it, and receive it. He hadn't known he'd hungered for that rare commodity until that moment.

He wanted to erase the sadness in her eyes. But the timing was wrong for them. If they had met years ago, before Luke came into both their lives, ruining everything, things might have been different.

She'd melted into his arms when he held her, but she'd stiffened once she realized she was safe. Still, he'd felt her initial response. She fit him perfectly, like a custom-made saddle. Again he regretted meeting her under the current circumstances.

He still didn't know where she stood with Luke. And he'd begun to care for her in a way that went beyond desire. He didn't want to see her hurt.

Rob watched her, wondering what went through her mind, especially in regard to Luke.

She opened her family Bible. She traced the family tree on the front pages with her index finger. Tears filled her eyes and the look on her face made him want to pull her close again, a rash urge he had to control.

Then he remembered. She couldn't read. From the look on her face, she must long to read her family Bible.

Rob cleared his throat. "I could teach you to read, if you'd like."

She looked up, surprise filling her face. "Yes, I'd like that very much."

Rob nodded and turned back to the fire and swallowed.

He couldn't make love to her. But he could do this one small thing. He'd leave her with one more skill to make her way in the world.

It was the least he could do.

He threw another piece of wood on the fire and thought again of the kiss, the way his body now craved the touch of her.

He didn't know what had gotten into him to act so rashly

and against his better judgment. Oh, he'd wanted to kiss her, but not that way, not with fear filling her wide blue eyes. Not because she'd felt gratitude for him pulling her out of the river and definitely not until he'd settled the score with Luke.

He couldn't allow it to happen again. Traveling with her, watching her every move, it was difficult to tamp down the desire he felt for her. Even at night he dreamed of her. His desire for her wasn't going to go away and now it waged war with his desire for revenge. Tamping down one only managed to heighten the other. And he had no release for either of them until he found Luke.

Life had become a bitter potion to swallow since meeting Luke.

A noise startled him out of his thoughts. He glanced over his shoulder. The fire had attracted Indians.

Sally followed his glance and gasped.

Moss and Rob reached for their guns.

The old Indian who led the party had a weathered face, which reminded Sally of a walnut. He raised his hand in greeting then dismounted. "This woman is wet from the river."

"Yes," Rob said.

The Indian handed Sally a dry blanket. "I call you Running Water." He turned to Rob. "Is this woman taken?"

Sally stiffened as the Indian appraised her.

"Yes." Rob stepped close. "She is my woman."

His strong arm wrapped around her again, his body warm against her. Her fear subsided as a heated glow took its place. In the safety of his arm, she felt a stirring. She tried to pull away, but his grip held her firm.

The Indian nodded. "She is named well. Even now she tries to run like water."

His men laughed.

"You get tired of this woman running, you send her to me." He mounted his horse, and they rode away.

Rob released her.

Sally turned to glare at him. "Why did you tell him I was your woman?"

He crossed his arms. "I could call him back." He gave her a

slow grin. "You might be worth another blanket. Want to be his woman?"

She sputtered.

Her reaction only amused him more.

"Rob did good to say that." Moss shook his head. "Sally, ye don't know nothin' 'bout Injuns."

Still disgruntled, she wrapped Carolyn and herself in the dry blanket. "It was nice of him to give us the blanket."

Rob's mouth quirked with humor and his brow rose. "Moss, we could've gotten much more if we'd traded her."

Moss didn't reply. Instead he huffed off to salvage what he could of their goods by laying them out to dry.

Rob watched him go then leaned close to whisper in Sally's ear. "The quickest way to dry out is to take off all those wet clothes and spread them by the fire."

His breath in her ear sent tingles down her spine. Blood rushed to her cheeks. "Absolutely not."

The nerve of the man, wanting her to completely disrobe in front of him. What kind of woman did he think she was?

Her cheeks burned in remembrance of how she'd clung to him by the river. Blood pounded in her temples as he watched her with a mischievous grin.

Carolyn tugged at her skirt. "I'm cold, Mama."

Rob gestured to Carolyn. "You don't want her to catch pneumonia do you?"

"Of course not." He was right, but the thought of removing all her clothing still disturbed her.

She removed Carolyn's wet clothes while avoiding his gaze. She wrapped the dry blanket around her daughter and rubbed her arms to dry her.

Rob collected Carolyn's clothes and spread them by the fire to dry. He held out his hand. "Next?"

"Turn around."

He sent her a slow smile then turned away.

Sally removed her dress but kept her underclothing on, though the threadbare chemise did little to cover her breasts.

Oh no. Then the men would see the necklace the Indian has given her, and she didn't want to explain it to them. Moss would be upset. Quickly she unfastened the necklace and kept it hidden in her hand. Then she slipped beneath the blanket with Carolyn. She tossed her dress toward Rob. "There."

The dress landed by his feet.

He picked it up and spread it near the fire. "And your other things? Your unmentionables?"

"I've no intention of removing everything."

"Suit yourself." He watched her with amusement.

Sally shivered, conscious of his scrutiny. She thought of the way he'd held her after he'd saved her from the river. The damp chemise against her skin only made her more aware of how her body continued to respond to him.

Her face flushed with humiliation and anger at herself. The deeper he grinned, the angrier she became.

Moss took in the scene when he returned with more firewood. "What in blazes? Cain't leave 'em alone long enough t' spit."

Sally unbraided her hair and let it down to dry as she looked away from the men.

She heard them moving about as they took off their boots and hung their shirts and trousers to dry along with the bedrolls.

"We're decent," Rob said as they came near the fire.

Each man held a saddle in front of himself.

Sally tried to avoid looking at Rob but couldn't help herself. She saw the muscles in his powerful legs as he strode toward the fire. With each step she was aware of his restrained energy. The flames sent a golden glow across his bare arms and chest. Now that she knew how it felt to be held in those firm arms against his chest, she couldn't tear her gaze away.

Rob sat by the fire cleaning the well-polished gun that he kept cleaner than his clothing or boots.

Her grandmother's words came back to her.

"Look to what a man takes care of," she'd said, "for that's where his heart lies."

Rob was a gunman. Those bullets were meant for Luke.

Luke's long fingers, adept at shuffling cards, were fast. But how fast was he with a gun?

Who would win? Luke had a ruthlessness she doubted Rob

possessed. Still, the look in his eyes when Luke's name came up was as cold as the grave.

Sally shivered. Who knew what any man was really capable of? Despite the chill she felt and the anxiety churning inside her, curled next to Carolyn she soon fell into an exhausted sleep.

Rob sat on a log near the fire and watched Carolyn and Sally as they slept.

"Don't get no ideas about sharing her blanket," Moss growled.

Rob glanced at the old man and decided not to respond. But he had a warning of his own. "Luke won't like them showing up out of nowhere."

"Nope."

"You taking her all the way back to Kansas, if you don't find the boy?"

"She won't hear none of that. Says she'll stay in Texas until she finds him."

Rob scowled. Luke didn't deserve Sally. He took what he wanted then moved on. But his past would catch up to him. Rob would see to that.

Moss spat and squinted at him. "What're ye fixin' to do when ye find him?"

"Repay an old debt."

"Must be a big one."

"Big enough."

"I reckon it ain't none of my business, long as Sally an' them children ain't hurt."

"I'd never harm a woman or a child."

"Fair 'nough." Moss paused and stared off into the flames. "I drove cattle fer a time." He took a stick and stirred the fire. "Luke reminds me of a feller I knew named J.D. We drove a thousand head of stock. Trail boss slept with a bag of seventy-five silver dollars under his saddle. One mornin' the bag was gone. J.D. now, he put all the blame on this other feller jus' fer spite. Well, they searched fer it an' found it under a rotten log, where it'd been drug by a pack rat." He spat. "J.D. swore up an' down he seen the man take it. Trail boss told J.D. to get on down the road an' don't come back." Moss sent Rob an intense look. "I don't accuse no one of nothin' less I know the truth. I'll hear the truth from ye any time yer ready to tell it."

"I'll keep that in mind."

Moss nodded. "Night then."

"Night."

Moss rolled over to sleep and left Rob to his thoughts. Thoughts of what unlikely company he now traveled with and how strange it felt to be accepted by the old man. He'd forgotten what that felt like after the long years in jail.

The next morning as they headed out, Sally's mind was on the trail ahead. She'd seen enough of rivers to last her a lifetime, but there was no choice but to cross the others. She hoped they wouldn't have trouble crossing the Cimarron. But they'd left behind ruined supplies and Moss said traveling light they'd make better time.

The winter sun came out, warming Sally. She still felt chilled from the river. She'd been foolish making such a fuss over undressing last night. Everyone else's clothes were dry, while her dress was damp from the underclothes beneath it.

She hadn't braided her hair, but left it down, something she never did. It felt good to wear it loose. When she got to Texas she'd leave her hair down all the time. Luke had made so much of her hair that she'd stopped wearing it loose, that being one of the things that kept his mind on bedding her instead of work. But he had no claim on her now. From now on she'd wear it down or tie it back with a ribbon.

Rob rode ahead to scout and Moss brought up the rear while Carolyn rode with Sally.

Carolyn played with her soggy rag doll until Sally made her put it away. Carolyn liked to make her dolly climb Sally's arms, which made it hard for Sally to control her mule.

As Carolyn whined about her doll, Rob rode back to them. "You have to keep her quiet. There may be Indians nearby."

"Easy for you to say. You keep her quiet." Sally was damp, sore and tired from her river dunking. She'd even begun to wish she hadn't started this journey.

Rob reached for Carolyn. "You can ride with me and help

me listen for Indians if you'll be quiet."

"Okay." Carolyn held out her arms and smiled.

He lifted her onto his saddle and rode ahead.

Sally watched him in stunned amazement. She couldn't imagine Rob with children, and her nerves were frayed from worrying about Carolyn, but he seemed gentle enough with her, so she supposed it was all right.

How unusual for a man like him to give her a break from Carolyn. Sally was either carrying her or caring for her constantly.

She squinted into the sun, watching them. Carolyn seemed quite taken with Rob and was even giggling behind her hands at something he'd said.

He was quite good with her.

Luke never offered to help with the children. He'd been too concerned with his own wants and needs. Her job had always been to keep them out of his way so he could do whatever he wanted. He thought only of himself.

But the month before he left, he'd watched Matthew with a strange look in his eyes. She should have suspected something then.

She would never give up until she found her son, and she knew Rob wouldn't give up until he found Luke. How strange that this man she barely knew was better to Carolyn than her own father. Rob would make a good father if he wanted to settle down. But he wasn't that kind of man.

As Sally watched them, all her loneliness and yearning came together in one surge. She rebuilt in her mind the romantic picture of the father she wanted for her children. One remarkably like Rob.

Sally dozed in the saddle. But she dreamed of Rob coming toward her with his shirt off and a gun in his hand. Startled, she woke.

Moss rode beside her. "Sally Mae, you feelin' all right?"

"Yes, I'm just tired."

"Yer plumb tuckered out from the river, I reckon."

"Yes, I am."

The river. Rob had saved her, and he'd held her as if she was the most important woman in the world. Then he'd held her again when the Indians came. No wonder she dreamed of him. She longed for the protectiveness of his arms. She had to keep more distance between them. Keep him from touching her again. His touch upset a balance within her.

Rob slowed his horse and put out his arm in warning. "Slow down. I see horses and riders up on that hill."

"I see 'em," Moss said.

"Go slow. Stick close together." Rob nodded to Moss.

"This is Injun territory an' they don't like no one else passin' through."

Sally's shoulders stiffened. She didn't want to be taken captive. Without Rob, she easily might've been. She owed him for saving her and felt bad about trying to leave him behind. If only she knew why he wanted Luke. But she was afraid to ask.

Had she misjudged Rob? Confusion filled her mind. She needed his help to reach Texas. Moss had aged more than she'd realized. It had been foolish to set out with only an old man to guide her.

Rob, who'd dropped back, rode up to Moss. "Take Carolyn."

Indians appeared on the ridge and Sally caught her breath.

War-like whoops sounded.

Chills ran down her spine as she gripped the reins tight. Her heart raced.

Rob glanced at her. "Keep riding and stay close. Don't let them separate us."

"That yer only plan?" Moss said.

"There's too many of them. Keep your gun in sight but don't shoot."

"I ain't never held back from no Injuns an' we ain't got nothin' to trade. Nothin' they want."

"There's Sally and the child. I'm not losing them to Indians."

Moss nodded in unspoken agreement.

Indians poured down the hill.

"Now!" Rob yelled as he kicked his horse faster. But the mules couldn't keep up.

To Sally, it happened too fast. Indians rode closer and surrounded them.

Rob rode on Sally's right and Moss on Sally's left. Each held a rifle. In a flurry of dust, everyone stopped.

The horses snorted in impatience.

As the winter sun beat down, Sally smelled the sweat of the Indians and the men who protected her. Her heart pounded in her chest. Surely they'd hear how loud it was as it thundered in her ears. She tried to stay calm and remain still.

The Indians wore fierce expressions under their war paint. One brave with a red paint stripe across his broken nose rode up and stopped in front of Rob. Fear seized Sally, and her stomach clenched. Their horses snorted.

This brave didn't ask if she was Rob's woman.

The two men sized each other up. What would happen? No one spoke. What could Rob do? Indians surrounded them. There was no way out.

Another brave with a terrible scar on his face rode next to Sally and lifted her red- blonde hair. He crowed in triumph. The expression in his eyes made her shake.

"Ain't you gonna do nothin'?" Moss tightened his fist on his gun.

"Wait," Rob said tersely. "Something is off."

An Indian chief approached. He wore many feathers in his hair and bear claws around his neck. A strip of cloth wrapped his muscular shoulder.

As he rode closer, Sally recognized him as the Indian she'd seen at the creek. She'd looked into his eyes for an eternity it had seemed. Now his face held black marks that highlighted his strong cheekbones and chin. He appeared even more fierce. Atop his black horse, she could see how strong and dangerous he was.

She reached into her blouse and pulled out the necklace.

He stared at her as his powerful legs guided his horse next to her mule. His eyes briefly met hers in recognition, then he reached his hand out to touch her hair as she held her breath. He reached for the turquoise necklace, lifting it for all to see. He spoke in his language, and then let the necklace drop back upon her quivering breast.

As his fierce eyes looked into hers, a slow-growing security came over her. He wouldn't harm her. He'd protect her as she'd protected him. But would he let the others go? Raising one hand he backed his horse in silence then made a gesture to the north. As quickly as they'd circled the group, the Indians turned and rode off.

"Hurry," Rob said. "He may change his mind."

They rode hard. Sally's mind was a crazy mixture of serenity and fear. Her heart beat rapidly. She watched the flanks of Rob's horse working and heard her mule breathing in the wind. She felt the mule's muscles work beneath her, moving in rhythm, trying to keep up.

She wanted to ride forever. Wind tore through her hair, and she didn't care if they ever stopped. She felt alive for the first time in her life.

Reaching the Cimarron River delayed them, but they crossed it and continued on. But the mules couldn't keep up with Rob's horse and finally Moss said they'd reached their limit and called a halt.

Sally couldn't tell how many miles they'd ridden.

"I don't think they'll follow us," Moss said. "Reckon we ken rest a spell." He reached for his water jug, took a swig, swished it around in his mouth then swallowed. He glared at Sally. "What went on back there?"

"Nothing."

"Nothin'. Don't seem like nothin'. Where'd ye get that there necklace?"

Sally hesitated. "I'm not sure how to explain it."

"Say it straight, that's how."

"I saw him at the creek a few nights ago. He was wounded."

"Tarnation, Sally, how ken I protect ye when you ain't tellin' me things?"

"Go on," Rob said, "let her finish."

"I gave him some food and he went home to his family."

"He ain't home with his family. He's out huntin' white men." Moss shook his head. "If that ain't the dumbest..."

"Not so dumb," Rob interrupted. "She made a powerful friend with that chief. Saved our lives." His eyes dropped to her gaping blouse. "You'd best wear that necklace out where all can see it."

Sally blushed as her fingers drew the blouse together.

Robs eyes lingered on her hands, then he looked into her eyes.

She knew her face was sunburned and her hair tangled.

Wonder filled his expression as he reached out to touch her hair. He gave her a look of appreciation.

Sally tucked her hair behind her ears with a shaking hand. "I must look a sight."

He smiled. "Like the wildflowers in the mountains, rambling everywhere, but beautiful."

She blushed. He'd called her beautiful. No one had ever called her that before. Her confidence spiraled upward and she smiled back at him.

He stepped closer. She could smell his scent and the dust of the ride. His finger traced the line of her cheekbone and jaw. "Most beautiful sight I've ever seen."

His finger continued across her lips. She stood frozen, unwilling to move away from his light touch.

Would he kiss her again?

"Here." He handed her his water jug. "You must be thirsty."

Their fingers touched, and her cheeks burned with heat at the way her body reacted. She drank several gulps then handed it back to him and watched his Adam's apple bob as he drank.

He wiped a hand across his mouth and gave her a slow grin.

"They done forgot everythin'," Moss mumbled to his mule. "That's what comes of gettin' the blood up."

The heat in Sally's cheeks burned hotter as she overheard him. Her lips still tingled from where Rob had touched them.

"See to Carolyn," Rob said gruffly and turned away.

Whatever was the matter with her? Of course she should be taking care of her little girl. Her mind spun.

Carolyn was perfectly fine. Sally hugged her.

"Momma, that Injun liked my hair."

Sally shivered. Indians liked to scalp, she'd heard, and though they didn't usually scalp children they'd capture them for slaves. She could have lost not only her son but her daughter as well. Sally gulped hard as tears rolled down her cheeks.

"Mama, what's wrong?"

Tears blinded her and choked her voice.

"Now, Sally Mae," Moss said, "Carolyn is fine an' yer fine. Ye jus' had a scare."

Rob fiddled around with his horse. His stomach growled, and he was damned tired. Let Moss play nursemaid.

The corner of his mouth twisted with exasperation. Crying women bothered him because he never knew what to say. He usually stayed out of their way.

The sooner they reached Texas the better, but they still had a long way to go. And he had to keep his reaction to Sally to himself.

Fighting had always made him look for a warm woman afterward. Moss was right about one thing. His blood was up. Every inch of him had wanted to fight that Indian.

Moss approached. "How far off the trail ye reckon we are?"

Rob squinted at the setting sun. "I'm not sure." He nodded over to where Sally sat rocking Carolyn from side to side. "Think she'll be all right?"

"Ye know womenfolk. Fierce in battle then cries out of the blue like a rain cloud."

Rob grunted. "Sounds more like a thunderstorm to me. When do you think it'll let up?"

"Hard tellin'. Seems every man on this prairie wants her. She's more trouble than a wagon full of gold. We'd best git settled in fer the night. Want me to take the first watch?"

"No. I'll wake you when I get tired."

Rob remembered what had happened when Moss kept watch before. He'd just as well sit up all night. Take no chances. He wouldn't sleep anyhow.

Thoughts of Sally filled his head. The vision he'd had of her hair spilling over her shoulders would haunt him tonight. The way the wet cloth had clung to her body as her eyes looked to him in gratitude when he saved her from the river. The way her body fit against his, the fullness of her curves. Her soft skin and her lips just begging for another kiss.

Rob kept his distance as he watched her.

Sally rose and spread out the bedrolls. Carolyn helped then Sally bent down to tuck her in. Tilting her head, she looked over at him as if she'd felt his gaze.

He turned aside. He'd best quit watching her. He closed his eyes but it did no good. Images of her were blazed into his memory. He'd get no sleep tonight. And if he did, he'd only dream of her, something that happened more and more frequently. It didn't bode well.

Rob clenched his mouth tight. He had a score to settle and Sally would only get in the way.

Carolyn screamed out in the night.

Sally woke and Moss grabbed his rifle.

Rob tossed another log on the fire. "She's having a bad dream. She tossed and turned most of the night."

"Mama, Injuns took you away," she sobbed.

Sally soothed Carolyn's forehead. "It's only a dream, sunshine. Mama isn't going anywhere."

She glanced over at Rob, who sat watching. His eyes studied her with a curious intensity.

What he was thinking?

"Go back to sleep," she told Carolyn. Then she began to sing a lullaby.

Rob enjoyed her soft, low voice as she sang. Even the animals quieted. Soon Carolyn slept.

"Want me to spell you?" Moss said.

"No. I'm not sleepy."

After Moss went back to sleep, Rob went for a short walk nearby, unable to quiet his new worry. Suppose something happened to Sally? Then he'd be saddled with the responsibility of what to do with her children. He hadn't considered that.

His father had always said, "Don't ever interfere with something that isn't bothering you."

Sally and Carolyn hadn't bothered him until he'd gotten involved. Now he felt responsible for them because they'd come to depend on him.

Why hadn't he stuck with his original plan to follow their trail, and let them fend for themselves? What was he going to do with them when they found Luke? What would Luke do about them once he knew they'd come to Texas?

Rob liked things clean and simple, but he'd stepped into a big mess. And stepped willingly. He'd never spent much time with children and was surprised to discover he'd grown attached to Carolyn.

He'd also become attached to Sally. She was a better class of female than the women he'd taken up with in the past. Even better than May Belle, who'd been educated and came from a wealthy family. She hadn't been wholesome like Sally. He'd had plenty of women. They always came around when the cards were good. But just as cards could turn on you, so could women.

Sally was loyal. He'd seen that right away. Even if her loyalty was misplaced. He planned to stay away from wholesome women. They always asked too much of a man.

Rob stopped pacing and walked back to the fire. He watched Sally and Carolyn as they slept.

Sally's delicate wrist peeked out from under the blanket. She didn't belong in this situation. He had to protect her. He was in it for the long haul.

Can't turn your back on her, can't trifle with her emotions either.

He'd keep his hands off of her, hard as it might be.

How had she'd ended up with a scoundrel like Luke? And how had she stayed so sweet, married to Luke or thinking she was?

She deserved better. He'd keep himself in check and see that she got her meeting with Luke.

Then he'd settle things.

Rob settled down across his bedroll and leaned back to look at the stars that gleamed sharp in the dark sky as the moon floated full and shining. He hadn't seen clear open spaces for many years. He would never tire of open sky.

Out in the open range a man could see things better somehow.

And what he saw as clear as day was his gun barrel leveled straight at Luke Wheeler's chest.

Chapter Seven

Sally's body ached. The day dragged on as a bitter, biting wind blew. A snowstorm had come upon them the night before and they'd stayed put, huddled together for warmth, hoping the storm would soon pass. By morning it had cleared and they'd set out.

She'd seen nothing but snow and rocks for miles. They were out of food, and except for the rare jackrabbit Moss had shot at and missed—no buffalo, deer or elk had been spotted.

Moss had shot prairie dogs and sage hens on the Kansas trip but he was older now, a filmy haze beginning to cover his once clear blue eyes, and his aim was slow.

Sally had collected roots to put into a stew, if only they could find game to add to it. Hunger gnawed at her belly. It didn't do to dwell on food when there wasn't any to be had. She glanced down at her hands, the red knuckles raw from the wind.

Now there was too much snow for her to find roots and wild vegetables. Despite her attempt to think of something besides their lack of food, her mind kept returning to it as the never-ending trail gnawed away her hopes like the constant hunger inside her belly.

The mules moved sluggishly and Moss called them to a halt. "Time to rest 'em," he said. "We'll walk."

Sally dismounted then carried Carolyn on her hip. Tides of weariness and despair engulfed her whole body. The trail was relentless and she had no idea how far she'd have to go to find Luke and Matthew. But she would walk until her legs gave out if that's what it took.

Moss checked his mules over and muttered under his breath, shaking his head.

"Is there any water?" Sally felt as hollow as her voice sounded.

Rob handed her his water pouch. It was almost empty. She offered it to Carolyn then drank from it before wiping her mouth. They wouldn't have more water until they stopped to build a fire and melt more snow.

"Mama, I'm cold." Carolyn began to cry. "I don't want to go to Texas. I want to go home. I'm hungry."

"We can't go back to our old home, sweetheart. But soon we'll have a new home in Texas."

How would she ever provide her children with a new home? Doubt crept in. What if they didn't make it to Texas? What if she didn't find Matthew? The thought was almost more than she could handle. Doubts had been dogging her for the last few miles and now she was too tired to fend them off.

Her back ached between her shoulder blades, and her heart was filled with a deep sense of loss for the son she might never see again. Each day on the trail drained more of her strength.

"We'd best move on," Rob said.

"Carolyn can ride Critter." Moss patted his favorite mule. "She's light an' ole Critter don't mind."

But by evening, Critter could go no farther. The old mule stumbled and sank to her knees.

"Take Carolyn," Moss said in a harsh raw voice.

"Why?"

"Don't ask me, dagnabbit, just do it!"

Rob gestured for Sally to bring Carolyn over to stand beside him and his horse. He stood in front of Carolyn and covered her ears. Then he gave a nod to Moss.

Sally understood when a shot rang out.

Moss stood holding his gun, tears in his eyes.

Rob released Carolyn.

She wrapped her arms around Sally's skirt and began to cry. "Mama, why did he shoot Critter? I love Critter."

"I know, sunshine." Sally hugged her back, thinking of how everyone she loved had gone away until she was left with only

114

her children. "It's hard to say goodbye."

Moss stood silently blinking away his tears. He'd been terribly attached to his mules and had traded all but his favorite for fresh mounts. And now that one too was gone.

"He had to do it," Rob said. "The old mule gave out. She was in pain."

Moss put away his gun. His whisper was hoarse. "Poor ole Critter."

Rob began to remove the saddlebags and spoke to Sally. "We need to lighten these loads."

"I don't know what we can do without."

Moss growled, "Nothin' ye can do without." He began tossing her things on the ground. "Food and water. Ye have to have 'em. Ye see them here?"

"No." She pursed her lips.

He picked up her sewing kit. "Plannin' to do yer fancy stitchin'? Mebbe ye ken sew up our stomachs when we get hungry. Here's a fancy little plate. Think ye ken use that when ye ain't got nothin' to put on it?"

Her mouth dropped open and she recalled his earlier hostility. Why was he so angry with her? It wasn't her fault his mule was dead.

Moss stalked off.

Rob had remained quiet. Now he spoke. "Sally, he just lost his favorite mule. And he doesn't have the load he was paid to deliver. He's right. We can't take all those things."

His cool manner irked her. His belongings weren't being thrown around.

Rob sorted through and rearranged until he was satisfied. Moss sat on a rock cleaning his fingernails with a knife. When Rob finished, Moss stomped back.

"Wasted half the day fiddlin' with them female gee-gaws."

They left behind everything but their bedrolls, one pan, the rifles, Sally's wooden box, which held her Bible and the whiskey. She didn't see the harm in taking her silverware but Rob said they'd eat with their fingers.

They only had one horse and one mule between them.

This journey had been nothing like she'd planned. She longed to confess her doubts to Rob. She had to talk to someone, and Moss wasn't speaking to her.

"Nothing has gone the way I thought it would," she said.

"How did you think it would go?" Rob spoke in an odd, yet gentle tone.

"I thought we'd be in Texas by now, along with my furniture. I never dreamed we'd be in all this trouble and traveling on foot."

He didn't reply but watched her with steady eyes. She grew uneasy under his silent scrutiny and turned away, trying to hide the pain of steadily losing everything she could call her own. He always saw too much. Awkwardly she cleared her throat.

Moss spoke. "I warned ye trail rides is hard an' long, especially with children."

"I know you did."

Rob watched her, his thoughts unreadable. "Life has a way of turning out different than you plan." He turned away.

Was he referring to her life or his?

He didn't speak of his past. And she hadn't the nerve to ask him, knowing she'd hear of more bad things Luke had done. Things that put Matthew in harm's way. Things she didn't want to know when she was too far away to do anything about them. When she was too far away to save her son.

Moss spoke to his mule. "I'd tell her what I think 'cept she wouldn't never listen. Has to larn the hard way."

"Do you think we'll ever reach Texas?" Sally asked with despair. Her head swirled with doubts, as strong as the river that had tried to carry her away.

"It won't be for lack of trying." Rob set his jaw. "We'll do it. I'll see to that."

Before now, she'd never considered they might not make it to Texas. The thought of losing Matthew was more than she could bear. She could only keep going and pray they'd reach Texas safely.

That night she got down on her knees and prayed with her daughter before they slept. "Lord, help us reach Texas safely. Help me find Matthew. Keep us in your sight as we travel this desolate trail. Amen."

Carolyn whispered, "And send me a new papa."

Sally choked back tears as she listened to Carolyn's small voice. Her last waking thought before drifting into sleep was that she had to keep going. She had to press on and make a better life for her daughter.

Rob had tried to keep his distance though it was difficult with such a winsome child. He shouldn't get attached to the little girl, but Carolyn's small voice asking God for a papa broke through his resolve. His eyes misted.

Poor little darling. Praying for a papa.

He brushed away the moisture in his eyes.

Luke had plenty to answer for. Rob's eyes narrowed in the dark. Plenty.

To Sally the current of the North Canadian River appeared strong and lethal.

They came upon a flat, barge-type boat that sat heavily on the side of the river. Normally it would have been used to transport traders' goods. It seemed strange to see no one about. They'd use it to cross.

Rob smiled at Sally. "Don't worry. I'll see you both safely across."

The dark circles ringing her eyes showed she had slept no better than he. The shadows had deepened with each difficult day and it was obvious her spirits were low.

She looked at him through exhausted eyes. "I hope your luck holds."

He'd been lucky enough to shoot two rabbits the night before, and that kept the hunger pangs at bay.

She was lucky he'd saved her from drowning. The thought of crossing another river made her stomach turn, but she would trust him in this.

Once the horse and mules were loaded, Moss pushed off one side with a pole while Rob pushed off the bank.

They hit shallow water and the boat scraped bottom on part of a sandbar. The swirling brown waters of the Canadian coursed around and past them, but for now the river let them be and the crossing was uneventful.

Sally breathed a sigh of relief. This river wouldn't take her with it like the other one had tried to do.

Running Water, the old Indian had called her. It was a good name. She'd survived the running water.

The river keeps on going, just like me. I will keep on going until I get to Texas. Until I find Matthew.

She'd felt listless all day, but Rob's encouragement buoyed her spirits. It was strange how he seemed to know just what to say to keep her going and just the right time to say it.

She regarded him with curiosity. What sort of a life had he led? She wished she knew more about him.

Her thoughts filtered back to the day they'd met. She'd been afraid of him at first, yet he'd been kind. Despite the fact he clearly hated Luke, he hadn't taken it out on her.

She hesitated, watching his profile. In some ways, she felt as if she knew him though she knew nothing of his past.

"Mama, when can I have a new dolly?"

Carolyn's rag doll had fallen apart after the soaking it had taken from the river. And all that was left of her sun babies were the few seeds Sally had stored in the wooden box.

She'd fixated on wanting a new dolly ever since they'd left their home. And Sally had promised.

"Yes, sweetheart, we'll find you a dolly in Texas."

"I'm tired, Mama. When can we stop?"

"Soon, sunshine, soon."

Rob approached Sally. "Set her down. I'll take her."

She put Carolyn down. Her hip and her back ached as she bent then straightened.

Rob lifted Carolyn onto his shoulders.

She giggled "whee" as she bumped into his hat.

"That won't do." He removed his hat and placed it on Sally's head. "Keep the sun off."

She looked up at him, flustered.

His smile widened.

Carolyn quit whining and made up songs about the new dolly she'd been promised.

Rob said to Moss, "Now I know why Sally calls her sunshine. I've never seen a happier little girl."

They soon reached the outskirts of an Indian village near

the South Canadian River. Smoke rose from the dozen teepees clustered together. A dog ran out, barking.

"Ever been here before?" Moss asked Rob.

"No."

"What kinda Injuns ye reckon they are?"

"Could be a tribe from up north, here for the winter." Rob glanced behind them. "We need food and horses if they'll trade."

"Humph. If'n they'll do it."

"Move slow. Just because no braves met us coming in doesn't mean they aren't nearby."

"We ain't got nothin' left to trade 'em."

Rob didn't reply.

As they rode closer, Sally saw only women, children and an old man who sat outside his teepee.

Rob raised his hand in greeting. The old Indian raised his but didn't speak.

As they stopped, Rob set Carolyn down. "Go to your Mama."

She ran to Sally.

Carolyn's chatter had worn him out. That must be the reason women talked so much. They were born that way. He watched as Sally hugged her daughter close.

Sally didn't chatter like most women. She had a shy way about her, and he'd seen from the very first it wasn't only her fear of him that made her back away. He was a much better reader of people than he'd been before he spent time in jail.

He turned his attention back to the old Indian, who gestured to the men to sit then called for his woman to come out of the teepee. He spoke and she offered them water in a gourd.

They each drank eagerly, then the old Indian spoke again and the woman led Sally and Carolyn away.

The woman who led Sally to the Canadian River walked with a gracefulness she'd never seen before, her long braid swinging behind her back. They stood in silence by the river as Sally washed the dirt from Carolyn's face and hands, then cleansed her own in the cool water.

A fish swam by and the woman laughed as Carolyn tried to catch it with her small hands.

Then she led them back to the camp.

Later, she brought fish, and Sally and Carolyn ate. After they finished, a little girl came over to Carolyn and they began to play.

Sally watched Carolyn anxiously. No words were necessary for the children. They found it much easier to communicate.

The men had commenced trading. The old Indian kept shaking his head, his eyes drifting back to their rifles.

"Old timer, can you part with that rifle to get Sally to Texas?" Rob asked.

"No. Trade your'n."

"I'm not the one who promised to take her there. That foolish agreement was yours."

Moss spat. "I'm a dang fool." He squinted. "Ain't got nothin' else he wants. Dagnabbit, first my wagon, then my mules, an' my load an' now my gun." He shook his head. "This ain't no good."

Rob reached for the gun before Moss could change his mind and held it out to the Indian for inspection.

The Indian gave him a wide smile, which crinkled up the lines in his dark cheeks and his missing teeth. He grasped the gun and gestured to the two horses Rob had indicated.

Rob nodded with a smile.

The deal was done. The animals and rifle for two fresh prime horses.

Sally traded her corset for a pair of soft doeskin moccasins. Her shoes had worn through the soles, but as she slipped the moccasins on and set her old shoes to the side, a child ran up and carried them off as if he'd captured a prize.

"We'd best not linger," Rob said as he and Moss packed the horses. They'd travel faster now.

Sally's feet felt wonderful in the soft moccasins. She stretched her toes. Why would anyone want to wear shoes when these were so much more comfortable? Why would anyone want to wear a corset?

No wonder Indians didn't take easily to white men's ways. She supposed it was a curiosity to the other woman.

The woman's dress was lovely. Beaded and soft like the moccasins. Sally wondered how it would feel to wear one.

Maybe a squaw's life wasn't so bad. Surely this woman's life had been no worse than Sally's. She had a serenity Sally could only dream of. What was her secret?

But as Sally remembered how fierce the braves had looked when they surrounded them, she shivered. No, she wouldn't want to be at the mercy of such a fierce warrior.

What was she thinking? She'd had enough of violent men. If she ever married again, it would be to provide a father for her children and he would have to be a kind and loving man.

"Ye trust that Injun?" Moss asked.

Rob had asked the Indian how to find Red River Station and the old man had pointed west.

"Yes. He's Cherokee."

"What's that got to do with anythin'?"

"I was in jail with a man who was half-Cherokee. He was a man of his word. Indians have more honor than most white men I've known."

"*Humph.*" Moss nodded at Sally who rode watching them. "The two of ye make a pair, takin' up fer Injuns."

Sally's eyes widened when Rob said he'd been in jail. She regarded him with renewed fear and awe.

Moss hadn't missed her reaction. "What were ye in fer?"

"Murder."

Sally gasped, her arms tightening around Carolyn.

She'd known the minute Rob said he was in jail that he'd done something terrible. You didn't go to jail unless you did something bad. The man was a murderer. An outlaw. But how was he connected with Luke?

"Who did you kill?"

Leave it to Moss to ask the questions she'd never dare.

"I didn't kill anyone. Then."

It was clear things had changed once he got out. The look on his face said he had no distaste for killing and his tone brooked no further discussion of the subject.

They rode in silence, an occasional song from Carolyn filling the air.

When they reached the South Canadian, crossing the river was easy. Sally breathed a sigh of relief. Now with fresh horses it seemed possible they would find Matthew again.

But Moss wasn't pleased since giving up his rifle.

"I wished I'd never set out on this here trail," he said to Rob. "From now on I won't take no women nor babies anywhere's. It's bad luck, jus' like them sailors say. Ain't had nothin' but bad luck since we started."

So he blamed Sally for his bad luck. Maybe he was right. Maybe bad luck followed her wherever she went.

"Luck is what you make it," Rob said. "Sometimes luck is what happens when you aren't aware of what's going on." He glanced at Sally. "You can change your luck if you're willing to accept the consequences."

She wasn't sure what he was trying to tell her, but the sooner she changed the subject the better. "How far is it to Red River Station?"

"Ain't I told ye not to ask? Always puttin' bad luck on us, ain't we had 'nough?" Moss rode off.

She didn't know why he kept snapping at her.

Rob rode next to her and they watched Moss ride away.

"What has him so upset?" Sally asked.

"A man needs his gun and his horse to survive."

"Well, he's got a horse now."

"But he hasn't ridden far enough to feel like it's his. And he doesn't have his gun. It isn't something a woman would understand."

Now he sounded like Luke. Always talking about what a man needed. Never thinking she might have needs. She didn't understand men. Maybe they were all selfish.

Rob watched her expression. He could see how Luke had fooled her. She honestly didn't understand men. She had no idea of what it took for a man to give up the things that made him a man. The things Moss had given up taking her to Texas.

"The old man made quite a sacrifice for you, Sally."

Puzzled, she looked at him.

"He's given up everything for you. His wagon and mules, those were his livelihood. He lost his load. Now he's given up his gun. It isn't like he's your kin. He doesn't have to do anything for you."

Sally felt stunned. She'd always thought of Ozzie Moss like

a grandfather or an old uncle. She'd been young when he took them to Kansas. He'd looked after her.

But she was grown now and Moss was the one who needed looking after. She'd been acting like a child. Never thanking him, expecting him to behave as if he was kin. He wasn't.

"You're right." She looked to where Moss rode up ahead. "Will you take Carolyn?"

"You know that I will."

She handed Carolyn over then raced up beside Moss.

He scowled at her sideways.

"It was mighty nice of you to trade your gun for the horses."

He grunted. "*Humph.*"

"I can't tell you how much it means to have you take me to Texas to get my son back."

"I give my word."

"Yes, you did. But I'm sure you'd no idea how hard it would be. What sacrifices you'd make."

"*Humph.*"

"Well, I want you to know it means the world to me. You're the only family I've got, Ozzie, other than my children. I know you aren't really kin, but you feel like family to me."

"Confound the gal," he muttered as his old eyes watered. "She don't even let me be mad at her." He blinked a few times.

"You've a place at my hearth any time, Moss. When you get too old to ride, you come stay with me."

"Well, now." He choked up. "Well, now."

They rode quietly together.

After a while Rob and Carolyn caught up with them. It looked to him like they'd made up. That was good. But he hoped he didn't have to play peacemaker again. It was a role he wasn't used to.

This was the strangest journey he'd ever been on. He wouldn't mind getting his hands on a bottle, finding a woman and sleeping for a day. If it weren't for Sally he'd have found a woman by now. But she filled his thoughts.

She was completely different from May Belle who'd always been the center of attention, who constantly flirted and was unhappy unless surrounded by a crowd of people. He'd mistaken her vivacity, her demand for his attention for love.

Sally had a shy manner. Self-conscious in the way of those who didn't like being the center of attention. Her mannerisms told him this, like the way her hand rose to play with her brooch when she was nervous, or the way she blushed under his gaze. And that combined with the sensuality bubbling beneath that surface attracted him more than any woman ever had.

More even than May Belle.

He couldn't act on the attraction he felt for her, and the pent-up desire built with each day on the trail. There was no release here on the trail and no chance he'd leave her alone for even a quick interlude in the saloon.

Every time he left her alone, she took off without him.

As evening settled in, Sally heard a coyote howl. She saw no one nearby. No sign of life, only earth and wind. The howling blew out across the land, sending a chill down her spine. She shivered.

Carolyn's eyes grew wide. "What is it, Mama?" she whispered. "Is it wolves?"

"No, sunshine, they're called coyotes."

"Coyotes are something like a wolf," Rob added. "Both will eat little children. Stay near your Mama and don't go wandering off when we make camp."

Sally glared at him. Why would he want to scare her little girl?

"Don't worry, Sally, I'll shoot any that comes near. They'll stay away unless they're hungry."

Now he was trying to scare her. Well, she wasn't going to let him know it had worked. He probably wanted her to fall into his arms again. But that wasn't going to happen, despite her growing attraction to him. Despite the way she longed for him to hold her again.

She'd noticed how much attention he paid Carolyn. The closer they got to Texas, the more he changed. Carolyn liked him and it would be easy to fall for the handsome maverick. But she wasn't going to forget who he was and what he was here for.

She had to figure out a way to keep Rob out of the way until after she'd dealt with Luke and had Matthew back. There were too many things that could go wrong. Simply being in another man's company was enough to set Luke off.

A week after their wedding, she and Luke had gone to a barn dance. He danced with her once then went out back to drink whiskey with a few other men. He'd been angry when he returned to find her talking with a nice young farmer. Luke had accused her of cheating.

She'd been a loyal wife, but he had looked for reasons to be angry. He'd hurt her that night after his rage built all the long way home. And he'd enjoyed hurting her.

He'd kill Rob if he knew Rob had kissed her. She couldn't let anything like that happen.

But she also didn't know how she'd keep Rob away from Luke until she got Matthew back.

She'd have to think of something soon.

The sun slowly eased down behind a scrub oak on a lone hill. Its red glow framed the tree in black.

A coyote stood underneath howling to his mate, sending his call across the desolate plain.

"Ain't that one o' the purtiest sights ye ever seen? This here's why I love the trail. Follow it long 'nough an' it gives ye somethin' back." Moss seemed happy for a change.

They made camp as the sun receded behind the hill.

Yes, it was beautiful here, but deadly too. Sally couldn't see the coyotes. Hearing them but not knowing where they were kept her awake.

By morning she was tired and cranky and her eyes burned from sleeplessness as she made coffee.

The others woke to the scent.

She glanced down at her work-worn hands as she rinsed out the coffee pot. Her nails were cracked and dry, her knuckles red and rough. When she got to Texas, she'd have a good meal and take a long, hot bath.

Her hair was a tangled mess, though the others didn't seem to notice. They all looked as rough as she. No man would find her attractive. Yet she'd have to either find a job or a husband once she had Matthew back. She hadn't fixed up for a man in years. Her looks had been wasted on Luke. Completely wasted.

Rob watched Sally.

She was a rare beauty. He'd been on the trail with her long enough to see her at every time of day, and what he'd seen only made him appreciate her more. She wore no paint as other women chose to wear. Her beauty was natural yet she didn't seem aware of it.

He enjoyed watching her calf as she slipped down from her horse and the way her limbs moved as she stretched and as her hand rubbed the stiffness from the back of her neck. The way she looked and the way she moved made him want to gather her in his arms.

She was more enticing than a roomful of painted ladies. Sally was the real thing.

He glanced away, ignoring the tight knot in his throat, the aching need to look at her.

Moss stretched. "Time was I'd be up afore the sun," he told his horse, now named Coal Miner. "These bones ain't gonna take this much longer. Too bad them two ain't married," he muttered, watching Sally and Rob. "Tarnation, I done promised her I'd take her to Luke, an' I'm a gonna do it. 'Course I ain't promised nothin' else." He chuckled. "Never ken tell what'll happen. Mebbe Luke will get himself shot a'fore we git there."

His words startled Sally, but before she had time to react to them, she saw Indians in the brush.

She caught her breath. This time there'd been no warning.

They waved weapons and made war whoops as arrows started to fly. She barely had time to shout to Rob before one struck Moss in the shoulder, and he cried out before slumping over.

Rob had dropped on one knee and was firing his rifle. He wounded several before the small but fierce hunting party turned away, retrieving their fallen warriors.

Sally exhaled and turned to Moss, his complexion pale.
"Is anyone else hurt?" Rob asked, concern filling his face.
"No," Sally said.

He looked at Moss. "We've got to stop the bleeding."

She tore a strip off the bottom of her underskirt to tie around the wound.

Rob grasped the arrow, but as he tried to pull it out of Moss's shoulder the shaft broke.

"Damn." He looked at Moss, who sat clenching his teeth. "I'm sorry."

"Wish I had me some whiskey. It do deaden the pains."

Rob gave him what was left. "I wish I had more to give you, old timer." He tied the cloth strips around the wound and stood. "Can you ride?"

"Yep. Ain't the first time I been shot."

They rode until midday when they reached a stream and stopped to water the horses and refill their water jugs.

Sally cleaned Moss's wound, and tore more strips to wrap it. She held back her tears.

So much had happened to Moss, and it was all her fault. She should never have asked him to take her to Texas.

She tore up the rest of her petticoat to stop the bleeding after rinsing her hands in the stream.

"We won't stop until we reach Red River Station," Rob said.

Sally feared for Moss as she watched Rob help him onto his horse. He was so weak. And she worried even more when he dozed in the saddle and Rob led his horse.

"How old do you suppose he is?" Rob asked.

"It's hard to tell," Sally replied. "Do you think he'll be all right?"

"He needs a doctor soon. He's lost a lot of blood."

Sally was concerned about Moss. She had dragged her old friend into her problems and she could not bear to lose him this way. All on account of her. They had to find a doctor, but what if they moved him when he shouldn't be moved? What if that made him worse?

Rob frowned as he checked his gun. "One bullet left. Damn. We need to keep riding."

Moss moaned.

"Moss needs to rest," Sally said. "And bouncing around in that saddle can't be good for him. It will start the bleeding again. Please, let's stop. We need to rest too."

Rob's glance raked her up and down. She knew she looked a sight in her torn dress and no petticoat and with her legs exposed and her feet adorned in the Indian moccasins.

"We can't stop. He'll be in his final rest if we don't keep going." Rob urged his horse faster. "Keep up with me."

Sally tightened her arms around Carolyn and rode after him.

They rode through the night until morning broke through the clouds. Rob couldn't remember a time when he'd had less sleep.

Carolyn pointed to the sky. "Look, Mama, a hawk."

"That's no hawk," Rob said.

Sally looked up. The vulture spread its wings and swooped as it followed them.

You want Moss. Well, you can't have him.

Moss's groans had given way to silence. He hovered on the brink of consciousness.

They pressed on and by nightfall, finally approached Red River Station.

Sally hoped they'd find a doctor. Moss's situation had grown more desperate.

It was dark, and the outskirts showed no sign of people.

An owl screeched at their approach. Sally felt like screaming along with it. Would Moss make it? She couldn't bear the thought that if not for her, he wouldn't be in this trouble. Moss was right. She'd brought him nothing but bad luck. She didn't want to think of losing him.

And if he didn't make it, how would she find Matthew?

She'd be alone with Rob.

Sally eyed his back and his broad shoulders. She didn't want to contemplate what he would do if he had her alone on the trail. But her mind filled with all the possibilities.

Chapter Eight

"Mama, someone's hurting a baby," Carolyn said.

"No, honey, that's a screech owl."

"Is it crying?"

"No, that's just the sound it makes."

"I don't like it, Mama." Carolyn snuggled closer to her.

Sally was relieved they'd soon be in the settlement, but she was also worried. First they had to cross another river. The Red. Even the name sounded dangerous.

"Now listen to me, Sally," Rob said. "Hold his mane tight, and let your horse swim. He'll carry you both across just fine, long as you hang on. You go first. I'll follow behind you."

"I don't know about this."

"Let your horse feel his way. If he hesitates don't force him. This river has soft spots that can sink a horse quick. Carolyn, hold tight to your mama."

Sally hesitated. Her thoughts spun as fear filled her mind. This river looked a whole lot meaner than the one that had tried to carry her away.

"You can do this, Sally. You've come through every obstacle we've met. Now grit your teeth and go."

Rob would bring up the rear in case she or Carolyn fell off. But he also had to guide Moss's horse. She glanced at Moss.

"Sally Mae, a man don't never step in the same river twice, they's always changin' on ye." He clutched his wound. "A body ken always stand more'n ye think it ken."

"You hold on, Moss." Sally gripped the reins tightly. "We're crossing this river."

If Moss could keep going in his condition, so could she.

Sally concentrated on the opposite bank and gave her horse a kick. As they started across, the horses hesitated but with Rob's encouragement they entered.

The current pulled strong against them, but the horses fought their way through.

Sally blew a sigh of relief as they reached the other side.

"Ye done it. 'Member this, Sally Mae. Life is kinder like bustin' broncos." Moss caught his breath with a painful gasp. "Yer gonna get throwed. The secret is to keep gettin' back on. Don't never let 'em keep ye down."

Tears filled her eyes. Here Moss was wounded and thinking about her. "Don't you worry, Moss, we'll get you to a doctor."

"Let's go," Rob said. "His color doesn't look good."

When they finally rode into Red River Station, an army officer greeted them and glanced off into the distance. "Looks like you've had Indian trouble."

Rob nodded. "But they didn't follow us."

"How far away were they?"

"On the other side of the Red River," Sally said. "But right now we have a wounded man who needs help."

The officer ignored her. "Any idea which tribe?"

"Nope." Rob's lips sealed tightly. "The lady was speaking."

"Our friend needs a doctor," Sally said.

"Doc will see to him. Second building on the left. After you take him in, report to the commander's office." He pointed to a small building. "He'll want to know all the details of any Indian attack." He gave a curt nod then walked away.

They reached the doctor's quarters then Sally helped Carolyn down and tied the horses. Rob lifted Moss from the saddle and carried him up the steps as Sally knocked on the door.

The army surgeon who opened it looked as if he hadn't bathed in months, and he reeked of whiskey.

She wrinkled her nose and looked past him. Surely he wasn't the doctor. But the dismal room was empty. She frowned. "Is the doctor in?"

"Yes, ma'am," the man hiccupped. "Enter."

He gestured in a drunken manner that didn't improve Sally's opinion of him and pointed to a small cot. "Put him there."

Rob laid Moss down and stepped back. "He took an arrow. It broke off when I tried to remove it."

"Indians have gotten smarter," the doctor slurred, "make arrows thin. Rougher arrow heads so they'll catch." He wiped his mouth on his shirtsleeve then ripped Moss's shirt open to see the wound. Moss moaned but didn't open his eyes.

Sally's breath caught.

The doctor was drunk, his movements rough.

He turned to Sally. "Bring me that whiskey bottle on the table."

"I think you've had enough," she said.

"It's for Moss," Rob said. "Doc here wouldn't waste liquor when there's an ailing man who needs it." His steely gray-blue eyes looked into the doctor's bloodshot ones.

Doc got the message.

Sally brought the bottle and handed it to him. He looked at it with longing, gave a sigh then poured some over the wound.

Moss groaned and turned his head.

"He's alive. Doesn't mean he'll stay that way," the doctor said.

"What are his chances?" Rob asked.

The doctor shrugged. "Depends. I make no promises."

A man with a long, black beard stepped inside. "Who're you butcherin' this time, sawbones?"

Sally gasped. The man had a peg leg and a fierce expression.

"Like what you see?" He leered at her.

When she offered no reply, he turned to the doctor. "Don't all the ladies love a man with a wooden leg?" His gaze returned to Sally. "Pretty ain't it?"

She stepped backwards and gripped the edge of the table.

The man stepped closer to her. "Bring your friend in here for doctoring, no telling what he'll lop off."

Rob moved between them. "Step out of here, mister. This isn't any of your concern."

"Ask him," the man said. "Ask him how many Reb arms and legs he lopped off. Ask him when he closes his eyes don't them arms and legs hunt for him in the night. Ask him why he stays drunk. Ask him why he don't hear the cries of the men he killed with his sawing blade."

Rob put a hand on his gun. "I told you to leave."

The man's lips curled into a thin smirk as he headed for the door. "Ask him."

Sally turned to look at the doctor who'd taken a swig out of the bottle when she wasn't looking. He hastily set it down and stared at her with tortured eyes.

Rob glared at him. "I've got just one question. Can you doctor this man, or do I need to take him out of here?"

"I can do the job."

"Then do it."

The doctor's hands worked, cleaning and digging out parts of tattered pieces of arrow, the hand that held the knife shaking.

Sally's gaze drifted over to the table where the doctor kept his tools. There was a saw that looked like a miniature of the one her Papa had used to saw logs.

So that was a bone cutter. She imagined it cutting through living flesh. All the arms and legs the man with the peg leg had spoken of made a grisly picture in her mind. No wonder he'd been so unhappy.

She watched Moss and prayed the doctor knew what to do, but she had her doubts.

The doctor's hands dripped with blood as he dug around the wound. He removed several splinters of wood from the broken shaft before he finally withdrew the bloody arrowhead. He tossed it to the floor by Sally's feet.

She jumped.

He wiped his hands on his pants and eyed the whiskey bottle. Rob silently handed him clean bandages. The doctor bound up the wound again after he'd cleaned it once more by pouring whiskey over it.

Finally, he stood. "I've done all I can."

"Will he be all right?" Sally asked.

"Too soon to tell."

Rob planned to have a talk with the doctor once Sally was out of earshot. He needed to know the old man's chances and he wanted to hear it straight.

"Sally, see to Carolyn. I'll be along in a minute."

"If you think Moss will be all right. I know Carolyn is tired. We're all tired." She walked over to Moss, lifted his hand then bent down and kissed his cheek. "Don't you go on any other trail rides, Ozzie Moss, you stick to this one. You promised, remember?" Tears welled in her eyes and she stood. "I'll pray for him."

"You do that," the doctor's voice rang bitterly, his eyes those of a lost soul. "For all the good it will do."

Rob walked Sally out to where Carolyn had curled into a ball on the porch to sleep. She woke when Sally lifted her.

"Mama, will the doctor fix Moss like you fix my dollies?"

"I hope so."

"Tell the commander I'll speak to him once you've found a place to sleep. I'll see to the horses and catch up with you later," Rob said. He watched Sally and Carolyn walk away. He could use a drink and some grub. But he'd take care of the horses first.

He stepped back into the doctor's quarters. "How's he really doing?"

"I told you."

"Is there anything else that can be done?"

"He'd have a better chance if I had more whiskey." He lifted the bottle and shook it.

Rob's eyes narrowed. "I'll bring back whatever he needs. But you'd better care for him like he was your own."

There was a knock on the door. The commanding officer of the fort had sent for Rob.

The commander, a tall thin man with a weathered face, stood and pointed to a rough map covering a table. "Here on the Red River we're on the border of Indian Territory. We see plenty of action. Do you have any idea which tribe attacked you?"

"No, sir, I don't."

"Had to have been Comanche," he said. "About one hundred of them attacked Rangers right here on the Red a week ago. They may have scattered to hunt with winter coming on, or they may be regrouping. How many of them do you think there were?"

"They were a small hunting party, four at the most and none of them had guns. They took off quick once I started firing. Hit two of them. "

"You must be a good shot."

"Fair." Rob shrugged. "Sir, about the doc. Is he any good?"

"He was once. He's all we have now. The Indian Territory has become a hideout for renegades and deserters from the army. At least he hasn't deserted, which is more than I can say for the last doctor we had. Fort Worth is the closest doctor if you want another one. And if you want laudanum or other medicine, you'll have to ride there, since we have none."

"He won't make it that far," Rob said somberly. "If he needs medicine, I'll bring it back."

"It's a dangerous ride, unescorted. And I can't spare any of my men right now."

"I understand."

A soldier stepped in and waited until the commander dismissed Rob.

After he cared for the horses, he went to find Sally and Carolyn in the tent they'd been assigned. She'd already put Carolyn down for the night.

"Listen, Sally, there's a large band of Comanche who killed Rangers right here along the Red just last week." Lightly taking her hand he added, "I don't think it's safe for you and Carolyn to stay here. I want you to ride with me to Fort Worth, out of Indian Territory."

The mere touch of his hand sent a warming shiver through her and she felt her pulse leap with excitement.

Did this mean what she thought it meant? Did he want her to ride away with him?

Her heart leapt at the thought, even though she knew he only meant to see her to the fort for safety. Even though she knew he was only traveling with her to find Luke and settle his vendetta. Part of her was tempted by the thought of riding away with him and leaving all her troubles behind.

But she couldn't. "No." She pulled her hand away. "I'm not

leaving Moss."

"Sally, I'm telling you, it's not safe. If the Rangers couldn't protect themselves, how will they protect you? And if Indians attack this fort, you won't be safe inside these walls."

"We can't leave until Moss is able."

"I'll check on him again." He cupped her chin tenderly in his warm hand, brushing his thumb along her cheek.

She leaned her cheek into his palm, savoring the gentle touch. A touch that was gentle and strong. A touch that reached into the secret heart of her.

She closed her eyes, savoring that brief moment and knowing it couldn't last.

"We won't make the decision tonight. Get some rest. And think about what I said. We'll talk about it in the morning. But, Sally," his hand caressed her cheek again, "I won't let anything happen to you."

She opened her eyes as he leaned in to kiss her and she drank in the sweetness of his kiss, the warmth and tenderness of lips sending uncurling desire radiating through her body.

His tongue teased her lips open until his tongue met hers lightly teasing, tasting.

Her hands eased around his neck, touching the back of his thick hair as he held her by the waist, pulling her closer, deepening the kiss. Making her aware she no longer wore a corset or a petticoat beneath her dress. Feeling the warmth of his body, his strength, the easy way he savored her, holding back so as not to rush her.

In sensing all these things, a sob rose in her throat.

This was the one man she wanted, and if not for her children she would give him her all, her everything. Give it all for just one night with him.

She pulled away, breaking the kiss with a gasp. "I can't go with you."

He knew she was speaking about more than just leaving Moss.

"I can't leave until Moss is better."

Rob studied her set chin. He could see there'd be no reasoning with her about this. He hadn't counted on her stubbornness. This was the first time he'd encountered it.

She was willful. Had more spirit hidden inside than even she knew. He'd get nowhere with her if he pressed the issue.

And he was painfully aware that she wanted him as much as he wanted her. It did neither of them any good to keep pursuing her, teasing them both in this way.

He had no control when it came to her and he prided himself on control. So he wrestled with himself as he stood watching the way her breath came quicker. The way her breasts rose and fell and the way she bit her lip.

"Then goodnight, Sally. Sleep well."

He went back to check on Moss, leaving Sally to settle in and trying not to think about the fact they would share a tent. He forced himself to think of Luke, the one thing guaranteed to tamp down his desire.

The doc agreed it wouldn't be wise to try to move Moss to Fort Worth. So Rob made plans to ride there and bring back medicine to fight the infection and ease the pain. He'd catch up on lost sleep tonight then ride out tomorrow. But he'd leave at night to avoid notice from roving Indian bands.

It was also another way of putting distance between him and Sally. He resolved to find a willing woman to release his frustrations before he returned.

The next evening, as he prepared to leave, Sally came up to him and grasped his hand.

Her touch surprised him. He'd never known her to be forward. But tonight there was a desperate longing in her eyes. He eased her into the back of the stable.

"I'll be back, Sally, don't worry."

She pressed something into his hand as her eyes filled with tears. "For Moss," she whispered. She swallowed and blinked, tears rolling down her cheeks. "Come back safe."

He looked down at his hand. She'd given him her locket. There was a picture of her mother inside.

"No, Sally. I can't take this."

He circled his arms around her neck to fasten the locket. She smelled of lavender soap now that she'd had a chance to wash, and he inhaled deeply before whispering through her hair into her ear. "I'll take care of the medicine. You keep this."

Her hair was soft against his cheek. Tickling, teasing him. The feel of her breasts brushing his chest as he fastened the locket destroyed all sense of the restraint he'd kept in place.

His slid his hands down her back to her waist and pulled her close, pinning her arms lightly.

He'd kiss her, once more before he left. Just this once.

Dipping his head, he covered her soft lips with his. Touching, teasing, tasting. She tasted like mint. His tongue traced the soft fullness of her lips, coaxing until her mouth opened wider.

His tongue explored her mouth with feather touches, encouraging her to give him more.

She returned his kiss and he held her closer, feeling her warm, womanly curves.

Yes, he wanted her. Wanted all of her.

She leaned back, her spine stiffening.

Still holding her, he gazed into her eyes and saw tears. She stood silently crying, and her shoulders shook.

"Sally, I'm sorry," he said.

Had he hurt her in some way? He'd been as gentle as he knew how. Yet the tears rolled down her face.

Rob frowned. He'd never been any good with crying women. What was he supposed to do? Damn tears. Why was she crying? He hadn't hurt her. He'd been gentle and persuasive, and she'd responded to him.

She looked into his eyes, pleading for something.

Lord, he could drown in those eyes.

"Rob, I —"

He waited for her to explain but something stopped her from speaking and the expression in her eyes was more than he could take. He let her go and stepped back. "I've got to go."

He spun and mounted his horse then rode away without a backward glance. But his thoughts remained on Sally. Thoughts of her eyes, her lips and the way her body felt next to his.

Sally watched him go.

Soon the darkness swallowed him, and she could only

picture him in her mind. She crossed her arms and fought to bring her emotions under control.

She trusted him. He could so easily have taken the locket but instead he'd pay for the medicine himself. The generosity of that compared with the way Luke had taken and taken from her made her love Rob even more.

It was in that moment she knew he was a man worth loving. A man who would give his all for his woman.

A man who could never be hers.

Then he'd kissed her again. And she'd shattered with the hunger of his kiss.

He was strong like Luke. Strong enough to do things Luke had done. Hurtful things.

Rob's kiss had sent the pit of her stomach into a wild swirl, and she'd responded without thinking until he pulled her to him, crushing her, his belt buckle rubbing against her. It reminded her of Luke and his belt, his demands.

When Luke had wanted to make love, it was now, not later. He'd given her no teasing kisses, only quick demanding ones.

Her mind relived the velvet warmth of Rob's kiss.

But he could be just like Luke. Charming until he got her where he wanted her, and rough and fast later on. She couldn't go through that again. She wouldn't.

Rob had been good to them. He'd been there for her and Carolyn and now Moss. He didn't have to ride out for that medicine. And with so many Indians around, it was likely he'd never make it back.

What if he decided not to come back and rode off like Luke? It wasn't Rob's responsibility to take care of them. He could go off on his own, hunting for Luke.

But the look in his eyes had told her he'd return, more so than his words ever could. She'd trusted words before. She'd trusted in vows and look where that had gotten her.

Her mind spun in turmoil and she tried not to think of the ache his leaving created. The deep aching need within that had grown daily.

What would she do if he kissed her again? For she knew without a doubt that if he returned he would indeed kiss her again. How would she stop him?

She feared the next time she would be unable to stop herself from giving in to her desire.

Chapter Nine

In her dream, Sally and her daughter wore yellow dresses. Sunflowers grew in abundance in the yard by a little white house. She sat on the front porch snapping beans into a bowl. Matthew chased a giggling Carolyn around the yard.

A warm hand closed over her shoulder and a kind voice said, "It's good to be home. I've missed you and the children."

She knew that voice. It was the one that soothed her when she was afraid, the one that calmed her when she was worried. She turned to face him and woke.

It had been Rob.

The dream had left her in a lazy, floating feeling.

Outside, a bird warbled a soft song. It was early, the sun just coming up. She would rise and face the day. Face the fact that Rob had gone, he didn't love her, Luke still had Matthew and Moss was wounded.

Reality was about as far from her dream as she could get.

But one fact from her dream remained.

She'd fallen in love with Rob.

Short of Matthew being hurt, it was the worst thing that could have happened.

A cold wet rain fell. As she stepped outside, the cold surprised her. She'd heard Texas was hot.

She wondered if Rob had ridden though the night and reached the fort before the temperature dropped. Every day he'd been gone made her worry more. Had something happened to him? Had he changed his mind and gone looking for Luke?

Moss was awake now and asking about Rob. He was still

pretty bad, but at least he'd lost his gray pallor.

"Come along, Carolyn. It's time to visit Moss." Carolyn slid her hand into Sally's and skipped along beside her.

At the doctors quarters she knocked then stepped inside when Moss called, "Come in."

"How do you feel today?"

"Better."

"I know it must hurt something terrible."

"It do hurt some."

As the doctor changed Moss's bandages, she saw the gaping wound. "I wish we could do more for you."

"Cain't be heped."

"I'm sorry I brought all this on you. You're a brave man."

"I ain't brave. Ain't never seen no wild critter feelin' sorry fer itself. I ain't no different. Don't do no good to complain."

The rain poured down harder, hitting the roof in a steady rhythm. Moss dozed.

Sally walked to the window to look out at the vertical streams of gray.

"He'll sleep. That's nature's medicine," the doctor said.

She turned to face him. "Does he feel the pain?"

"It wouldn't make a difference to you if he did or didn't. There's not a damn thing you can do about it. Many a man's been brought to his grave without a drop of relief." He gripped the whiskey bottle by the neck.

Where he'd gotten his hands on a new one, she didn't know.

He took a swallow. "At least this one takes it like a man. But I've seen that too. They all die just the same."

He walked out onto the porch with his whiskey, leaving Sally and Carolyn to sit with Moss.

She watched through the window as the doctor drank then leaned back in the chair with closed eyes. Maybe he did see the war dead all around him.

She wasn't afraid of the doctor any more. He battled his own personal ghosts and took no notice of her. One of the soldiers had told her they brought in new supplies every few weeks. And whiskey for their doctor was a priority or he would've deserted long ago.

Sally remained in the cabin until late afternoon when a soldier brought word there'd been an Indian raid a few miles out. Four men had been killed.

Her heart was in her throat. "Was Rob one of them?"

"No."

Relief coursed through her.

How long would it be until he returned? She was surprised to realize how much she missed him.

Days passed with no word. Then it was Thanksgiving. Sally and Carolyn woke to a blanket of new fallen snow that made everything sparkle.

The fort filled with a festive air as preparations were made for the meal. There was so little to look forward to in the life of a soldier, other than routine and more routine. The soldiers grasped any excuse to hold a festivity. They'd feast on venison, roast wild turkey, fish, rice pudding and dried apple pies.

Sally helped prepare the food and Carolyn helped set the tables.

Everyone came together, except for the men posted as lookouts and Moss. Sally hardly tasted her food as she worried about Rob. He should have been back by now. What if something had happened to him? She'd not even had word that he arrived at the other fort.

Moss was recovering, but slowly. How soon could he be ready to travel?

She'd begun this journey without considering the dangers to herself and the others.

Left on her own, how would she ever find Luke and Matthew? She was no tracker.

She was supposed to be thankful, but it was hard when everything seemed so hopeless. She wondered how Matthew was spending Thanksgiving. Luke usually spent any holiday nursing a bottle of whiskey. She'd had to fight to keep a sense of joy during Christmas when he'd been at his worst.

The more joy she felt, the more he tried to trample it. But she realized that having both her children together and healthy was all she'd ever need for a joyful Christmas. Luke could drink himself into oblivion. He'd ruined enough holidays. Fury almost choked her and she set down her fork. She had to stop thinking about what he'd done to her. Dwelling on it would poison her mind.

When the meal was over and Carolyn went to play with a visiting family, Sally fixed a plate of turkey to take to Moss. He hadn't had much appetite, but maybe he'd feel like eating once he smelled the food. She'd be sure to stay until he ate it.

As she started across the compound, a horse rode up behind her in a hurry.

Before she even turned around, she sensed Rob's presence. She turned.

Rob was grimy, wet and grinning at her. He climbed off his horse and came toward her, holding the reins.

Her breath caught. Relief flooded over her. As he walked, she noticed his swift movements, full of grace and virility.

"Well, now, what've you got for me?" he asked with that irresistible, devastating grin. "You wouldn't believe how hungry I am."

"Got for you?" She blushed. "I... I don't have..." Her emotions whirled and skidded.

His dark eyebrows arched mischievously. He gave a deep warm laugh and pointed to the plate she held.

How silly of me, he only meant the food.

He wasn't hungry for her.

"Looks like you've saved me dinner."

"Yes." She shoved the plate toward him.

He accepted it with a grin. "Might need to see to my horse first." He sniffed the food. "Smells mighty good."

"Let me help." She reached for the reins.

Their hands touched, his fingers warm and strong.

She blushed, breathless as a girl.

He appeared faintly amused.

"How's the old man?" He asked between bites as he walked along beside her, eating heartily.

"He's gaining strength."

"Good." He smiled down at her.

She'd forgotten how alive she felt when he was near. He'd returned. And his smile told her he'd done it for her. "I was afraid something had happened to you."

She couldn't believe she'd let the words slip out.

"Something did happen." Drops of moisture clung to his damp forehead.

With a pang, she realized he might've been hurt. "Are you all right?"

"Had to backtrack to keep away from Indian scouts. They're moving in circles, hunting."

"I suppose they need meat for winter."

"That's not what they're hunting."

"Oh." She peered closer. "You said something happened."

"One of them chased me."

"But you're all right."

"Notice anything different?"

"No."

To Sally he looked fine, though wet and dirty.

"He shot me with his arrow."

Sally dropped the reins and grabbed his muscular arms. His muscles felt hard beneath her fingertips. "Where are you hurt? Take off your shirt and let me see."

He threw back his head and let out a great peal of laughter. She let loose as if burned. Her temper flared. "What are you laughing at?"

"He shot me all right." His deep laugh reached his eyes. "But it was my hat that he hit."

Sally beat on his shoulder with her fists. "You, you...oh, you rotten..." She couldn't get the rest of the sentence out she was so angry. "I thought you were hurt!"

"Well, I'm gonna be hurt if you don't quit pounding on me." A wry but indulgent glint appeared in his eyes.

Sally stood panting. Tears of frustration filled her eyes. "You don't know how worried I've been."

He hadn't meant to shake her up so, only to tease her. He reached his arms around her and held her close.

She wrapped her arms around his waist and held on, crying as if the world was ending.

He stood, patting her awkwardly with his free hand while eyeing the plate in his other and wondering what to do with it.

He didn't know what to do with her either, so he stood patting her back until she calmed down.

He'd missed her too, not that he'd tell her. He'd arranged to spend the night with a Mexican woman when he reached the fort. But it was a mistake. He'd thought of nothing but Sally all evening, even when Carlota had taken off her clothes. It was the first time he'd ever paid for a woman and walked away. Not something he was likely to tell anyone.

He'd wanted to get away from Sally, feeling caged by his ever growing feelings for her. But Carlota had made him think of nothing but how she compared to Sally, and she didn't measure up. He had a feeling no woman ever would.

So Sally had worried about him. He grinned.

She looked up at him again.

"Let's see to these horses, shall we? Then we'll go see Moss." He squeezed her shoulder softly.

"Yes." She sniffled and wiped her eyes. "Don't play any more jokes like that, Rob."

He gazed into her watery eyes. "No, Sally," he said seriously, "I won't play any more jokes like that."

He'd never be the one to cause her pain if he could help it. The question was what to do about Luke. What would she do when he killed Luke? Likely that would also kill any chance for the two of them.

When Moss had recovered enough to be out of bed, out of the blue he said to Sally, "Ye ready to head out tomorrow mornin'? I know how ye like to light out at the last minute."

"Moss, are you sure you're well enough?"

"I'm held together good 'nough. I'll be ready at sunup."

Sally rushed to tell Rob about Moss's decision when he came back from riding with the soldiers to hunt for meat.

He handed her a brace of ducks he'd looped over his saddle. "Think you can clean these?"

"I can clean anything you bring me."

He grinned. "Maybe you'd make a good squaw after all."

She smiled in return.

She'd finally learned how to take a little teasing from him, though lately he'd been careful about what he said and how he said it. "Moss says he's ready to ride at sunup."

"Does he now?"

Rob strode toward the doctor's quarters.

He stepped into the room and saw Moss sitting up in bed. "Well, old timer, Sally tells me you're itching to ride."

"Ye done aimed that right. I ain't staying in this here bed all winter. It's time we get Sally to her son before Christmas."

"Now listen. I'm in charge." Rob pointed his finger. "We'll ride in the morning, but we do it on my terms, not yours."

Moss crossed his arms over his chest as his chin jutted out. "I ain't made ye no deal."

Rob was glad the old man would make it, but the injury had changed things. Moss was no longer in charge and he needed to know it. "We'll leave at sunup then. And there's something you should know."

"What's that?"

"Luke's made a name for himself."

Moss frowned. "That don't sound good."

"It isn't. I heard he robbed a bank."

"Think he done it?"

"I'd put my money on it."

Moss eyed him with a serious expression. "This is more than I bargained for. More than Sally bargained for. Does she know?"

"I'm not going to be the one to tell her." Rob remembered the look in her eyes when he'd told her she wasn't married.

Let Moss give her this piece of news.

"If he's ridin' with outlaws we'd best keep her away 'til we git the boy."

Rob nodded. "I agree."

They shook on it.

A chill sat in the air the next morning as they rode out.

One of the soldiers had told Sally that Luke had been seen on his way to Fort Worth. She could hardly contain her enthusiasm and the cold morning air added to it. She hoped to make it to Fort Worth as quickly as possible.

Moss rode bundled up, but still she worried. "Are you sure

you have enough blankets?"

"I done told ye. Stop fussin'." Moss sat crooked on the saddle and held the reins with one hand as he struggled to get comfortable. "Well, what're ye waitin' fer?"

"We're waiting on you, old timer," Rob said.

Sally bundled Carolyn up tight. "The wind is picking up."

As they rode, the sun sent a bright glow across the snow, yet its warmth was absent. The chill wind grew fiercer as the day went on.

About midday they came over a rise and stopped abruptly.

Sally caught her breath. In the valley below, a small herd of buffalo grazed on the wisps of grass that poked through the snow like whiskers on an old man's chin. Their steamy breath rose in spurts as they snorted and pawed the ground, hairy heads bent low.

Even Carolyn remained silent as they gazed upon the sight.

The crack of a gun split the silence.

"Drive them west," a man shouted.

Another shot was fired and the herd took off running. Men had ridden just past a clump of trees. Rifles flared as they pursued the massive beasts.

"No buffalo meat for our dinner," Rob said regretfully.

"Ain't that somethin' though," Moss said.

"They're huge," Sally noted with surprise. "And how heavy their fur is."

"That fur makes warm blankets and coats," Rob said. "We could use a few of those right now."

"Best we move on," Moss said with a shake of his head. "I ain't gettin' in the way of no buffalo hunters an' that sun ain't getting' any younger."

They rode until dusk as the snowdrifts became deeper and the horses grew tired. When they stopped for the night, Rob built a large roaring fire using the buffalo chips that were abundant under the snow.

Soon everyone slept except Rob.

Moss snored raggedly. Since he drank whiskey at night, he slept soundly, but he snored. He had the bulk of the blankets while Sally and Carolyn curled together sharing theirs. Rob walked from time to time to stay awake and warm. The fact that he got little sleep on this trail made it harder and harder to stay awake, keeping watch.

He'd just stepped beyond a tree on his way back when he heard riders.

The men crept close to the fire. He counted four.

"On my signal," one man said.

Rob positioned himself behind the man who'd spoken. He must be the leader. He'd be the one to shoot first.

If only Moss still had his gun. But the shoulder that was wounded was on his gun arm side. So it was no matter.

Rob could take these men. He froze and listened, waiting for the right moment.

The leader fired a shot into the air.

Sally, Moss and Carolyn woke at once.

"Don't move," the man said.

Sally gathered Carolyn close in her arms. Both stared, their blue eyes wide with fear.

The leader leered at Sally. "Well, now, look what we got here, boys. Ain't she a mighty fine looking filly?"

The other men snickered.

Panic filled Sally. Rob wasn't here. Where had he gone? Had they shot him? Was that the shot that had waked her?

Moss kept his eyes on the leader. "We ain't got no money. Nothin' here ye want."

"Not so hasty," the leader pointed his gun toward Sally. "Stand up, give us a look-see."

Sally glanced past the men into the darkness.

Where was Rob? Had he deserted them?

"Sit very still," she whispered to Carolyn.

She rose slowly.

One of the men hooked the corner of her blanket with his rifle and yanked it away, letting it fall on the ground.

"Well, now, ain't she purty, boys?" The leader chuckled. "Seems we found us some treasure after all, old man."

More snickers followed from his men.

"Come on over here. We ain't gonna hurt you. We know how to 'preciate a fine woman." He smiled.

Sally could see his rotten teeth. She froze, mind and body

numb with cold and fear. Goose bumps covered her skin.

The man who'd pulled off her blanket said, "Oh yeah, she's gonna feel real 'preciated when we're done with her." He looked at the leader. "I call seconds."

The leader nodded. "Long as you keep in mind who's first." He gestured with his rifle. "Move on over here, gal. Ain't any need to be so cold."

Sally forced herself to move forward slowly, hugging her arms to herself. She tried not to look at the men.

If they wouldn't hurt Carolyn, she could endure anything.

Fear filled her. She couldn't feel her body now but she knew she was still moving. When she stepped barely within arm's length of the leader, he stopped smiling and a look of surprise came over his face.

The barrel of a rifle pressing on his back made him freeze. Rob stepped out of the shadows. "Drop your guns. Slowly. Then kick them over here."

"You heard him, boys," the leader said.

"Now your boots."

"What?"

"You heard me."

The men removed their boots.

"Now back away."

Sally watched Rob's steely eyes, which didn't blink or waver. The look in his eyes told her he was a dangerous man, but it didn't frighten her like the eyes of the men who'd followed her movements as if they'd pounce at any moment.

Like a pack of wild dogs, the men backed into the shadows.

Rob released the leader. "If you or any of your men come around fifty feet of my family, I'll shoot you on sight. Now get out of here before I change my mind."

The men ran into the darkness.

"Ye jus' gonna let 'em go like that?" Moss squinted at Rob. "They'll come back."

"Not on foot. I've got their guns and boots, and their horses are gone."

"Gone?"

"I cut them loose and sent them running. It'll take them a

while to round them up again. Best we mount and put some distance between us though."

"Why didn't ye jus' shoot 'em?" Moss shook his head. "Now they'll come lookin' fer us."

"I didn't want Carolyn or Sally to get hurt in a gun fight."

"We'd best be movin'." Moss gathered the guns.

Sally stood frozen in place, her color drained.

Rob knew she was cold. He bent down to retrieve the blanket. Gently he said, "Sally Mae, come on, let's get you warmed."

He placed the blanket around her shoulders and rubbed up and down her arms creating friction.

She broke out of her frozen position and started to shake. Her eyes raked the area wildly.

"Are you sure they've gone?" she whispered. Her voice died away as she looked around again.

"If they weren't I'd have shot them." He said it matter-of-factly. He knew she'd been terrified.

She turned to look at him. "Don't leave us again."

"I was right here all the time, Sally."

She grabbed his arm and looked up into his eyes. "Don't leave me again."

Her voice was fragile and shaking.

He moved in an instinctive gesture of comfort and gathered her into his arms. "All right, Sally. I'll stay close by." He kept his voice calm and steady. "I'll keep you safe."

He held her until she relaxed then moved away reluctantly and held her at arm's length. "You're safe, Sally. They can't hurt you."

He guided her to the horse Moss had readied.

"We need to go, Sally."

He helped her onto the horse and noted how her legs shook. Then he mounted and they rode into the dark night.

He considered what he'd promised. Keeping her safe wasn't in question. But when you made that kind of a promise to a woman, she began to expect certain things.

Things he wasn't able to give her.

If he'd been courting her, it would have been fine. But he

wasn't. He'd come to kill Luke. And the moment he did, her eyes would fill with the fear and loathing he'd seen when Moss has asked him why he was in jail.

Any way you cut it, the action made him a murderer.

She wouldn't take kindly to Rob killing Luke, even if she wished the man dead herself. That was no way to court a woman. There was no hope he'd win her heart.

Rob snorted. A fine mess he was in. He'd promised to protect her, and he'd keep his word. He'd stay close by and make sure Luke didn't hurt her. And he'd see her settled with her children after he took care of Luke.

It was the first time he'd thought about what he'd do after Luke was dead.

Carolyn slept as they rode and Sally kept nodding off.

She would've liked to stop to rest, but they kept moving, putting as much distance between them and the rogues as they could. All her strength had fled, and she wished she'd never set out on this journey.

She doubted she'd ever find Matthew. Terrible things kept happening, and if not for Rob she'd never have made it this far.

They rode through the night until the sun began to rise over a valley with snow-covered trees. Fog sat low on the land.

"I never imagined there'd be this many trees in Texas," Sally said. Her mind was so tired she felt as if she were dreaming. It was like nothing she'd ever seen before.

"Texas is a big place," Moss said. "It's got 'bout ever'thin' ye ken think of, rivers, lakes, desert, trees an' grassy plains. This here's the hill country. In summer it's as green as can be."

Sally looked out at the snow and thought of how different her life would be now. Soon she'd confront Luke. He'd put her through so much. Everything that had happened on this trail was his fault. But he'd better not have let anything happen to Matthew or he'd be sorry. She would take Rob's gun and shoot Luke herself.

Though the fact that she didn't know how to shoot a gun might be a problem. She would ask Rob to teach her, but like the promise he'd made to teach her to read, nothing would come of it. He'd probably even forgotten he'd made the offer.

That was just like a man, making promises he didn't keep.

Even Moss had wavered between keeping his promise and trying to talk her out of it.

She was glad she had Rob to look out for her and Carolyn.

But Matthew only had Luke. What would Luke do if Matthew got tired, hungry or cold? What would Luke do if one of the terrible things that had happened to her on the trail had happened to Matthew? If Matthew got scared he'd never tell his Pa. Luke preyed on weakness and he didn't allow it in his son. Matthew would probably be more afraid of his father than anything they encountered on the trail.

She closed her eyes and pictured his small, bony frame and the freckles that crossed his nose, so like hers. She had to find him, but how? Like Moss said, Texas was a big place.

If only someone had seen Luke. When they reached the next town, perhaps someone would have seen him.

Chapter Ten

Over the next hill, they came upon a man camped beside a wagon. The man brewed a pot of coffee as the smell of bacon lingered in the air.

"Do you think he's friendly?" Tension rose in Sally's shoulders. She'd not met many friendly folks on this trail.

Rob grimaced at the gaudily painted wagon. "With that getup, he's probably too friendly."

As they rode closer, the man raised a hand in greeting then smoothed his hair back. His bulbous nose dominated his meaty features. His black and white striped suit did little to slim his rounded figure. He looked a bit like the zebra Sally once saw in a picture book.

"Morning, folks. Royal J. Huckabee is the name."

"Mornin'." Moss nodded to him. "Ken ye spare some coffee?"

"Yes, sir." His fat face melted into a buttery smile. "I have plenty of that and more. You're welcome to join me for some morning nourishment."

Mr. Huckabee bowed low and a part of his white hair drifted forward over his forehead. He stood and smoothed it back.

Rob dismounted, still wearing his frown. He didn't care for the man despite his warm welcome.

After tying the horses to a tree, they washed their hands and faces in the barrel Huckabee pointed out.

The man had everything imaginable tied to his wagon. Bells and signs hung around all sides. Another sign across the top read *Royal J. Huckabee's Fantastic Elixir of Spirits*.

Rob sat just as Huckabee dished out thick slabs of bacon and biscuits. Once they'd all been served, he joined them.

"What brings you folks down the trail so early this fine morning?"

"We had trouble a ways back." Moss would volunteer more information than this man needed to know.

Rob interrupted. "We thought it best to keep moving."

"That's the best way. Always move away from trouble, I say. Before it finds you." Huckabee smoothed his shiny, silver satin vest and removed his gold pocket watch. He clicked it open, glanced at it and closed it again. "Well, now, I do believe I shall be moving on very soon. I hope to make it to town before evening."

"Thankee for them good vittles." Moss patted his stomach.

"Friend, I see you have need of medicinal care." Huckabee fingered one side of his mustache.

"Oh, I been doctored."

"Might I ask what medicine the good doctor has provided you with?" Huckabee linked his thumbs into his vest pockets and assumed an official air, rocking back on his heels.

"Well, he done give me whiskey at first, but I don't know as I'd call him a good doctor. 'Course he ain't killed me like them others. He's the sawinest doctor I ever heard tell of. An' Rob here went and got me medicine, but I done used it up."

"Friend, whiskey won't cure you. It only helps the pain."

"That it do."

"Now my elixir here, it cures many ills. Not a pain medicine but a cure. Why if you were to try this elixir it would change your life. It'll make you feel young again. No more morning pains, no more aches upon rising. My elixir will grow hair on a bald head and will quiet a colicky baby." He hardly seemed to pause for breath once he'd gotten started. "This elixir will ease the pains of childbirth—" he nodded wisely to Sally, "—as well as take the toothache away."

Sally looked at Rob, who only rolled his eyes and snorted before walking off to stand near the horses.

"This elixir will mend your wound quicker than anything a doctor could give you." Huckabee held out a bottle that seemed to appear from nowhere. "My elixir has no bad taste and no bad smell. Here, take a whiff."

He waved it under Moss's nose to demonstrate.

Moss sniffed it and opened his mouth to speak but Huckabee interrupted.

"Unlike most medicines, this one is a pleasure to take." He handed Moss the bottle. "Now, friend, you just try a taste of this elixir and no charge to you for the first dose."

Moss took the bottle and drank a swig.

"Now, doesn't that go down smooth?"

Moss nodded, unable to get a word in.

"Unlike other medicinal potions, my elixir will even clean your pipes as it goes through."

Rob shook his head.

Carolyn watched Mr. Huckabee with her mouth open. He had her completely mesmerized. And Sally was fascinated as well.

Rob couldn't stand much more of this nonsense.

"I'd wager you feel better already. Tell me, what do you think of it, friend?" Huckabee draped his arm around Moss's shoulder.

"Well, I cain't say as I feel no worse, nor no better."

Rob snorted again.

"Give it time, friend," Huckabee patted Moss's shoulder. "Let the elixir work. I guarantee this will have you mended in no time at all."

Enough of this foolishness.

Rob spoke up. "We don't have any money. He can't afford your elixir."

Huckabee hooked his thumbs into his vest pockets again and rocked back on his heels as if he were thinking. "Perhaps we can make a suitable arrangement to both parties."

"That so?" Moss seemed eager to get some of the special potion for himself.

"You come with me to the next town and help me sell some of my elixir, and I'll give it to you for helping."

"That sounds fair."

Rob rolled his eyes. Royal J. Huckabee was a smooth-talking snake. Couldn't Moss see that? "We're headed south, and we're not backtracking."

"Why, that's just the direction I'm headed. We can travel together, and I'll share my meals with you."

"That's mighty kind of ye." Moss shook the man's hand.

Rob grunted. So much for Moss understanding that Rob was in charge. The old fool. Huckabee's food tasted good, but Rob never put himself in a position to owe anyone.

Men like Huckabee would always make a deal. He didn't trust the man, but Moss had made an agreement.

Carolyn skipped around to the back of the wagon and peered through the black cloth that hung down.

Huckabee hurried over to her and pushed her away saying, "Time to pack up." He patted her back. "Go help your mother."

Rob watched with amusement.

He doesn't want her to see what he's got back there. I wonder what it is.

He wasn't sure it was a good idea to be in this man's company when they entered a town. They'd best part on the outskirts of town before the man got them into trouble.

Rob had heard of old Indian remedies, old folk remedies and old African remedies, but he'd never heard of Huckabee's Fantastic Elixir. He wouldn't be surprised if it turned out to be creek water, molasses and whiskey.

Soon they'd packed and were moving again.

Huckabee never seemed to quit talking. He was telling Carolyn stories and once he finished he lit into a song. She giggled and clapped, entranced by the man.

Sally smiled when Rob rode up beside her. "Mr. Huckabee certainly keeps her entertained doesn't he?"

"That man could charm a rattle off a snake," Rob replied.

Since he's familiar with their ways, being a snake himself.

Rob's brows drew downward in a frown. He didn't like Carolyn spending time with the man. "He wants something. Mark my words. And don't let her out of your sight."

Sally gave him a considering glance, but said nothing.

He wished he knew what she was thinking. Especially as that look of sadness came over her.

Rob watched Sally and wondered what went through her mind. What made a woman stick with a man who was no good? It would shock her to hear Luke was robbing banks. How would she take the news? Would she panic in worry over her son and confront Luke? She'd likely do something foolish and get herself shot.

She needed a good man to take care of her. He wished he could be that man.

Huckabee started talking to Sally, and Rob watched as her features became more animated. What was it about that stuffed suit that fascinated everyone so? He'd never heard so much blather in his life as what came out of that man's mouth. Huckabee talked more than a woman.

Moss muttered to his horse as he rode along behind. "That gal is in love and it ain't with Luke. I ain't never seen a pair like them two. Her lit up like a house afire, and him flyin' like a bee to the flame."

What was he saying? That Sally and Huckabee were falling for each other? Surely not.

He watched them and his mood darkened. Perhaps Moss was right about Sally. "House afire" indeed. Well, Rob was no bee, and he sure as shooting wasn't flying into any flame. He'd keep control of himself with Sally. But he'd best throw water on her "house afire", before Huckabee got any ideas.

He motioned Moss closer. "How's that elixir working?"

"Not so good."

"Maybe you ought to tell him."

Moss rode up to Huckabee's wagon. "I done took that elixir agin' an' I ain't noticed no change a'tall."

"It takes time for my elixir to work," Huckabee reassured him. "And sometimes an extra dose helps to get things started."

"I wished I never packed that whiskey away," Moss muttered to his horse. "I'll swipe me a quick swallow when we stop. Them pains is bad, Coal Miner."

The horse's ear twitched.

They reached the outskirts of town as evening approached. They rolled into town and Huckabee took his wagon to the blacksmith shop to have one of his horses re-shod.

Soon, a heavy-bodied sheriff walked toward them as they

tied their horses. He was out of breath. "We don't want any flim-flam shows here in this town."

Huckabee straightened and solemnly said, "Oh no, sir. Of course you don't. I'm having my horse shod and we'll rest here tonight, then tomorrow we'll be on our way."

"You do that." The sheriff walked away.

Huckabee watched him quietly for a moment, then smoothed his vest as if wiping away any worries and began to hum.

"But, Mr. Huckabee," Sally said, "why didn't you tell him about your elixir? And how can you sell it if you can't stay in town?"

Huckabee smiled an oily smile. "I'll camp on the edge of town, in the middle of the road. Then I'll walk into town and ask the people to come out and visit before we leave."

Rob frowned with distaste. It was a sneaky plan. The man wouldn't be selling inside the town, a mere technicality, but he'd be selling. And then he would move on. By the time the townsfolk figured out the potion was no good he'd be gone, taking their money with him.

Rob knew he was right about the elixir. It had done nothing for Moss. He'd seen the old man take sips of whiskey when he'd thought no one was looking.

Though every time he mentioned the elixir, Moss said, "It's workin' on me insides," and pretended he was fine.

Rob waited until Sally took Carolyn to the general store and Huckabee went into the blacksmith's to pull Moss aside.

"Listen, I don't think it's a good idea for you to help him sell his elixir. You heard what the sheriff said."

"I give my word on it. An' I done drank that whole bottle of elixir too."

Rob looked at Moss with a frown. "You can't believe it's done you any good."

"Well, now it's takin' some time."

"That's why you've been sipping whiskey when you thought no one was looking."

"Now he said it don't kill pain. I'm jus' takin' it 'til it do work."

"It's never going to work. That's why he moves on right after he sells it."

Moss shook his head. "Now you ain't a doctor. "

"And that's nothing but creek water. Tell me, what did it taste like?"

Moss considered. "Well, it didn't have no taste, or no scent, but he done told me that."

"Like creek water, no taste, no smell, no color and no cure."

Moss grew quiet and a muscle in his face twitched.

"You don't want to go to jail for working a flim-flam."

"I done give my word. More's the pity."

Moss looked sad and Rob felt sorry for him. "Sell it if you feel you have to, but once you're done we ride away, fast. Else he'll have you selling in every town between here and Mexico. If you don't end up in jail first."

"I din't say I'd do it ferever."

"No."

"He only give me one bottle."

"That's right."

"Well, have them horses saddled and ready. Soon as he's done we'll ride off."

"That's all I'm asking." It was all he could hope for, since Moss was intent on honoring his word.

"I don't s'pose we ought to eat no more of his vittles."

"That's the bargain he made. See that he holds up his end of it."

Moss nodded. "I reckon if he done fed me creek water I ought to get more out of it than that if'n I'm gonna hep him."

Rob clapped him on the back. "Let's go have breakfast."

They found Huckabee in the blacksmith shop talking excitedly about his elixir.

The blacksmith had streams of sweat rolling down his face. He grimaced as he worked.

Rob suspected the grimace was as much from having to listen to Huckabee as the hammering of the anvil. He watched as Huckabee pushed his sale, barely taking a breath before winding up again.

The blacksmith pounded harder on the horseshoe to flatten it as if he could drown out Huckabee.

Moss winked at Rob then interrupted. "Say, Royal, the little gal is hungry. Ye reckon we might set up camp soon an' rustle up some grub?"

Huckabbe turned and smiled. "Why, certainly. I'll be along as soon as I'm finished here."

The blacksmith spoke. "I'll send a boy to fetch you when I'm done."

He clearly was glad to be rid of the salesman.

"No need," Rob said, "I'll wait here. You two go on ahead."

Huckabee nodded to Rob. "Why, thank you, sir." He grabbed Moss's arm and whispered in his ear as they went out the door.

Rob watched them go. "That man never stops talking."

"Never complain about a paying customer, my Pa always said." The blacksmith wiped the sweat from his brow. He looked as if he would've said more but held back.

Rob chuckled. "But that one would wear a man's ears out."

"That's right and I was hoping I'd lose my hearing what with all the pounding. But I couldn't be so lucky."

They both laughed as he went back to work.

Once he'd finished Rob said, "I'm looking for a man named Luke Wheeler, might've come through here a few months back."

The blacksmith grew solemn. "Why are you looking for him?"

Rob explained about Sally.

The blacksmith shook his head. "He's bad news. Cleaned out a few men at poker and robbed a poor widow woman, skipped out without paying room and board and left her daughter brokenhearted. The daughter tried to follow him and ended up working at a saloon the next town over. She's with child. Says it's his. You sure your Sally wants to find him?"

"She's determined. Was he traveling with anyone or was he waiting for anyone?"

"I got the feeling he was a loner. I heard he had a young boy with him, but I never saw the boy. I don't know if he met up with anyone or not."

"Thank you for your help. Do me a favor though and keep the information about Sally quiet."

"I won't mention it."

Rob strode off toward the campsite. He smelled chicken and biscuits as he neared. He was glad he'd had time to walk and consider what Luke was up to.

Carolyn danced out to greet him and his heart gave a lurch.

She skipped along singing and took his free hand in her slight one.

"Mr. Rob, can you play the guitar? Mr. Huckabee gots one."

"It's been a while, but I've played some."

"Oh!" She gave a high skip and a bounce as she squeezed his hand then went running off toward the fire, pulling him behind her. "Mama! Will you sing, Mama?"

"After dinner."

Rob fed the horses then they ate.

Huckabee lectured about what he expected of each of them tomorrow at the show. He'd thought up something for everyone.

Annoyance crossed Rob's face. "Absolutely not. Carolyn will have no part in this."

"But I assure you, she will enjoy helping and no harm will come to her."

"Carolyn will be with me. We have other details to see to," Rob said firmly.

Huckabee settled his hands on his hips. "What?"

"We'll be looking for people who've seen her papa."

It was the first thing he could think of to shut Huckabee up. But he'd spoken without thinking. And as soon as the words were out of his mouth he realized he'd made a mistake.

Sally gasped and put her hand to her brooch. She came toward him and placed her hand on his arm. "You've had word of Luke and Matthew?"

He nodded. "He stayed at a boarding house near here."

"Then we'll go directly and ask."

"We'll go in the morning after breakfast. The proprietor is an old widow and can't be disturbed this late."

"Oh." Sally sagged, but her eyes were lit up like candles. "Does the widow know where they headed? Has she seen Matthew? Is he all right?"

"We can ask those questions tomorrow. Get Carolyn to bed. Tomorrow will be a busy day." He stepped into the shadows.

"Mama, sing."

Sally looked toward the shadows of the tree where Rob stood. "Sweetheart, not tonight. We have a big day tomorrow and we need our rest. Go to sleep now."

Rob leaned against the tree watching her smooth Carolyn's brow. He'd made a mistake telling Sally. Now he'd have to follow through. But maybe this could be useful. The proprietor might take pity on a woman and child who'd been deserted. They might learn more than if he went alone.

He'd gotten himself into this particular mess out of concern for Carolyn. But he didn't want her selling the elixir and he couldn't understand why Sally would allow her to help Huckabee. She'd even asked him to give Moss another bottle of elixir.

But Moss had patted his pocket where the bottle lay and said he'd aplenty and was doin' fine.

Rob closed his eyes to think. Tomorrow would be a busy. Huckabee would stir things up and in the commotion, they would all slip away.

Away from one mess and into another.

He'd stop in the saloon the blacksmith had mentioned, but Sally had no business in such a place. He'd never felt such a combination of responsibility and lack of control. And he didn't like the way Huckabee stared at Sally. If she were Rob's woman and the child his, he'd have plenty to say about what Huckabee had in mind for them.

If he couldn't have her, Huckabee damned sure wasn't going to have the honor.

Chapter Eleven

The next morning Sally woke long before the others. She'd laid awake tossing and turning most of the night. Soon she'd find Matthew.

She cooked an early breakfast and hoped the smell would wake the others. Huckabee had asked her to cook for them while he got his wares ready to sell. She'd happily agreed.

Finally, she heard the others stirring.

Huckabee woke cheerfully. He sat up and smoothed a hand through his hair. "Well, now. It's nice to have a woman along. What a smell to rouse a man!"

His chatter broke the silence, waking the others. Rob seemed to have woken in a bad mood.

Sally sent him a smile as she served the bacon and biscuits. Soon they'd visit the boarding house and she'd learn where Luke and Matthew had gone. Nothing could spoil her mood.

Once she'd rinsed the breakfast dishes, she smoothed her dress and gave Rob her best smile. "Are you ready to visit the boarding house?"

"Yes. Get Carolyn."

They headed off toward the other end of town where the sign, *Mrs. Bailey Stamps - Boarding House* hung from a whitewashed building.

Sally smiled at everyone she passed.

Moss and Huckabee had set up everything for the show and they headed into town to collect customers.

To Sally, it seemed as if it took forever, but at last they reached the building and stepped onto the porch. She looked at

Carolyn, smoothed her hair and stood tall.

Rob knocked on the door.

A short, pudgy woman opened it. "Rooms are taken this evening, but one will open tomorrow. I can lay pallets in the parlor if there's no other place in town."

"May we step inside?" Rob inquired with a calm smile.

"Certainly." She glanced at Carolyn and softened. "Perhaps your little girl would like a sugar cookie."

Carolyn tugged at Sally's skirt. "Mama, please?"

"You may."

They followed Mrs. Stamps into the kitchen where dishes stood stacked high after the morning meal.

"I've been short-handed since my youngest left home."

Rob twisted his hat in his hands. This was a tricky subject. He'd made Sally promise to let him do the talking. Out of the corner of his eye, he could see her bite her lip, forcing herself to remain silent.

He waited until Mrs. Stamps settled Carolyn on a tall stool with a cookie and a glass of milk.

"Ma'am, one of the reasons we've come is that Sally here is looking for her husband and son. They came through here a few months ago and she's come to find them."

Mrs. Stamps looked at Sally and Carolyn then clucked, "Poor dears."

"We heard they might've stayed with you for a night."

"Lot's of folks come through here."

"His name is Luke Wheeler."

Mrs. Stamps glanced at him sharply. "Luke Wheeler!"

Her face puckered as if she'd tasted something sour.

Sally gasped. Mrs. Stamps had recognized his name. And her reaction said it all. She must have seen him. "Did he come here? Did he have my little boy with him? How long did they stay? Did he say where they were going?"

Mrs. Stamps hesitated as she looked back and forth between Rob and Sally.

Rob took a step back where Sally couldn't see him and shook his head.

Mrs. Stamps watched him as she answered. "He came

through." She hesitated. "He stayed here. He never paid for his room."

"I'm so sorry." Sally blushed. No wonder the woman looked sour when she heard his name. "I'd pay you if I had the money."

"You aren't the one that owes it." Mrs. Stamps looked as if she wanted to say more but wouldn't in front of Carolyn. Only the tensing of her jaw betrayed her deep frustration.

"Did he say where they were going?" Sally pleaded, anxiously. "Was Matthew all right?"

"No, he didn't say where. I heard he went on to the next town and stayed for a while."

"Can you tell me anything else?" Sally implored.

Mrs. Stamps walked over to a sideboard where a daguerreotype of a beautiful young girl stood. The girl's innocent eyes shone from out of a heart-shaped face.

"No." For an instant, wistfulness stole into her expression. She caressed the frame then looked at Rob. "I have nothing else to tell you."

"We'll be going then. Thank you for your time," he said.

Sally reached for Carolyn's hand. "I'm sorry about the money. I wish I had it to give you. Thank you for the information and the cookies."

The woman nodded but didn't reply.

Rob led Sally and Carolyn out as the woman stood running her fingers over the photo.

Sally seemed oblivious to the subtle clues Mrs. Stamps had given him.

Rob watched her captivating smile and listened to her all the way back to the camp.

Now they'd have to go on to the next town. The girl in the photo was the one he'd heard about. The girl had fallen for Luke. Word was she lived at the saloon now.

"We'll find Matthew soon, I just know it," Sally said.

He watched the bounce in Sally's step as she walked along with Carolyn.

Rumor was the saloon girl carried Luke's child. If it were true, Sally had more disappointment coming. He'd convince her a saloon was no place for her to visit.

"Won't be long," he replied as he watched her face.

What was it with women and Luke? Couldn't they see what a liar he was? He felt bad about the girl and wondered why she didn't go home to her mother. Mrs. Stamps seemed friendly and obviously liked children. Someone ought to convince the girl to return home.

Here he was again, caught up in problems Luke created. Problems that were none of his business.

He'd grown soft traveling with Sally. Before he met her, he'd have ridden through without any notice of anyone else's problems.

As they neared the wagon, he noted that a crowd had gathered.

Huckabee stepped up onto the platform in front. He wore a tall black hat and a silver vest under a black coat.

Stuffed peacock.

He glanced at Sally. Her eyes shone with excitement, and she smiled with an air of pleasure. Surely she didn't find that fat bird attractive?

Carolyn began to run toward the crowd, but Rob reached out a hand and drew her back.

"Stay with me," he said, "I'll need you to help me get the horses ready."

Sally looked at him in confusion. "Get the horses ready for what?"

"To ride."

"Shouldn't we wait to see the show? Mr. Huckabee won't be ready to ride for some time."

"Exactly."

"Rob, I'm surprised at you. Ready to ride off and leave a man after he's helped us out, feeding us and all."

In the silence that followed, Sally realized what she'd just said.

Rob looked straight down into her eyes. "You're one to talk about riding off and leaving a man. Seems despite what I'd done for you, you didn't mind leaving me behind."

Sally swallowed as he continued to look deeply into her eyes. She'd gone off and left Rob after Carolyn recovered. He was right. Ashamed of herself, she broke eye contact.

Yes, she'd done it and he'd not said a word to her about it.

He'd continued helping them out. He was a good man. She didn't understand why he wanted to ride off but she wouldn't say any more. He must have a good reason.

Rob stood watching her closely and waiting for her to say something.

She looked up at him and smiled. "All right, Rob, whatever you wish."

Rob felt surprised. He'd expected her to excuse her behavior or deny it or argue with him about leaving. He hadn't expected the gentle angelic smile she gave him and the look in her eyes that told him she'd do what he asked, no questions. He felt such a surge of tenderness, protectiveness and love for her that he could hardly speak.

Love. Yes, that's what he felt for her, love. Like nothing he'd ever felt before. He'd felt it creeping up on him but hadn't put the word to it before now. Here it hit him, full blown. Love.

Men did crazy things for love. He'd never meant for it to happen, but it had.

And now he had to deal with it. Briskly he said, "Come on. You can listen to his speechmaking while we get ready."

They walked around to where the horses stood and packed their belongings.

The crowd appeared mesmerized as Huckabee spoke.

Moss stood stiffly by his side with his shirt off as Huckabee pointed to him as an example of the miracle cure. Moss shifted from one foot to another as his skin turned blue from the cold. He kept glancing down, embarrassed.

Huckabee rolled along, talking at a mighty pace.

Sally stood holding the reins as Rob packed Moss's mount.

Soon hands raised in the hair as Huckabee called for his "friends" and "neighbors" to purchase the fantastic elixir.

Moss threw his arms into the sleeves of his shirt and handed out bottles wherever Huckabee directed him. Huckabee pocketed all the money.

"Let's move along behind the wagon," Rob said. "Moss will join us when he's done."

"Shouldn't we at least thank Mr. Huckabee for all he's done?" Sally asked.

"No need. Moss has thanked him enough."

They waited behind the wagon.

Moss rushed around the back. "Let's go."

He mounted and they rode away.

"You left in a hurry," Sally said. "Is something wrong?"

"Nothin' the sheriff cain't fix. He's fixin' to close down Huckabee's show an' we ain't gonna be nowhere's nearby when them folks start complainin' 'bout their ills."

"Why, Moss, you mean that elixir didn't work?"

"No more'n horse spittle. An' I ain't goin' to spend my nights in no jail for fancied up crick water."

Sally appeared shocked.

When they stopped to water the horses Rob asked, "Sally, how old were you when you got married?"

"Almost seventeen. We celebrated my birthday a week after our wedding."

Rob didn't reply. He peered at her. He'd figured her to be at least twenty-one when she married. But she'd married young. Being isolated on that farm at the age of seventeen must've kept her from learning about folks like Huckabee and their tricky ways.

He forced himself to bring up the unspeakable subject that he'd put off asking her for so long. "Have you thought about what you'll do once you find Matthew?"

"I haven't made any plans."

"If Luke were dead what would you do?"

"He's alive." She spoke with quiet but desperate firmness then glared at him stubbornly.

He'd made her angry.

He could tell by the way her chin jutted out. Well, she might be angry, but she had to think about what he'd said.

"Sally, he owes a lot of people money. Any man who owes that many people, eventually he's gonna get himself shot."

Her eyes widened as tears hovered on her eyelashes, ready to fall. "What a mean thing to say."

"No. Not a mean thing. A true thing." He let out a long, audible breath. "A mean thing is when a man lies to a woman, because he doesn't want to see her cry, because he doesn't want to put himself out."

Tears began to trickle down her face.

Doggone it.

He pressed on. "Sally, a man who cares about a woman tells her the truth even when she doesn't want to hear it."

She continued to cry and as he watched her, it occurred to him that tears were one way to keep men at a distance. Something he'd never thought of before.

In spite of the fact he still felt mighty nervous around a crying woman, he grabbed her by the elbows. "Sally Mae, look at me."

Her accusing eyes met his, as tears ran down her face.

"I've never done a single thing to hurt you, and I never will. Sometimes a person doesn't want to hear a truth because it causes them pain, but not to tell it true would hurt them more. Now I know you're upset but I want you to think about this. What will you and the children do?" He let go of her. "Because you need a plan and you need to be prepared for the worst."

He'd said all he had to say.

Sally turned her back to him, folded her arms and stood crying. She still wasn't speaking to him.

Well, confound it he couldn't do more than that. He stomped off. He'd never known a woman who frustrated him so.

Sally sat by the stream and cried until she ran out of tears. How could he be so mean? Luke couldn't be dead. He couldn't. Because if he was dead what might have happened to Matthew? Just the thought of it shattered her. She didn't want to think about it.

Her only plan until now had been to confront Luke and get Matthew back. Then she would worry about what she and the children would do.

Luke couldn't be dead. She'd find him alive, and she'd get Matthew back and then she'd worry about the rest.

She fought to keep the fragile control she'd held onto since finding Luke's note. In her heart she'd always been afraid that she'd never find Matthew.

But what was wrong with Rob?

Sally had noticed the way he'd choked out Luke's name like it was a word he couldn't stomach. She knew then that Rob hated Luke enough to kill him. She knew without being told that this was Rob's plan.

Yet Rob was gentle with Carolyn. How could a man be both hard and gentle?

When Carolyn whined about missing out on the guitar singing, he'd promised to play for her once they got settled. He said he'd come by to visit after he got his own guitar. Then he'd taught her cowboy songs while they rode.

Sally wondered where he'd learned the songs. She didn't know much about him, where he came from, what he'd done with his life, how old he was. Why had he wanted to know how old she was? He'd seemed intense lately, watching her even keener than before.

She looked down into the creek at her dry skin and her tangled hair.

I probably look like an old woman. No man will want me.

But there weren't many options for a woman with two children to feed and no family or money to help her do it.

"Be alive, Matthew," she whispered.

The rest she would worry about later.

Rob waited patiently for Sally to return from the creek.

He and Moss made stew out of the fish the old man caught. They'd started to eat by the time Sally walked slowly back toward the fire. She sat as if she'd been walking all day.

Rob could see the remainders of tear streaks on her face.

Moss glanced accusingly at him but didn't speak.

Carolyn chattered and Rob answered her questions, all the while watching Sally.

She ate then got up to clean the dishes. She still hadn't spoken.

Rob didn't feel inclined to make conversation with her. She put Carolyn to bed then everyone went to sleep except Rob.

He sat awake wondering. Had he done and said the right thing? She'd been thinking about something. He wished he knew what it was.

She seemed wilted, not like the Sally he'd come to know. He'd apologize in the morning. He wouldn't take back his words, for they were true, but he felt bad about hurting her.

Once again, he'd get no sleep. He hadn't been able to keep the truth from her any longer. He'd as much as told her he'd kill Luke.

What would she do about that?

He'd just thrown a bucket of water on the "flames of love" as Moss had called it.

Rob wrapped his blanket around his shoulders and hunched down to brood. Nothing even remotely connected with Luke had ever been anything but bad for Rob.

He didn't know why he'd expected Sally to be any different.

Chapter Twelve

All the way to the next town where the saloon girl lived, Rob waited for the best time to tell Sally about her. But a good moment never presented itself and he continued brooding.

When they reached town he said, "I'll check in the saloon."

"Carolyn, you stay here with Moss," Sally said.

Rob turned to her. "A saloon is no place for a lady. You and Carolyn go with Moss to see if the sheriff has seen Luke."

Moss agreed. "Sally, ye don't want to go in no saloon. Likely the sheriff will know more 'bout him anyhow."

Sally reluctantly watched Rob mount the steps.

He'll look for a woman while he's there.

The thought displeased her and she scowled all the way to the sheriff's office.

Moss muttered to Coal Miner, "She cain't have him, but she sure don't want to share him neither."

Moss got on her nerves with his mumbling. She was fairly fed up with it.

As Rob stepped into the noisy saloon, heads turned to watch him belly up to the bar before turning back to their card games. Once he had the bartender's attention he asked for whiskey. While he waited, he asked the man if he'd seen Luke.

The barkeep placed the whiskey on the counter, but kept his hand on it. He seemed less friendly than before. "Pay in advance."

Rob reached into his pocket, removed a coin and tossed it on the counter. Then he explained the situation with Sally.

The barkeep relaxed and shook his head as if he felt sorry

for her. "Lou Pearl's upstairs. If you'll wait a bit, she'll be back down soon."

Rob took his glass over to an empty table and sat. He sipped his drink as he waited. The young pregnant woman would be better off at home with her mother than turning to prostitution. Here was another life Luke had ruined.

The wait was longer than he'd expected, but he enjoyed the whiskey. It'd been a long time since he'd sat in a bar.

Sally and Moss had no luck finding the sheriff. He'd ridden out to one of the ranches and the deputy who lounged in his boss's chair with his feet on the desk had no intention of working until his boss came back.

"When will the sheriff be back, ye reckon?"

"Hard telling."

"Maybe you can help us," Sally said. "I'm looking for my husband, Luke Wheeler. He's traveling with my son Matthew who is seven. Have they been through here?"

"Might've been. Hard telling."

Sally looked to Moss for advice.

He kicked around a chair and sat. "Well, I reckon I'll jus' set here an' wait for the sheriff."

"Could be dark before he comes along."

"These old bones don't mind none. I ken set fer days." Moss leaned back in the chair and tipped his hat down just far enough so the deputy couldn't see he was being watched. "Sally, go on and see the town with Carolyn. I'll wait here."

"I suppose we could look for Rob. Perhaps he's done asking questions at the saloon."

"Ye wait outside for him, ye hear? Carolyn don't belong in no saloon."

"I know that," Sally said with exasperation.

She tugged Carolyn along after her. It was hard to be patient when she'd waited so long for news of Luke and Matthew.

Rob watched as Lou Pearl came slowly down the steps. She looked fresh and pretty, with her heart-shaped face and shiny golden curls. Several men watched her pass as she neared Rob. Pregnancy had given her a glow. But as she came closer he saw the dark circles under her eyes.

He stood and pulled out a chair for her.

"You sent for me?" Her voice sounded tired.

"I did. My name is Rob. I'm looking for Luke Wheeler."

Her eyes narrowed. "How do you know Luke?"

She hadn't asked what he wanted with Luke, so he decided only to answer her question. "He and I used to gamble together a bit. I heard he'd headed to Texas to improve his luck."

This much was true. When they'd first met they'd been friendly toward each other.

She relaxed. "Yes, he's been through here. He stayed for a time." Her hand grazed her stomach in an unconscious gesture. "He'll be back, though I don't know when."

"I stopped at Mrs. Stamp's boarding house. That's how I knew to come and see you.'

She sat quiet for a moment. "And what did Mrs. Stamp have to say?"

"Only that Luke had been through about the same time her youngest girl left home. Said she's hard up to do all the work now that her daughter left her all alone."

Lou Pearl looked down at her hands. "How did she seem?"

"Old. Sad." He cleared his throat. "There's something you should know about Luke."

"I know all there is to know about him." She smiled and her hand moved across her stomach again.

"I see. Tell me, where's he from?"

She hesitated. "Up north somewhere, he said."

"North is a big area."

"Well, you've known him longer. Where is he from then?"

"He lived in Kansas for a time. Did he ever mention that?"

She shook her head.

"Did he ever mention the wife he had in Kansas?"

From her expression, Rob was fairly sure the subject had never come up.

"He said he was a widower. He had his son with him."

Rob nodded. "He has a daughter also."

Shock filled her face. "Why he never said a word." Her hand went again to her stomach. "Not a word about her."

174

"Her name is Carolyn. She's four years old."

She sat up straighter. "Where is she? Who keeps her?"

"She's here in town. I brought her with me."

"Carolyn," she mused. "You must be a good friend to care for his little girl."

"He hasn't seen her for a long while."

She frowned. "You never said what happened to his wife."

"That's right, I didn't." He watched her face and sat quietly waiting for her to catch on.

Her eyes mirrored her dark thoughts. "Where is she?"

"Here in town. She's looking for Luke and wondering why he ran out on her. The same way he did you. The same way he did his first wife who is still living. Just rode off into the night. Or did he tell you he was leaving?"

She pressed a hanky to her forehead. "No, I woke and he was gone. He left a note."

"That's Luke. He never stays in one place long. In fact his first wife lives in New Mexico. He seems to have a habit of leaving wives. No telling how many more he has out there."

He didn't have the heart to tell her the marriages weren't legal. It wouldn't matter once Luke was dead.

"Does he ever come back to them?"

"No."

She fainted into her chair. Rob hollered at the barkeep to bring smelling salts and water.

When she came to he said, "Do you feel all right?"

She barely whispered, "Yes."

He bent down to hear her say it again.

Sally stopped in front of the doorway to the saloon and looked in. She'd grown tired of waiting for Rob and wondered what had taken him so long.

Rob held a painted lady in a red dress. He whispered into the woman's ear.

With an odd twinge of disappointment Sally drew back and called Carolyn to her side. She walked briskly back to the sheriff's office, tugging Carolyn along.

Really, men were disgusting. Whiskey and women, that's all

they wanted, even the ones who seemed nice.

She felt so thoroughly disappointed with Rob that her stomach churned. She stomped up the steps.

"Any word on the sheriff yet?"

"Nope," the deputy said. "Told you I didn't know when he'd be back."

Sally leaned over the desk and shouted, "Then I suggest you go and find him!"

The deputy sat up. "Yes, ma'am." He picked up his hat. "I'll go directly."

Sally watched the man walk out the door. She turned around to glare at Moss.

He still sat with his hat over his eyes.

Sleeping through it all. Men. Intolerable creatures!

She found a chair and sat.

Carolyn wanted to play outside so she let her. Sally watched her though the window.

She crossed one leg over the other then switched them again and glanced at Moss. The corner of his mouth twitched. She suspected he was awake.

Rob saw that Lou Pearl was taken to her room to rest. The last thing he said before he took his leave was, "Mrs. Stamp seemed like a kind woman. She really took to Carolyn."

Lou Pearl sniffled and he saw a tear in her eye. "Seems lonely. She could use some help. You can't keep working here."

Lou Pearl sniffled again. "I'll write to her."

Rob tipped his hat and left.

The sun had begun to go down. In the windows as he passed, lamps were being lit. The noise of the saloon would soon pick up. The smells of various meals prepared in homes and boarding houses hung heavy in the air.

He wondered what Sally would fix for them tonight. He enjoyed her cooking. It really was very good.

Carolyn played in the street near the sheriff's office.

Rob watched her for a moment before he went in.

Children bounce back. Look at all she's been through and she takes it better than her mother.

In the office Moss looked like he was dozing and Sally glared at him from her chair with burning, reproachful eyes.

"Sorry it took so long. I had to wait a bit."

"Oh, don't mind us." She sounded bitter. "You go on back and see to *your* business." Her face filled with anger. "I'm sure you have plenty to occupy you back at the saloon."

He looked at her quizzically. "I learned that Luke and Matthew have been through here."

"Well, I guess I should say thank you for finding the time to fit that into your busy schedule." She threw the words at him like stones.

He glanced at Moss and could've sworn the old man was grinning. He didn't blame him for playing possum. What had her so riled?

"I'd think you'd be glad to hear the trail is still warm. But I guess if you don't want to know..." He started to leave.

She rushed to him and grabbed his arm. "Rob, you'd better tell me everything you know."

He looked into her wild eyes and flushed cheeks. "Everything?"

"Yes, everything." She folded her arms and stepped back. "Every single thing," she replied in a low voice, taut with anger.

"All right then." He pulled up a chair and rested his boot on it. "You'd better sit down. It's no short tale."

She sat and fluffed her skirt like a ruffled hen. "Well, fine." She looked at him again. "Tell me."

He told her about Mrs. Bailey and Lou Pearl and the baby on the way. He told her what had taken place in the saloon. She sat with a blank expression on her face.

Moss tipped his hat back, sat up, then shouted at her. "Sally Mae! Best we hit the trail agin' fore it gits too late!" He acted as if he hadn't heard a word.

Sally had listened. She'd known what a skunk Luke was. But learning of another young girl who now carried his child brought it home hard.

How young she'd been when she'd had their first child. The memories all came rushing back with a vengeance.

She walked to the doorway looking out at Carolyn. Her child was beautiful, full of life and love.

Luke had never liked children. He'd left a child he'd known for years and didn't care to know about any more children.

But he'd taken his son. He'd talked about having a son all the time even though he'd never paid any attention to the boy until just before he'd left.

He'd made her think she was the only woman he'd ever wanted. He was a charmer, but for a handsome man he was ugly inside and his looks didn't extend to his ugly soul.

She didn't want to feel bad for the girl. Maybe she'd pursued him. She'd seen the way the girl had gotten Rob to hold her close in the saloon, and he'd only just arrived. That's what those women did, wasn't it?

Rob was a good man.

The girl wasn't content to sleep with Luke—she wanted Rob too. The thought washed away any sympathetic feelings she had for the girl.

She turned and said, "Let's ride and make camp away from this town. I've had my fill of it."

The sooner she got Rob away from that girl, the better. He might want to stay here instead of helping her find Luke.

Rob felt surprised at her response, but he wasn't about to argue with her.

The sheriff had never arrived and the deputy had disappeared. He'd wanted to ask about the bank robberies Luke was accused of, but he'd learned all he could and the longer they stayed, the colder the trail would get.

They mounted and rode, with Sally in the lead for once. Rob gave her space so she could blow off steam.

"That gal has a temper," Moss said. "Best let her cool down some."

"I've never dealt with redheaded women," Rob said. "I guess it's true what they say about their tempers."

Moss chuckled. "Yessir, that's the way of it."

"I wonder what set her off?"

"Somethin' you did."

"Me? What did I do?"

"How'd I know? First she set off to the saloon to fetch you, then she come runnin' in here, tossed the deputy out on his feet, then commenced to stew 'til ye come back. Whatever ye done in the saloon must've set her off."

Rob thought back to what had taken place in the saloon. He'd done nothing wrong, but if she'd seen him holding Lou Pearl in his arms, she'd have gotten an eyeful.

That must have been what had happened.

He grinned. She'd been angry before he'd even mentioned Luke. She was jealous. He'd seen fire in her eyes before he'd mentioned Lou Pearl and explained.

"I know'd ye done somethin'. What was it?"

"I was holding a lady who'd fainted. It might've looked like something else to Sally."

"Ye mean ye was holdin' a fancy woman in a saloon in a swoon? She must have thought ye was makin' love to the woman right there."

Rob grinned wider. "Sally was red hot about that, wasn't she?"

"That's a fact."

Rob's mood suddenly felt light. Well, maybe Sally felt something for him after all.

He grinned as he rode along and hummed to himself.

"I'm goin' to tell ya what my Pa told me. A woman's heart is like a campfire, if ye don't tend to it regular, it'll go right out. That's why I ain't never settled with no woman. I was always too busy ridin' an' rovin' an' never had no time to tend to no home fires."

"What're you saying, old timer? Sally still acts like she's married to Luke."

"Remember this, son. The first blaze always grows big an' hot, but it don't last. It ain't hard to start a fire. It's keepin' it goin' that's the work. So 'fore ye go lettin' that fire blaze up, ye need to think 'bout whether ye plan to tend to it or not. That's all I'm sayin'."

Rob thought about what he'd set out to do when he'd first seen Sally and decided to trail her to Luke. He thought about the old score he had to settle with Luke.

"I always finish what I start."

He rode off to take the lead again, and to think.

He stayed well ahead of the group until he thought his horse needed a rest and eased up.

Sally caught up to him. Carolyn slept, snuggled into her left arm, which sagged with the weight of the child.

"Let me have her for a while," he said. "Give your arms a rest. We'll be stopping soon."

"Thank you." She handed Carolyn over. "I am tired."

He smiled at her.

This was the Rob Sally had come to know and care for. She was glad to be away from the town.

Being on the trail with Rob felt right somehow.

He took charge with quiet assurance and the world seemed safe, even when it wasn't.

When they stopped to make camp, Sally woke Carolyn and tried to get her to eat. Her forehead felt slightly warm, but not enough to worry about. Sleep would be the best thing for her.

Carolyn slept fitfully most of the evening and Sally wondered when any of them would sleep soundly again. The trail seemed as if it would never end.

In the morning, Carolyn was still warm, but Sally decided to keep it to herself until they reached the next town. She hoped the trail to Luke and Matthew would get warmer. She worried they'd lost so much time she might never catch up.

When they broke camp and rode out again, Moss asked her, "What do ye reckon ye'll do once we find Luke? He might be in a saloon or somewhere's ye ought not to go."

"I hadn't thought of that."

"Lot's of things ye ain't thought of," Moss muttered under his breath. Louder he said, "I reckon I ken go in an' talk to him fer ye."

"Thank you, Moss."

"Be thinkin' on what message ye want me to give him."

"I'll do that." Sally rode on, holding Carolyn who slept.

What should she say to Luke? There were so many things.

She played and replayed conversations in her head. She wanted Matthew back and she never wanted to see Luke again. But she had to see him.

She'd let Moss find him, since she didn't want Luke to know Rob had traveled with them all this way.

Though he could hardly accuse her of anything after the way he'd lied to her. But he'd find some way to twist it the way he wanted it. He was good at that. And he would be angry if he knew about Rob.

It was safer not to mention him. She wondered if Carolyn would be able to do the same. He'd become such a part of their lives and she didn't think her little girl would keep quiet about a man who'd traveled this far with them. Then Luke would find out and he'd lose his temper.

She dreaded her reunion with Luke and she'd rather he wasn't around her daughter at all. So she would make sure Carolyn was nowhere near him. She only wanted to grab Matthew and run.

Hopefully he wouldn't come after them. She knew how mean he could be and how strong he was. She'd have to outsmart him.

Rob was right, she needed a plan.

Chapter Thirteen

Nacogdoches bustled, and there were no rooms to be had.

Rob hoped Luke had done more than pass through town, otherwise it might take a while to find anyone who'd seen him. Lou Pearl had said Luke mentioned meeting a partner, but she didn't know who or where.

The man at the livery stable gave Rob directions to a house several miles past town where an older couple took in boarders.

The elderly couple needed wood chopped and fences mended. Rob arranged to work for their room and board, which kept him busy, while Moss and Sally inquired in town about Luke. But no one had seen or heard of him.

And Rob discovered the reason when he heard the story of a card game gone bad.

Luke no longer went by the name Luke Wheeler. Now he was known as Lucky Draw. He'd killed three men in a card game before he and another man stole three horses and rode out of town with a small boy.

No one in Nacogdoches had known his real name, but Rob made the connection once he saw the wanted poster inside the sheriff's office. It said Lucky was traveling with a young boy fitting Matthew's description.

The sheriff had posted a reward.

Rob rode back to the house. He had to tell Sally but he dreaded it.

Now that Luke was a wanted man, bounty hunters would be after him. From now on, the more trouble he got in, the higher the reward would climb. And people would be watching for him and remembering what he looked like, new name or not.

Eventually someone would catch or kill him.

Matthew was in danger. Any day now some bounty hunter could ride up and start shooting.

Luke had crossed the point of no return. He might even be dead by the time they found him.

Rob's hand went down to the gun at his hip.

I've got a bullet with your name on it, Luke. You'd better stay alive until I get there.

Rob found Moss outside chopping wood and told him what he'd learned in town.

"I ain't surprised. Man goes lookin' fer troubles is gonna find 'em sooner than later."

"Sally needs to know. I don't suppose you'd care to deliver the news?"

"Nope. She ain't gonna be happy. Jus' say it plain an' leave some room fer breathin'."

"I'm not looking forward to that temper of hers and there's no telling how she'll take it."

"Problems are like doggin' steers. Ye got to dig in yer heels on 'em, or they'll turn on ye."

Rob kicked at the dirt with his boot. "Guess I might as well get it over with."

Moss went back to chopping wood. "Ye ain't got it near as bad as me. I'm the one who's gotta tell Luke she come fer Matthew. He ain't gonna like it. He'll turn mean as a rattler and quick too." Moss looked at his gnarled hands that held the axe. "An' I ain't quick as I used to be. But fer Sally..." he turned to look where she stood hanging out the wash, "...I'll do the best I ken."

Rob walked over to her and she smiled at him.

He wanted to tell her about Luke but he stood twisting his hat in his hands, trying to find the right words.

She looked happy and he hated to destroy that mood. He saw it so seldom. First she'd been upset about Lou Pearl and then she'd realized Rob hadn't told her everything he'd learned about Luke. He guessed she'd hold that against him for a while.

Sally studied Rob's face. The happy expression washed away from her face as if he'd dashed cold water on it.

"You obviously have something to tell me. What is it?"

Rob struggled to find the words and his hesitation served only to make her angry.

"You're keeping secrets from me, and I don't like it."

He watched as she placed her hands on her hips. "Tell me everything, Rob. No holding out on me like you did at Mrs. Stamp's."

"You'd better sit."

"I'm not sitting, you just tell me." Her voice was hoarse with frustration. She stood glaring at him.

"It's not good news."

She tapped her foot.

"Luke shot three men, stole some horses and skipped town. There's a price on his head."

Her anger at Rob evaporated. "Are you sure it was him?"

If it was true then Matthew was in danger.

Panic filled her mind, and her stomach clenched.

"Fits his description, but he's changed his name."

Her fists bunched at her sides. "Changed his name?"

"Yes. He goes by the name Lucky Draw."

"Oh, that's ridiculous." She turned away, her hands still clenched, then turned back to face him and waved one hand in a gesture of dismissal. "It makes him sound like an outlaw. I don't believe it. Why would he do something so stupid?"

"Others believe it, and they'll hunt him for the bounty. If we find him, it won't be safe for you and Carolyn. No telling who he's riding with."

He let the news sink in and stood without speaking.

What he'd left unsaid was that Matthew was now surely in danger. There was no more doubt about it.

Sally walked over to the fence and leaned on it, looking out into the pasture.

He followed her.

She took a deep breath. "There must be some mistake. Lucky Draw doesn't even sound like a man's name."

"The likeness on the wanted poster is his."

She turned to look at Rob. Her eyes shone with tortured disbelief. "This can't be true."

"I'd never lie to you, Sally. You can talk to the sheriff

yourself, but you'll get the same answers I did."

"I need to be alone. I'm going for a walk."

Her dress was thin, and her shoulders shook slightly under the worn wool shawl. He wanted to put his arm around her, but she wouldn't welcome that.

"Fine." He draped his heavy coat over her shoulders, letting his hands linger briefly. "It's getting colder. Take this to keep you warm."

She grasped the coat and gathered it close around her shoulders. "Thank you."

A deep chill coursed through her body that had nothing to do with the weather. Like someone had walked over her grave, as her grandmother used to say.

She walked away from Rob. She didn't want to be near anyone right now. She needed to be alone with her thoughts.

It couldn't be true. If Luke had changed his name, that made her the woman who thought she'd married Luke Wheeler who turned out to be Lucky Draw. It was crazy.

She supposed it shouldn't be a surprise he'd turned outlaw. He was suited to it. If he'd killed someone, more than likely it was his terrible temper. She didn't know him, not really. There was a side to him she'd never understood.

Sally stepped over a log and sat on it to think. Remembering his temper, her hand rose to touch her cheek. One time he'd hit her so hard her jaw had gone numb.

Even now her jaw clicked sometimes.

She'd thought back then he might do anything, anything at all. How afraid she'd been. He'd said it was her fault, for burning his supper. He'd always claimed everything was her fault, crazy as that now sounded.

Why had she ever believed him?

She closed her eyes, and her shoulders hunched. A chill wind blew across the back of her neck. She drew Rob's coat tighter around her body, but couldn't get warm.

Taking a deep breath to try to calm herself, she caught a whiff of Rob's scent.

She felt safe with him, felt it instinctively now. He'd proved himself through their long ride.

She'd not allowed her fears of what would happen when she found Luke to fully surface until now. In the past she'd always pushed her fear of him to the back of her mind. But once Luke had left her, she'd begun to see him for what he really was.

He was a terribly dangerous man and she was no match for him. She could never outthink the crazy turns his mind would make. She needed help to protect her children.

She sat until the cold and her fears became unbearable then went back to the house.

All remained quiet inside.

Moss snored in a rocker by the fire and Carolyn sat playing in the warm, rosy glow of the crackling fire.

Rob glanced at her and gave her a reassuring smile.

Sally stood inside the door for a moment. What a peaceful scene it was. How good it would be to come home to a scene like this every night. They'd become a family of sorts though they weren't related by blood or marriage.

If only the men didn't have to leave when she found Matthew. She'd been isolated on the farm for so long she'd forgotten what it was to be surrounded by adults who cared for her. That sense of family had been missing from her life for a long time.

But what could she do? They wouldn't stay.

She'd press on alone as she always had. Even after she'd married she'd felt alone though she'd told herself otherwise.

Sally settled down near the fireplace with a cup of tea and drank it slowly, savoring the warmth of the liquid and storing the moment away, for she knew it wouldn't last.

The next morning, they rode away from Nacogdoches.

In other circumstances Sally would have enjoyed her stay. The town had been settled early and was more civilized than most places they'd passed through. But she couldn't wait to get away. Posters of Lucky Draw had gone up all over town. Her stomach hurt and her head pounded when she glimpsed one. Knowing what had happened was bad enough, but seeing the picture posted for all eyes to see made it worse. But she hadn't told anyone she knew the man named Lucky Draw, so no one had asked questions.

The only good thing was that Matthew hadn't been in the saloon when it happened. He hadn't seen his father kill those men. Thank God for that.

The quietness of the trail eased her pounding head. All she heard as they traveled in the early morning light were birds singing. No one spoke.

Later a shout broke the stillness.

Suddenly, coming toward them through the snow, she saw longhorn cattle. Men on horses worked each side of the ranging cattle, shouting at them.

"Odd time of year to drive beef," Rob said.

"Yep. Maybe they don't have no choice."

Moss headed toward the closest cowpoke.

The man didn't slow, but continued to work, making Moss catch up with him.

Moss spoke to him, then rode back to the others.

"Feller said they was drivin' them cattle fer a widder woman who don't have no choice but to sell the herd. She's gettin' up in years."

"Poor woman." Sally could easily sympathize with any woman left alone to cope with a ranch.

"But good news fer us." Moss grinned. "That feller said we might stop on by an' pay her a visit. It's on our way an' she gets mighty lonesome."

"If she'll put us up for the night, we can do some work for her before we leave in the morning," Rob said. He glanced at the sky. "There's a storm moving in. We need to find shelter."

They rode until almost dusk, when at last Sally saw the rise of smoke from over a hill. The gray sky seemed to reflect the whiteness of the snow. Everything around them stood under blankets of cold. Snow lay in the firs and ice needles hung down as a blanket of white covered the ground. The temperature had dropped.

Moss rubbed his mustache to break the tiny icicles that had formed there.

"That must be the ranch," Rob said. "We'll be too late for supper, but maybe we can find Carolyn a warm bed."

Carolyn was coughing again, her cheeks a rosy flush. They needed to get her inside where it was warm and dry.

It was odd to Sally the way Rob thought in terms of Carolyn. He'd changed since she'd first met him. He seemed to genuinely care for her little girl and Carolyn thought he was wonderful.

Like the father she'd never had.

As they neared the ranch house, Sally saw the glow of lamps in the windows and a bunkhouse a little further on, both surrounded by fences. Other fences enclosed immense stretches of land, occasionally broken by trees, which hung heavy with snow like large white lollipops.

As they rode nearer to the house, the corner of a curtain moved slightly but no face was seen.

"What a pretty house," Sally said. "I hope the widow has room for us."

After hitching the horses at the post, Rob lifted Carolyn down.

The curtain moved again. Then the door opened wide and an old woman holding a shotgun stepped out onto the porch.

Sally's breath caught.

The shotgun drooped heavily in the woman's hands, and she gestured them inside.

"Come." Her voice cracked with age. "Bring that child over by the fire. Get her warm. It's too cold to be out traveling with a young one."

"Yes," Sally said. "It's getting colder every minute."

The old woman set the gun inside the front door. "I knew a snowstorm was coming. My bones told me that a few nights ago."

"Thank you for your hospitality, ma'am," Rob said. "The weather is steadily growing worse."

"I knew. These old bones speak plenty, but they never lie."

Sally led Carolyn close to the fire and began to remove her snow-covered blankets.

Rob introduced everyone using first names only in case the woman had heard of Luke. They'd learned to do this since Luke's name wasn't always welcome. He moved over to Sally. "Let me take those blankets outside and shake them."

Moss hadn't said a word, which wasn't like him. He seemed to be struck silent by the woman.

"My name is Dorothea, but everyone has always called me Aunt Doe."

"Was your Mama a deer?" Carolyn put her hand over her mouth and giggled.

Aunt Doe's face crinkled in a smile that deepened until every wrinkle assumed lines like a raisin. "No, my Mama was a lady. She named me Dorothea, but Papa used to take me hunting, and I hit a doe once that was going to have a baby. It wasn't a mortal wound. I was a very poor shot. But I felt so badly that I brought her home and nursed her back to health. When her baby was born, it was a doe. Both of them took to following me around."

Moss interrupted her. "Then some of them boys in town teased an' called you Doe. Good name fer a purty gal with doe brown eyes."

She turned her old brown eyes to his and squinted as she walked nearer.

Moss took off his hat and smoothed the hair on his head.

She stopped in front of him and peered closer to see past the beard and mustache.

"Why, Ozzie Moss, is that you?"

He stood a bit straighter. "Yes, ma'am, it is myself, certain an' sure."

She chuckled. "Certain and sure, that always was you. Why I could tell tales on you and you on me, I suppose. Your granddaughter wouldn't know what to think."

He looked down at his feet. "'Ceptin' she ain't my grandchild." He glanced over at Carolyn. "Though I love her as if she was."

"I have neither children nor grandchildren either. My husband passed on not long ago."

"Well, now," Moss shuffled his feet. "I'm sorry to hear that."

"And your wife?"

"Never had one," he said with a deep sadness.

Aunt Doe looked sad as well. But she soon pulled herself together. "Well, come on everyone, set yourselves down and get warm. I'll fix Carolyn some warm milk and coffee for you folks. I have leftover cornbread and beans if you're hungry. I don't cook much now that my Sam's gone, and the cow hands are off to take my cattle to market."

"Cornbread sounds wonderful," Sally said. "Can I help you?"

"Land, no. You just rest by the fire."

The food and beverages warmed them and Carolyn grew sleepy.

Aunt Doe said, "Sally, you and Carolyn can have the spare room, and, Ozzie, you and Rob will have to sleep in the bunkhouse if you want beds. I don't have a fire going there, so you can either build one or bunk here by the fire with your bedrolls."

"They ain't the cleanest bedrolls, Doe," Moss blushed as he said her name. "We'd best bunk out there."

"Ozzie Moss, do you think I care about a little dirt or bugs when I haven't seen you in over fifty years? I only mentioned the bunkhouse thinking your old bones could use a soft bed like mine."

He turned as red as a ripe tomato.

She seemed unaware of what she'd just said and Rob spoke up before the woman could catch on and be embarrassed. "I'll build a fire in the bunkhouse and be glad to do any jobs you need doing tomorrow."

"Why thank you. Yes, there are some things..." Her voice trailed off as she watched Moss's embarrassment, still puzzled by it.

"Good night," Moss snapped as he went out to gather his things and take them to the bunkhouse.

"Breakfast is at sunup. We rise early here. Force of habit, I suppose. Though I don't know what I'll do with myself now that the cattle are gone and no hands here to feed."

"Yes, ma'am," Rob said. "We'll be ready."

Moss might be more ready than she knew. Rob wondered if a late love was brewing for the old man.

Moss didn't speak as Rob walked into the bunkhouse.

Rob noted that he unpacked his things and laid them out slowly, looking at them in turn as if he'd never seen them before.

"Everythin' I own right here," he mumbled. His expression turned gloomy, and he sat on the bunk. "Nothin' to offer her."

190

Rob built a fire, still watching as the old man sat looking into space. "I'll see to the horses."

Moss didn't move or reply.

Aunt Doe had explained to Rob which barn held feed and the location of the water pump. He eyed the large barn as he entered.

Her husband must've been a smart man. There were shelves and strange-looking gadgets everywhere. Along one side of the barn was a long trough, which had a pump. He'd never seen anything like it.

He pumped water to fill the trough. A connection to an underground spring brought it up right into the middle of the barn. The water tasted clear and clean.

Rob smiled to himself.

If that old woman takes a liking to Moss, he's got it made.

This wouldn't be a bad place to settle in, and she'd make a good wife. Though she might want to tidy Moss up and fit him out with new clothes.

He laughed at the thought of Moss duded up and living on this ranch. Stranger things had happened.

When he came back to the bunkhouse, Moss was still sitting where he'd left him, staring into the fire.

"Old timer, we'd better get some rest, daylight comes early."

Moss lay back on the bunk, put his hands behind his head and stared up at the ceiling. "Life don't ever do what you expect."

"No. It sure doesn't."

"I went west with my brother, back when Doe was a young woman. She said she'd wait on me."

"I guess she didn't wait."

"No, she waited all right. I come back an' then I was a goin' off agin' an' she said, 'If ye ain't back in a year, I'm goin' to marry somebody else.' I asked her who an' she said she didn't know, but somebody. Well, I didn't believe her. Then I heard she done it."

"At least she warned you, and gave you a year. She didn't throw any surprises at you."

Moss was quiet for a minute then said, "When I finally come back she'd up an' married an' had a baby on the way. She was pretty shook up to see me so I rode off an' didn't see her again 'til just now."

"What do you think happened to the baby?"

"Don't know, an' I ain't goin' to ask." He rolled over with his back to Rob and his face to the wall.

It would be a long night for the old man. No wonder he went on so about "tendin' the fires of love". Though it looked like his fire had never gone out, Rob wondered how Aunt Doe felt. She'd found someone else, so maybe she'd been happy.

Rob realized he'd been thinking an awful lot about love lately. A subject he used to never think of.

In fact he'd been doing more thinking than usual these days. He lay back on his bunk with a groan and placed his arm over his eyes.

Moss wasn't the only one who would have a long night.

Rob had glanced at the main house as he'd walked from the barn to the bunkhouse.

Sally had stood by the window looking out.

He'd caught a glimpse of her in a white nightgown, which must've been borrowed. Her hair hung down as she'd leaned toward the window.

She'd spotted him and raised her hand to say goodnight before she backed away. She'd looked like an angel beckoning, and even now through closed eyes Rob could see her again, like a vision.

No, he wouldn't sleep well tonight. Sally would fill his dreams again.

After Sally put Carolyn to bed, she changed into Aunt Doe's old nightgown. The soft white gown had silk ribbons and looked like something to be worn on a wedding night.

The soap in the washstand smelled of roses, and Sally inhaled deeply as she washed. Then she brushed her hair until it gleamed.

Her thoughts returned to Rob. The moon drew her to the window, and as she looked out she felt as though she were in a dream. The soft fabric caressing her body and her hair down her back made her feel like a desirable woman.

Then she saw him walking from the barn to the

bunkhouse.

Hardworking Rob, who did so much for her and never asked for anything in return. Here she'd been indulging herself, enjoying the fancy soap, the fine nightgown and he was still working. Working to provide a place for them to stay.

He looked up and she raised her hand to wave to him, longing to tell him all she felt in her heart and didn't know how to put into words.

She wanted to say come look at the moon with me, let me wash your hands and your tired face, let me ease your boots off and rest. Rest here with me.

He stopped and stared at her almost as if he'd read her thoughts.

She realized then that she wore only the thin nightgown, her breasts visible against the white cloth, the lamps illuminating everything in the room.

She blushed and drew back behind the curtains. Then placed her palm against her breast and felt her quick breathing, as if something had scared her.

She climbed into the downy bed and pulled the covers up before she realized she'd forgotten to blow out the lamps.

When she went back to blow out the wick, she looked out the window again, to see if he was still there, but he'd gone.

The moon had drifted behind a cloud, and she felt loss and disappointment.

She longed for the protectiveness of his arms and for the touch of his lips on hers. Longed for what she could never have. She climbed back into bed and fell asleep to dreams of Rob.

The sun rose early for everyone but Carolyn.

She coughed in her sleep, and Sally worried that the sickness she'd come down with earlier on the trail had returned.

Aunt Doe had given Carolyn some cough medicine, which had put her back to sleep.

They ate breakfast while she slept, then the men went out to work on the fence while Sally took a spot in the corner rocker where she could watch and listen to Carolyn.

Aunt Doe popped her head through the doorway. "May I

join you?"

"Of course."

"If she's not better in the next day or two, I'll send for the doctor."

"Thank you, Aunt Doe. I appreciate all you've done. It's a terrible feeling to know your child is sick and there's nothing you can do for her."

"It sounds like you've had some experience with sickness."

"My mother died just after we left for Kansas on a wagon train. She'd been sickly for many years and I left school to care for her and my sisters. She should never have left home, but she was following Papa's dream."

"Sometimes we do things for our men that we shouldn't."

"My sisters caught the fever from Mama and they passed on too. There was nothing I could do. Then Papa died of a broken heart and guilt over what he'd done to Mama."

"And you were all alone then?"

"Not for long. I met a man on the trail. He was a charmer, made me feel like I was something special. But he was a liar. He went through all the money Papa left me, then he ran off with my son just before our homestead was auctioned off."

"Oh, Sally. How awful."

"But I'm going to get my boy back."

"I hope and pray that you will."

"I'm so afraid something will happen to him. He's only seven and Luke is so irresponsible."

"Surely he'll take care of his own son?"

Sally didn't reply, but Aunt Doe must have guessed by the pain in her eyes that it wasn't likely.

"You've been through so much." Aunt Doe patted her on the knee. "If there's anything I can do, you'll let me know?"

Sally nodded.

The kindness in this woman's eyes showed what a gentle soul she was. She reminded Sally of her grandmother who'd died when she was ten. Grandmother had taken care of Sally once when she was sick and she'd made honey cakes and lemon drops to ease her sore throat. But it was Grandmother's presence that had soothed her the most.

After a few hours, Sally woke Carolyn so she would drink some water. She still had a cough and a slight fever. Sally sang her back to sleep.

When it was time for supper, Sally went into the kitchen where she found Aunt Doe sitting at the table with an old letter and a lock of hair.

She looked up at Sally, folded the letter then tucked it into her pocket.

"Sit down, my dear. How is Carolyn?"

"She's still asleep, but I'll wake her for dinner."

"No, let her sleep. There's no hurry. When she wakes, we can feed her if she's hungry."

"What can I do to help with dinner?"

"Not a thing. The roast and vegetables are cooking. Bread is in the oven. You rest. I'll make us some tea."

"It sounds wonderful, Aunt Doe. I'm sure the men will be hungry."

"Working men are always hungry. It's a blessing you came along when you did. I've been lonesome since my Sam passed on. It's nice to have a woman's company." Her hand reached across the table and squeezed Sally's.

Sally watched Aunt Doe make the tea.

Long slim fingers handled the blue and white china gently. Her hands were speckled like a robin's egg, only brown, but they moved like a graceful young girl's.

"I'd like for you to stay on a bit," Aunt Doe said. "Little Carolyn needs to rest and get well, and it'll be nice to visit with my old friend Ozzie."

Sally felt the warmth and restfulness of the place. "I wish we could, but I must find my son."

"I understand, my dear. Well, take it one day at a time. Let's see that Carolyn gets well and enjoy each day we're blessed with. Perhaps she'll feel better in the morning."

Sally was thoroughly exhausted from the trip and the news that Luke was now a wanted man. She wished she could rest, but that would never be possible as long as Matthew was in danger.

Yet she couldn't remember when she'd last been in such a restful place as this. Part of her wished she could curl up in

Aunt Doe's big bed and sleep like Carolyn.

She let Carolyn sleep as long as she dared then woke her and tried to get her to sip some beef broth.

Afterward, Carolyn felt well enough to climb out of bed.

The men came in at noon after washing up, and Carolyn joined them as they sat at the long table.

Carolyn looked around at the rest of the chairs. "Do you got children?"

Aunt Doe laughed. "Well, I guess you could say I've got a lot of boys. The fellows who work the ranch usually take their meals here with me. We've had as many as twenty around this table. But most of my boys have gone to sell the rest of my cattle. I don't know what they'll be doing after they come back here."

It was a quiet meal.

Aunt Doe didn't seem to mind the lack of table conversation. She didn't mind the way Moss dropped gravy onto his shirt. She simply handed him another napkin and passed him more food.

Sally had never seen him eat so much.

It was as if he had a hole that emptied as quickly as it filled. And Aunt Doe gave him more and more.

After dinner the men lounged in the big room with the stone fireplace, while Sally helped Aunt Doe with the dishes after putting Carolyn to bed.

Soon the ladies joined the men, and the conversation turned to Carolyn.

"I don't like her running these fevers," Rob said.

"We ain't goin' nowhere 'til that little girl is well ag'in," Moss said. "She wasn't hardly awake no time when she fell asleep eatin' her dinner."

"She's sleeping soundly. I gave her some more of the cough medicine." Sally twisted her apron ties and sat with a frown. She hoped Carolyn didn't get worse.

"I'll send for the doctor, if she worsens," Aunt Doe said.

They couldn't leave until Carolyn was well enough.

And Sally felt torn between her worry for Matthew and worrying over Carolyn's illness.

The choices were impossible. No matter what she did, if she

stayed here or kept chasing after Luke, she feared losing one of her children.

Chapter Fourteen

They'd been at the ranch for over a week while Carolyn recovered from her illness.

The doctor had said her lungs were infected and it could have been hovering there since her last illness. If they left before she was fully recovered, she might never get well.

Aunt Doe reassured Sally there was no way of knowing this would happen, but still the guilt ate heavily at her. If she hadn't been in such a hurry to find Matthew, would Carolyn be this sick? She couldn't help but feel partly at fault.

But Aunt Doe kept Sally busy. She'd fit into the routine at the ranch as easily as a custom-made slipper.

It was almost Christmas.

Aunt Doe was thrilled they'd be spending the holiday with her. She and Moss were sparking, and her joy was infectious.

Sally hated the thought of being away from Matthew at Christmas. She'd never been away from her children before Luke took Matthew and the holiday only intensified her feelings.

Rob and Moss rode out to find a tree while Carolyn and Sally made decorations for it. Carolyn still had a cough, but the fever had gone.

The men came back with a big, fat tree that barely fit through the door. They set it in the corner near the fire and stood back to admire it.

Sally had bundled Carolyn up and carried her out to watch the goings on.

Carolyn pointed toward the top of the tree. "Look, Mama, a bird's nest! I want to see the baby birds."

Rob stretched to his fullest height to peer into it. "It's

empty, but let's leave it there."

"Maybe Saint Nicholas will bring me a baby bird. Mama, that can be my one special gift."

Carolyn had talked for three days about the one special gift Saint Nicholas would bring.

She wanted a fancy doll.

Sally knew the others were aware her little girl would have no gifts.

Aunt Doe seemed to sense her embarrassment. "Tonight after dinner we'll decorate the tree. We'll make cookies and popcorn and sing songs."

"Mr. Rob can play the guitar."

Carolyn hadn't forgotten the promise he'd made at Mr. Huckabee's campsite to play the guitar for her.

"But I don't have guitar, little one," Rob said.

"Well, now, I just might have an old guitar around here somewhere," Aunt Doe said.

Carolyn clapped her hands, which brought on a new bout of coughing.

"Stay still," Sally warned. "Or I'll have to put you back in bed."

"If Aunt Doe can find a guitar, I'll play it for you tonight," Rob promised.

They gathered for a supper of stew, biscuits and dried tomato pie. Carolyn had her appetite back, an encouraging sign.

After supper Sally helped clean up then Aunt Doe went to find items to decorate the tree. She returned with ribbons and dried fruit, paper to cut and popcorn.

Rob popped the corn over the fireplace while the women helped Carolyn cut out figures to tie to the tree with ribbons.

"Got to go work in the barn." Moss slipped out the door.

Later, Rob went to tell Moss the celebration was ready.

Moss was working on his project. He nailed one board to another. "Well, now, let me jus' finish this here piece."

"What is it?"

"Jus' a little somethin' fer Carolyn." Moss stood and stretched his back.

"You should smell the cookies Aunt Doe made. That woman can cook up a storm."

Moss nodded. "She sure do make good cookies. I remember that from when she was a girl."

The freshly fallen snow crunched as they walked across the yard leading to the house. It glittered in the evening light. Inside, the scents of popcorn, cookies and pine filled the air, while the fire crackled in the hearth.

Rob spotted the old guitar Aunt Doe had placed in the corner of the room and went over to tune it.

"It hasn't been used in some time," Aunt Doe said. "One of my boys left it here. He angered another man by mistakenly shooting his horse then he rode off in the night, and I never heard from him again."

"Must've been a green hand to shoot a horse." Moss chuckled.

"Or a terrible shot," Rob added.

"He was a fairly nervous lad. Young, had only been here a week. Most of our hands were off to the war. We were left with young boys and men who wouldn't fight except among themselves." Aunt Doe shook her head. "Those were hard times, those war years. We barely made it through."

"Is that why you're sending cattle north in winter?" Rob asked.

"Yes. I should've sent the men on the trail last fall, but Sam was so close to death I didn't want to leave his side. I had no time for the ranch. Many of the hands left for other jobs. I couldn't blame them. I buried Sam a week before Thanksgiving."

"Wished I'd a been here to hep ye," Moss said.

"Our trail boss stayed along with our cook. I thought we'd pick up boys like we always have in the past, but it was so late, finding hands was hard." Aunt Doe sighed. "I didn't think I could wait it out until spring. There's plenty of land, but there's too much pressure to sell it cheap. Plenty of men came with offers. Some friendly and some not so friendly. But to stay on I have to pay my hands. And my cousin in Missouri agreed to buy the cattle for a fair price. So I'm selling them off."

"Them cattle is bound to be lean an' ye ken lose half o' yer herd time they get 'em to Missouri," Moss said. "Ye sure ye ken trust them hands?"

"Yes." Aunt Doe smiled. "I need to get out of the cattle business. I'm too old for it. I thought I'd spend one last winter here then move into town. I haven't decided what to do about this house yet though."

"Well, now." Moss said.

"This is my last Christmas in this house and look at what I've been gifted with. A ready-made family. It's as if I'd had children and grandchildren." She looked over to where Carolyn played. "I never thought to hear the sounds of children here."

Rob cleared his throat. "Let's see how this thing sounds." He began to play a few tunes.

Carolyn sat enthralled.

The others recognized the tune of "Silent Night" and started singing.

When they'd sung all the songs Rob knew, Moss said, "Let's step out onto the porch. Them stars is bright on the fresh snow. It's a purty night."

Carolyn slipped her hand into Rob's, linking Rob, Carolyn and Sally in a human chain.

Sally saw the look that passed between Aunt Doe and Moss as they smiled at each other.

This felt like a real family even if Sally could only imagine it so. No law or blood joined this group, but their heartstrings tied them to each other.

It proved to be a miracle that the trail had brought the little group together and dropped them right into Aunt Doe's mournful but welcoming heart. Even more so that this journey had brought Aunt Doe and Ozzie Moss back together again after all these years.

Aunt Doe grasped Moss's hand and squeezed it as she looked across her land sparkling under the stars.

No one spoke. There was no need for words. The stars and the crispness of the evening would be etched on Sally's memory for a lifetime.

Then Aunt Doe said, "Children must be in bed for Saint Nicholas to come."

Carolyn was too tired to argue. She even took the cough medicine without complaint.

Sally tucked her in and kissed her forehead before singing her to sleep.

When Sally rejoined the adults, all sat silently.

Rob nursed a glass of scotch and stared into the fire.

Aunt Doe's eyes softened as she watched the back of Moss's head. Then she noticed Sally's presence and stood. "Come with me, I have some things to show you."

Sally followed her into a room filled with old trunks.

Aunt Doe stooped to unlock a trunk and pull out a china doll from underneath a quilt. "This is for Carolyn, from Saint Nicholas."

"Oh, but I couldn't," Sally said.

She had no gift for her little girl, but she couldn't accept this beautiful china doll. It was too dear.

"Yes, you can and you will," Aunt Doe insisted, placing the doll into Sally's hands. "This was meant for the daughter I never had. She needs a good home."

Sally held the doll in her hands, its blue eyes and black hair striking against its pale face.

She'd always dreamed of being able to give Carolyn a doll like this, one that wouldn't fall apart the way sun babies or rag dolls did.

The blue dress emphasized the doll's blue eyes. Carolyn would love it.

"Thank you," she whispered, past the lump in her throat.

"Thank you for sharing your precious child with me." Aunt Doe placed her hand over Sally's. "Now come, I have something for you too." She reached into another trunk and removed a green velvet dress trimmed in gold lace.

"Oh," Sally gasped. "It's beautiful."

Aunt Doe held up the dress. It was out of fashion but still elegant and looked as if it had never been worn.

Sally touched the fabric, feeling its softness as her eyes took in the rich color.

"You must try it on. I think it will fit, but we may need to alter it some."

"I don't know what to say."

"There's nothing to say." Aunt Doe took the doll from Sally's hands. "Try the dress on now, it's getting late."

Sally slipped out of her old dress and into the green velvet and Aunt Doe fastened the buttons in the back.

The dress fit as if it had been made especially for Sally.

Aunt Doe drew her toward the mirror in the corner.

"Oh," Sally sighed.

"It looks lovely on you."

Sally took in the sight of her figure in the beautiful dress. It actually made her look pretty, not like a worn-out woman. The deep green dress brought out her skin tones and the red-gold color of her hair.

Aunt Doe rummaged until she found several green ribbons to match the dress. She stood behind Sally and pinned her hair up.

"Now with a little curl here..." she tucked at a piece, "...and a little curl there..." she moved to the other side, "...your dance card would be filled every evening."

Tears streamed down Sally's cheeks. "Oh, Aunt Doe, you have no idea..." She reached up to swipe at her tears. "My dance card..." she shook her head, "I'd never danced with anyone until Luke. And then he..."

Aunt Doe put her arm around Sally's shoulders. "Why don't you tell me about it, my dear."

Sally unburdened her life story. She told of the beatings and the horrible things Luke had done to her. Things she'd never told another living soul.

She cried until she was all cried out. When she was done, Aunt Doe's eyes were misty as well.

"Sally, do you still love Luke?"

"I did once. But he wasn't the man I thought him to be. All I ever wanted was for him to be a good husband and father."

Aunt Doe sighed. "Even good men aren't always ready to settle down, Sally. Sometimes they take a long time."

"I used to think it was something I did that made him act that way. Because he'd been so different before we married. And afterwards, all he ever did was complain. I had no idea he'd lied to me from the start."

"Some men are no good. You can't change them."

"I'm glad he's gone. But he didn't have to take Matthew."

Sally's hands fisted. "He didn't have to steal my son."

Aunt Doe was silent for a moment. "Tell me, Sally, what did you love about him? What made you fall in love?"

"He's tall and slim, very handsome. I used to watch him practice dealing cards on our kitchen table. He has long slender hands. It's almost pretty the way they move when he deals a hand, though I never liked card playing. I guess it was his looks and his smooth talking ways that made me fall for him."

"Yes, but what qualities of his did you love?"

"He was kind to me after Papa died. But I wouldn't say he has many good qualities."

Whatever redeeming qualities Luke had once had he'd drowned with whiskey and lies.

"And how is he with the children?"

"He doesn't like children," Sally said abruptly.

"I see. Then it doesn't make sense his taking Matthew."

"No. It doesn't, unless he wanted to get back at me for something. He hated the farm. But I never thought he'd leave. I never thought he'd steal Matthew."

"What did he do before you met him?"

"I don't know. He wouldn't talk about his past."

Aunt Doe drew her near and gave her a hug. "Sally, I'll pray that you find them so you can get your son back. But you need to settle things with Luke before you can start a new life. You must clear the air."

Sally listened to her advice, but it was useless in her situation. Luke hadn't discussed things with her when they were married. He was unlikely to do it now.

"There are plenty of other men out there. Good men. You're young. You can love again. But you don't want the shadow of Luke hanging over your life when you find a good one."

"I gave my whole heart once, and it wasn't enough."

"But you gave it quickly and to the wrong man. The best love is one that grows slowly over time."

"Our marriage wasn't even legal. I think he just wanted my inheritance."

Aunt Doe inhaled sharply. "Then he's not legally entitled to Matthew either."

Sally sat in shock. It was so obvious. But it simply hadn't occurred to her.

"You'll be wiser next time." Doe hugged her again. "It's late. We must get the presents ready."

They settled Carolyn's doll under the tree.

Rob watched from his seat near the fire. He looked as if his thoughts were far away. He stretched his long legs casually before him and looked over at her.

Sally wanted to cry. She was too emotional from her talk with Aunt Doe to speak to him right now. And he reminded her of Luke, sitting there with the glass in his hand, but he didn't glare at her like Luke used to do.

She'd never been around Rob when he'd been drinking, though she'd seen him glance at saloons as they rode past. She hoped he wasn't the heavy drinker Luke had been. Men who drank made her nervous.

How quiet he was nursing that glass. What was he thinking?

"It seems to me that everyone is tired," Aunt Doe said. "I suggest we get some sleep. Carolyn will likely be up early."

The men went back to the barn, and Sally went to her room, but not to sleep. She kept reviewing her conversation with Aunt Doe.

Her last waking thoughts before she drifted off to sleep were of Matthew. She hoped Luke remembered to give him a gift for Christmas. That had always been her job. With silent tears she hugged her pillow and prayed for her missing son.

Her sleep turned into a nightmare.

She'd found Luke in a dirty little town full of men with guns. The dark musty house he'd hidden Matthew in had no windows and only one door.

Luke shot the bar across the door to lock it and stepped menacingly toward her. He grabbed her arms and shook her. "Why'd you come here, woman? Did you bring the law?"

"I came for Matthew. My son needs his mother."

"He doesn't need you."

"Yes, he does." She looked at Matthew who sat tied to a chair in the corner.

Luke slapped her face. "I thought I taught you never to sass me." He yanked off his belt and began flailing at her. "I'll teach you for good this time."

As the beating grew fiercer, Sally screamed for help. But no one came.

Just as she called for Rob and he burst open the door, she woke with a start.

Carolyn bounced on the bed, a big grin on her face.

Sally rubbed her head, disoriented, hoping to ease the headache that now pounded.

Her dream had been a warning.

"Mama, get up." Carolyn pushed her on the shoulder.

Sally sat up.

"Hurry, Mama." Carolyn bounced again. "I want to see if Saint Nicholas has come."

Sally rose and splashed cold water on her face. Her bleary face in the mirror showed no bruises, and she told herself it had only been a dream. But some marks never showed. She was well familiar with those. The dream had left her feeling slightly sick and Carolyn was tugging at her hand.

"Come on, Mama."

She put on the green dress and tied her hair up in the ribbons. Aunt Doe had been kind in giving her the dress. Though she felt no joy this Christmas morning, she'd show how much she enjoyed the gift by wearing it.

Carolyn's eyes sparkled in fascination. She'd never seen her Mama look so fancy. She kept running her hands along the sides of the green skirt, touching the velvet.

"Mama, you look like a dolly. So pretty."

Sally hugged Carolyn.

How precious her little girl was. She wanted to protect her and give her a home where no bad things happened.

Carolyn squirmed. "Are you ready?"

"When the others wake, we'll see what Saint Nicholas brought you," Sally said.

Carolyn tiptoed into Aunt Doe's room with her hands behind her back. "Aunt Doe," her voice sang. "Wake up."

Aunt Doe peeked one eye open. "Do I hear a little bird calling me?"

"Yes, a baby bird and he's in my nest."

Sally called to her from the doorway. "Come, Carolyn, let Aunt Doe alone so she can get dressed."

Carolyn ran over to her and held her hand. "Mama, I want to see the baby bird in the nest."

"Remember, Carolyn, the bird's nest is empty. There isn't any baby bird."

Rob came in just in time to hear the last part of their conversation.

He came up behind Sally, touched her on the shoulder and she jumped as if scorched.

He frowned. What was wrong with her?

Sally stepped around him and followed Carolyn as she danced into the kitchen.

Rob poured the coffee he'd made earlier.

Sally seemed out of sorts this holiday morning. Was it because she missed her boy? It had to be hard on her.

Rob knew just the thing to take her mind off of Matthew temporarily, but that could wait until this evening. He planned to kiss her again.

Listening to Moss lament about the years wasted that he could have been with Aunt Doe had made Rob rethink the feelings he had for Sally. Maybe she'd turn away from him once he took care of Luke. But they were here now and the feelings between them were strong. He would take things as far as she'd let him. And hope it would be enough.

He watched her move about the room. The green dress fit her like a glove and was meant for touching.

Perhaps she'd had thoughts similar to his. If she'd worn the dress for him, well the effect was working. He wanted to touch her but he'd restrain himself.

He'd hinted to Moss and Aunt Doe that he wanted some time alone with Sally this evening and they seemed agreeable.

It was their last evening at the ranch, and he wanted it to be memorable. Memorable enough that when Sally saw Luke again, she'd have no thought of going back to him.

Inside her shy, nervous exterior there burned a passionate

woman. Tonight he'd unleash that passion.

He'd been thinking about one thing for some time.

Some "no's" really meant "yes".

She'd wanted him to kiss her. There was no mistake about that. Her initial response had proved it.

But perhaps he'd been too much the gentleman. Tonight, one way or the other, he'd have his answer.

Chapter Fifteen

Rob touched Sally's shoulder.

She jumped.

He'd come up behind her so quiet, he'd scared her.

Now he studied her with a strange look in his eyes.

Carolyn started toward the Christmas tree then froze with a squeal. "Did Saint Nicholas bring this dolly for me?"

Sally smiled and glanced at Aunt Doe. "Yes, sunshine, he was especially good to us this year."

Carolyn cradled the doll, rocking her. "Her name is Bell, Baby Blue Bell."

"I have somethin' fer ye too," Moss said.

Carolyn's eyes widened. "For me, Uncle Moss?"

"Jus' you stay there, darlin'." He put on his coat, went outside then came back in with a cradle for her dolly.

"Uncle Moss, Baby Blue Bell can sleep there!"

"Yes, darlin', I know." His eyes twinkled.

Aunt Doe laughed softly and they shared a glance.

Carolyn sat rocking her dolly. Then, as if she'd suddenly remembered something, she ran to the tree and jumped up and down. "The baby bird, Mama, I want to see the baby bird!"

"I told you there isn't any baby bird, Carolyn."

Rob picked Carolyn up and lifted her high above his head. "Tell me what's in there. Can you see anything?"

"Ooh, a baby bird!" Her small hand reached into the nest and drew out a tiny wooden bird.

Sally couldn't believe her eyes.

So that's what Rob had been carving. A warm glow filled her heart as she watched him with her little girl.

Carolyn wore a big smile as she sat on Rob's shoulders and flew the bird around his head.

He laughed. "That little bird won't fly away like a real one would."

She set the bird on his head and made it hop. "No, little bird." She giggled. "You can't fly away. You are a baby bird." Sally watched them, amazed at the way Carolyn had taken to Rob. He appeared relaxed with her daughter, as though he enjoyed her playful antics with the wooden bird as she bounced it on his head. Not a shred of irritation showed on his face.

If only Carolyn could have had a father like Rob.

Sally memorized the shape of his back, his shoulders, his stance and the waves of his hair.

He turned and her gaze drifted down his arms. Those strong arms had held her, saved her life. The cuff of his shirtsleeve barely touched his wrist. She longed to trace her finger from his wrist to the veins that ran just under his skin.

If only she could memorize each inch of him, to keep him with her forever.

She had to remember each part of him in detail, imprint him on her memory so he wouldn't drift into the blur of those she'd cared for and lost.

Soon he'd be gone.

The vengeance that drove him would no longer direct his path and she would never see him again. He had no reason to stay.

Yet her heart cried out to him.

Please love me, stay with me, want me with all your heart and never leave me. Never abandon me.

She closed her eyes and choked back the sob that threatened to make a spectacle of her in the midst of this happy Christmas celebration.

Rob was an honest man. He'd made no promises.

The burden of a woman with two children was more than most men would take on.

Even if he were to fall in love with her, what man would want to raise the children of his enemy?

She turned away to pull herself together.

Rob noticed the sudden change in Sally's expression and set Carolyn down.

He didn't know what had made those sparkling blue eyes so sad, but he guessed it had something to do with Luke.

Carolyn skipped around the room with the bird in her hand until she reached the cradle. Then she stopped and knelt down to introduce Baby Blue Bell to the baby bird.

Rob studied Sally as she turned away.

She was the most beautiful woman he'd ever known. Her beauty was in her spirit, not merely in her outward appearance. Even the time spent with Luke hadn't turned her away from the goodness within her.

She didn't even realize how stunning she was. The green in her dress brought out the blue in her eyes and the reddish gold highlights in her hair. Ribbons trailed down her neck, and his gaze followed them to the curve of her shoulder.

Sally would have made a fine lady in other circumstances.

He could picture her wearing that dress to a ball or riding in a fancy carriage.

Instead, she'd wasted her time on a man like Luke.

Rob's jaw tightened and he clenched his fists.

Luke could be smooth when it suited him. Would Sally be taken in by him again? What pack of lies would Luke tell her?

Sally had never voiced her feelings about Luke.

Though Rob knew she was angry at having her son stolen, what would she do once she had Matthew back?

He wasn't sure how to handle this situation.

It would be easy to shoot Luke dead if not for Sally and Carolyn and the boy.

He didn't want to cause them heartache but he could see no way to avoid it.

They'd leave tomorrow now that Carolyn was well. Soon they'd catch up to Luke.

Around noon, Aunt Doe served a huge Christmas dinner.

Moss ate as if it were his last meal.

But even he couldn't put away all the pies, meats and

breads Aunt Doe and Sally had made.

Aunt Doe poured hard cider all round, and they raised their glasses in a toast.

"To those we love, those we've lost and joys yet to come," Aunt Doe said.

As evening arrived, a sense of sadness settled over Sally. This was the most peaceful time she'd spent since she'd met Luke.

She'd miss Aunt Doe. It was hard not having any female relatives or close friends to share her troubles with. A burden had been lifted telling Aunt Doe about her marriage to Luke. She'd named the unspeakable things and now she could move on with her life. They would no longer have power over her.

"Do you mind if I tuck her in tonight and do the storytelling?" Aunt Doe asked. "I'm going to miss this little girl."

"I'm sure she'd love that," Sally said.

Aunt Doe treated her daughter like her own grandchild. And Moss hovered over them both, doting. He'd replaced his mumblings with real conversations between himself and Doe. He was downright jovial and hardly ever grumbled.

"Sally, why don't you come with me to bed down the animals?" Rob hinted with a wink, "Give the old folks some time alone."

Sally collected her coat and joined him.

A coyote far off in the distance howled a mournful sound as Rob opened the door to the barn. Once inside, he shed his coat, rolled up his sleeves and grabbed a pitchfork to give hay to each of the horses.

Sally sat on a bale of hay and watched the muscles of his back strain against the fabric of his shirt. Her gaze followed the curve of his belt and the way his pants fit his body. The muscles in his legs flexed as he walked past her.

She sensed the barely controlled power coiled in his body.

Unable to turn her gaze away, she remembered the way he'd held her by the river. She longed for the protection of his arms. How could a man be so strong and yet so gentle? He was also gentle with Carolyn.

He turned and caught her looking.

Sally's cheeks flushed. Her gaze had dropped to the seat of his pants and he knew exactly where she'd been looking.

She needed to quiet her thoughts. She moved into the stall furthest from him and picked up a comb to curry his horse. The barn was quiet, all the animals settling into their beds. Chickens dozed on their nests, and the goats slept in their stall.

Sally daydreamed, stroking the horse, unaware of the passage of time. The horse huffed softly, enjoying her gentle handling.

Rob spoke to her from where he worked. "I think Carolyn enjoyed the bird."

"She loves it." Sally smiled, picturing her little girl's face.

Rob moved into her stall. His gray-blue eyes stared into hers with concern. "I didn't mean to startle you this morning."

"That's all right. I just don't like people coming up behind me all quiet like."

"I'm sorry. I was trying to keep the secret until it was time."

"You're good at keeping secrets."

"I won't keep secrets from you, Sally. Anything you want to know, you just ask."

He'd given her the opening to ask the hundreds of questions that had filled her head.

"Have you ever been married?"

"No. Though I came close once."

Sally mulled that over.

"Now it's my turn. What do you plan to do once you find Matthew, will you go back to Luke?" he asked, his voice velvet-edged and strong.

"Never." She spat the word out. "I want nothing more to do with him." She looked up at Rob. "But I want my boy."

The horse shifted under the pressure of her brush.

"I'll do everything in my power to see that it happens." He reached across and placed his hand over hers, his gaze soft as a caress. "Careful now, you don't want to brush so hard. And you shouldn't be working in the barn wearing that fancy dress." He took the brush from her and laid it aside.

The small window in the barn suddenly blew open, and Sally jumped. The horse snorted and moved beside her.

Rob walked around past her to close the window, pulling the latch across. Turning back, he noticed her shiver. He stepped up behind her and ran his hands up and down her arms.

Moving closer, he put his arms around her. "You're chilled," he whispered into her ear.

She shivered against him.

He glanced over her shoulder at her white alabaster breasts in the low-cut velvet gown. "Have I told you how beautiful you look tonight?"

"No."

He flicked his tongue against her ear lightly, and her breathing quickened.

"Your gown is beautiful, just like you." He whispered in her ear. His lips grazed her earlobe then moved back up to whisper again. "This velvet fabric calls out to be touched."

He slid his arms around her waist slowly as if feeling the fabric, then turned her around to face him. He gazed into her eyes and drew her nearer, rubbing his hands across the bottom of her rib cage. "This dress is as soft as it looks."

Her goose bumps had nothing to do with the chill in the air and her breathing quickened.

His lips brushed hers as he spoke. "But it's not the dress that makes you beautiful. It's what you bring to the dress— what hides inside."

He kissed her, feeling the softness of her lips and waiting for her mouth to part.

His hands explored the hollows of her back, moving slowly across the muscles beside her spine. He kissed her until he felt her relaxing under his fingertips. Then with slow careful movements, he eased her back toward the hay piled in the corner. He moved slightly around beside her, and still layering kisses down her neck, laid her down slowly.

Under sensually lowered lids, she gazed upon him.

Yes, there were hidden depths of passion inside her.

Still keeping his arms around her, he kissed her ear, her neck, and finally again her mouth.

She parted her lips, her tongue tentatively meeting his.

He kissed her slowly and thoughtfully, drawing out her

response with each breath, and she relaxed into each movement as if sinking slowly.

Sally soaked in each kiss as they moved ever so slowly, and with each kiss she relaxed deeper and deeper into his arms.

His lips were more persuasive than she remembered.

She'd dreamed of this but the reality was more intense than her dreams had ever been.

The heady sensation of his lips against her neck turned her knees to jelly. She longed to sink deeper into his arms, so safe, so warm and so loving.

As he finally touched his lips to hers she wanted to melt. He continued showering her with kisses.

She relaxed more deeply into the warm hay. His lips left hers to nibble at her earlobe again and moved back to her neck. Slowly he kissed her there.

Oh yes, there, and then here again.

She let herself relax completely, thinking only of how glorious it felt.

His hand moved around back up her ribcage and stroked her breast through the velvet dress, his finger making circles that warmed her. He edged the shoulder of her dress down, his fingers lightly moving over her skin. He deepened his kiss and moved his hand again but she no longer noticed their moves, and soon he had moved her dress until her breasts spilled out.

Sally no longer cared.

His lips and hands moved across her body, making her think of nothing else. Slowly his tongue trailed down toward her neck, across her collarbone, and to the swell of her breasts where her dress had slipped.

Her skin craved his touch.

His lips caressed hers again and she abandoned herself to the whirl of sensation.

Her breast surged at the intimacy of his touch as he rubbed across the peak with his warm thumb.

Instinctively, her body arched toward him as his thumb moved in a circular motion, teasing.

His lips soothed hers. He kissed her chin, her neck, down to the hollow in her throat and on to the valley between her breasts. He slid the dress further to her waist.

She yielded to the searing need that had been building in her. She would have this night of passion. She wouldn't think about tomorrow, only here and now. Every word he'd spoken to her, every touch of his hand had been leading up to this moment. She was his, and he was hers, their bodies meant for each other. No awkwardness existed. No fumbling. Only a coming together of what had to be.

His tongue traced a hot trail across her breasts and she longed for release. His hands settled on her hips, grasped the dress to pull it away.

A coyote howled.

The animals in the barn came awake. The quiet broken by chickens squawking, goats bleating and horses moving nervously in their stalls.

Sally pushed Rob away.

The coyote was close. Very close.

Rob sat up. "Damn." He ran a hand through his hair.

Sally watched him with flushed cheeks.

"Stay here. I'll be back."

He picked up his rifle and went out the door.

Damn coyote.

Everything had been going well. He would have to start over again, if she'd let him.

Rob peered out into the darkness, watching for movement.

He saw the coyote and fired a shot, then waited to see if the animal moved.

Aunt Doe and Moss came running out of the house.

"What happened?" she asked.

"Coyote."

Sally heard a shot.

The goats bleated and the horses shifted in their stalls nervously, making her afraid.

She tugged the sleeves up over her cold shoulders and holding the dress to herself, ran to the door, the back gaping because she couldn't do the back buttons up.

Rob stood over the coyote he'd killed.

Aunt Doe and Moss approached the middle of the yard and

stopped suddenly. Both stared at her with wide-eyed concern as though she were standing there naked.

Her face flamed.

Moss stood with his mouth hanging open in astonishment.

Aunt Doe elbowed him before he could speak. "Hush, you old fool. Remember when we were young?"

With tears of embarrassment filling her eyes, Sally clutched her bodice tighter and ran into the house.

In her room, she closed the door and leaned against it, breathing heavily as tears rolled down her face.

The evening had been so wonderful. Now it was all ruined.

What had she been thinking? Nearly making love with a man who'd said nothing of marriage.

A man who would ride away. Another man who would abandon her.

She slipped on her nightgown and climbed into bed, curled herself into a ball and wept tears of frustration.

It had felt so good. She'd been willing to forget everything. But how could she forget about her son?

She couldn't let this happen again.

Getting Matthew back was all that mattered.

Morning came early for Sally as she'd slept hardly a wink last night. With effort she forced herself to enter the kitchen for breakfast, acting as if nothing had happened.

Every time Rob looked at her, she blushed and she couldn't look at him.

Her hand shook as she ate her eggs.

Aunt Doe eased the situation by keeping everyone busy packing the gifts she kept pressing on them. She gave them food and insisted on paying Rob and Moss for their work.

"You go on now. The sooner you go, the sooner you can come back to visit." Aunt Doe hugged Carolyn. "Be good for your Mama, you hear?"

"Yes, ma'am."

Moss stood twisting his hat and looking pained.

Aunt Doe placed a hand on his arm. "You make sure to let me know how you are, old friend. I don't expect a visit, though

I'd welcome one."

"I surely will."

She embraced him and stood back to look at him. "I don't expect you to settle down, but if you ever feel the urge to come and rest a spell, you come and see me."

"I'll do that."

Aunt Doe stood on the porch waving until they could no longer see her.

Moss looked back only once, but Carolyn waved until they were out of sight.

The brisk clear air nipped at Sally. She was anxious to move on now that they'd said goodbye. Gripping the reins tight, she forced her gaze ahead.

Rob watched her as she rode without speaking, lost in her thoughts.

As Sally replayed the events of the previous evening, heat filled her face. She snuck glances at Rob under her eyelashes. The seductive thoughts she was having about him should be reserved for his wife.

If she wasn't careful she'd be acting the wanton woman.

She had to think of Matthew and Carolyn.

When they reached Austin, Rob learned Luke and his gang had robbed the noon stage.

The sheriff said they'd headed southeast, but he thought Luke might lay low in Houston.

Rob decided to set up camp outside the Austin city limits.

In a few days, it would be New Year's Eve. The saloons were full of early revelers. There were no rooms to be had in respectable establishments. Rob thought they'd be better off away from town, so they pressed on.

A few miles outside town, they came upon an abandoned shack near the Colorado River. It held no furniture, only an old cook stove in one corner.

Moss started a fire for Sally and Rob led the horses to the river where grass grew just under the snow.

Sally started a pot of beans, bacon and onion. So far she'd avoided speaking to Rob, but she was aware of how he watched her.

It was late by the time supper was ready. As they ate Sally listened to the wind howl around the shack.

Rob and Moss had stuffed twigs and debris into the cracks in an attempt to stop the onslaught of cold brittle air, but they could hardly seal every crack.

Sally washed the dishes then tucked Carolyn into her bedroll and sang her to sleep.

The horses in the lean-to behind the shed were out of the wind. Neither Rob nor Moss felt the need to watch over them. They'd hear anyone who came near to steal them.

As Sally listened to the wind, she wondered what they'd find when they reached Houston.

Rob had warned her about New Year's revelers. Would Luke be among them, drinking and shooting off his guns in the middle of town? Would Matthew be with him in that chaos?

Sometimes she thought the trail would never end, Luke would just keep moving and they'd keep on tracking him.

What would happen when she did find him? How would he react when he learned she was there to take Matthew back?

She'd give her children a good home, whatever it took. She could hire herself out to a boarding house or some other decent job for a woman. Everything involved struggle and hard work. But she would not work in a saloon.

No, she wouldn't be with a man again, unless they were really and truly married.

She might not own property, but now her decisions were hers, for good or for bad. She had to make sure she made good ones. She would find the strength to press on.

The next day they reached Houston by nightfall.

Rob knew Sally was exhausted, but he saw the gleam in her eyes as they neared the end of the trail. He would handle the situation before she became emotional and the tears started.

"Sally, you and Moss and Carolyn will settle in at the boarding house."

"But where will you stay?"

"Out of sight, so I can keep an eye on you. Tongues wag. There's no need to rile Luke and tip our hand."

She didn't argue. Even if Luke didn't want her any longer, he'd not like her traveling with Rob. And they said Luke had already killed three men. He'd not hesitate to kill another. She couldn't bear for Rob to get shot.

"I'll come if you need me. Send Moss. He'll know where to find me." Rob headed for the other end of town.

Sally and Moss approached a large, white two-story house. The sign hanging over the front porch read *Jane Steeple Boarding.*

Moss knocked on the door. A thin, prim woman opened it.

"Ma'am, I was wonderin' if'n ye had rooms fer us." Moss gestured to Sally and Carolyn.

The woman gave them a critical glance. "Come in. Room and board are paid upfront and include breakfast and supper. Men lodge on the first floor, ladies on the second. No exceptions. I'll have no misbehaving under my roof. Is that clear?"

"Yes, ma'am." Moss patted his hat on his pant leg.

"Ladies' baths are extra. Men bathe down the street."

"Thank ye kindly. I could use me a bath."

"You'll not sleep on my sheets until you've had one. That goes for all of you."

Sally glanced down at her dress. She must smell as bad as Rob had when she first met him. Suddenly she felt filthy. She stood in silence, her cheeks burning.

"I'll not have bugs in the bedding. I keep a clean establishment."

"Yes, ma'am," Sally said.

The landlady looked Sally and Carolyn over then tossed her head. "Follow me."

She led them to the men's quarters first and pointed out the room to Moss.

"That'll do jus' fine," he said.

"Settle the bill, then I'll show the lady to her room. And you head on over to the bath house."

"Yes, ma'am." He counted out her fee.

Sally and Carolyn followed her up the stairs and down a long hall to a room at the end. Mrs. Steeple opened the door.

"This is fine," Sally said.

Carolyn started to walk in.

The woman laid a hand on her shoulder. "Just one minute, little missy. You may enter your room once you've had a bath."

Carolyn stared up at Mrs. Steeple in awe.

"Young ladies do not gape with their mouths open. It's impolite." Mrs. Steeple looked at Sally. "You are married."

"Yes, ma'am."

"I take it your husband will be joining you."

"I hope so, ma'am." Could the woman tell she was lying? Her heart raced.

"I'll not have men visiting. Your husband may meet you downstairs."

Sally nodded. After picking Carolyn up, she followed Mrs. Steeple down the stairs.

Carolyn snuggled against her shoulder.

Sally whispered, "It'll be all right, sunshine."

Moss waited below. He told Mrs. Steeple he would pay two more days in advance, but he didn't know how much longer they'd stay. Later that evening, Rob sent a note to Moss.

Luke had been seen at one of the card tables.

Sally paced on the porch after hearing the news. Her sudden energy had no outlet.

Moss noticed the landlady peering out the window. "Sally Mae, set down before you get Mrs. Steeple a goin'."

Sally sat and wrung her hands. "What should I do, Moss? How should I handle this?"

"Well, I been thinkin' on it. I figured I'd go an' tell Luke yer here an' lookin' forward to seein' 'im. I ken find out what kinda mood he's in, an' if'n he's ready to see ye."

"Yes, that's a good plan. How soon can you go?"

"I oughtn't ter get that woman riled." He nodded toward the window where a curtain moved. "I'll slip on over to the saloon later, while folks is in bed."

"But you'll come and wake me, when you know?"

"Sally, that ain't a good idea, me comin' to wake ye. That woman would as soon toss us out as look at us an' we done paid a'ready. I'll tell ye at breakfast."

"All right." Sally nodded. But she had no intention of waiting until breakfast. She'd stay up and watch for his return.

After dinner, Moss played checkers with a lodger while Carolyn played in the corner.

Sally chatted with the other woman until it was time to put Carolyn to bed.

As she climbed the stairs carrying Carolyn, Sally wondered about the strange house.

How different it was from Aunt Doe's. She doubted Aunt Doe would enjoy moving into town if these were the kind of neighbors she'd have.

When it grew dark enough for Moss to go unnoticed, he snuck out the window and headed for the saloon.

Though it'd been several years since he'd seen him, Moss recognized Luke at once.

Moss bellied up to the bar. "Whiskey."

Luke sat in the back corner eying two soiled doves as they walked past in their red gowns and purple feathers, flirting.

Moss could tell they knew Luke well.

He watched Luke long enough to know he held good cards and was in good spirits tonight.

One of the ladies sat next to Moss. "What's your pleasure?"

"Ma'am, ye ken tell the tall feller in the corner that I have a present waitin' fer him. Tell him I knowed him back when he traveled to Kansas."

Her eyes narrowed. "What kind of present?"

"Don't worry. I ain't packin'. It ain't that kinda present."

She agreed after he passed her a coin. She stood and walked over to Luke.

Luke's eyes hovered over her breasts as she bent down to whisper in his ear. Then his gaze lifted and flew directly to Moss.

Moss raised his glass and nodded.

Luke's eyes narrowed, but he nodded back and lifted his own glass. He returned to his card game while Moss waited.

Finally Luke won, swept his winnings into his hat and stood. His spurs clanked on the wooden floor as he strode over to Moss.

"Ozzie Moss. You've come a long way."

"Not so fer. Trailin' an' trackin's my life I reckon."

Luke's eyes narrowed. "You trailing or tracking this time?"

"Little o' both. But I ain't here fer the reward."

"Keep your voice down," Luke said in a low growl as he glanced at the bartender.

"I ain't here fer that. A woman asked me to find ye."

"That so?"

"Yep. Her feller done left her high an' dry."

"What was the lady's name?"

"Sally Mae. She's here in town an' wants ter know if'n her feller would pay her a visit."

Luke appeared stunned. "Sally. Here in town?"

"Yep."

"Why'd she go and do a damn fool thing like that?"

"Mebbe she didn't know ye was wanted fer murder."

"Shut up, you old fool. Let's go outside where we can talk."

They left the saloon, and Moss kept to the sidewalk, near the lamplight.

"Don't think you'll turn me in." Luke fingered his pistol.

"If'n I was a gonna turn ye in I'd a done it afore now, an' I wouldn't be such a damn fool as t' come an' tell ye about it."

"See that you keep your mouth shut."

"Ain't none of my business."

"And bringing Sally here? That's your business?"

"I give her my word. Didn't know ye was turned outlaw."

"Hell. No point in living a small man's life. This way I have plenty of money for whiskey and whatever else takes my fancy." He frowned. "So Sally wants to see me?"

"She's stayin' at Mrs. Steeple's. That woman don't even let husbands an' wives share a room but you ken visit in her parlor."

"I'm no parlor man."

Moss eyed the gun belt strapped to Luke's leg. "Ain't said ye was. Perhaps ye ken suggest a more fittin' meetin' place."

"Tell Sally I'll meet her tomorrow for a late supper. If she came all this way she must've missed me pretty bad. Or she wants Matthew back."

"All the way down it was Luke this an' Luke that. She wants to work things out." Moss nodded. "I ken watch the children fer ye. I ain't seen that boy in ages. Bet he's grown fast."

The plan was for Sally to act as if she wanted to reconcile with Luke. She'd keep Luke busy while Moss spirited the children away. And Rob would keep an eye on Sally to make sure nothing went wrong.

"Matthew's fine where he is." Luke's eyes narrowed again and a clever look crossed his face. "But I wouldn't disappoint a lady, especially such a pretty redhead. Tell her I'll meet her by the general store about seven."

Moss nodded. Luke hadn't asked once about Carolyn.

Soon after Moss climbed through the window, he heard a tap on it. "What in tarnation?"

Sally lifted her skirts to climb in the window.

Moss held up his hand. "Stay out there. Mrs. Steeple will have a fit if'n she catches ye."

Sally dropped her skirts and leaned in through the window. "Then tell me," she whispered. What did he say?"

"He's meetin' ye fer supper tomorrow night at seven."

Her eyes widened. "He was friendly?"

"Yep."

"And Matthew?"

"He said Matthew's fine. Now get back in yer room 'fore ye get us throwed out." Moss shook his head. "I'm getting' too old fer this."

Sally couldn't believe it. Luke wanted to meet her for dinner as if nothing had happened.

The liar. The thief.

She crept barefooted up the stairs. As she rounded the corner, she came upon Mrs. Steeple in a long flannel nightgown holding a lamp.

Sally stopped and her hand went to her throat.

"What is the meaning of this?" Mrs. Steeple eyed Sally's shoes in her hand and her eyebrows rose.

"I didn't want to disturb the boarders."

"The best way to avoid waking them is to stay in your own bed."

"I was visiting the outhouse."

"There is a chamber pot in your room."

"Yes, ma'am. I'll think of that next time."

"See that you do."

Sally walked to her room and opened the door. She felt Mrs. Steeple's eyes on her back as she entered. She closed the door, leaned against it and closed her eyes.

After tomorrow night she'd have Matthew.

She blew a breath out.

Soon it would all be over.

But now that it was near, her thoughts raced. She replayed all the things she wanted to say to Luke. All the speeches she'd practiced in silence over the long trail.

He wouldn't talk his way out of this one.

She'd wear the green dress and do her hair up. She'd show Luke she was a lady and one not to be messed with. He'd be so swept away by how she looked he wouldn't know his son was gone.

She'd trick the trickster.

Sally was in bed before she realized she didn't remember climbing into it. She pulled the covers up and lay watching the night sky through the window.

The next morning at breakfast she couldn't contain her excitement. Soon she'd have Matthew back. She hummed as she ladled gravy over Carolyn's biscuits.

The chatter at the breakfast table was lively. Mrs. Steeple entered and left the room many times bringing food from the kitchen. Her boarding house was full.

She frowned at Sally each time she passed.

After breakfast Moss said, "Sally Mae, keep away from that woman, she don't care fer ye none."

"Don't worry."

"I cain't hep it. There's plenty that can go wrong." Moss shook his head. "I been studyin' on this plan an' I don't like it, Sally."

"Our plan will work. It has to."

"Luke ain't agreed to let me watch Matthew. I got to find him an' steal him away an' that ken take some time since none of us knows where he is."

"I'll keep Luke busy long enough for you to grab Matthew. I'll do whatever it takes. If he doesn't let you watch the children then we'll know we have to go to our second plan. You'll have to go to his hideout and steal Matthew back."

"Remember to signal Rob if ye need hep. He'll be watchin' out fer ye."

She'd do anything to see both her children safe. Even have dinner with Luke. It was dangerous. She hoped Rob would pay Luke back in full for everything he'd done and then some.

Chapter Sixteen

Late in the afternoon, Sally and Carolyn went with Moss to check on the horses and to get away from the eagle eyes and ears of Mrs. Steeple.

"It ain't too late to change yer mind, Sally."

"No, we have to steal Matthew away. I just wish I knew someone who could watch Carolyn."

With Rob keeping an eye on her meeting with Luke and Moss heading to Luke's hideout to snatch Matthew, there was no one to stay behind at the boarding house with her little girl.

But she didn't want Carolyn anywhere near Luke.

"It ain't such a good plan."

Moss had been trying to talk her out of it all morning. Since meeting Luke he seemed to have lost his nerve.

"It will work, Moss. I've never done anything sneaky. Luke won't think me capable of it."

"Well, I ken put Carolyn to bed an jus' hope she stays asleep. But that means ye'll have to stretch out yer dinner as long as ye can to give me time to get the boy."

She hated the fact she'd have to pretend to want Luke back. She loathed him. And she'd never been a good liar.

But Luke was so self-involved, with any luck, he might not even notice.

"I'll do whatever I have to. Now I'd best start getting ready. If you'll keep Carolyn, I'd like to take a long bath."

She needed time to prepare for her role. To settle her nerves and think of how she'd handle Luke.

"Mama, you and me had a bath yesterday."

"I know, sunshine, but that was a fast one. Tonight I'm going to dinner with your Papa."

She and Carolyn had shared a bath to save money. Mrs. Steeple charged by the bath and by the time spent in the bath.

Carolyn danced around her. "Can I go, Mama? Can Baby Blue Bell come?"

"No, sunshine, not tonight. Your Papa and I have a lot to talk about."

"I'll keep Carolyn busy. Go on an' git fixed up."

"Mama," Carolyn tugged at Sally's dress as she turned to go.

Sally knelt. "Yes, sunshine?"

"Will you give Papa this for me?" She put her arms around Sally's neck and kissed her on the cheek.

Sally's eyes misted. "I'll tell Papa how much you've missed him."

Such love in her little girl's heart for a man who didn't deserve it.

"Come on now." Moss patted Carolyn's shoulder. "Let's go to the saddle shop an' watch the blacksmith."

As Sally walked back to the boardinghouse, a tangle of mixed feelings engulfed her. She'd have a long bath and hopefully that would be enough to sort things out.

At the boarding house, she requested a bath in Mrs. Steeple's fancy tub. "I'll pay extra for a long bath. My husband is coming to town and we're going out to supper."

The landlady pocketed the extra money for special soap then she left Sally alone to bathe in the large claw-footed tub.

Sally soaked and thought. She scrubbed her fingernails and rubbed at her elbows and knees until they were bright red.

When she was clean and thoroughly wrinkled from the water, she finally exited the tub and wrapped the dressing gown, another gift from Aunt Doe, around herself.

She went back to her room and lay on the bed to nap briefly while her hair dried.

She woke late then had to hurry to dress.

Sally held the green velvet dress up and looked into the mirror before slipping it on. Her hair had dried while she had slept and one side had more bounce than the other. She

228

twisted, twirled and curled until she'd created an unusual cascade of curls and ribbons, which came down to the top of her left shoulder, barely brushing it.

She looked in the mirror and pinched her cheeks. Luke had never seen her look this ladylike. She had to capture his attention for an entire evening, while keeping things from going too far.

Below, she heard the other boarders head to the parlor after finishing their supper.

It was time for her to go.

At the bottom of the stairs, Mrs. Steeple stood ready to pounce. She looked Sally up and down and sniffed. "Be in at a decent hour or the door will be locked. And no wild carryings on here in this establishment."

"Yes, ma'am." Sally went over to Carolyn and kissed her forehead. "Goodnight, sweetheart."

"She'll be fine," Moss said.

"Thank you, Moss, good night."

She hurried to the meeting place, slowing only when she saw that no one waited there.

Had she arrived early? No, she'd actually been running late. But then Luke had never been punctual.

She forced herself to stand quietly on the sidewalk though her nerves were a riot. The evening's darkness had moved in.

How long should she wait? Would she be safe here in her fine dress, alone?

Her hand went to her throat where the brooch normally resided. Touching bare skin, she shivered and glanced down at her cleavage.

This dress was too fine for Luke, too fancy.

Would he wonder where she had gotten it? That was something that hadn't occurred to her. He thought he'd left her with nothing. Certainly not enough money to purchase a dress like this.

What if she couldn't carry this off?

Fear gathered in her stomach.

The future loomed vague and dark again as shadows lengthened on the street.

Rob watched her from across the street where he stood in the narrow space between two buildings. Every muscle in his body was tensed as he watched Sally and waited for Luke.

Anger at Luke had driven him for so long it seemed a part of his nature. But tonight his anger multiplied as he watched Sally. His emotions were ready to blow.

She was so beautiful standing there alone and unprotected. Put there dangerously by Luke's choice of meeting place.

His hands fisted at his sides. He'd make sure she came to no harm. But watching her with his enemy would be one of the hardest things he'd ever done.

Sally looked at the ground, about to break into frustrated tears. Had Luke left town? Tricked her again?

He wasn't coming. This was another one of his tricks.

Her hair felt lopsided, and she felt discarded once again.

"Hello, Sally." Luke's familiar voice spoke behind her.

She inhaled a quick, sharp breath and turned.

He'd leaned against the building with his thumbs in his pockets. An air of dark isolation reeked about his tall figure.

It had been so long since she'd seen him that she'd forgotten what he really looked like. The picture in her mind didn't quite match.

When he stepped away from the building into the moonlight and stood before her, she was struck by how he'd changed.

He was still tall and lean and he hadn't lost the good looks he prided himself on. But she no longer saw him as the handsome man she'd married.

He was clothed in black, from head to toe and wore a silver buckle and spurs. The buckle had shiny silver initials LD on the black leather.

Lucky Draw.

She inhaled sharply.

So it was true.

He'd apparently embraced the outlaw image.

She'd hoped it was a mistake. That some other man had done those things and any day now the mistake would be cleared up, clearing away the danger to Matthew.

But his belt buckle gave truth to the rumors.

Now she stood before him, the man she'd thought was her husband, this outlaw. Her stomach clenched.

Matthew had been stolen by an outlaw. What had Luke taught him in the time they'd been gone?

Luke gave her a wide smile, his teeth strikingly white in his tanned face.

Nervously she moistened her dry lips.

He was an outlaw, and she no longer knew what to say or how to act around him.

When she spoke, her voice wavered. "I didn't think you were coming."

He drew his lips in thoughtfully then gave her a sly smile. "And after I invited you...*tsk, tsk*."

This was when he was most dangerous. When she couldn't gauge his mood. She smiled at him tentatively.

She had to keep him busy long enough for Moss to find Matthew and get her son to safety. "It's good to see you."

Because seeing you means I'll have my son back.

She had to twist the lies she spoke in her mind, to make her words believable.

He gave her a smooth smile. "It's good to see you too, Sally."

So he'd decided to be charming this evening. She exhaled. Good. That made her job easier.

He took her elbow and led her to the other end of the street. There was a restless energy about his movements, but she tried to keep pace with him.

"I've reserved a private room." His arm snaked around her waist as he led her down the street. "We'll dine in style tonight."

He led her into a saloon.

She heard the clink of silver tossed on the gaming tables and the maudlin laughter of a dancehall girl swinging past in the arms of a drunken man.

"Never mind the other patrons," Luke said soothingly into her ear. "We'll be undisturbed."

His voice at her ear made her want to jerk away. But she

couldn't. She had to stay in control.

Luke was in his element in a saloon. But she didn't like it. The men eyed her and the women seemed to know secrets she didn't.

He guided her through the back of the main room into a smaller room decorated with red and gold and mirrors. A lone table stood in the center covered with a white cloth, candles and a service for two.

"Oh my." He'd gone to a lot of trouble for this dinner. This wasn't what she'd expected.

Luke seated her and went to close the door. She watched him and wondered; could he really be hoping for reconciliation?

He sat across the table from her and reached for her glass, pouring wine into it.

"This will make up for the fine wedding night we never had," he said with a smile as he handed her the glass. He looked her over seductively before reaching for his glass.

You couldn't have a wedding night without a real wedding.

She bit the words back and fought to hide her feelings.

Luke was never this nice without having something up his sleeve. Could he honestly think she'd take him back? But that's what she wanted him to believe and it was working.

She'd never let him make a fool out of her again. This time she was in control.

Sally fell back into her old pattern of watching him silently under her eyelashes to see what he'd do next. This was what he would expect of her.

She had to act as if nothing had changed. As if all her actions centered on what he would do.

He'd never been predictable. She was afraid to mention Matthew's name. Luke's moods could turn quick. And she'd never liked being around him when he drank.

He lifted his glass. "To us."

"To us."

He tipped his glass to touch hers.

"Us" didn't exist for them. It never had.

But she had to keep him busy thinking otherwise.

She sipped the wine.

He smiled at her.

She forced a smile back, playing along and wondering how she would ever manage to eat with her stomach turning.

Dinner was served. Roast duck, fancy potatoes, carrots and fresh bread. The beautiful food tasted like sawdust in her mouth as nervousness made her mouth dry.

She had to take sips of wine just to get her food down.

Luke kept pouring more wine into her glass before it was even halfway gone.

Then he asked her to dance, and as Sally stood the room spun. The wine must have gone to her head.

Luke quickly moved to her side and slipped his arm around her. His touch made her feel sick but she didn't let on.

He led her out into the main room and requested a song from the piano player.

Then he swung her into the circle of his arms and began to dance. They hadn't danced together since the barn dance when he'd lost his temper. He still danced smoothly but he wouldn't sweep her off her feet this time. She wasn't naïve any more.

What she was was dizzy and flushed. The room seemed incredibly warm.

Another couple danced by, and the evening ladies watched them. The room spun. Her head spun.

She had to stop before she fell.

"I need to talk to you about Matthew," she said.

"I wondered how long it would take you to bring him up." He spun her around.

"How is he?"

"He's just fine and he's waiting to see you."

"I can't wait to see him. I've missed him."

"You'll see him soon. I'll take you upstairs in a little while." With another spin he was almost holding her up.

"Upstairs?"

"Yes. To see Matthew." He spoke slowly as he spun her around again and gave her a slow smile as she sank into his arms.

Matthew? Upstairs?

She frowned slightly before she could stop herself.

This was something they hadn't counted on.

How could Moss steal her boy away when he was right here under Luke's nose?

The plan had gone wrong, just as Moss said it would.

She was no longer in control. She couldn't even stay on her feet. If she could just think what to do next.

She was supposed to signal Rob to come to her rescue. But she couldn't do that now, with her son upstairs.

But she felt dizzy and her thoughts wouldn't focus. Something was terribly wrong. She needed to call Rob. But she couldn't remember the signal.

"Let's go see Matthew now, shall we?"

Yes. She needed to see Matthew.

Luke wrapped his arm around her, leading her up the stairs. Her limbs were slow and heavy and she was forced to lean on him to keep her balance, though she hated his touch.

Upstairs he opened the door to a room where a fireplace blazed. The room was too hot and she felt faint. "Where is Matthew?"

He wasn't there.

Luke closed and locked the door.

"You didn't honestly think I'd keep him here in this room? When his Ma and Pa planned to put their marriage back together?"

He released her and she sank onto the bed, her knees weak as a roaring sound filled her ears.

"What's wrong, my dear?"

Something was wrong.

She had to get away. But the room spun.

He came up behind her and fastened something heavy around her neck.

Sally glanced down.

A ruby necklace.

He kissed the back of her neck and ran one finger down her cleavage. "A beautiful woman deserves a fine bobble every now and then. Especially when her neck is as lovely as yours."

She had to get out of this room.

"It goes well with your dress." His eyes narrowed. "This very expensive green dress. Now how did you come upon that, I wonder? I didn't buy it for you."

She knew better than to respond.

He forced her up and over to stand in front of the mirror, his hands tight as iron on her arms.

"Look at how it displays your breasts so well." He released her and she swayed.

"But not well enough." He grasped the gown and ripped it, splitting it down the middle where it hung on her hips.

She gasped and clutched her hands over her breasts to cover them as the ruby swung between her breasts, blood red next to her white skin.

He'd always wanted to make love immediately after giving her a gift. He called it payment rendered.

She stumbled backward and stepped on the hem but his hands circled her waist and gripped her tight.

"You're mine, remember? Mine to do with as I please. Wife." His words mocked her, that smooth voice of his dangerous as a rattler ready to strike.

She had to get away.

"Such beautiful red hair." He yanked the ribbons out of her hair, bringing tears to her eyes. "But you know better than to wear it up." He wrapped one hand around her hair and yanked her head backward as he watched her expression in the mirror. "I prefer it down."

Tears of frustration, pain and anger welled in her eyes and poured down her cheeks.

"Let me go."

He froze, his eyes widening in pleasure. It had been years since she'd told him no. It only served to fuel his urges.

Fear and anger mixed with the pain in her head as the room spun. This was a nightmare. No one could save her.

There was no escape.

But if she held him off long enough, Moss would save Matthew.

Still yanking her hair, his other hand gripped her by the neck, under her chin. "Drop your hands."

She felt ill. This was worse than what she'd imagined.

The room grew increasingly warm as he cut off her air.

"Do it."

She dropped her hands to her sides as he watched her in the mirror.

"Unresponsive as ever." He laughed and released her neck. "Some things never change."

She watched him in the mirror without speaking, trying to gather her fuzzy thoughts.

Loathing was all she felt for him. Loathing and fear. She wanted to kill him for all he'd done to her and to her children.

But her body wouldn't respond.

He was a monster.

She had to stretch the evening out. "I need to sit down, it's so warm."

"Not so fast." He released her hair, turning her around. "I'm not ready for that yet. One more dance will do it, I think." He grasped her in a dance grip and spun her around the room.

It only took two spins.

"Stop."

"Of course, my dear." He threw her onto the bed and pulled out a knife. "That's what you get for wearing such a heavy gown." He cut the rest of the dress away. "Velvet holds heat you know."

No, she didn't know. She'd never owned a velvet gown before. And what did he know and care about gowns?

He was always throwing her off balance, changing the subject, confusing her mind.

"Luke, please, we need to talk."

"No. The last thing we need to do is talk."

He kissed her hard on the lips, bruising them as his weight crushed her.

She struggled to push him away.

His arms tightened.

"I didn't come here to talk." His face hovered inches from hers, his gaze drilled into her. "I've been a long time without a woman," he growled. His knee pressed between her legs. "And I'm not waiting any longer for my own wife to give me what's due."

"I'm not your wife. I heard about your trick and the other women too. You have no right to Matthew or Carolyn."

He slapped her face hard.

"I say you're mine and I'll take you whenever I want." He grabbed her by the throat. "And I want it now."

She gasped for air and clawed at his hands but he was too strong. He pinned her with one hand and reached below to pull her underclothes down.

Oh, God no. Not again.

She couldn't breathe. She raked her nails across his face and saw the anger in his eyes turn to deadly rage.

He fought to enter her and she fought to keep him out. As he cut off her air again the room began to go dark.

Someone knocked on the door.

"Who is it?" Luke growled, releasing her.

She gasped for air, her hands rising to her throat.

"Jethro."

Luke shoved Sally down before rising.

"Don't move," he growled.

He went to the door and opened it a crack.

Gasping for air, she slid off the bed and backed into the corner. Frantically her gaze searched the room for a weapon. Where was Rob? Why hadn't he saved her?

She was on her own.

Luke's back was tense with rage.

Her heart pounded. He'd turn back around any minute and finish what he started.

"Will said to tell you to get on back right away," a man's voice said.

"Ten more minutes."

He slammed the door, locked it and crossed the room with fast and furious strides.

"Get back on the bed, woman," he growled.

"No. You're never touching me again."

"I'll touch you any damn time I please."

"Not this time."

Rob watched the doors of the back room as he played cards. He'd seen Sally and Luke enter the back room, but he'd kept his hat low so Luke wouldn't recognize him if he came out.

Each time the door opened, Rob's eyes strained to see Sally. That is, until they came out and danced.

Then a small doubt crept into his mind over Sally.

What if she were as fickle as May Belle?

Luke had stolen the girl of his heart once before.

He kept telling himself she was just playing along until Moss took Matthew to safety.

But then she'd gone upstairs with Luke without even attempting to slow him down as he swept her up the stairs.

In fact she leaned against Luke like a woman in love.

Rob felt gut-punched.

They'd reconciled.

He folded his cards, left the pot on the table, and grunted "Good night" to the other card players.

Thoughts of Sally and Luke together churned in his mind, reminding him of the way May Belle used to dance with the devil.

That's just what Luke was. A devil.

Sally had fallen for his lies again.

Rob had promised to protect her from Luke, but not from herself.

She was just another fickle woman.

He'd been a fool to fall in love with her.

Rob pushed through the swinging doors of the saloon.

He'd find Moss and warn him. Then Luke would pay.

The deed had been postponed long enough.

Chapter Seventeen

What was she doing on the floor? Where was she?

In a rush it all came back to her.

Thank God she'd survived.

She hadn't been raped, but he'd come close.

His friend had been impatient and that had saved her. That and the way she'd fought.

Sally sat up and using the dresser, pulled herself to her feet. Her body ached. Her head pounded.

The sun through the curtains was just beginning to come up. Her heart sank. She'd spent the whole night here.

What had happened to Rob? He hadn't charged in.

But then she hadn't signaled him either.

If the man who'd knocked on the door hadn't returned, it would have been much worse.

She was fairly certain Luke would have killed her though she'd fought with every ounce of her being. She would never cower from him again. Never.

But the question remained. Had Moss found Matthew in time? Was Matthew safe?

She'd thought she could trust Rob to save her, but she'd been wrong.

Men. They were all unreliable.

She would never count on one again. Especially not a man with his own agenda.

If Moss had found Matthew, he would have sent word to Rob and found a way to see that she was told so she could get away from Luke. She had to get Matthew. Now. Before Luke did something worse. Now she'd made him angry and he was capable of anything. If she wanted her son, she'd just have to take him.

Sally stepped in front of the mirror and gasped. One side of her face was black and blue. She gingerly placed her fingertips on her swollen and split lip.

Oh God help me.

She hugged her arms around herself. He'd never hurt her this bad where others could see the marks. She'd make a spectacle going down the street. And her beautiful dress was ruined. If only her shawl was still downstairs where she'd left it. She had to cover herself somehow.

What if Luke had returned and taken his anger out on Matthew?

Panic like she'd never known before welled in her throat and her stomach heaved. She lost the contents of her dinner on the floor, dropped to her knees and rocked back and forth, hugging herself as tears streamed down her face.

Oh God. Oh God. Oh God.

What would she do? Luke was so strong and if he still had Matthew...

She breathed in shallow, quick gasps. She was going to be sick again.

Later, after she'd cleaned herself up, she looked in the mirror once more.

The stone hanging from the necklace wasn't a ruby but a cheap piece of glass. How could she have thought it was anything else? The necklace looked even cheaper beside the green velvet dress that had been a gift of love from Aunt Doe.

Sally wrapped a blanket around herself and went downstairs to collect her shawl. It was still there in the corner. No one had wanted the threadbare thing and for that she was glad.

The bartender watched her as she passed. She covered her face with her shawl to keep the bruises from showing and hurried out of the building.

Her mind returned to last night. It was just like Luke to take what he wanted from her and then leave her in a defenseless position. He hadn't locked the door behind him. Her mind filled with sour thoughts of all the things that could have happened to her.

He treated her this way because he did not care. His words of love when they had first met were just that. Words. A man who loved a woman would care about what happened to her. Even if he had to ride off and leave her. Luke had never cared for her in that way. She'd just been too young and naïve to understand that a man like that only cared for himself.

She was fortunate something worse hadn't happened to her.

When she reached the boardinghouse, Moss was pacing on the porch. Carolyn was with him but not Matthew. He didn't look at her as he spoke, his agitation too great. "It must've gone well, since ye was out all night."

"No. It did not go well. We have to find Matthew. Have you seen Rob?"

"I ain't seen him since he told me ye made up with Luke."

"Made up with Luke?"

So that's how it had looked to Rob. No wonder he hadn't come to her rescue.

"We didn't make up. It's a long story, and I don't have time to tell you right now."

Moss grunted then stopped pacing as he looked at her for the first time. "Sally Mae."

His shock quickly turned to anger. "If Rob don't kill him, I will."

"Rob won't do anything. Just like last night. He doesn't care about me. He has his own reasons for wanting Luke dead."

"Don't be too dad-blamed sure."

"Did you find any trace of Matthew?"

"Found him with Luke's gang. There's three of 'em not counting Luke. Regular den of outlaws. One man ain't enough to take 'em on. Not if ye want yer boy back safe."

"You told me the plan wouldn't work. I should've listened. Now he knows we're here and we won't take him by surprise."

"What do ye aim to do now?"

"First I need a bath and a change of clothes. Can you buy me a dress, Moss? I'll give you my size. Anything will do. I don't care what it looks like. But I can't go around like this."

"No, I reckon ye cain't." He stomped his foot. "Dagnabbit. Rob shoulda kept a better eye on ye."

"We can't count on him." She changed the subject, not wanting to think about Rob. "Help me sneak past Mrs. Steeple and I'll wait in my room until you bring the dress." She frowned. "Where's Carolyn?"

"Takin' a nap in yer room."

Sally breathed a sigh of relief.

At least Carolyn was safe.

While she was waiting for Moss to return, Sally sat on the bed watching her daughter sleep.

Carolyn rolled over and opened her eyes. "Mama, Papa hurt you."

Sally closed her eyes. How many times had her daughter seen her father raise his fists to her? "Yes. But he'll never do it again."

Carolyn's small hand crept into hers. "I don't want to live with Papa."

Rob trailed Luke to the edge of town. Luke appeared nervous so he stayed back. He wasn't about to give his position away by riding out in the open where a lone rider could be seen for miles.

Luke's pattern was consistent even though it appeared random to anyone who hadn't followed him as long as Rob had.

Luke couldn't stay away from cards, whiskey or women. But this time he seemed to be holding back. Something was keeping him in check.

He'd seen Luke and another man in a sombrero eying the bank, while buying supplies. Odds were they planned to rob the bank after the shipment of gold came in. Then they'd be on the run.

Rob had to strike before that happened.

But he'd see the boy safe first like he'd promised. He kept his promises even to women he couldn't trust. His biggest worry now was that Sally had told Luke that Rob was coming for him. That was just the sort of foolish thing a woman in love would do.

But he was the biggest fool of all for falling for her.

Luke arrived back at the hangout where his three partners had holed up.

It was time his youngest son knew how to take care of himself. Time he acted like a Wheeler. The boy had turned whiney. He kept asking when they'd go back for Mama.

He had to learn you could never trust a woman. Use them before they use you was Luke's rule. It had never failed him.

Luke rode up to the mud hut and shouted out, "It's Luke."

"You alone?"

"Yeah."

"You ain't been followed?"

"No."

The door cracked open. A rough, unshaven face looked out.

"You said the boy wouldn't be no trouble."

Luke went inside.

"I'm hungry, Pa." Matthew's stomach growled as he whined.

"Hush up. I'll find you something." Luke nosed around. He spooned the beans from last night's supper into a tortilla, rolled it then handed it to Matthew.

From under his sombrero, Will spat. "We didn't ask for another mouth to feed."

"He don't eat much." Luke rolled a tortilla for himself and took a bite.

Matthew watched how his Papa ate and copied him. He understood he was there to learn how to be a man. He swallowed the cold beans even though they made him want to gag and tried to make his Papa proud. Except Papa had said not to call him Papa no more 'cause that was a little boy's word. Now he was to say Pa. He was trying to remember all the things his Pa had told him since they left home, but it was hard. He mostly tried not to talk much and said, "Yes, sir."

He watched Luke eat. His Pa had left him alone all evening with these bad men. He didn't know why Pa called them friends.

"Pa." The word felt odd in his mouth. "When am I going to see Mama again?"

"Damn it, son, we ain't going back. Now hush your mouth."

Matthew sniffled but didn't cry. He knew better. He didn't want to give his Pa any reason to hit him.

But Pa had said they weren't going back. Before now he'd always said they weren't going back *today*. Had something happened to Mama?

The man watching out the window said, "What did you bring him for? He'll just get in the way."

"No, he won't. I'll see that he don't."

"You can't take him back. He knows where we are, and he'd bring us trouble."

"No chance of me taking him back."

Matthew choked on his breakfast. He'd never see Mama again. Would she come looking for him? Could she find him here? He doubted it. Suddenly, Matthew was no longer hungry.

Sally wondered what Rob would do.

He'd said he'd help her find Matthew and make sure he was safe. But he hadn't promised anything more.

But after last night she didn't expect anything from him. Moss would help until they were safely away from Luke.

She fastened the new gown Moss had bought her. It was a high-necked plain dress with light blue flowers on a tan background. For an old bachelor, he'd done well. But he wouldn't let her pay him back.

"Least I ken do after lettin' ye down last night. Now I'm goin' to see if I can find Rob."

Sally brooded as she paced in her room.

He'd probably taken up with a saloon woman. That's why Moss couldn't find him. The more she paced, the angrier she became.

Luke ruined everything. The liar. The thief.

He wouldn't keep Matthew from her.

A cold knot formed in her stomach. She knocked the contents of the dressing table onto the floor. Her anger and the fear she might never see Matthew again knotted inside her and made her want to throw things. She wanted to break something.

She eyed the necklace Luke had given her.

Grabbing it, she yanked on the chain and it broke, rolling the fake ruby across the floor.

Mrs. Steeple knocked on the door. "What's going on in there?"

Sally opened the door. "Nothing. I knocked something over." She kept her tone civil in spite of her anger and turned her head to keep the bruises on her face hidden.

She didn't need trouble.

It was too late.

Mrs. Steeple stepped inside. "I told you before. This is a respectable house." She gave Sally a look of disdain. "I should have known you weren't married." She inhaled with a hiss and drew herself up to her full height. "I want you out."

"I have to wait for Ozzie Moss. And we don't have anywhere else to go."

Mrs. Steeple barely glanced at Carolyn who sat wide-eyed on the bed with her arms wrapped around the dolly. "I wouldn't have rented you a room if I'd thought you were anything but a respectable mother." She gave Sally a keen look. "There are other places in town for your sort. I want you out now. And your gentleman friend too. I'll give you five minutes to collect your things."

Sally's blood pounded as her face grew hot with humiliation.

Mrs. Steeple slammed the door and went back downstairs.

Where would they go?

Sally sagged against the door, looked at the broken necklace on the floor and gave a choked laugh. Just like Luke, the stone wasn't genuine.

He'd set her up. And she suspected he'd drugged her wine.

She seethed with mounting rage.

Who did he think he was?

He'd never given her anything of lasting value other than the children. Everything about him was fake.

She closed her eyes. No. He'd taken back all the jewelry he'd bought her and then sold it again.

Sally had given until she could give no more, but all he did was take. And now he'd taken away a beautiful thing that had grown between her and Rob.

She wept.

She'd probably lost Rob forever.

Moss would find him. If only he'd keep his promise to make sure Matthew was safe. That would have to be enough. She couldn't think of herself now. She couldn't think of how her heart was breaking.

She gathered their belongings and Moss's, then she and Carolyn headed for the livery stable. They'd wait with the horses where Moss could find them.

He wasn't going to be happy about losing rooms they'd already paid for.

Moss was in the saloon speaking to a dancehall girl when Rob approached and motioned for him to come outside. Rob pulled Moss around the corner of the building into the alley. "You shouldn't be asking about me. If Luke knows I'm in town he'll be on guard. He might take off again."

"I had to find ye. Sally needs yer hep. I know how it looked." Moss squinted at him. "But things ain't always what they seem."

Rob snorted. "That's an understatement."

"I thought mebbe ye'd light out after ye seen them two together last night. Why did ye stay?"

"I gave my word. I'll see nothing happens to the boy. And I still have a score to settle with Luke. But Sally doesn't need my help. I saw her with Luke. Looked like a friendly meeting to me. She's still in love with him."

"No, it ain't what it looked like. She ain't gone back to him. If ye'd take one look at her, ye'd know."

"What do you mean?"

"He 'bout beat her to a pulp."

Rob's whole body seethed with rage. He knew where to find Luke.

I'll kill the son of a bitch.

"We got to get Matthew away from here afore somethin' worse happens."

"Luke is holed up out of town with his gang. He leaves Matthew there when he rides into town. We can't just go riding in or the boy could get hurt."

"I shore don't want the little feller hurt. What's yer plan?"

"Wait for Luke to make a move."

"Sally ain't gonna like that."

"No, I'm sure she won't. But it's no good involving the sheriff. No lawman will interfere with a man who wants his son. And if she tells him bank robbers are in town, they'll send out a posse and Matthew could get killed."

"She ain't gonna sit around and do nothin'. I cain't tell ye what she's likely to do."

"Tell her not to do anything but wait. Tell her you met with me, and I've given my word to bring her boy back safe."

Moss didn't hesitate. "It's dangerous. Luke's quick." He frowned and fingered his beard. "What ken I do to hep?"

"Keep an eye on Sally and Carolyn. Keep them safe and out of the way." Rob raised an eyebrow. "With Sally that may be asking a lot."

Moss put his hand on Rob's shoulder. "Be careful now, son. I wouldn't want nothin' ter happen to ye."

Rob nodded. "You, too, old timer. I know a ranch where a lonely widow wouldn't mind your company."

They shook hands and Rob walked away.

Moss found Sally in the stable.

"Sally Mae, what are ye doin' here?"

Sally looked past Moss, expecting Rob.

"You didn't find him," she said flatly.

"Yes, ma'am, I did."

"But he won't come."

"No, he ain't comin'."

Her heart fell.

"But he's goin' after the boy."

She felt a moment of joy and her hands flew to her bruised mouth. "Oh, Moss."

"He said ye was to wait an' take care o' Carolyn an' he'd make sure Matthew was all right."

"What is he going to do?"

"I ain't sure, exactly."

"But he may need our help."

"He don't want our hep. An' in case you was thinkin' of getting' the sheriff, Rob wanted me to tell you the law ain't no hep in cases like this 'un."

"But Aunt Doe said Luke has no legal right to him."

"We ain't in no court of law an' ye'll never get Luke into one except to hang."

"What does Luke plan to do with Matthew? Why does he want him?" A faint thread of hysteria threatened to take over as panic rose in her again.

"I don't rightly know. But don't ye worry none. Rob's a good man."

A war of emotions raged within Sally.

Matthew had to be safe.

Everything rode on Rob's success.

But Rob could be killed. Luke was already wanted for murder.

She felt ill at the thought of harm coming to Rob.

Luke was a brute and a killer.

What would he do once he found out Rob had come for Matthew?

Chapter Eighteen

Luke was teaching Matthew the various parts of a gun, when Jethro came back with three chickens hanging from his saddle.

"Where'd you get them?" Luke asked.

Jethro grinned without answering then tossed the reins to him and pushed open the door.

"Hell, yes, boys we've got us a feast." Will clapped Jethro on the back. "Where'd you find them?"

Jethro's grin lit up his whole face.

"That *señorita* of yours is back, ain't she?" Will asked.

Jethro nodded, still grinning.

Will's eyes narrowed. "Did you check on the bank like I told you?"

"Yep."

"Any changes?"

"Nope."

"All right. Nick, you keep watch next. We can't have Jethro running off and missing the stage because of his woman." Will spat. "Hell, women, children and more women. If I got to carry off this job on my own then I ain't splitting' the gold. You understand?"

"Yep," Jethro said.

"It was bad enough Lucky wantin' to bring along Lou Pearl. Good thing I came along when I did. A woman with big bosoms like that's fine for the evening, but hell you can't spend all your time with her."

'Don't know why not," Luke said.

"Hell, you were so drunk you didn't even know what day it was. I'd been lookin' for you for two days. Hell, we're lucky you didn't tell everyone our plan. Now I don't blame you for havin' the woman, but you got to stick to business on a job." He looked over to where Matthew stood against the wall taking it all in. "Lucky, put that boy to work plucking them chickens."

Luke stretched. "Sure, Will. Ain't I always paid my way?"

Will nodded.

Luke picked up the chickens. "Come on, son, I'll show you how to cook these scrawny yard birds."

"Pa?"

"What."

"Are we going to eat all them chickens?"

Luke laughed. "Hell, yes! This ain't your Mama's kitchen where it's 'no, we got to save this to make it last'. Here, when we get a lucky strike we ride it 'til it plays itself out. You got to live big and think big, boy."

Matthew watched him but didn't speak.

Luke plucked the first chicken, showing him how to do it. Feathers blew in the wind.

He handed one to Matthew. "Get started."

When Matthew finished, Luke got out his Bowie knife and prepared them for cooking.

Matthew felt sick at the way his Pa cut the chicken parts off. Like he enjoyed it and blood was everywhere.

"You squeamish, boy?"

"No, sir."

After all the chickens were roasting on a spit over the fire, his Pa walked over to his saddlebags and removed two bottles of whiskey.

"Jethro ain't the only one with bounty to share," he said.

"You been holdin' out on us?" Will said.

"Naw, just waiting' to see if you'd accept the boy first."

"Long as you keep him out of the way." Will scowled. "But if he ruins this job, all the whiskey in Texas ain't going to make it right."

Luke set one bottle on the table and scooted it over to him. "I told you. He won't get in the way. He's my blood. He ain't a problem."

Will grasped the bottle with one hand then lifted it to his lips. "See that he ain't."

When the chickens were ready, the men ate with their fingers, wiping their greasy hands on their pants.

Matthew copied them.

"See?" Luke grinned and ruffled his hair. "Just like his Pa."

He took out a deck of cards and tapped it on the table. "Anyone up for a game?"

Matthew watched as the men pushed the food to the side and set up the table.

His Pa wiped the table off with a rag and water. He wouldn't allow his cards to get dirty.

Matthew could see the men took cards more seriously than supper. He sorted his rock collection off in the corner while he watched them.

They played for a long time until it'd been dark for a while.

Matthew didn't have bedtime any more but he was tired. And this was when he got homesick the most. He missed Mama telling him goodnight and giving him a squeeze and a kiss on the top of his head.

The men were drunk and paid no attention to him.

He slipped out the door, walked around behind the hideout and looked out into the darkness. How far was it back to where his mama was? Was she looking for him right now?

He missed her and Carolyn. A tear formed in the corner of his eye but he brushed it away with the back of his hand. He felt all alone out here.

But he wasn't alone. Something moved behind a nearby bush.

Matthew stepped forward to see what it was. A tail stuck out of the bush as the animal backed up. Afraid he'd scare it away, Matthew slowly backed up a few feet then stood still and tried to breathe quietly.

Soon a long, thin nose emerged from the other side of the bush, sniffing cautiously. It was the mangiest looking dog Matthew had ever seen.

Its eyes glowed in the night as it watched Matthew.

Slowly a thin paw came forward. Then another cautiously,

one after the other until the animal stood outlined in gray against the snow.

Matthew sucked in a quick breath, afraid to make a noise.

The animal was skeletal thin and covered with mangy fur. Its tail sagged down as it crept closer, still watching Matthew. It looked hungry. Then Matthew remembered the uneaten chicken. He moved slowly away, back around the corner of the building, hoping the animal would still be there when he got back. He slipped inside as quietly as he'd slipped out. The men paid no attention to him. His father dozed in a chair, empty bottle in his hand.

Matthew picked up a piece of the chicken and skipped back out. He moved slowly and quietly and peered into the dark night.

It had moved. When it saw Matthew, it backed into the bush again, where it eyed him.

Matthew held out the chicken and moved slowly forward.

"I know you're hungry. Come on, I won't hurt you."

The animal put a paw forward.

"That's it. Come on." He tore off a piece and threw it on the ground between them. "See, it's good."

The animal darted forward just enough to take a bite of the chicken, ate it quickly and stood eyeing Matthew, who held the rest of the chicken out.

Inside, Will kicked Luke's chair to wake him. "If you can't keep an eye on that boy, you'll have to leave. I ain't hanging for no boy."

"Wuh?" Luke sat up. "Where is he?"

"Ain't my job to watch him."

"Oh, hell." Luke grabbed his gun. "How long has he been gone?"

The other men shrugged.

Luke walked around the building just as the coyote drew near enough to Matthew to almost take the outreached chicken.

Matthew watched him, thinking, *yes, that's it, come on*. He hardly dared breathe.

Crack! The animal yelped and jumped into the air, then fell to the ground. Blood dripped from a dark hole in his fur. Its eyes still gazed at Matthew.

Matthew's hand dropped, still holding the chicken. He wanted to cry.

Pa had killed the dog just as they were making friends.

He grabbed Matthew by the shoulders and shook him.

"What's wrong with you, boy? Didn't your mama teach you about coyotes?" He let loose of Matthew's shoulders and shouldered his rifle.

"It was hungry, Pa."

"They're no good and you can't tame them. He would've eaten you next."

Matthew followed his Pa back inside. He'd thought the animal was trying to tell him something. He'd always wanted a dog. He didn't know it was a mean coyote.

They entered the cabin to pointed gun barrels.

"You're lucky we ain't shot you," Will said. "What was that shot I heard?"

"Coyote."

Will looked at Matthew. "That'll teach you to go sneakin' around outside. Stick with your Pa."

Matthew nodded. He followed his father over to the pallet on the floor where they slept.

His Pa pointed to it. "Time for you to go to bed."

Pa lay down next to him on the pallet, pushed his hat over his eyes and was soon snoring.

Matthew pretended to sleep so the other men wouldn't get mad at him. They got mad easy. His Pa was mad all the time too. Matthew couldn't do anything the way Pa wanted him to.

I got to work hard at bein' a man.

But he was sad and homesick and he didn't know how to please his Pa.

Nick had been sent to watch the bank. He rode back to the hideout to report the gold shipment had arrived.

They planned to wait until just before the bank closed, when the gold had been counted and tucked away in the safe and the bank employees were leaving for the evening.

Matthew sat in the corner, listening and trying not to worry about the bad men his father called friends. They scared him.

And he didn't want to go rob the bank.

He handled his lasso, twisting it around and around in his hands, trying not to think about it.

Will reached over and snatched it from him. "Cut it out."

Matthew's heart hammered. He froze, unsure of what he'd done wrong.

"What's the problem, Will?" Luke asked.

"Damn thing looks like a hangman's noose."

"Hell, they'd need a bigger rope than that to hang your fat head."

Will cocked his pistol and the click made Matthew jump.

"I ain't fixin' to hang no time soon," Will said.

"Neither am I." Pa got out his deck of cards, smiling. "Relax. Everyone's nervous."

"Keep that kid out of my way. I told you, I ain't hangin' for no one, not you and not that kid," Will said.

"I understand." Pa nodded.

Will grunted.

Pa tapped the cards on the table. "A quick game will keep our minds off things."

Jethro and Nick were willing.

"We ain't got time for that," Will said. "Keep your minds on the job. Nick, get the horses ready and don't forget the dynamite."

Nick put on his hat and stepped outside.

Matthew had noticed Nick didn't talk much, but spent a lot of time cleaning his gun and spinning the cylinder like a toy.

Pa put the cards in his pocket. He looked at Matthew as if he'd never seen him before, then walked over and sat next to him.

"Son, I'm going to teach you how to deal cards. Something my Daddy taught me."

He set up a barrel to use as a table.

Pa had never played games with him before.

Excited, Matthew pulled up a chair.

Pa's hands flew as he shuffled.

Matthew watched in awe. Then Pa handed the cards to him. His hands wrestled to shuffle the cards as his Pa watched.

Pa thumped the flat top of the barrel with his thumb and scowled. "Not like that."

Nervously Matthew tried again and dropped some cards.

"Be better off teaching the boy to shoot," Jethro said.

"I started to then I remembered I didn't have an extra gun."

"Don't waste the bullets," Will said.

Nick came back in.

"You ready?" Will asked.

Nick nodded, then the men stood.

Matthew looked at Pa to see what he should do.

"Come on," Pa said.

Matthew followed them out to the horses. They mounted and he sat with Pa on the big black horse.

They were going to rob the bank.

The bad men didn't speak as they rode toward town, and Matthew was afraid to talk to Pa. He had that look again.

Rob watched the bank and wondered when they'd hit it. He'd given Moss strict instructions to keep Sally and Carolyn off the street after noon.

He didn't know how the old man would keep Sally away. She could be stubborn. But it was partly her stubborn determination that had brought her this far.

His thoughts came to a halt when he saw the riders coming into town. A small boy sat on the horse in front of Luke.

Rob slipped inside the building and watched through the window.

"Something I can help you with?" the storekeeper asked.

"No. Just staying out of trouble."

"Trouble?" The shopkeeper stepped to the window and looked out. "I see what you mean."

The air crackled with tension. It would come to a head now. Rob was ready.

Sally followed Moss.

He was up to something.

She couldn't stand by hoping the men would take care of

things. Hoping Matthew would be all right. She couldn't stand by doing nothing.

Moss should've realized the absolute worst way to make sure Sally stayed in the room was to vehemently object to her leaving.

She would make sure he didn't know she was behind him.

Sally stopped behind a lady on the street who was staying at the boarding house. "Please take my little girl inside. There's going to be a shootout."

"Oh! Of course." She took Carolyn's hand and stepped inside the newspaper office.

Sally hurried after Moss.

Rob watched as Luke's gang rode up to the bank and stopped just outside the door with pistols drawn.

They moved quickly, glancing all around. Luke placed one hand on Matthew's shoulder and pushed him forward as they disappeared quickly into the bank.

"That man has a small boy with him," the shopkeeper said as he reached for his rifle.

"He sure as hell does." Rage filled Rob.

Luke was using his own son as a shield.

The boy could be killed.

Luke pushed Matthew to the side once they entered the bank.

Nick covered the door.

Jethro pointed his gun at the teller and the bank president. "Get your hands up." He ground the words out between his teeth. "Get over in the corner and don't move."

The bank employees raised their hands and moved to where he'd gestured.

Will set the saddlebags on the ground. He unloaded the dynamite and wired it to the safe. "Ten-second fuse. Get ready, I'm going to light it."

Luke spoke to Matthew. "Get down and cover your ears."

Will lit the fuse.

They ducked and waited for it to blow.

Even with his ears covered, Matthew jumped as the blast from the dynamite rocked the bank.

Smoke filled the room.

"Everything's going according to plan." Will sounded pleased.

The bad men grinned at each other.

"On second thought, Lucky, that was pure genius, bringing your boy," Will said. "The sheriff ain't likely to shoot a boy." There was a cold edge to his voice.

Matthew's knees began to shake.

"Maybe we should all get ourselves a boy," Will sneered.

Matthew was glad the men weren't mad at his Pa anymore. But he felt scared, and he wondered what they'd do next.

Pa and Will quickly filled the saddlebags with gold. Will threw a saddlebag over one shoulder. "Let's go," he said, "you know what to do."

Jethro turned and pointed his gun at the teller and the bank president.

"No. Please don't shoot," the bank president said.

Jethro cocked the hammer and fired.

The man slumped to the floor. The teller died next.

Matthew felt sick to his stomach. Then he chanced a look into Jethro's cold eyes and fear swept over him completely.

The gang headed toward the door.

"You go on out first and keep him in front of you," Will instructed Luke. His voice was stern with no vestige of sympathy.

"Go on, son," Pa said in a hard voice as he nudged Matthew's back with his gun.

Matthew didn't want to move. He wanted to hide somewhere far away from the bad men and his Pa.

But his Pa pushed against his back harder.

Matthew slowly pushed the door open and walked out, Pa right behind him.

A shot buzzed past Matthew's head.

When the sheriff heard the explosion, he and his deputy came running with their guns out, ready for a fight.

But when he saw the boy he called a ceasefire.

Luke's gang had fired wildly in every direction then backed into the bank again, where they crouched down like animals.

"Let the boy go and come out with your hands up," the sheriff called.

"Like hell!" Will answered. His voice had hardened.

"He ain't going to shoot us with Matthew here," Pa said.

Matthew wasn't so sure. Sometimes Pa was wrong.

"Didn't stop him the first time," Will said. He stood just inside the door reloading. "Go on and try it again. We ain't named you Lucky Draw for nothing. Maybe it'll work this time."

Pa again pushed Matthew ahead of him through the doorway.

Matthew trembled with fear. He scraped one foot slowly in front of the other, feeling Pa's hand on his shoulder, the fingers like long claws digging into his soft flesh.

"Move, son. Move."

Matthew couldn't.

"Keep moving," Pa said, his voice cold and disapproving as his fingers dug deeper.

Brandishing their pistols, Will and the others followed Luke out the door, riding his good luck.

The sheriff fired another shot, this time in the air.

Sally heard the shots and ran toward the sound.

Seeing Matthew and Luke, she froze. She couldn't breathe. Time stood still.

"That's far enough," the sheriff commanded. "Now let the boy go."

Will pushed the muzzle of his pistol against Matthew's head. "I'll let him go when we get to the edge of town if no one follows."

"No."

Positioned inside the doorway of the store facing the bank, Rob had a good shot at Luke, if only Matthew would break away. He doubted Luke or the sheriff would shoot the boy.

But how could he be sure?

Sweat formed on Rob's forehead. He eased off the trigger a hair. He'd have to wait.

Moss had a good position in the alley to shoot the big man,

but Matthew was too close to Luke.

"I ain't gonna let that boy get shot," Moss mumbled.

So far the big man hadn't seen him. Moss had to either shoot him straight or draw his fire so Matthew could run.

Moss's heart beat out of rhythm as blood rushed to his head. "Ticker, don't quit on me now," he mumbled and willed himself to live.

He had to save the boy.

But his left arm grew numb and as he fired at Will, he missed.

Startled, Will turned and began firing at Moss.

The shots came close.

Rob took aim and waited.

He could see Matthew was paralyzed with fear.

He almost had the shot, if only the boy would hold still. "Stay there, boy," he breathed. "Don't move."

He was ready to pull the trigger when Matthew stumbled.

Rob hesitated and Luke fired a quick shot from the hip.

The bullet ripped through Rob's right shoulder. He dropped his gun, and it thudded. He gripped his shoulder and went down on one knee for the gun.

Holding Matthew's shoulder tightly, Luke's eyes flashed.

He'd recognized Rob. He smirked briefly.

Moss and Will exchanged two more shots, each missing and splintering wood chips in the other's face.

Matthew stood still as if frozen.

"Run, boy!" Moss shouted. With a last surge of effort he aimed steady and fired a shot that hit Will between the eyes.

Suddenly Moss was very tired. The numbness was stronger. He couldn't hold his gun up.

Luke turned, and without hesitation, shot Moss.

He collapsed against the building and lay still.

Sally ran to him and knelt beside him. "Ozzie Moss," she cried, "don't die on me now."

But Moss was dead.

Anger roared through her like the raging river that had almost taken her life.

Her son still lived, but bullets zipped past Matthew as his father's fingers dug into his shoulder and held him.

Matthew stared at his Mama. Mama had come for him. Joy bubbled up inside. But what could she do? The bad men had guns. Mama shouldn't have come. Now she'd die too. They would all die here.

Sally lifted Moss's heavy revolver. Using both hands she cocked the hammer and rose with a cold hard fury.

She pointed the pistol at Luke and stepped forward.

"Luke!" she screamed. "Let Matthew go!"

Luke turned. A look of surprise covered his face. "Sally?"

Realizing what she was about to do, Rob yelled, "Matthew, down!"

His voice penetrated the boy's stupor.

Matthew jerked away from Luke, dropping to the ground.

Sally fired.

Her shot hit Luke in the thigh. He grabbed his leg.

Now with a clear line of fire, the sheriff and his deputy opened up. Another bullet hit Luke in the shoulder. A third pierced his heart.

Wearing a look of disbelief, he crumpled across Matthew and lay still.

Bullets had flown like a swarm of hornets, but now the gang lay dead around Matthew, splayed out like the numbers on a clock.

Matthew wiggled out from under Luke and stood covered in dust and his father's blood, looking like some child angel who'd walked through death.

The sheriff called, "It's all right now, folks."

People slowly emerged from buildings.

Sally looked at Matthew.

The gun hung from her hand.

She glanced from Matthew to Luke and back to Matthew again. She heard the sheriff's words from a distance saying everything was all right now. She couldn't believe it. Was it finally over?

The sheriff gently took the gun from her hand. "Ma'am. My guess is that's your boy."

She nodded, speechless.

"He'll be all right now that it's over."

Tears streamed down her face as she walked toward Matthew. She held her hands out to him.

But he didn't come to her. He stared. But he didn't seem to see her.

A fear began anew deep down in her belly, below the pain that already existed there.

Matthew wasn't all right.

Behind her the sheriff directed his deputies to drag the bank robbers over to the jail where they'd be out of the way until the undertaker could measure them for boxes.

Her hands reached Matthew's shoulders and she knelt. "Matthew, its Mama. Come with me, it's over." She looked into his glassy eyes. "Matthew?"

He neither looked at her, nor answered. Dullness swept over his eyes as she led him to the other side of the street away from the dead bodies and the stench of gun smoke.

Away from the body of his father.

Sally reached the store across the street.

Rob had been wounded and he was surrounded by women fussing over him. But he only had eyes for Sally.

"I did my best," he said.

He'd lost the ability to shoot without thinking of anything else. He cared for Sally and her children, and he'd lost his edge, the ability to put everything on the line as when he had nothing to live for.

He'd failed to kill Luke.

But the boy was safe.

He noted Matthew's vacant stare. The boy might be scarred forever.

"Rob, you did fine." Sally's hands caressed Matthew's shoulder. "You told me you'd bring him back safe. Not a mark on him." She started to cry. "Thank you."

"You don't need to thank me. You were very brave today, Sally. I'm proud of you."

"Moss is dead." Tears ran down her face.

"Mama, Mama." Carolyn had fought her way free of the

woman who'd held her back. Now her arms found their way around Sally's skirt. "I was afraid."

"We were all afraid, sunshine."

"Mr. Rob, are you dying?"

"No, Carolyn. I just need a little doctoring."

Her hands went onto her hips like she'd seen Sally do when she took charge. "That doctor better come fast, or I'll give him some piece of mind."

Rob smiled at her mistake.

"Matthew!" Carolyn squealed. She ran to him and hugged him. "I missed you."

Matthew put one arm around her but didn't speak.

"She didn't see it, Sally," the woman from the boarding house said. "When I saw you out there, I covered her eyes."

Sally nodded. At least her daughter had been spared the horror of it all.

At this moment the men moving the bodies came past with Moss on a flat board and Carolyn saw them. "Uncle Moss!" she cried. "Is he sick?"

"I'll tell her, if you want me to," Rob said.

He felt concerned about Sally and disgusted he couldn't help her without bleeding all over the place. And these blasted women hovered, fussing at him like hens.

Sally nodded.

He was about to speak when Matthew spoke his first words.

"Lucky Draw done it. It was his fault." His tone was flat, like the expression on his face.

Carolyn had no idea who Lucky Draw was and she hadn't seen her Papa. So she accepted this without question. A bad man named Lucky Draw had killed her Uncle Moss.

The doctor directed Rob to be moved to his office. He glanced briefly at Matthew before saying, "It's shock, Ma'am. It'll fade with time."

Matthew stood stony-faced, not seeming to care about anything. He'd seen his father dragged away and his eyes seemed too old for a child's face.

Sally gathered her children and walked to the boarding

house. Perhaps Mrs. Steeple would let them stay one more night. Sally had paid for one more night and Matthew could take Moss's room. And even if the woman wouldn't let them stay, she still owed Sally for two rooms Sally wouldn't use. Sally would demand her money back. She was tired of being a victim.

It hit her then, and she stopped just short of the boarding house porch. The children stood, holding hands and waiting.

She'd shot Luke.

She saw his face again—full of surprise as he'd called her name. What had he wanted to tell her? She'd never know.

She squared her shoulders and walked up the steps.

Mrs. Steeple met them at the door. "You can't stay here. We don't want your kind."

"We paid in advance," Sally said. "I'll get the sheriff."

The woman tossed her change onto the ground. "I'll not take your money. The sheriff would want to know where it came from. Likely from another robbery. Get out of here before I call the sheriff myself."

Sally picked up the money and the children followed her back down the steps.

"There are places for such as you." The woman's voice trailed after her.

Sally walked to the doctor's office, holding her head high. She'd check on Rob. Then they'd find lodging, somewhere.

Had Moss been carrying the rest of their money? She hoped it would be with his possessions when she collected them.

Poor Aunt Doe. Sally would have to wire her and tell her Ozzie Moss wouldn't be coming back. She could have broken down and cried except the children were with her and the townsfolk stared and whispered as she walked by. Still she held her head high.

"That's the woman."

"I was there, I saw the whole thing."

"That boy, he'll never be right."

Their words spun through her head.

What would happen to them? Where would they go?

Chapter Nineteen

The doctor's wife met Sally and the children at the door and led them into a room where two of Rob's lady admirers waited.

"The doctor is seeing to your friend," she said. "Once the bullet is out, he may have one visitor. That's all. One. Do you understand?"

Sally nodded but the other two women looked ready to argue. Carolyn's eyes welled up with tears. "Mama, is Mr. Rob going to die?"

"I don't know, sweetheart. But I don't think so."

The doctor called for his wife and she went back inside.

"What's your relationship to Rob?" one woman asked Sally.

"What's yours?" Sally retorted.

She spoke with enough authority that the two women must have felt uncomfortable, since they departed soon after she'd spoken.

Sally was left with one unanswered question.

What *was* her relationship to Rob?

Now that Luke was dead and she had Matthew back safely, Rob owed her nothing. He'd kept his promises.

She didn't want him to go, but there was nothing to keep him here. And that one thought wrenched her heart.

Visiting Rob would instigate talk. But what did it matter? With all that had happened, she could hardly avoid the town's gossiping tongues now anyway.

When it came to Rob, she didn't care what they thought. The Steeple boardinghouse was no longer an option. She'd have to find another decent place to lodge. She didn't want her children to stay in a saloon.

The one night she'd spent there was enough.

But what if no one would rent to them?

Once again Luke had managed to place her in a bad spot.

But Luke was dead. He'd trouble her no more.

It was with surprise that she realized her rage was gone. It had fled the moment she'd had the courage to pull that trigger.

When she'd discovered he'd stolen her son and gone to Texas, she'd been angry enough to kill Luke. But she'd also feared him. It had taken everything she had to face him down in the street.

And even though she hadn't fired the final shot, she could have. Did that make her a cold-blooded killer?

No. She was only defending her family.

"Sally Mae," the doctor's wife said. "You are Sally Mae? If you are, he's asking for you. You may go in."

"What about the children?"

"They'll have to behave, but they may come in. I see the other two have gone."

"Yes."

"Good. I'd had enough of their squabbling over whose beau he is. Rob says you're family."

"Thank you for letting us see him. I wondered who those women were. I've certainly never seen them before."

Sally was babbling, but she couldn't help it. She was nervous about seeing Rob and wondering if he'd tell her goodbye.

She stepped past the doctor's wife without responding to the remark about being Rob's family.

They weren't family, and any day now he would leave.

Rob lay on a cot. His shirt had been removed and his shoulder bound with white strips of cloth. His hand gripped the side of the bed, arm muscles flexed in pain.

"Sally, I'm glad you came." His gray-blue gaze searched hers.

The doctor moved away. "Keep this visit short. You may come again tomorrow."

"Is he going to be all right?"

265

"Yes. The bullet is out but he needs to rest until the bleeding stops. It'll take time for him to mend, but he'll recover."

"Thank you, Doctor."

He nodded and turned away to wash his instruments.

Sally knelt beside the cot. "I'm glad you're going to be all right."

Rob's eyes crinkled as he smiled. "Are the children here?"

"Yes." She turned and motioned them forward.

Carolyn planted a little kiss on his cheek. "You get better, Mr. Rob."

"I'll do that just for you, honey."

Rob looked at Sally as if he wanted to ask her something.

Matthew moved to the other side of the bed. "I want to talk to Mr. Rob," he told her. "Alone."

Surprised, she agreed. She told Rob she'd be back later and took Carolyn to the outer room to wait.

Once the doctor left the room Matthew spoke. "He ain't my Papa. He told me not to call him that, so I ain't going to. But I ain't ever calling anyone Pa again."

Rob swallowed hard, wondering what to say.

This boy had been wounded beyond what any bullet could do.

"I can understand why you'd feel that way."

"You been good to Carolyn and Mama. I want to thank you."

"You don't need to thank me, Matthew. I wanted to take care of them."

I still do. And you too if you'll let me.

Matthew turned to leave then turned back again. "But don't ever tell Carolyn what Luke Wheeler did. She don't need to know. You promise?"

"All right, Matthew."

"I got to go."

Rob watched him leave, wondering if he'd ever be a little boy again. He'd aged beyond his seven years.

What had Luke said or done to the boy beyond what Rob already knew? Anger mingled with the pain of his wound.

"I'll give you something for sleep," the doctor said.

"Yes, I'm tired." It felt like years since he'd slept well.

Sally and the children headed to the sheriff's office.

The sheriff met her at the door. "I have questions to ask you."

"Matthew, watch your sister, please."

"Yes, ma'am." He took Carolyn's hand.

She pointed to the schoolyard. "Matthew, let's play."

"I don't feel like playing."

She seemed content to sit with him on the steps, holding his hand as he stared down the street.

The sheriff opened the door for Sally, and she entered his office. He asked questions, and when he was finally satisfied that she knew nothing about the gang, he said she could leave.

Then he reached behind his desk and brought out Moss's things. "The money is all here, minus the undertaker's fee."

There was Moss's new gun, his knife, an old folded letter that looked barely readable from being weathered and wetted, and a braided lock of hair tied in a ribbon. The once yellow ribbon was now a faded brown.

"Not much is it?" the sheriff said.

"It was everything he owned in this world," Sally said.

She unfolded the letter and read.

My dear Ozzie,

May the days pass quickly until you return. I keep my promise though two men have asked Papa for permission to court me. I tell him I only have sparks for you, and he laughs because he likes you. He says you are a fine man and will work hard all your days. Papa is glad we will wait the year he has asked. He hopes as I do, that you will exercise your restlessness and return ready to settle down here.

I miss dancing, but I think of you when I wear the pin you gave me to hold your lock of hair. I trust you haven't lost mine in the wilds. I braided it extra tight so not one strand will slip loose. Like my love for you, it will remain steadfast.

What is one year when love is true, Mama says. One year is an eternity when I cannot see you or talk to you. Mama says many daughters marry the men their fathers choose, and I am fortunate. I know this is true and will try to be brave until we can

be together again.
> *With all my love,*
> *Doe*

Sally closed her eyes. How sad to lose a love like that. Then to lose him again after finding him so many years later.

The sheriff cleared his throat. "Ma'am, do you have a place to stay? It's getting late."

She shook her head. "No."

The sheriff stood. "I'll put a word in at Diana's. Once folks know I've cleared you of this mess they'll settle down."

"Thank you."

"My pleasure. How's your boy?"

"He's talking now, but I don't know. He seems different."

"I expect things will be different for all of you."

He accompanied her outside and waited while she gathered the children.

Darkness had come. Sally held the children's hands as they followed the sheriff. Diana's Boarding House wasn't far. "She's a kind lady. I take my meals here. She won't quibble about putting you up. But you wait here while I talk to her." He stepped inside leaving them on the porch.

Sally waited nervously. As people passed by, she felt their glances and heard their whispers.

The sheriff returned and introduced her to Diana, a rosy-cheeked woman who exuded cheer.

"I'll check on you folks later," he said.

"Thank you for everything," she said.

"Good night." He tipped his hat.

She watched him go then followed Diana to their room.

The room was plain, clean and homey. Diana had no rules about bathing, though she pointed out where the bath was and told them what time meals were served.

Sally settled the children in then realized she hadn't seen to the horses. "Matthew, stay with your sister while I check on the horses."

"I can do that, Mama," he answered in a serious voice.

"Not tonight, son. I need you to stay here with your sister."

"Yes, ma'am."

Sally walked to the livery stable and spoke to the owner about keeping the horses a while longer. He asked her if she wanted to sell Moss's horse.

That would give her extra money for a fresh start. And if she sold both horses they could always take the stagecoach. She wanted to be far away from this town, but didn't know where.

Where did you go when the whole country was open to you?

Except for the places where Luke had burned every bridge for her, her choices were unlimited.

She'd have to tell Aunt Doe what had happened and she should do it in person. But she wouldn't be able to.

First, there'd be the funeral, and Rob's doctor bill. She felt she owed him that much. But she could easily be out of money soon, if she weren't careful.

She walked back to the boarding house.

The children slept soundly. Sally kissed their foreheads then prepared for bed. She lay down but her mind replayed the shooting and she wondered if Rob could sleep or if he was haunted by it as well.

How soon would he tell her goodbye? It couldn't be long.

Now that Matthew was safe, she should be happy.

But her heart was breaking.

After breakfast, she took the children with her to the undertaker's. The children walked around the wooden boxes while she talked to the undertaker about the inscriptions for the markers.

She'd decided on, "Ozzie Moss, trail leader, beloved grandfather". He wasn't really their grandfather, but he'd loved them as his own, and they'd loved him as well.

Luke's inscription had taken more thought. "Luke Wheeler, father" was as far as she'd gotten. She was dissatisfied with the sound of it, but didn't know what else to say.

The undertaker waited patiently, suggesting words, but none felt right. The man had tormented her. She had no good words for a man like that.

"Put Lucky Draw on it," Matthew said. "Put killed robbing banks. It don't need to say father. He didn't want to be my Papa, so don't say it."

Sally gazed at him in despair. Luke had been a terrible father. And Matthew needed one so desperately.

And was that Luke's real name? If he'd changed his name once, why not again? She didn't even know the date of his birth.

Carolyn played with her dolly, jumping it into and out of the wooden coffins.

Luke had brought them to this. Her daughter now played in coffins.

She'd had enough.

Let the marker read "Lucky Draw, bank robber". They wouldn't claim him as their own. If she left Wheeler off the tombstone, fewer people would make the connection with her and the children. Tongues wagged freely, and she'd had enough of that. They would move away where no one had heard of him.

"Mama, Baby Blue Bell is in her boat."

"Come away from there, Carolyn."

"Is this where Uncle Moss will sleep?"

"Only his body. He's up in heaven now."

Carolyn looked up. "Can he see us?"

"I believe he can."

Carolyn smiled at the sky, and waved.

Sally turned to the undertaker. "My son is right. Make it as he suggested."

Then she paid the man and they left.

"Where are we going, Mama?" Carolyn asked.

"To see Rob."

Carolyn skipped along beside her. "Can Mr. Rob play today?"

"No. He'll need to recover first, sunshine."

They entered the doctor's outer office and his wife looked up from a stack of papers on her desk and smiled. "He's better today. He had a full night's sleep and ate a big breakfast."

As they entered the back room, Rob sat up straighter in bed. His breakfast tray had just been removed, and he blotted at his mouth with a napkin.

"Mr. Rob..." Carolyn skipped over to the bed, "...can you play?"

"I'm afraid not, little lady." Rob winked at her. "Doc here says I'd better rest another day."

"More than just another," the doctor said sternly from the corner, where he was making a notation. "I'll leave you folks to visit but no bouncing on the bed, young lady," he said, shaking his finger at Carolyn.

"Yes, sir," Carolyn said with a solemn nod. She sat on the chair next to the bed and wrapped one leg around the other.

The doctor smiled and closed the door.

Sally looked for another chair, but didn't see one.

Rob patted the bed. "Sit here, Sally." He grinned. "But no bouncing on the bed now."

She sat gingerly, afraid to jostle him.

Matthew leaned against the wall and crossed his arms.

"What've you been doing this morning?" Rob asked Carolyn as she swung her legs back and forth.

"We went to the coffin place, and Baby Blue Bell played ship 'cause they're so big." Carolyn hugged her doll. "Uncle Moss is up in heaven. He can see us from there. So you need to come outside soon." She stopped swinging her legs and looked at the ceiling. "Can he see through roofs? Can he see me now?"

Rob smiled sadly. "I don't know, but there's a window over there if you want to see the sky."

When she jumped up and ran to the window, he reached for Sally's hand. "What are the arrangements for Moss?"

"The funeral is in two days. I'll wire a message to Aunt Doe." An acute sense of loss came over her. She closed her eyes.

"Sally, is there anything I can do?"

She opened her eyes, her gaze clouded with tears, and she dropped her lashes to hide the hurt. "You can get better."

He squeezed her hand. She felt a strange numbed comfort.

"Carolyn seems fine, but what about you and Matthew?"

"We're fine. I sold the horses to pay for the undertaker and our room."

She didn't tell him she'd also paid the doctor. She sensed his male pride wouldn't have allowed that.

Rob silently added figures in his head. "Your money won't last long. What are your plans?"

Sally stared toward the window. Was she listening?

"Sally?"

She looked disoriented. "I don't know," she said. "I'll deal with that after the funerals."

"Where would you like to settle?"

He knew she'd want to be away from this town.

She shrugged. "I don't know. Not here. Not Kansas."

"That leaves a whole lot of country. Do you think you could narrow it down some?"

She answered in a rush, "I want to be away from here. Away from any town *he's* been in."

Rob took encouragement from her tone. He didn't want the ghost of Luke rising between them.

"Would you like to hear what my plans are once I'm well?"

She clutched her brooch and her eyes widened. "No, Rob. Not today. I couldn't bear to hear your plans just yet."

He wouldn't say more.

"I'm going to attend the funeral with you," he said.

He'd propose to her directly afterward. He wanted to see Luke in the ground first.

"Do you really think you'll be well enough? Has the doctor said you'll be up by then?"

"I'll be well enough."

After Sally and the children said goodbye, she sent a wire to Aunt Doe. She couldn't remember a time when she'd had to send such a sad message. She didn't know how to say so much in so few words.

Aunt Doe, Ozzie Moss killed saving Matthew. Rob wounded. Funeral in two days. Sally Wheeler

That's the last time she would use the name Wheeler. From now on she would sign as Sally Adams.

Would Aunt Doe come to the funeral? She missed her comforting presence. What would her advice be?

As she and the children walked back to their room to rest,

she wondered what to do after the funeral. Rob was right, she'd need a plan. How would she support the children?

She wanted both of them to go to school. She didn't want Carolyn to grow up not knowing her letters.

Perhaps she'd take in sewing. Mama had taught her to sew, and she'd always made her own clothes. She tried to think of other skills she could use. She could take in laundry.

Sally sank onto the bed. There weren't many jobs in the west for women. Not the kind a respectable mother could take. What could she do?

She'd have to marry again.

But he would have to love her children.

She pictured Rob in the role then put him out of her mind. She loved him, but he'd never want to be saddled with the children of a man he'd hated.

And he hadn't said he loved her.

It didn't matter. She'd settle for a good father for her children. And she wouldn't even hope for love this time.

She dozed until she heard the call to supper.

After supper, she and the children walked back to the doctor's house. Sadness crept into Sally's soul like when Papa died. She barely noticed the people in the streets.

She knocked on the doctor's door.

His wife opened it. "We didn't expect you this evening."

"May we visit Rob?"

"Of course." She led them into his room after knocking on the door and asking if he was decent.

"Decent as I'll ever be," he'd answered with a laugh.

The woman left them to visit, and Sally sat in the chair and held Carolyn. She snuggled in as if sensing Sally was the one needing comfort. Matthew sat on the stool.

"I didn't think you'd come back tonight," Rob said.

"Why ever not?" she replied, puzzled.

"I didn't think you'd come unescorted on New Year's Eve."

Sally frowned and her slender hands unconsciously twisted together. "I hadn't thought of that."

"You've had a lot to handle these last few days."

"Yes. I sent a wire to Aunt Doe, but I fear she won't arrive in time."

"She may not have anyone to travel with and may not wish to travel alone."

"Then we'll send his things to her." She handed him the letter and the lock of hair. "Ozzie would've wanted her to have these."

Rob held the letter in his hand then turned it over and read it. He refolded it gently.

The old man had missed the love of his life and nothing could ever make up for that. If Sally wouldn't have him, Rob would ride forever alone just like Moss.

He handed it back to her and their hands touched briefly. He smiled, but she seemed lost in thought. She'd begun to feel the loss. He knew she missed the old man, as he did. He wanted to comfort her but was unsure of her reaction. And it was late. The noises on the street grew louder.

"You'd better go, Sally. I wouldn't want anything to happen to you or the children."

"Yes," she stood. "We should get back."

He frowned and raised himself up on one elbow. "I should come with you."

"No." She put out her hand. "The doctor said you weren't to be out of bed yet."

He leaned back. "Go on then before things get out of hand."

Sally told him good night and headed for the boarding house, staying near the side of the street with fewer saloons and dance halls.

The noise was loud and rowdy. Across the street a bar fight had begun in The Welcome Hotel, while laughter spilled out of The Eureka Dance Hall as a man stumbled through the door. The sound of glass breaking and music playing mingled with shouts and laughter.

They should have been off the street long ago. People stared when she passed. She walked with dignity, hoping that by acting like a lady, she'd be treated like one.

"Hey, little lady. How 'bout a kiss?" A drunk stumbled toward her after staggering out of the Palace of Pleasure.

Sally hugged the children closer and hurried past him, setting her chin in a stubborn line. Maybe if she didn't speak to him, he'd leave her alone.

The man reached out a hand and his mouth took on an unpleasant twist. "Where're ya goin' in such a hurry? A little kiss won't hurt you none."

Rob was right, what had she been thinking?

"Hurry, children," she said.

At the boarding house she had to pound on the door before it was unlocked and opened.

"Sally," Diana said. "I thought you were in your room. Respectable citizens lock their doors and go to bed on New Year's Eve here. The boisterous ones really whoop it up."

Sally breathed a sigh of relief upon entering. "Thank you, Diana. It's good to be safe inside. I'll put the children to bed."

In their room, Sally put a chair under the doorknob as a precaution. She laid Moss's gun next to the bed after checking to see if there were any bullets.

"Don't touch this gun, either of you," she warned the children. "It's loaded."

Once they'd climbed in bed, Carolyn said, "Mama, tell me a story about Texas."

"No, sunshine, I don't have any good stories about Texas."

She felt restless and irritable listening to the noises coming from the street.

"Yes, you do, 'member?"

"I'm too tired to think of them tonight."

She told the story of Daniel in the lions' den instead. Matthew had always liked that story, but tonight he listened without enthusiasm.

When Carolyn drifted off to sleep, Sally said, "Matthew, aren't you sleepy?"

"Mama, them stories are all fibs." His expressionless voice chilled her.

"I see," she replied. She didn't know how to help him. Would he ever again be the little boy he once was? The question was a stab in her heart.

"I'll stay awake an' watch out for you, Mama. I'm the man of the family now. There are lots of bad men in town."

"Matthew, you don't have to do that. You need to sleep,"

she said firmly.

He was only seven, much too young to be the man of the family. Much too young to feel he had to be.

Luke had caused so much pain. Wouldn't it end with his death?

"Ain't sleepy."

"Well, all right. Just sit with me then." Like all stubborn little boys, he'd fall asleep soon.

They sat quietly until late in the night as the sounds became louder out on the street. Sally was surprised Matthew could stay awake so long.

When he looked at her, his eyes held knowledge beyond his years. She missed the boy who so eagerly gave her hugs and teased his sister. She missed his smile and his laugh.

Sally heard a woman scream and glass breaking. She ran to the window and looked out.

Fire had broken out in the Red Shoe Hotel across the street. People ran out of the building and piled furniture and bedding in the middle of the street. Men staggered out with billiard cues and a roulette wheel, women carried silly things like frilly lamps and fancy dresses.

Sally and Matthew watched from the window as others ran buckets of water inside to dash on the flames. The wind changed and the flames climbed higher. The revelers stood around the pile in silence, watching.

Hours later the fire was put out. Only smoke and ash remained. Slowly the crowd trickled away.

Sally turned away from the window. "It's late, Matthew."

Matthew looked at her with serious eyes. "Mama, are you going to marry Rob?"

"He hasn't asked me. And he isn't a man to stay. Now will you go to sleep?"

He turned over and pulled up the covers.

Rob would want to get on with whatever he did before. Like with Luke, she didn't know what Rob had done before. But Rob wasn't like Luke. He was a good man, though restless, like Ozzie Moss had been.

A tight pain squeezed her heart.

If only Rob would love her, just a little.

Chapter Twenty

Carolyn woke Sally early by bouncing on the bed and asking when they'd eat breakfast.

Only a few people had come downstairs for the morning meal. Diana had made scrambled eggs, ham and golden biscuits.

Sally and the children had extra helpings, with Diana insisting the food would go to waste if they didn't eat it.

"I don't know why I cook so much on New Year's Day," she said. "There are never enough folks to eat it. But the one time I don't fix it, they'll all be up early. The lunch crowd will likely be a sorry looking bunch, and I won't need much food."

Mostly women gathered at the table, and Sally enjoyed their conversation. The woman in the blue dress turned to her. "I'm surprised you aren't wearing mourning."

"I don't own a black dress. There hasn't been time to make one with all the arrangements to be made."

The woman reached for a biscuit. "There are plenty in the general store."

The woman was either being helpful or critical. Sally wasn't sure which. "Thank you."

She changed the subject and asked one of the other boarders how far it was to Galveston. If she were going to choose a place to live, she'd better start asking questions.

Rob was right, she needed to make a decision. It would be nice to live near the ocean. The children would enjoy that.

The woman in the blue dress persisted. "When do the funerals take place?"

"In two days."

Conversation hovered around the topic of the men to be buried, until Sally had had enough and took the children back to their room.

She was sitting on the bed wondering how much a new dress would cost when there was a knock on the door.

It was Diana. "Come with me."

Sally and the children followed her down the hall to a tiny room. Diana reached into her pocket, removed a key then unlocked the door and swung it open.

Traveling bags, trunks and shoes filled the room. Clothing lay folded and stacked on shelves.

"This is where I store the things people leave behind. If they don't come back to claim it, I give it away where I see the need," she explained. "You might find something suitable here. I'll leave you to look through these and be back in a bit. Take what you want."

The children helped Sally look through the trunks and bags. There were fancy hats with feathers and plumes, cowboy hats and worn-down boots, dresses, men's pants and shirts, long johns and frilly ladies' underthings.

Carolyn tried on several of the hats. She giggled as they slipped down over her head.

Sally smiled at her daughter then turned her attention back to the task at hand. In the bottom of the last trunk, she found a black dress. Despite it being huge, Sally could take it in and make it fit if she worked on it all day and evening. The only black hat she'd found had long plumes and had obviously belonged to a lady of the evening. Maybe she could do something with it.

A little while later, Diana returned. "Did you find anything?"

Sally held the items out to her. "Is this all right?"

"Why sure," Diana said with a laugh. "That hat belonged to a woman who came here looking for her man. She took off in the wee hours after he'd snuck out the window trying to get away. She followed him right out that window and rode her horse through town still wearing her red chemise. Left that red dress over there with the black lace trim and the hat." She walked over to the dress. "You might take the lace off the dress and do something with it."

"Oh, yes, I hadn't thought of that."

"And that black dress belonged to a large woman who died here after choking on a chicken bone. I never saw a woman who could eat so much. Fairly swallowed her food whole without chewing. Her death didn't surprise me, but I was afraid for a time that I'd lose customers who thought it was my cooking. It scared me silly. I don't ever serve fried chicken any more unless someone asks for it special."

Sally held the black dress up. She could fit two of herself inside the billowy silk gown.

Diana laughed as Carolyn put a pair of ladies gloves on that came to her shoulders. "You just go on and have fun with those, you sweet thing. You'll grow into them."

Sally thanked her and walked to their room with her things. She laid them on the bed and made a mental note of what she'd need for the alterations. Needle, pins, thread, scissors.

"Let's go to the store, children."

"Can we go see Mr. Rob?" Carolyn asked.

"Not until later."

The children looked around the general store, and Sally let them pick out candy while she shopped. It didn't take long for her to get the supplies she needed.

She returned to her room, settled herself on the floor and began cutting and pinning.

All she needed was a basic dress. She'd wear it for Moss but not Luke. She couldn't mourn him.

Carolyn played with her new gloves and seemed content.

Matthew sat in a corner whittling a piece of wood he'd found. The knife had belonged to Moss, and Matthew was trying to teach himself how to carve with it. He worked slowly and methodically, a small frown of concentration on his forehead.

"Be careful with that knife, Matthew."

"Yes, Mama, I am."

The call came for supper, and they went downstairs. Sally asked the children to eat quickly so she could return to her sewing. The dress had to be done by tomorrow evening. She'd have to work all night.

After dinner, Carolyn asked, "Mama, can we go see Mr.

Rob?"

"Not tonight."

Back in their room, Sally sewed. With no sewing machine it was slow and tedious work. She didn't waste time trying to make the dress special in any way. It was very plain.

The children put themselves to sleep as she sewed into the wee hours of the morning. Her eyes grew tired, dry and sore from focusing on the tedious tiny stitches as she worked by the dim light of the lamp. Her fingers bled when she missed and jabbed them.

Her head drooped as she sat on the floor leaning against the bed, and she woke with a jerk.

How long had she been sitting like this?

Finally, she stopped and slept on the bed in her dress, not bothering to remove her shoes.

When she woke, Matthew and Carolyn weren't in the room. Panic seized her. She swung open the door, ready to do battle with the devil himself.

Then she saw them coming up the stairs. Relief flooded her senses. "Where have you been?"

"Breakfast," Matthew replied. "I can take care of Carolyn, Mama. Go on back to sleep."

"No, I have work to do." She herded the children into the room then picked up the dress. She held it up. Plain it would be, but she'd do something with the hat.

She took off the plumes and let Carolyn have them to play with.

Carolyn giggled.

Sally removed the lace from the red dress and fashioned a veil, sewing the strips of lace together. She tried it on. It looked like a dark wedding veil as the long pieces of lace hung down over her head. How fitting.

"White to black," she said.

By midday, she'd completed the entire outfit. She tried it on before the mirror. Oddly enough the simplicity of the lines fit her form in a striking way. She smoothed her hands down past her hips, feeling the black silk.

She hadn't intended it to fit her like that.

Carolyn tugged on the dress. "Mama, now can we go see

Mr. Rob?"

"Yes. I'm finished." And she needed to talk Rob into resting instead of going to the funeral with her.

They left the room with Sally carrying the hat. Carolyn skipped ahead of her singing and Matthew walked behind her keeping an eye on his sister. As Sally passed women on the street, she heard the comments again.

"Isn't that the woman who shot her husband?"

Heat stole into Sally's face. Luke wasn't her husband.

"Yes, he was an outlaw and she a sporting woman."

"Look at her dress and that red hair."

"Black widow."

"She's been visiting that man who was shot. I heard she entertains him right there in the doctor's office."

Sally felt their eyes on her. She held her head high as she walked down the busy street, but her cheeks flamed and she was helpless to halt her embarrassment.

She was completely absorbed in herself when she suddenly saw Rob in the middle of the street.

He walked toward her with a strange expression.

She felt the blood drain from her face.

She rushed up to him. "Rob! You shouldn't be out of bed."

He grasped her by the elbows. "Do you have any idea how worried I've been?"

Puzzled, she frowned. "Why?"

His expression clouded in anger. "You came to see me late on New Year's Eve and then you didn't come in the morning. I worried, but thought the noise had kept you up late and you'd slept in. But when you hadn't come by suppertime and I heard about the fire, I thought something might have happened to you." He let loose of her arms and stood there, tall and angry.

"I didn't think."

"No, you never do." Though still angry, he looked as if he needed to sit.

"You mustn't be out on the street like this. Let's get you inside." She worried over him. She'd never seen him look this way. And he wasn't healed yet.

As they walked back to the boarding house Rob didn't

speak, but he grimaced with each step.

The silence lengthened between them.

Sally wanted to speak, but felt guilty about causing him such worry. He'd roused himself out of bed before he was ready on account of her. At last she got him seated in one of the chairs in the parlor.

Diana entered. "May I bring you tea?"

"Yes," she answered.

Beads of sweat formed on Rob's brow. She could see he'd overdone it.

As the tea was served, he muttered, "You have no idea what you put me through."

"I'm sorry, Rob," she said softly.

He grunted. "Sorry is a sorry word." He sipped his tea and studied her. "New dress?"

"I made it yesterday and last night."

"Thunderation." His fingers tightened on the cup.

She rushed over. "Where does it hurt? Are you in pain? Is there anything I can do?"

He gazed up into her eyes. "I don't know if you can give me what I need."

His steady gaze impaled her. Silence loomed between them like a heavy mist and the room felt warm and heavy.

A clock chimed. It would be time for the funeral soon.

"We'd best be going," Sally said. "Wait here until I get the doctor to come for you."

His firm hand closed over her arm. "No. I'm coming with you to the funeral."

"But you need to rest."

"I'll rest once I've paid my respects to Moss and seen Luke buried where he belongs."

"At least wait while I get a buggy," she said.

He raised one eyebrow. "Buggy?" He scowled and eyed her dress. "Where'd you get the money for a buggy?"

He gritted his teeth and waited for an answer.

Sally knew he was angry with her and she couldn't bear the way he was looking at her. She dashed outside and down the street to where there were carriages for hire. "Please, I need a carriage and driver right away."

The man eyed her black dress. "Lots of folks going to the funeral. I have one left, but it will cost you."

"How much?"

He named a price.

She paid him then pointed to the boarding house.

Rob had sat stewing while she was gone.

When the carriage arrived, Sally asked the man to come in and help Rob out to it.

"I want to ride with Mr. Rob," Carolyn said.

"No," Matthew said harshly into her ear. "He's mad at us. Remember how Papa was when he got mad?"

"Did Mr. Rob drink that smelly stuff?" she asked.

"Maybe," Matthew said. "Come on." He helped her climb into the back of the carriage and sat next to her.

Sally was about to speak to the children when Rob interrupted her.

"I guess you'll have to sit with me," he said in a dry tone.

Several men glanced at her appreciatively as they walked past.

"We'll be late if you don't hurry."

Rob's quiet voice held an undertone of cold contempt and her spirits sank even lower.

She climbed in, adjusted her hat and pulled the lace veil over her face. At least the veil would shield her.

Rob stared straight ahead.

They rode in silence to the graveyard on Cemetery Hill, where folks who'd arrived early stood just close enough to watch.

Sally felt their eyes staring. One woman pointed at her and whispered to another.

The driver helped Rob and Sally down, and the children jumped out.

Rob looked at Sally and scowled.

Sally watched him from under her veil.

He must be in pain.

She slipped her arm around his waist to help him along

and held her head high as they walked to where the preacher stood.

The silk dress rustled as she moved along beside him. Her hand held his waist and she felt so small beside him. His body was warm, his muscles firm. He was all male. She liked the feel of his body next to hers. He was tall and solid. She'd never be able to hold him up if he fell.

She wished he was the one holding her.

Her hips moved next to his and she was aware of the way their gaits now matched each other. They were walking in step, together.

The gawking townsfolk continued to whisper. A few women snuck enticing smiles at him, but he scowled back.

The children followed behind them.

Sally glanced back. "Come along now."

Rob walked stiffly beside her.

Was the pain unbearable when he moved? Was this making him worse?

She readjusted her hand on his side.

He gave a low groan. So low she almost missed it.

The preacher began the ceremony for the five dead men. They buried Luke's gang with little fuss in the boot division of the cemetery where those who died gloriously or otherwise in the thick smoke of guns were laid to rest.

The preacher read a few verses about reaping what you sow. He didn't mention Luke as a father or husband.

Sally had asked him not to mention that she and the children were related to Luke in any way. He was buried under his outlaw name, Lucky Draw.

Her main concern was to get through this ordeal by telling Carolyn they were only there to bury Uncle Moss.

The gathering then moved to the community section of the cemetery, where Ozzie was given a respectable plot. When the preacher began to speak of Ozzie as a hero, Sally started to cry.

"Mama, I want Uncle Moss to come back," Carolyn sobbed.

"He's up in heaven, sunshine," Sally said between tears.

Carolyn stopped crying. She smiled. "When we go to heaven, Uncle Moss will lead us on the trail."

Sally glanced at Rob and he gave her a gentle smile. "Yes, sunshine, Uncle Moss will be there to show us the way."

Her little girl had put it so beautifully.

Sally saw a rider in the distance riding hard toward the cemetery. When the horse drew up beside the tree that stood at the far end of the fence, a woman climbed down and hurried over.

Sally gasped. It was Aunt Doe.

"I came as soon as I got your message," she said and hugged Sally. "I rode hard. Only stopped to rest my horse. I used to race horses with Ozzie when I was a girl." Her gaze scanned the crowd of onlookers and hangers on and dismissed every one of them. "I see we have an audience. Have I come too late?"

The preacher overheard her. "The service is over, but you may stay as long as you wish."

"That is exactly what I wish. Now if you'd usher these good townsfolk back to their safe little houses, I'd appreciate it."

Her sarcasm wasn't lost on Sally.

The preacher nodded and said in a voice loud enough for all to hear, "Let's leave the relatives to their grief."

"Nosy good-for-nothings," Aunt Doe muttered. "Look at them. Vultures. The same sort arrived for my husband's funeral. Some even met me at the gate to offer their condolences along with offers for my land." She glanced sternly at Sally and Rob. "Never make decisions in your grief. Wait a few days."

Carolyn hugged her. "Hello, Aunt Doe."

"Hello, little darling."

Carolyn squeezed her small arms around the older woman's neck. "I missed you."

Matthew stared at them.

"I missed you too," Doe said. She nodded to Sally. "Let's take a walk, just the two of us, and you can tell me what happened. Rob will stay with the children."

Sally walked with her and told her the story from the time they left until the fatal shootings.

Aunt Doe stopped and put her arm around Sally. "How do you feel about Luke now, Sally?"

"I won't use his name. I don't want Carolyn to know she

had a father like that. And Matthew." She shook her head. "I don't know what to do about him. He isn't the little boy he once was."

"And Rob?"

"He'll mend and go off to do whatever it is that he does."

Aunt Doe stopped and put her hands on her hips. "And you don't even know what that is, do you? Have you ever asked him? I can't imagine Rob would give anything but a straight answer to a direct question."

"No. I haven't asked him."

"So you haven't learned a solitary blessed thing from Ozzie's death."

Surprise overwhelmed Sally. She'd never heard Aunt Doe speak harshly.

"I've seen the way you two watch each other when you don't think the other is looking. I can't believe he hasn't asked you to marry him, unless he's waiting for you to go through a mourning period. By then you're both likely to have gone in different directions."

"No, he's only asked me what I plan to do next."

"Well, what did you tell him?"

"That I didn't know."

Aunt Doe shook her head abruptly. "Now, listen to me and listen well. If he doesn't ask you, then you ask him. I don't care if that isn't the way things are done. You just do it. Life is short. Look at that man over yonder." She pointed to Rob. "Do you love him?"

"Yes, but he'll be leaving as soon as he's well enough."

"Don't be too sure. He loves you, Sally. Now you quit acting like a schoolgirl who's waiting for someone to ask her to dance and go over there and talk to him. Leave this old woman alone to mourn."

Aunt Doe turned away and marched up to the top of the hill.

Sally walked to where Rob sat talking with the children.

He looked up when she came near and nodded toward Aunt Doe. "Is she all right?"

Doe stood on the hill, like a statue silhouetted against the setting sun.

"More than the rest of us, I believe."

He looked into her eyes. "And how are the rest of us?"

"We'll be fine. I suppose you'll be riding off soon. Once you're well enough."

"That depends. I might settle down somewhere."

"Where?"

"That hasn't been decided yet."

She smiled sadly. "Somehow I can't see you settling down. You'll be riding off as soon as you're well enough."

"I would settle for the love of the right woman."

Sally looked away, hurt.

He didn't mean her.

"Matthew, take Carolyn over to Aunt Doe so I can talk with your mother," Rob said.

"Yes, sir."

Rob patted the log next to him. "Sit here, next to me."

Blinking away the tears that threatened, she sat.

Now he'd tell her he was leaving.

"Why are you crying?" he asked.

"No reason."

He took her hand in his to comfort her. "It's been a difficult day for you."

She smiled thinly and a tear escaped to run down her cheek.

He wiped it away with his thumb.

"Could you ever marry again?"

"I'll have to, so that my children will have a father. But he would have to love them."

"Is that all?"

Disappointment hit Rob hard. He'd hoped for much more. He'd hoped that she loved him. That she needed him.

"Matthew needs a good father to teach him how to be a good man," she said. "And Carolyn wants a Papa to play with her."

"And what do you want?"

"I'd like to move to Galveston and live by the ocean."

That surprised him. "Why Galveston?"

"I don't want to live where Luke's ever been. I don't want Carolyn growing up knowing how bad her father was. And they say Galveston is a good place to raise children."

"The children. Always thinking of the children. But what about you, Sally? What would you like?"

She didn't answer. It wasn't about what she wanted.

Every time she'd wanted something or dreamed of a happy ending, it all turned out wrong.

All she wanted was for Rob to love her. But she couldn't have that.

His gray-blue eyes looked into hers, the depths unreadable. He was very still. "I'd be happy to be their father."

Her eyes welled up with tears. This was more than she could have hoped for. So why was she still sad?

"Carolyn loves you already."

"And I love her," Rob said.

"You'll be a wonderful father." She felt as if a great weight had been lifted, but her heart was still filled with pain. He still hadn't said he loved her.

He gave her a sad smile.

She smiled back at him through her tears. His fingers threaded through hers.

She had a moment of panic. She didn't know his past.

"What did you do before I met you?" she asked.

"Lots of things. I worked on a ranch, took steers to Virginia. Tried my hand at mining once for a few weeks. I've traveled and played cards."

Sally's heart plummeted to the pit of her stomach. He was a card player like Luke. She didn't want to think of Luke. She looked away, unable to bear the thought he might resembled Luke in any way.

"I'm no angel, Sally, but I'm not a cheat or a liar and I keep my word."

Rob watched her fleeting expressions and began to understand what was going through her mind.

She was really asking what kind of a man he was. She was really asking if he would turn out to be like Luke. If he would beat his wife. If he would steal from her and leave her stranded. That she felt the need to ask after all the months on the trail together surprised him. Didn't she know by now what kind of man he was? Would she ever come to trust him?

There was one thing he had to share with her now. She'd been deceived enough.

"Sally," his fingers squeezed hers. "I want you to look at me."

She turned to face him again.

"I want us to be honest with each other. No surprises. I'm going to tell you about Luke, so we can leave him in the past, dead and buried."

She caught her breath and nodded.

"Luke killed my fiancée and then paid a drunk to say I did it. All because he couldn't beat me at cards. I spent five years in prison for that murder. He beat her to death. That's why I wanted to kill him. I know what kind of man Luke Wheeler was. I know what kind of husband he was to you. But I've never hurt a woman in my life, Sally. And I'd never hurt you."

Rob looked into her eyes, hoping to see her fears drop away. Hoping she would say she loved him and would trust him.

He waited, watching her, yet he saw only her relief that she'd found a father for her children. She wasn't happy about this marriage. She hadn't said she loved him. And this wasn't what he wanted.

She deserved to be happy. She deserved to be married to a man she loved. She'd find some other man and fall in love.

He closed his eyes as the pain of that thought hit him. It would just about kill him, but he had to let her go. He wouldn't allow her to marry him simply because she felt she must.

He let her hands drop. "Sally, I can't marry you."

"What? Then why did you say you'd be their father?" Tears welled in her eyes, and she stood.

"I can't marry you because you deserve someone better than me. Marriage without love is an empty shell."

He stood and began a slow painful walk back to the carriage.

Sally was stunned. She felt as if her heart had been lifted into the sky and dropped again.

She'd never marry another man. She couldn't let him go.

She loved him.

And he was leaving her forever.

"Wait!" Sally ran.

Rob stopped and turned.

Sally ran toward him, throwing off her black veil. Tears streamed down her face. But she didn't care. He had stopped and was waiting for her. And that's all that mattered.

"I love you," she cried.

His arms reached toward her, and she fell softly into his warm embrace like a drop of rain falling slowly into a closing flower at night. He held her and gently rocked her from side to side.

"I love you too, Sally Mae," his voice choked.

Into his shoulder she cried, "Please don't leave me."

"Hush, I've got you. I'm not going anywhere." He brushed a gentle kiss across her forehead. "I love you, Sally." He began raining kisses over her cheek, her ear, and her lips.

"And I will never willingly leave you as long as I live." He drew back to look down into her eyes. "Will you marry me?"

"Yes." Sally looked up into his eyes and laughed and cried at the same time. "Yes. I will marry you."

He smiled. Then his lips slowly descended to meet hers.

Her knees weakened as his mouth took control. She drank in the sweetness of his kiss like water from a desert. It was a kiss for her tired soul to melt into. He sweetly drained all her doubts and fears away until she knew the flooding of uncontrollable joy. This man loved her with all his heart as she loved him, and he'd never leave her.

Aunt Doe watched from the hill and smiled. "Looks like there's going to be a wedding." She looked up at the sky with tears in her eyes. "Someday, Ozzie, you and I will have a good laugh about those two. But you'll have to wait until I can join you on the trail. This time I'll be coming with you."

She placed a hand on each of the children's shoulders. "Let's go join your Mama. I think she has something to tell you."

Chapter Twenty-One

When they reached the boarding house, Sally turned to Aunt Doe. "I have some things for you that belonged to Ozzie."

Aunt Doe sat on the bed and Sally unpacked Moss's saddlebag. She handed Doe a letter.

"Oh," Aunt Doe gasped. She opened the letter and a lock of hair tied with a faded ribbon fell out. She lifted her tear-filled gaze to look at Sally and reached into her pocket to pull out another lock of hair. She placed them both together and put them inside the letter as she folded it again.

"Aren't you going to read it?"

"I remember every word. Every single word I wrote to him. Every word he said to me."

She held the letter to her breast. "The heart doesn't lie, you know. Neither time nor circumstance can change two hearts truly bound in love." She gave Sally a look. "Even when married to another. It doesn't change love or lessen it in any way."

She placed the envelope back in her pocket and stood. "Ozzie would be proud to hear of your engagement. I'm proud too. And I'd be pleased if you held the wedding at the ranch, unless you'd rather it be somewhere else."

"Of course not, Aunt Doe." Sally hugged her. "I wouldn't dream of having it anywhere else."

Rob smiled. "Aren't you going to ask me?"

Sally looked at him quickly. "Oh, Rob, I'm sorry. I should have asked your permission."

He gathered her into his arms. "Sally, you never have to ask for my permission. But we should make decisions together, don't you think?"

"Yes," she nodded. "I agree."

"Well, I think the ranch is the perfect place," he grinned, "especially if you'll wear that white nightgown you wore the night I saw you in the window."

Sally blushed. "Robert, please."

"Oh, it's Robert now. Sounds like we're practically married all ready. I'm just having fun, Sally Mae, best you get used to it."

Everyone laughed, and Carolyn began to sing. Sally looked over at Matthew and he smiled back at her. He was slowly beginning to come back to himself. Whenever anyone tried to talk to him about it he said, "It was a bad time," but he'd say no more. And Rob had been so good with her boy.

It almost didn't seem possible that all her dreams were coming true.

The ranch offered a restful spot for Sally to relax. For once, she didn't worry about the children. They followed Aunt Doe everywhere.

Rob's wound was healing well, and Sally made sure she fussed over him.

One evening, Doe looked out the window and saw riders approaching. She reached for the shotgun propped behind the door and waited near the window.

"Who is it?" Carolyn asked wide-eyed.

"I'm not sure yet, darling. Be still now," Doe replied.

The riders came near and a voice called out, "Hello in the house!"

Doe flung open the door. "Jack, I'm glad to see you!"

"Likewise." He slid down from his horse and grinned.

Everyone came out onto the porch and watched as the men climbed down from their horses and Aunt Doe greeted them with hugs.

"Come on in and get yourselves warm," she said. "I want to introduce you to my new family." She glanced back toward the horizon. "Sally, this here's Jack, my foreman, that's Andy, Marcus and Stuart." She looked back toward the horizon. "Where's Tom?"

"He's gone to take care of the horses," Jack answered.

"This is Sally, and her children, Matthew and Carolyn."

The men smiled and nodded to Sally.

"Now, fellows, before you get any grand ideas, Sally is marrying Rob." She gestured to where he stood. "Real soon now."

"She ain't married yet," Jack said and they all laughed.

Sally put her hand on Rob's arm. "No, but my heart already belongs to this good man." She smiled up at him. "And no other."

Rob put his arm around Sally. "I can't blame you for the interest though. Isn't she the prettiest lady in Texas?"

Joy filled Sally's heart. Rob loved her and didn't mind telling everyone about it.

"Who-ee, you been hit hard," Jack said with a laugh. "Better you than me."

With that they all laughed.

Everyone followed Doe into the kitchen where she poured cups of coffee while Sally cut large slices of cake.

"We've been testing cake for the wedding and you're just in time to try some," Sally said with a shy smile.

"So when's the wedding?" Jack asked.

"Soon as the circuit preacher comes."

"I heard he was two days away," Jack said before taking a bite of cake.

"That doesn't give us much time to get ready," Aunt Doe said. "Stuart, do you think you can play the fiddle for us?"

"Why, sure. You can't have a wedding without dancing."

"You're right about that," Aunt Doe said as she finally sat at the table with her own piece of cake. "Well, how did it go, boys?"

"We lost a few, like we knew we would, Doe," Jack answered. "But the ones that made it weren't too scrappy. We got a fair price for them." He reached into his pocket and handed her a bag of money. "It's all there along with the bill of sale signed by your cousin, right and proper."

"I knew it would be, Jack." Aunt Doe patted the money but didn't count it in front of them. "I knew I could trust you. But I see we lost a few men."

"We didn't see eye to eye on a few things once we got there."

"Good for nothing's," Tom said. "They didn't mind eatin' your chow, but just barely did their share of the work. Then when we got paid, all hell broke loose."

"I had my eye on them," Jack said.

"Good thing you did, too, or you'd have got a bullet in the back."

"At least we're rid of the troublemakers," Aunt Doe said.

"I don't know about that," Tom frowned. "I heard talk they might pay you a visit, now that you're all alone here."

Aunt Doe laughed. "Won't they be surprised when they come and find a house full?"

"Well, Doe," Tom began. He seemed embarrassed. "You ain't got no more work for me, and truth to tell, much as I like you and would like to stay on, I can't. Even if you are a better cook than me."

She laughed heartily. "Well, thank you, Tom. But you see, I've been waiting for you all to come back to tell you that I'm selling the ranch to Rob and Sally. And they'll need to hire on."

The men appeared stunned momentarily.

Aunt Doe laughed again. "Well, I'm glad you're all home safe. It's good to see this place carrying on in such good hands."

"Doe," Rob said, "this is your home, every bit of it. You are always welcome here."

The wedding took place two days later when the circuit preacher arrived. It was a small affair but the love surrounding the newly made family was as vast as the land spreading over the hills.

As the circuit preacher pronounced them "man and wife", Sally turned to her new husband. "I love you, Rob."

"And I love you, Sally. I'll love you forever."

Then he swept her into the deepest kiss she'd ever had as Carolyn giggled, and everyone cheered.

The fiddle started up and Rob held out his hand for her to dance.

"Soon we'll finally have a chance to be alone," Rob said.

"I can't believe Doe is sleeping out in the bunkhouse tonight with the ranch hands."

"She's a tough lady. And you should see the way they're fussing over her. Besides it's only for one night."

"Yes, and the children are excited about bunking with the hands."

"You're not worried about them, are you?"

"No. They'll be fine. And we'll be close."

"Do you know what Doe said to me about giving up the house this evening?"

"No, what did she say?"

He spun her in a circle, then held her close. "She said it's so you can make as much noise as you like."

Sally blushed. "So that's what she meant. She told me not to hold back if I feel like singing." She giggled. "That sometimes a woman wants to sing in the bed at night."

"Nervous?"

"A little."

He smiled and she lost all track of time as they danced the evening away.

Soon it was time to say good night to the children and she watched as Rob kissed Carolyn's forehead and ruffled Matthew's hair, joy overflowing from her heart.

Sally glanced out the bedroom window. Rob would be joining her any minute. She couldn't help but be nervous, remembering her first wedding night, though she tried to hide it from him.

The fact was, it was almost impossible to hide such a thing from him.

He seemed to read her so well. Though he could not read her thoughts, he came close enough.

She'd come to her first wedding night innocent and with a heart full of young love and the anticipation of all her romantic fantasies being fulfilled. Those fantasies had been dashed as surely as a lantern thrown off a runaway stagecoach.

Tonight, she came to her new husband experienced in everything but knowing the loving touch of a man who truly loved her. She told herself she knew what to expect and she would hold no romantic notions. That way they would not be so easily dashed.

She told herself this, yet deep within her heart, the longing remained.

Then his footsteps were on the stairs. The gait that was his, the one she'd memorized those many days on the trail, his step sure and steady.

She crossed to the dresser, picked up her hairbrush and prepared to take her hair down from the elaborate coils curling about her head. She didn't want him to enter the room and know she'd been pacing, nervously watching out the window for him.

Sally looked up to see him just as he paused inside the door.

His gray-blue eyes were gentle, understanding, and she felt a shiver of her nervousness slip away. His wavy hair brushed his shirt collar and one unruly wave curled itself over his ear, making her want to touch it, to run her fingers through it.

"I told Doe, I'd prefer helping you out of your wedding dress," he said. "I kind of like the thought of undoing all those buttons."

Despite all her thoughts on the matter of wedding nights, despite the fact she had been married before and had given birth to two children, she still found herself feeling incredibly shy, blushing like a schoolgirl. And then thinking of how it had started the last time with the unbuttoning.

"Unless you'd rather have Doe..." His voice trailed off.

The unspoken ghost of her past hovered between them.

"No, I'd rather have you," she replied, yet the memory of Luke's hands disrobing her was in her mind.

Rob's eyes reflected a sudden knowledge of her thoughts.

"Darlin', you are the most beautiful bride I have ever seen," he said, the warmth of his smile echoing in his voice.

A smile trembled over her lips.

"Thank you," she murmured, blushing, as happiness spread through her body along with a rising warmth.

He came toward her and took her hands in his, lifting her left hand to kiss it. "We'll take it slow, Sally. I won't do anything you don't want me to do."

She nodded, suddenly unable to speak what was in her

mind and within her heart.

His gaze searched her face as if he could read every emotion whirling within her, then he dropped her hands. "Turn around and I'll undo those buttons for you."

She turned, her shoulders tense as he began with the first button.

Oh why do they put such long rows of buttons down the back of a wedding dress?

She tried to relax and found it impossible as the silence grew.

I can't let memories of Luke ruin my wedding night. I can't, I can't. Oh, I don't want to even think of him now. Why can't I stop?

"Sally." Rob's hands settled on her shoulders, warm and firm. "I have a little surprise for you." He began to knead the knotted muscles of her neck.

She took a deep breath and released it. "You do?"

"Yes." His fingers continued to work on the knots, in a matter-of-fact way, as if it weren't their wedding night. As if he had no expectations of her this evening and was in no hurry. "I had a bath prepared in the next room as a surprise."

"Oh." She didn't know what to say. "But we had baths this morning."

"Not together, we didn't."

"Oh, my."

This was something she had never done with anyone. This bathing together.

"Can two fit into the tub?"

He laughed and kissed the side of her neck. "Yes, darlin'. We'll both fit. I promise."

"Oh. It sounds nice."

He turned her around to face him, the back of her dress gaping open. "It will be more than nice, Mrs. Truman, I promise you that."

She dropped her eyes and smiled, almost giddy with relief.

"Why don't you go ahead and slip into the tub and I'll join you in just a bit."

Her eyes widened. He was giving her the privacy to undress

without him watching. He wasn't going to examine her or leave her standing naked in the middle of the room while he was still dressed. She could sink into the tub and wait for him.

"Well..." she smiled up at him, "...just don't take too long, Mr. Truman."

The warmth of his smile lit up the room. "Oh I'll hurry. You just call me when you're ready."

"All right."

He bent and kissed the tip of her nose. "Go on now, darlin', the bath is waiting."

The moment she entered the other bedroom, she could smell the scent of rose petals from where they floated in the tub sitting in the corner.

"Oh, my," she whispered. "Oh, Rob." That he had thought enough to do this for her amazed her. That he would think of her first, was something that continued to take her by surprise.

She undressed and dropped her clothes to the floor, exhaling before she stepped into the water. Easing down into the water, she closed her eyes and leaned her head back against the tub.

So this was what it was to be truly loved.

Warmth flooded over and through her body and she felt a satisfaction bone deep. She sat breathing in, letting the scent and the water wash away every last remnant of her life with Luke. And when no thought of him remained, only thoughts of the man who stood on the other side of that door, she called for him.

"Rob?"

His name barely left her lips before the door opened and he stood, watching her, a towel draped around his waist. He was tall, and she felt the way his strength filled the room. A strength which came deep from within. A strength of character as well as of body. And he encouraged her to be strong as well. His was a true strength, never requiring the submission of others to make him feel strong.

"So beautiful," he said, his eyes widening. "I want to remember you just like that. My beautiful wife."

He took a step toward her and the love in his eyes warmed her to the core.

Her gaze slowly moved from his eyes to his smiling lips. The lines of his face reminded her this was the man she would grow old with. This was the smile she would wake to every morning. He was the love of her life and she was his. There was no doubting, no more fear. There was only love.

As he walked toward the tub, her gaze scanned his toned arms, his chest, his navel, the towel he had to grasp with one hand as it threatened to fall.

He stopped by the tub, bent and kissed her lips.

She melted into his kiss, her eyes closing, as she heard him step into the tub and felt the water moving.

When he moved away she opened her eyes, just as he eased down into the tub.

He reached for the bar of soap and said, "Let me wash you."

"Yes." She smiled as every pore of her skin responded to the suggestion, goose bumps of anticipation spreading.

"Relax. Close your eyes and lean your head back."

She did with a sigh. Warm soapy water trickled down her neck and then she felt the brush of his fingers. So warm. So tender. As he washed her from her neck to her breasts, the anticipation of where he would touch her next built and she caught her breath, only to sigh in the next moment. It was as if she was being reborn with each touch of his hands.

A rhythm built between her gasps and sighs and continued until he had washed every inch of her, murmuring words of love.

Then he cupped his hands and poured water over her again and again to rinse her.

He lifted her hand and kissed her palm, the inside of her wrist, then her arm to her elbow, and she shivered.

He chuckled as her eyes flew open.

She watched him heavy-lidded as he proceeded to kiss her other palm, making his way up her arm.

"Rob?"

"Hmmm?" He continued kissing.

"I think I would like to wash you too."

His smile grew even broader and his eyes lit as if she'd stoked a fire within. He leaned back in the tub, spreading his arms on each side of the tub. "Darlin', you can do anything you want to me. I'm all yours."

This bold feeling was new to her, but she liked it. She liked it very much. Reaching for the soap she smiled at him, knowing she would wash him every bit as slowly as he'd washed her.

And so she began.

She loved touching him, feeling the lean muscles beneath his skin, watching the way the water stirred as he grew even more aroused. And by learning every inch of his body, something clicked into place in her mind. A certainty that he was her perfect match in every way, in body and in heart.

By the time she finished, she sensed his impatience, though he never said a word to suggest he had waited long enough.

She stood in the tub. "Mr. Truman, I do believe I have kept you waiting long enough."

His eyebrows raised in surprise.

"Dry me off." She winked. "And I'll race you to the bed."

"Sally." He stood and reached for the towel. "There's nothing I'd like more."

If he'd been slow to wash her, he was certainly fast enough drying her off.

He'd just started toweling himself when she started to run.

Chasing after her, still toweling himself, he'd almost caught her when she scooted into the bed and pulled the covers up, giggling.

With a laugh, he lifted the covers and slipped in beside her. "Why, Mrs. Truman, I thought you'd never ask."

His lips closed over hers, and though he kissed her slowly, the impatience within her now would not be contained.

Wrapping her arms around his waist, she pulled him closer.

"Hurry, Rob," she gasped in between kisses.

"Are you sure?"

"We've waited long enough."

And as he touched her, and realized at once how ready she was, he waited not a minute longer.

"Oh," she gasped.

He stopped, and his eyes filled with concern.

"Why did we wait so long?" She looked deeply into his eyes and he laughed triumphantly as they rode into a blaze of glory.

About the Author

To learn more about Debra Parmley, please visit www.debraparmley.com. Send an email to Debra at debra@debraparmley.com

Exile...or love. Life...or death.
His demons will force him to choose.

Hell for Leather
© *2008 Beth Williamson*

Gunslinger Kincaid has traded his black clothes and pistols for a homespun shirt and trousers. Now he's Cade Brody, a man with dark hair, dark eyes and an even darker past. The blood money he's earned bought him a small piece of property in New Mexico territory, at the base of the Sangre de Cristo Mountains. But it can't buy him peace.

Sabrina Edmonds, a tough, no-nonsense widow, runs the post office and store in the small town of Eustace. She's made her way in life with an independent streak a mile wide. Sabrina doesn't want to get involved with Cade, but she finds herself drawn to the dark stranger who hides in his mountain retreat.

Cade wants nothing more than to be left alone, but an elusive wild child who delights in tormenting him, and a town full of people determined to befriend him, conspire to intrude upon his self-imposed exile. Then there's Sabrina, who should be afraid of him—but isn't.

Not even when the deadly demons of his past catch up with him.

Warning: This title contains lots of smart-ass remarks, a kick-ass heroine, a dark hero and some kickin' hot sex.

Available now in ebook and print from Samhain Publishing.

GREAT CHEAP FUN

Discover eBooks!

THE FASTEST WAY TO GET THE HOTTEST NAMES

Get your favorite authors on your favorite reader, long before they're
out in print! Ebooks from Samhain go wherever you go, and work with
whatever you carry—Palm, PDF, Mobi, and more.

Samhain
publishing ltd

WWW.SAMHAINPUBLISHING.COM